"What the hell?" Gordo asked when his ears caught the stuttering of an airplane engine. "Give me that thing." He took the headset from the man trying to operate the radio and not having much luck with it. Gordo frowned. "This dial is for frequency," he explained with a sliver of impatience. "See."

"Warrenton base," Amber's voice sounded faint but recognizable.

"Gordo here, Amber, what happened?"

"Gordo, I've been hit. I'm almost out of fuel and there's smoke and oil in the cockpit."

"Dump the rest of your fuel and land the damn thing," Gordo ordered. "The field is cleared."

"I can't land in the field. If I crash, the others will have trouble landing and I can't make a second pass. I don't think I can stay conscious that long."

Gordo felt the hair on his neck stand up. His heart began to race. "Clear the field!" he shouted to the troops serving as the ground crew and waiting for the planes to return. "Get me the fire extinguishers Cc imported. You know where they are."

What They Are Saying About

Cloud Walker

"Mary Ann you did it again. Cloud Walker has everything; the Civil War, aircraft, technology. I felts as if I were there taking part in the action."

Ed Kelemen,
Blairsville Dispatch

Other Works From The Pen Of

Mary Ann Mogus

The Lethe Gene August 2009

Archaeologist Keri St. Cloud is forced to unravel the secret of the Lethe Gene to save herself and those who carry it.

Shadow Hands July 2012

Trevor Towsen's investigation of his friend's murder leads him to a tangled web of alternate universe invaders attempting to exploit the American Civil War in his universe.

Hidden Alliances August 2013

Towsen didn't destroy the Khysids but set in motion the invasion of his universe and the Civil War has grown to encompass alternate universes.

Wings

CLOUD WALKER

by

Mary Ann Mogus

A Wings ePress, Inc.

Fantasy/Sci-Fi Novel

Wings ePress, Inc.

Edited by: Jeanne Smith
Copy Edited by: Joan C. Powell
Senior Editor: Jeanne Smith
Executive Editor: Marilyn Kapp
Cover Artist: Richard Stroud

Wings ePress Books
http://www.wings-press.com

ISBN 978-1-61309-792-2

Published In the United States Of America

November 2014

Wings ePress Inc.
403 Wallace Court
Richmond, KY 40475

Dedication

This book is dedicated first to the Craftique Fiber Arts Gang and Raggz & Friends for all their support and the stories they tell me and I tell them. They are always a constant source of ideas. It is also dedicated to the Greensburg Writers' Group for they helped with critiques and readings of the first draft. Finally it is dedicated to Seton Hill University's Writing Popular Fiction Program for the support and mentoring that comes with the program.

One

All universes are at the same place, but not
all are at the same time.
Codex of Flowering Butterfly

April 14, 1961 (Universe U0)

Gray Eagle climbed from the blue, gold and white airplane, while a mechanic hurried to greet him.

"Well, Medicine Man, how's the engine?"

"She's purring like a fat, sassy cat." Gray Eagle smiled at the use of the nickname he had acquired during his stint with the army. "Sam, you've worked miracles."

"It's easy when you have good material, as they say in Hollywood." Sam rubbed his hands against his greasy overalls. "But then Hollywood doesn't have an aeronautical engineer like you. I'll miss you when Connie and I leave to start the business."

"I'll miss you, too. The only mechanic I know who's better than you is Gordo."

Gray Eagle felt a sudden twinge of nostalgia for the man who had taught him so much about airplanes. He wondered where Gordo, R. Gordon Sykes, was now. He hadn't heard from the man since '52. *It is a shame the way once close friends often lose touch with one another.*

Sam interrupted his musings. "So you think you and the team will be ready for the August air show?"

"Yes, provided Amber doesn't burn out one of the engines."

"She's a little hellion," Sam agreed. "Not yet eighteen, and too smart for her own good."

Gray Eagle nodded, sobering at the thought of his pupil Amber Valic. She and the other six pilots were the children of the scientists and technicians working at ISIR, the Institute for Scientific Investigation and Research. But she was far ahead of her contemporaries in many ways, not all of them guaranteed to give her smooth flying in life.

"Check out the other planes, will you, Sam? I've a meeting with Julian at eleven."

Sam gave Gray Eagle a mock salute and hurried away. Gray Eagle watched for a moment, before staring at the sky, empty of clouds. He lowered his gaze as one of his team started a landing approach. The runways of the private airport baked under a sun the color of melted butter. The air had a hot, dry smell to it, a smell he identified with the season. It was in stark contrast to the North Dakota reservation where he had been born.

Gray Eagle glanced at his watch, an ever-present goad to action. No one kept Indian time here. He hadn't kept it since he left the reservation in '41. He hummed a song as he walked toward the hangar, set parallel to the north/south runway. It was a Quonset hut type building, the roof and walls supported by a metal skeleton. The hangar would house two of the Merlins Gray Eagle had designed.

The designs were based on the P-51 fighter used in WWII. He wondered if Julian Barstead, a man he considered a brother, was right about looking for a company to manufacture the new aerobatics planes. It would bring in extra money for ISIR, not that the institute needed funds. Barstead had a top engineering mind and the royalties from his patents were more than sufficient to keep ISIR in funds for years. It was Cc Rierdon, one of the anthropologists at the institute, who had the knack for investments.

"If Julian lets Cc have his hand in the stock market, we'll need no more government contracts ever," Gray Eagle said out loud as he made his way to the empty hangar. "What a blessing that would be. I hate the security issues."

He walked into the shade of the hangar with more spring in his step than he had felt for some time. *Yes, both the planes and his pupils were performing well. They would be ready for the air show.*

Buoyed by the thought, he turned to watch the second Merlin land. Heat flared in his stomach and he gasped as if he had been punched. He knew it was the sudden touch of a vision. The scene before him took on a mottled grainy appearance as if he were looking at billions of tiny colored dots. Gray Eagle grabbed at the side of the hangar entrance, anchoring his body to the earth.

"No," he pleaded. "Not now not after ten years." He knew there was no way to stop the coming vision; there never had been.

The graininess of his sight was followed by a prickling sensation as if he were passing through an electric membrane. Instantly his sight cleared. For a moment he thought the vision had passed. The scene before him was the same as when the sensations began, but the buzzing in his head was still present.

It's not stopped. He called upon his power animals to help him, but the answer was a sudden appearance of two Merlins leaping into the sky like young, winged colts. The planes gained altitude, did a snap roll, and climbed higher, before starting the Immelman maneuver, an old trick learned by pilots during the First World War to turn the tables on an attacker when both planes disappeared into a thick bank of clouds.

The sight of clouds in an otherwise cloudless sky reminded Gray Eagle that the vision was happening in his head and not on the airfield outside the confines of the hangar. As the vision continued, his mind was enveloped by smoke filled with the acrid stench of gunpowder, fear, and death. Voices called from a dark wind surrounding him, but their words were indistinct.

He was no longer in the hangar, but on a hill pitted by repeated shelling, and surrounded by two nebulous armies. His only clear view was of the sky and the hefty cloudbank into which the little Merlins had disappeared only moments ago. His eyes caught movement as the planes reappeared. But where two planes had gone into the clouds, three tore through, diving toward the ground in what he recognized as a strafing attack.

"What the hell?" he said, ducking to one side.

The planes were P-40s, just like the ones he had flown in China in '41 when he, Barstead, Gordo, and his old teacher, Murphy, had fought in the Chinese Air Corps. He would recognize the shark's teeth on the nose symbol anywhere. But his eyes caught a detail the planes he flew never had. It looked as if someone had painted white blotches on the body and wings in a careless attempt at what?

The scene collapsed. His sight readjusted to the airfield before him and two figures running toward him. The sound of engines filled his ears, followed by the routine crackle of static on the small radio in the hangar, and the smell of stale oil and grease. His forehead was beaded with sweat. His palm slid from the hangar's edge, catching on a sharp piece of metal, the bite of pain forcing him to full awareness.

"Gray Eagle!" Amber reached him as he dropped to his knees. "Help me, Roger!" she shouted to her companion.

They helped Gray Eagle to a chair beside the table that supported the radio and piles of books and papers. He nodded his thanks, strength slowly filling his body, some of it directed to him by the young people standing on either side of his chair. He was grateful he had taught them the ways of medicine just as he had taught them to fly.

"You had a vision?" Amber said, with the hint of accusation.

Gray Eagle nodded.

"What was it?"

He shook his head, not wanting to tell her what he had learned as the vision collapsed. That he knew she and Roger were two of the pilots in the planes of his vision and that he wasn't the third. He reached for the medicine bag he always carried around his neck. Warmth and energy touched his hand and filled his spirit.

"You've cut your hand." She unwound the silk flying scarf she wore as an affectation.

"I'll get the first aid kit," Roger offered, leaving the two alone for the moment.

Amber wrapped the scarf tightly around Gray Eagle's hand to stop the bleeding. "It must have been some vision. What was this one about?"

"War," he muttered, pulling his hand away from her. "I'm surprised you didn't sense anything."

"Only that you were in trouble. But I don't have one of those strange stones you carry."

Gray Eagle knew the allusion was to the pouch tied around his neck. The day in 1941 when he had left Bismarck, North Dakota, for California and the war, his mentor, Two Feathers, had given him what he at first thought was a white pebble. It was a sacred stone kept by his late grandmother, Red Moon. She had left instructions that it was to be given to him when he left the reservation.

After he met Julian Barstead, the two learned that the pebble was not simply a stone but a crystal formation. Later, after the war, after Barstead formed ISIR and Gray Eagle joined him, the two were able to finally study the stone they had come to wonder about. Scientific analysis suggested the stone was synthetic, and no one could discover exactly what it was constructed for or how to use it at will.

The warmth of the stone slowly ebbed and Gray Eagle sighed. “I’ve a meeting with Julian at eleven.” He stood on shaky legs, drawing on his new reserves of strength to shove aside the images burned in his memory. Time would not allow him the luxury of thinking about what had just happened. He would find a space for it later, and as he had done before, he pushed the images deeper back into his mind.

Roger came to him with the first aid kit. “At least let us put a bandage and some antiseptic on the cut.”

Gray Eagle agreed as Amber unwound the flying scarf from his hand, discarding it on the table. Roger opened the kit, and Amber used the alcohol to wipe away the dried blood. Gray Eagle winced as Amber painted his wound with iodine and bandaged his hand.

“I’m coming with you to that meeting.” She finished taping the bandage in place and returned the unused portion of the roll to the first aid kit.

“No,” he cautioned. “Weber will be there.”

She narrowed her blue eyes and drew herself up to her indignant five foot three height. “I don’t care.”

“He hates you,” Roger interrupted.

“He hates anyone under forty,” she retorted. “The man has the personality of a box of rocks.”

Gray Eagle chuckled. “The description fits. I wish Julian hadn’t been so insistent on hiring a plasma physicist.”

“You really wish Julian had hired someone else, say Dr. Hans Bechter?”

Gray Eagle nodded. “Bechter’s good, from what I hear. But he was too close to the Nazis for us to hire him.”

“I thought he worked for the underground during the war.” Amber snapped the metal tab, locking the first aid kit.

“No one really knows.” Gray Eagle looked at his bandaged hand, wondering how he was going to explain the accident to Barstead. It was true he and Barstead were like brothers: he the younger, Barstead the older worrywart. Barstead would demand to know what happened and his already graying hair would add a few white strands when he heard the nature of the vision.

“I’m still coming with you.” Amber poked at Gray Eagle’s shoulder.

"You'll need security clearance for this visit." Gray Eagle tried to temper her determination.

"I have it, so does everyone at ISIR. We live on the property, remember?"

"Yes and the others won't mind, but Weber..." Gray Eagle made a rocking motion with his bandaged hand.

Amber placed the first aid kit on the table. "Are you coming?" she asked as Roger brushed at an absent strand of blond hair.

"I'd rather chew on a rattlesnake."

"I'm going. Julian can be the one to kick me out."

Gray Eagle knew better than to argue with her when she had made a decision, and he didn't have the time for subtle persuasion. If Julian wanted her out of the meeting, he would be the one to tell her.

Dr. Stan Weber glared at Gray Eagle sitting across from him. The polished, round, walnut table was a tenuous buffer against the hostility radiated by the scientist.

"What the hell's she doing here?"

"I had an accident, and Amber agreed to come with me to the meeting," Gray Eagle replied. Both true statements but their relationship was questionable.

"I don't care if you had a heart attack," Weber blurted. "This is a secure meeting. The man coming to speak is from DC. You think he wants some dumb kid at the meeting?"

Dr. Margaret Aksawan toyed with the leather strap of her watch. The white skin beneath the watchband stood out against her darkly tanned arm. "Can it, Stan. We need to get the meeting with the secret service agent over with. I have a load of artifacts to analyze."

"Nobody gives a damn about your stupid potsherds. You've hogged half the instruments at ISIR in your study."

"She doesn't use the same equipment you do," Dr. Walter Reed said in defense of his colleague. He lounged at ease in his chair, his lanky body resting against the cushioned seat.

Weber's lips twitched. "When I took a contract with ISIR, I thought this place did serious research."

"It does." Margaret leaned forward, removed her watch and placed it on the table beside her notebook. "But not all serious research involves plasmas."

Weber said. "You don't know the meaning of serious." Barstead entered, interrupting Weber's criticism.

Dr. Julian Barstead, director and foundered of ISIR, entered with a man an inch shorter than he. The newcomer had dark auburn hair, hazel eyes, and the look of an agent. His navy suit, blue silk tie, button-down shirt, and wing tip shoes screamed Easterner before he opened his mouth.

"This is Mr. Arthur Beaumont, of the Secret Service." Barstead introduced the man with him. Barstead glanced at Amber, then at Gray Eagle.

When neither volunteered any information, he made the introductions, pausing only to assure Beaumont that the young woman had the necessary security clearance.

Gray Eagle suspected the assurance was redundant. If this agent had done his homework, he knew about everyone at ISIR, including Amber. What he thought about them was another matter.

Barstead directed the agent to a seat and took the chair next to him. "I've kept the number of people to a minimum as you requested. Now, would you like to tell us what the meeting is about? Your request said urgent."

"Since security clearance is not an issue for any of you, I'll get right to the point."

Gray Eagle sensed Amber shift in her chair. He felt it too, the silent anxiety gripping the stranger across the table from him in a bond so tight Gray Eagle wondered why he couldn't see an image of it.

"There's a problem at the White House that the president hopes you will be able to solve."

"What problem?" Barstead asked, training his blue eyes on the agent.

"We've had a visitor disturbing the occupants since March and it can't continue." Beaumont ran a hand through his hair.

Gray Eagle caught the liquid sibilance of a Virginia accent beneath the words. "Mr. Beaumont, isn't that the job of the FBI? Or even your agency?"

"Yes." Weber leaned against his chair. "Why bother us?"

"I'm working on this with two other agents, Mark Kraft and Aaron Stein. But this isn't, shall we say, within our area of training, let alone expertise."

"We don't do security work." Weber's nostrils widened. "Why would you even think this has anything to do with us?"

Beaumont met the scientist's gaze. "The visitor is a ghost."

"Ghost?" Margaret's eyes widened.

Beaumont nodded.

"Horse crap," Weber barked. "There's no such thing as a ghost."

"Shut up, Stan! Let the man finish." Margaret smacked the table with the flat of her hand, an action she had used to summon the wandering attention of numerous college students in the days when she taught at Stanford.

Beaumont smiled his thanks. Weber folded his arms across his chest and subsided.

"The visitations started in the Lincoln bedroom as just a glimpse of something, and when you turn it's gone. But the encounters have escalated."

"What do you mean by escalated?" Gray Eagle asked.

"The ghost has been seen by several people and we've been able to photograph it." Beaumont pulled out three photographs. "Would you look at these, Dr. Aksawan?"

She looked at the photographs, blinked, and shook her head.

Beaumont said. “Stein took, developed and printed the photos. The light from the visitor was enough to give us the image in a darkened hallway.”

“Let’s see what you captured.” Reed leaned closer to his colleague for a look at the photos.

“My God, it’s a picture of Lincoln!”

“Lincoln?” Weber casually ran the tips of his fingers along the edge of the table. “Surely, you’re not suggesting that Lincoln is haunting the White House?”

“I’m not suggesting anything,” Beaumont said. “I’m simply giving you what evidence we have. I’ve also brought along typed transcripts of interviews with the people who’ve encountered this ghost.”

“You say ghost with some hesitation,” Gray Eagle said.

“I don’t think this is a ghost. My gut tells me it’s something different.”

“Do you suppose the Soviets are doing this?” Barstead asked as he took one of the photographs that had made its way to him.

“I don’t know what to suggest.” Beaumont rubbed his forehead. “Kraft actually fired off two rounds at the thing when it appeared in the Rose Garden. The bullets missed the ghost, but it looked scared as hell.”

Gray Eagle sat upright in his chair. “The ghost looked scared?”

Beaumont nodded. “I couldn’t fire at it. I mean, it looks so much like Lincoln.”

Gray Eagle said, “But that doesn’t explain the reaction. Ghosts seldom interact with the person witnessing the scene.” He did not add that most witnesses ran in the opposite direction. Few drew a gun and fired at an apparition.

“That’s it.” Weber let out a deep breath. “I’ve got work to do. Count me out of this. I’m presenting a paper at the Plasma Physics meeting and I have some last minute calculations to finish.” He rose and strode from the room without looking back.

“Good riddance,” Margaret muttered.

Beaumont frowned. “Will he speak of this meeting?”

Reed shook his head. “No, this isn’t something he can add to his list of publications.”

Beaumont sat back in his chair, but his eyes strayed to the closed door.

“How would you like us to help you?” Gray Eagle interrupted the agent’s thoughts.

“I’d like you to come to DC and have a look for yourself.”

“When?” Margaret asked.

“Yesterday,” Beaumont quipped.

The ripple of laughter broke the tension in the room. Gray Eagle lifted a photograph and studied it as Barstead and the agent talked about the arrangements. Something was not quite right, he thought. The photograph was in perfect focus, but his mind insisted on blurring it, as if the focus of the action were elsewhere. He felt warmth from the stone he carried and quickly dropped the photograph.

"What is it?" Amber whispered to him.

"Nothing," he lied.

"You felt something from that stone."

Beaumont looked at her. "Is something wrong?"

"No, just discussing the flight east," she improvised.

"You'll be coming with them?"

"I'll pilot the plane. Roger will serve as my copilot," she said, keeping up the fiction she had just devised.

Beaumont glanced at the man beside him for an explanation, but none was forthcoming. He resorted to opening his briefcase and removing a set of folders that he placed on the table.

"Are these the interviews?" Barstead reached for a folder.

The agent nodded. "Seven, including mine. I know you people have top clearance. I've researched you at President Kennedy's request. But this has to be kept very quiet."

Reed asked, "Isn't that plasma physics conference Stan plans to attend in Washington?"

Barstead nodded. "It starts in a week. You thinking perhaps we could go also, but check out the White House ghost instead?"

"I'm thinking exactly that. It will serve as cover."

"Just what sort of cover will Cc and I serve?" Margaret asked.

Gray Eagle glanced at her. "You're coming to speak with colleagues at the Smithsonian."

"Good idea," she cocked a finger at him. "And you?"

"I'll check out the museum, maybe talk with some people about aviation research."

She winked at Amber. "And the dangerous duo?"

"I'll be responsible for them," he replied a bit too quickly. He suddenly wished he hadn't said it. He could easily have flown one of the newer eight-passenger planes cross-country without any help. But Amber's remark had seemed to commit ISIR to taking her and Roger as well.

"Then let's discuss what we've learned about the sightings and make some plans for your arrival and how we can integrate you into the White House routine," Beaumont offered.

~ * ~

April 14, 1861 (Universe U1)

Desiree Bouchard hurried toward her new residence on State Street in the western Maryland town of Frederick. She stopped outside her house, glanced at the sky, and said out loud, "It will rain this afternoon."

There was no hint of rain in the hazy sunlight filtering through the feather-like clouds, but she sensed the touch of moisture on the breeze. She was good at predicting the weather.

Returning her gaze to the house, she smiled, feeling again the thrill of freedom in her heart every time she looked at the two-story structure. The house was built in the Federal style of architecture, with window frames set off by black shutters. It was just the sort of house her late husband, Louis, would have hated. She absolutely loved it.

She hurried up the brick driveway and beneath the ornate portico with the two fluted columns, a later addition. She mounted the three steps to the door, inserted the key she carried in her hand and opened it, coming face to face with Harriette, the young woman she had raised from birth and considered her ward.

Harriette stepped back a pace to avoid a collision. “I heard you coming and meant to get the door.”

Desiree handed the young woman the package she was carrying. “I’ve brought the pastries. There was no need to worry that I would be late.”

“I’ll put these with the coffee.” Harriette took the package from Desiree. “A courier came for you while you were out. He left that.” She inclined her head to the petticoat table in the hall. A thick pack of papers sat inert on a silver tray.

“They’re from Henri.” Desiree knew without seeing the handwriting or the return address. She swore in French.

Harriette smiled, turned, and hurried toward the drawing room, her apricot taffeta day gown rustling as she walked. Desiree looked at her departing form. *She’s eighteen and there’s no one but me to support her.*

Harriette was the offspring of a liaison between

her late husband and one of his slaves. Harriette had been a gift to Desiree when Louis learned she could not have children. But Desiree had always known the truth. Louis preferred other women to his wife, no matter what the color of their skin.

Now Louis was dead, as was Harriette's mother. Harriette was free. And the dowry money Desiree had brought to the marriage was invested in stock and property in the North. At least Louis had known how to do that and see that she was provided for. The Louisiana plantation had gone to his younger brother, Henri. Desiree had all she would ever need and that she would share with Harriette.

She removed her bonnet, placed it on a wooden peg, part of an elaborately carved set of pegs fastened to the wall for just this purpose, and attacked the packet. She scanned the contents. *Mostly the remnants of the estate to deal with*, she thought.

"So he's still in Charleston," she muttered.

"What?" Harriette stepped into the hall.

"Henri, he's still in Charleston. He will probably lead the charge on that fort everyone is arguing about. What is it called?"

"Sumter," Harriette said. "But if the fort is fired upon, won't that mean war?"

"Yes," Desiree said. "Yes," she repeated to herself in a softer voice. "It will indeed mean war."

~ * ~

Universal Time 1. 00. 04. 14 (Universe 61)

General San felt that if Brie did not stop talking soon, she would reach across the table and strangle him, Supreme Commander of the Khysid Army or not.

"And I see that we are proceeding on schedule." He consulted a thin sheet of what looked like paper, but was really a computer.

San let her eyes travel over the domed Command Chamber, taking in the blue-gray color of the stone, and finally resting her gaze on the ornate chair occupied by Brie at the head of the crescent-shaped table. Since San had been granted a seat on the Command Council, the room had come to have a claustrophobic feel to it. She was still a junior member and the senior members seldom gave her words the seriousness she thought they deserved.

Brie concluded. "We will invade the 1861 universe shortly after they finish their battle at Gettysburg. That will give us a chance to get some good war footage."

San shifted in her chair. The natural highlights in her hair set off her dark skin. Her movement caused Elar to glance in her direction. San knew he was attracted to her, but he had yet to make his move.

"Any questions?" Brie asked.

She spoke. "Sir, I think we had better address this latest record of instability in the universe we are proposing to invade." She tapped the report before her with her beautifully manicured finger.

Brie made a dismissive gesture with his hand. "Have Colonel Val deal with it. After all, his new software has proved useful. I see no reason to interfere with the mission. He and Major Kester seem capable of dealing with any perturbations."

You wouldn't see your hand if it didn't come attached to your arm, she thought. She didn't like the data Val had sent to her. The incidents he related seemed too unstable. She knew the army was committed to invading the universe in question. The cache of Jewels, used to power the Source Gates that opened portals between alternate universes, was nearing depletion. The army had never been able to create synthetic versions of the original Jewels.

"I'm worried about committing a nearly intact Jewel to this invasion," she blurted.

"San, we need a large, stable portal at the Embassy Club. This is no simple long-term exploitation. We intend to take this universe. Are you worried about fighting?" Elar asked.

"I'm as anxious to see the troops trained, as ready to take to the field as any of your more experienced generals."

"Like Sig?"

"He's one of our best. But the instabilities in these readings worry me. I know they aren't large, but they seem persistent. That's not normal."

Cal waved her hand. "They'll dissipate in time."

"If we wait."

"General San." Brie poured contempt into the two words. "If we wait, fighting will begin, and we'll miss our chance at recording some good footage during the battle of Bull Run, or Manassas, or whatever they call it." He paused. "I mean *will* call it when they fight it."

The Command Council returned to deliberations as San felt, her temper moved up several degrees. She had rid them of Supreme Commander Hazen, paving the way for Brie to take Hazen's seat and control of the Khysid Army. But it was Kester, her mind whispered, who had Hazen killed. She smacked down the thought.

"I set the events in motion," she muttered beneath her breath. No one was paying attention to her.

She had learned one thing from the late Supreme Commander Hazen. Events not planned for were the problem in an army dependent for survival on the products and resources of the alternate universes. Events were history and before Hazen died, he had reminded her that history had a way of thumbing its nose at the best of plans.

Two

Visions become clearer with time.
Codex of Flowering Butterfly

April 19, 1961(Universe 0)

At four in the morning, Arthur Beaumont was keeping a lonely vigil on the second floor of the White House directly before the Lincoln bedroom. The East Wing was empty; only the creaking sounds of a very old house could be heard. He leaned back in the chair he had occupied since midnight when he had relieved Stein.

As of two days ago, Lincoln's appearances had been confined exclusively to the Lincoln bedroom and surrounding area. One of three agents, stationed there around the clock, could do no more than witness the appearances and record it. But the apparition was growing more solid with each appearance. Beaumont shivered, remembering his sighting of three days ago.

His eyelids drooped and his mind wandered. It was nearing morning. If the ghost hadn't appeared by now, it probably wouldn't. The low-pitched humming mocked his thoughts. It sounded as if someone had turned on a transformer. The air prickled with electricity and Beaumont jerked erect. He felt the hair on his neck rise.

"Oh shit; it's coming."

Before the closed door of the Lincoln bedroom a whirling mass of white vapor appeared. Tiny sparks of light danced in the vapor and at the center a region of darkness formed. Beaumont felt a rush of energy threading through this darkness and the ghost stood before him. Beaumont slipped from his chair, catching himself in an awkward movement while the specter watched his actions. He read recognition in the eyes of the ghost fronting him. *Not possible.*

"Who are you?" He demanded of the apparition. "What are you?"

"I might ask you the same question," the specter answered.

The sound was distorted and muffled, as if the speaker were talking through cotton. Beaumont rose to his feet.

"I'm Arthur Beaumont of the Secret Service." A part of his mind wondered that he had the courage to speak at all. "I'm here to protect the president and his family."

The specter looked puzzled. "I know you, sir. You and others raised your guns to me. Is that what you consider protection?"

Beaumont gave a quick shake of his head. “You’re a ghost. You’ve been appearing in the White House since March.”

“This place is my home for now.”

“You’re dead. You were assassinated almost a hundred years ago.”

It was the specter’s turn to shake its head. “I’m quite alive, and you are the ghost. You and others have haunted me since I came to Washington. Why are you doing this in such perilous times? We are cut off from the North since Virginia seceded and in Baltimore—”

“Mr. President, or whoever the hell you are.”

“There’s no need for profanity.”

Maybe you don’t think so, Beaumont whispered in his mind. “Look, President ah…”

“My name is Abraham Lincoln. Surely you know this?”

“Oh, I know.” Beaumont said. "Look, President Lincoln, you can’t keep appearing in the White House. You’re scaring the crap out of President Kennedy and his staff, not to mention his family.”

Lincoln’s brow furrowed. “President Kennedy? I’m president here.”

Beaumont arched his eyebrows. “Where’s here?”

“Are you daft, man? Here is Washington.”

Beaumont licked his lips. “The year is?”

Lincoln gave a sigh. “It’s 1861,” he said with the patience reserved for a slow-witted child. “What else do you need to know?”

Beaumont pulled his handkerchief from the pocket of his jacket and wiped the sweat from his brow. His head felt clogged, his mind grasping at what little science he knew. *Here I stand having a conversation with the ghost of a dead president, and one who thinks I'm daft, to boot.*

"Sir, where I am, it's 1961. It's a hundred years after the events you describe. Our Civil War has ended and you're dead."

Lincoln made a gesture as if to dispel Beaumont's words. "I'm quite alive and intend to remain so, as long as you do not shoot at me."

"I would never," Beaumont stopped when he noticed a smile tickling the corners of the specter's lips. "Lincoln always had a sense of humor."

"I have a sense of humor, sir. I wish you would stop talking about me in the past tense."

"Wait." Beaumont held up his hand, all fear gone for the moment. "I've got proof. Your image is on a five dollar bill." Beaumont, forgetting he still held his handkerchief, fumbled with his wallet, pulled out the bill, and stepped closer to the apparition.

"Bill?" Lincoln asked. "What is this thing called a bill? Are you referring to a bank note?"

Memory reminded Beaumont that in 1861 paper money consisted of bank notes and had not yet been introduced by the U. S. Treasury.

I'm losing it. I'm showing money to a ghost. Beaumont meant to display the bill, but the handkerchief he clutched in his hand stood out as if it were iron and the vapor a magnet. It was whisked from his grasp into the vapor. Beaumont jumped backward.

"What is happening?" Lincoln demanded.

"How the hell should I know?" Beaumont colored as he recalled the specter's comment about profanity. But where had his handkerchief gone?

Lincoln glanced at his feet, stooped, and lifted the handkerchief. "This is yours, I believe."

Beaumont's mouth opened wide, giving him the appearance of a beached whale. "But that's impossible."

"Shoot the damned thing!" Kraft bellowed running toward Beaumont.

Startled, Beaumont turned and looked in the direction of the shout. It suddenly crossed his mind that Kraft was there to relieve him. Kraft, gun in hand, aimed at the specter as the vapor began to dissolve. Reflexively, Beaumont stepped before Lincoln blocking Kraft's shot.

"Don't," he ordered. He turned to glance at Lincoln, but the space where Lincoln had appeared was empty. He looked at Kraft. "I'm calling those scientists. If they don't get here soon, all of us will end up in padded rooms."

~ * ~

Barstead cradled the phone between his ear and shoulder, making notes on the notepad at his desk as he listened to Beaumont. Across from him sat Gray Eagle and Weber.

"What do you mean your handkerchief was sucked through? Sucked through what? Well, I didn't see it happen. How the hell do I know where it went?" He winced, as the voice at the other end grew strident.

Rierdon opened the door and slipped into the office. Barstead made a gesture for the man to sit, and Rierdon pulled a chair beside Gray Eagle away from Weber.

"What is it?" he asked.

Gray Eagle explained about the phone call.

Barstead continued. "Our team is ready. We're planning to be there on April twenty-two. Besides me, the other scientists will be Gray Eagle, Dr. Aksawan, Dr. Rierdon, Dr. Weber, Dr. Reed and the two pilots, Amber Valic, and Roger Merit."

"Julian agreed to Amber and Roger going as well?" Rierdon whispered to Gray Eagle. "Their flying is guaranteed to have Margaret lose her lunch over Las Vegas."

Gray Eagle smiled, but Barstead made a gesture at the pair to keep quiet. He bit his lip as he continued to listen.

"Yes, we're bringing some equipment." He gave Beaumont a terse list of items. "We'll need unrestricted access and privacy." He listened. "Good, I'll phone just before we leave. Bye." Barstead replaced the receiver.

"Give, Julian," Rierdon demanded.

"Another sighting, this time the ghost took a handkerchief." Barstead offered a summary of the conversation.

Rierdon leaned his short, wiry frame against his chair. “You know, psychic literature talks about things called apports, items that appear during a haunting, or even disappear. But I’ve never read of an incidence where the ghost ended up with the item.”

Weber snorted. “Don’t you know ESP means ‘easily seduced people?’”

“There’s seduction even in science.” Gray Eagle shrugged.

“This isn’t a ghost.”

Gray Eagle smiled. “I agree. It doesn’t have the feel of a ghost.”

Weber pursed his lips.

Ignoring Weber, Rierdon said, “Gray Eagle’s right. This doesn’t sound like any ghost report I’ve ever read, but then I haven’t read everything on ghosts.”

“Well, if it’s a hoax, there will be physical evidence available,” Reed suggested. “And we’ll be able to record it.”

“Stan thinks it’s some sort of plasma discharge that affects the mind,” Rierdon explained.

Weber stood. “I told you that in confidence. I don’t believe in ghosts.”

“I know, but if it has a physical reality, we’ll detect it.”

“Excuse me,” Weber interrupted the anthropologist. “Julian, I only came to discuss the arrangements for the meeting and delivering my paper. I’ll fly with the rest of you, but I want it understood that Amber and Roger keep out of my way."

"I'll be responsible for them," Gray Eagle said in defense of his pupils.

"Good." Weber favored the Sioux with a narrow smile. "Have them see that food and drink is brought aboard the plane. I know we stop for refueling, but they seem to forget human comforts when they fly."

You mean your comforts. Gray Eagle clenched his fists. "The plane is already stocked. You may eat as you wish."

"Now if you will excuse me, I have to pack." Weber sauntered from the room while the others watched.

As the door closed, Rierdon said, "How about I make an herbal potion for Stan? Keep him sedated during the trip?" He nudged Gray Eagle.

"Leave him alone, for now," Barstead grumbled. He made several notes on the pad before him.

Gray Eagle's eyes widened. He sensed annoyance in Barstead. It took a great deal to annoy his friend. He wondered if Weber had finally overstepped the bounds of Barstead's patience.

"Will you see that the plane is ready?" Barstead asked Gary Eagle.

It was an unnecessary question. Gray Eagle knew something else was bothering his friend. "Certainly, I'll go now."

"No." Barstead looked at the others. "Would you excuse us?"

Reed and Rierdon exchanged glances. Reed answered. "Of course, see you in a bit." They stood and left the room.

When he and Gray Eagle were alone, Barstead asked. “Is this trouble at the White House related to the vision you told me about?”

Gray Eagle shifted in his seat. “I think it is.”

“How?”

“I have no idea. I don’t even have an idea as to what the vision means.”

Barstead sighed. “Too many times before you have had these visions and they spelled trouble.”

“You knew that about me shortly after we first met.”

“Gray Eagle, you are what I consider family. So are the people here. I’ve got no one else. And I have my own feelings about this. I want it over with quickly. If we can’t discover what’s going on, let’s turn it over to some other agency better equipped for this sort of study.”

Gray Eagle felt his stomach grow tighter. “It may not be that simple.”

“I don’t want to hear that.”

“Sometimes we are drawn into things because we are meant to be part of them.”

Barstead held up his hand. “We started this institute. I know you think I began it, but without your help it wouldn’t exist. Three hundred and fifty people work here. Most of us live here. This is all I’ve worked for and I don’t want to lose it.”

Gray Eagle sat upright. His friend may not know it, but he had just given a reason for the growing anxiety both of them felt. It was something that had blossomed in his mind the previous evening as he worked with Amber and Roger on readying the plane for the flight. If they took this assignment, there would be no going back. He felt it with an inner sense just as Barstead suspected it with his reason. But neither would speak the words. Once they left the West Coast, ISIR would become history.

~ * ~

April 19, 1861(Universe 1)

"Please forgive me, Mrs. Bouchard," Carl Denton, editor of the *Frederick Herald* implored as he lifted his hat to Desiree. "I did not mean to bump into you. It was my clumsiness entirely."

"That's quite all right, sir." Desiree straightened her new bonnet, acquired on a recent trip to Washington. "You seem in a very great hurry."

Denton bounced on the soles of his feet as if he were preparing to run. Desiree glanced at Harriette, but could read nothing in the fawn-like eyes of her charge.

"I've just received some very bad news." Denton glanced back at the open door to the telegraph office. "It's come from Baltimore."

"Oh? What has happened?" Desiree asked, knowing the man wanted to leave as quickly as possible.

"I fear it's too difficult a situation to tell such a delicate creature as yourself."

Harriette raised her gloved hand to her mouth to hide a growing smile, but Desiree caught the movement. Turning back to Denton, she too smiled ever so slightly.

"Mr. Denton, surely it cannot be that bad and I have been through many shocks. I think I can stand to know what you have learned." Desiree knew most men were easily disarmed, especially if they could be made to feel protective. A simple task with Denton, since he found her attractive.

He glanced along the dusty street to make certain they were alone, before returning his gaze to Desiree, ignoring Harriette. "There has been a riot in Baltimore. It seems Massachusetts troops were moving through the city on their way to a station to go to Washington, when fighting broke out."

"Was anyone hurt?"

Denton nodded. "Several people were killed."

"And President Lincoln, what has he done about this?"

The editor frowned as he spoke. "I've not heard, but the mayor of Baltimore had the railroad bridges and telegraph lines to Washington destroyed so this cannot happen again."

"But the president?"

Denton stepped from the wooden sidewalk into the dusty street. "I hope the rumors we have been hearing about him are but that, and that he will take some decisive action in this matter. Good day, Mrs. Bouchard." Denton tipped his hat and walked briskly toward his newspaper office.

"Desiree, you believe the rumors that President Lincoln is unbalanced and seeing spirits in the White House?"

Desiree looked at Harriette. “Lincoln is quite sane. It’s the country that has become unbalanced. There are so many hotheads among us willing to shed blood for what?”

Harriette did not answer, but looked away. Desiree went to her and placed her arm around the woman’s shoulders. She glanced along the street, watching the diminishing form of Carl Denton. She had sensed the country’s disintegration coming like a cold dark wind growing in her soul. It was death she felt, just as she had felt it before Louis had his last attack.

“They are coming for us,” she whispered the words that popped into her mind.

“Who?” Harriette asked, looking around the almost empty street.

“What?” Desiree’s attention focused on the woman beside her. “What did I say?”

“Oh Desiree, have you had a foreseeing?”

Desiree did not answer, though her breakfast rose in her throat. It was the gift, she knew, that took hold of her, whispering the thoughts and feelings that would come to pass. But in all her life she had never felt the chill that was inside her then. She wondered from what region of hell they would come, whoever they were.

~ * ~

April 22, 1961(Universe 0)

Beaumont walked the length of the small cul-de-sac on which his apartment building was situated beside several restored and refurbished houses. His destination was a gourmet coffee shop that beckoned with the aroma of fresh brew and homemade pastries. He tucked his copy of the *Washington Post* under his arm, slipped into the shop, and found a seat at the counter.

"The usual, Pam," he told the matronly waitress. She brought him a cup of steaming coffee and a small metal pot containing cream.

"Be right back with your breakfast."

Beaumont pulled out the paper, opened it, and began to scan the contents as he poured the cream into his coffee. "Shit." Two drops of cream fell on the pristine newspaper. Beaumont brushed them away from the headline '*Is There a Ghost in the White House?*'

Someone had talked and it had to be a source in the White House, otherwise the *Post* would never have printed the article. He glanced at the byline, but did not recognize the writer.

Pam stood before him with a plate containing an egg and cheese Danish. "Is something wrong?"

"Something is always wrong," Beaumont sighed. He was supposed to have the day to himself until he picked up the scientists.

"You had a call here from a Mr. Stein. He said to call when you finish your breakfast. I guess he couldn't reach you at home." She placed the breakfast before him, added a glass of orange juice, and left the bill.

Beaumont glared at the food before eating a few bites. He could just hear his sister, Mary Frances, once she read the newspaper. It amazed him she wasn't waiting at his usual breakfast spot demanding to talk to him. She was an expert on Civil War history, teaching at Georgetown University as an adjunct professor. She had been of help with one or two of his problems, mostly dealing with the history of the White House.

Shoving aside the thoughts of his sister, he wondered what Stein wanted, praying that the scientists were not delayed again. Yesterday, storms over Oklahoma had forced their plane to remain grounded until the weather cleared. When Barstead called to tell him, Beaumont explained the government would pay for commercial seats, but Barstead refused, saying he wanted his private plane.

After finishing his breakfast, he glanced at his watch. He realized it wasn't working and he had worn it from habit. The watch hadn't worked since his encounter with the Lincoln specter. Beaumont stood, paid his bill, and left the restaurant. He hurried back to his apartment where he called Stein.

"What is it, Aaron? This has been the first good night's sleep I've had since these incidents started."

"There were prowlers around the grounds last night," Stein explained.

"Prowlers, not more ghosts?"

"No, these guys were real. There were two of them."

"You see them?"

"Kraft saw them," Stein said. "He noticed them hiding in the shrubbery as he parked his car."

"How the hell did they avoid security?"

"No one knows. But they were dressed in black camouflage."

"What happened?"

Stein cleared his throat. "Kraft says they just vanished. He cornered them between himself and two other agents and the prowlers vanished into thin air."

Beaumont shivered. "The scientists will be in by four," he looked at his watch, grimaced and made a mental note to take it to a jeweler and get it repaired.

"I've got the cars ready. We can drop them off at their hotel and pick them up when they want," Stein said.

"I wish they would let us put them in private quarters."

Stein's laughter rang in Beaumont's ear. "I think they made the right choice. We start offering them protection and the press will be sniffing around. Didn't you see the paper? Did Mary Frances call you yet?"

Beaumont slammed down the receiver.

~ * ~

Beaumont opened the door to the limousine and stepped from the car. Stein was waiting for him at the smaller terminal used by private pilots. Dulles had separated commercial from private flights when the commercial carriers demanded more space.

"This isn't that bad an idea," he said as Stein dropped a cigarette on the ground and squashed it beneath his toe. "At least we can get to them without too much company."

Stein nodded. "It makes the fiction of being chauffeurs irrelevant."

"Not if those men Kraft spotted last night are around."

The two walked from the small, private parking lot through an open side door, and into the hanger cum terminal. The building was large, but the terminal section was cut off from the remainder of the hanger. Opposite the entrance, Beaumont saw a wall of windows and through them planes parked in designated spaces. He wondered which one belonged to ISIR.

To his left was a short corridor that ended in a padlocked door. From where he stood, he could see there was no handle on the door, hence the padlock. He looked at a man behind the counter, probably the manager since there was no one else around.

"There was a flight due at four," Beaumont said.

The man looked up. "Private planes come in most of the time, mister, but one just arrived."

"Where are the passengers?"

The man inclined his head to his right, and Beaumont stepped away from the counter. He hurried to the windows followed by Stein. Barstead was walking toward the terminal along with Reed and a man Beaumont didn't recognize. The two were pushing a transport cart loaded with supplies and some luggage.

Stein moved to the door, opened it, and Barstead thanked him. "I'm Aaron Stein. Are you Dr. Barstead?"

"Julian Barstead." He offered a free hand to the agent. Stein took his luggage instead.

"Let's keep it formal while we're here," he whispered to the scientist.

"I understand. You're our drivers?"

Beaumont nodded "Yes, the cars are outside. We'll give you a hand with the cart." He passed Barstead, walked outside, and directed the others around the terminal toward the parked limousines. However, Amber and Roger ignored him, walking inside.

They hurried toward the man behind the counter as Barstead said to Stein, "Just some paper work to do about space rental and payment."

Stein nodded and directed the scientist to follow him. As he passed by the two, he said. "The cars are outside when you finish."

Amber nodded.

Stein and Barstead left the terminal to find the group loading the luggage and equipment into the two cars.

Beaumont looked at Stein. "What about the others?"

"Paperwork," Stein replied as he removed a pack of cigarettes from his pocket. He offered one to Barstead, who declined. "Give them a few minutes to take care of that plane of theirs."

Beaumont watched Stein light the cigarette, take a puff, and sigh. He returned his attention to Rierdon. “I gather this equipment is necessary?”

Rierdon answered. “I’m Cc Rierdon. We haven’t been introduced, and yes, this is the latest in infrared and magnetic sensing equipment.”

Beaumont observed the bulky items filling the entire trunk space of one of the special limousines. He wondered what use it would be in dealing with the specter.

“What time do you have?” Rierdon asked him. “I forgot to set my watch when we stopped for refueling.”

Beaumont looked at his watch, made a face, and said. “Damn, I need to get this fixed. Keep forgetting. I’ve got too much on my mind. My watch hasn’t worked since that encounter with the ghost.”

“The encounter where you lost your handkerchief?” Rierdon asked.

Beaumont nodded. “Yes, why?”

“Let me see the watch.”

Beaumont removed his watch and handed it to the scientist. Rierdon took it, briefly examined it, and placed it on the car.

“What’s wrong?’ Beaumont asked.

Rierdon gently lifted the watch. Beaumont noted the man seemed to exert a slight pull as he did so.

“It’s been magnetized. It’s no wonder your watch doesn’t work.”

Beaumont took his watch and repeated the scientist's action. He felt a small tug as the steel car clung to the steel watch. "How did that happen?" He looked at Rierdon.

Rierdon shrugged as Gray Eagle approached them. "That's what we're here to find out."

~ * ~

"Seems to me you're awfully young to be flying that big plane." The manager behind the counter looked at Amber.

"I've flown for years." She ignored the implied accusation that not only was she young, but a woman.

Roger came to her defense as he usually did. "We had other supervision. Gray Eagle was with us."

"Why don't you finish this?" The manager shoved the clipboard to Roger, ignoring Amber. She and Roger exchanged glances, and she shrugged. He hurriedly filled in the information.

Amber studied the terminal while she fought to control her temper. Someday, she vowed, she would show them it made no difference if you were a woman. Change may be coming, as Gray Eagle often told her, but it wasn't coming fast enough for her.

Her gaze took in the institutional white paint that always seemed to be a part of utilitarian public buildings. She glanced briefly at a corridor to her right. A man dressed in a black suit was standing at the entrance to the corridor. He did what she could only describe as a double take when their eyes met.

"Hey!" she shouted, as the man turned and ran back into the corridor from which he had emerged. He was unfamiliar to her and she wondered about the implied recognition.

The hanger manager looked to his right in time to see the man disappear into the corridor that began at the edge of the counter.

"Hey, buddy, no one's allowed in that section." But the man was gone. The manager opened a small swinging door leading to the space behind the counter and raced into the corridor.

"What's going on?" Roger asked, looking up from his paperwork.

"Some guy was watching us. He was dressed all in black; I mean even his shirt was black."

"You've got to stop reading science fiction," Roger teased.

"This isn't fiction. The guy was for real, and I didn't like the feel of him. Besides, he had this emblem on the breast pocket of his jacket. It was a black circle with red around it and a red inverted triangle in the center. I've never seen that emblem."

"How did you see it was black if he was wearing black?"

"The circle looked metallic."

"What the hell are you doing?" The manager's shout drew their attention to the corridor. Sounds of a scuffle followed, and the pair hurried to the manager's aid. When they reached the start of the corridor, only the crumpled body of the manager lay on the tile floor. The stranger was nowhere to be seen. Amber raced to the manager and knelt beside him. She felt for a pulse. There was none. She looked up at Roger and shook her head.

Roger said. "I'll go for help."

Amber looked at the body beside her. There wasn't a visible mark on the manager, yet he was dead. Worse, the man she had seen was nowhere. How had he managed to escape from a dead end corridor into the very air?

Three

No event is ever certain.
Codex of Flowering Butterfly

Universal Time 1. 00. 04. 14 (Universe 61

San watched the colorful topology of equations unfold before her, created by the program used by the army to track perturbations and synchronistic happenings in the universe they were planning to invade. She studied a small point of coalescence that had appeared on the projected screen. It was a red warning blotch on an otherwise dynamic display. She studied a small point of coalescence that had appeared on the projected screen. It was a red warning blotch on an otherwise dynamic display.

"What is that?" she asked.

"General, it doesn't seem to be confined to the 1861 universe. It appears to be located in the buffer universe as well, but there it's in DC, not Frederick, Maryland."

San glared at the display that confirmed her growing suspicions. Val had lied to her. She could feel it and now she had the proof. San always knew one day that little rat would go too far with his scams. But she had not found anything out of the ordinary beyond this point of coalescence.

She would be forced to use Brac and Koru to help her ferret out Val's plans. Elar, searching for the operatives missing after a routine mission, had found them at an abandoned Source Gate in the middle Atlantic region of North America in a sixteenth century universe. It was the same universe where the Jewel Hazen had attempted to steal was located. The mission had cost Hazen his mind and led to San's attempt on his life.

Instead of avoiding that universe until the perturbations from the failed mission died down, Brac and Koru had been using it to hide some unregistered loot. The Khysid Army allowed for officers to skim a portion of the resources the army took from other universes during missions. But each officer had to log in what they kept and a part was returned to the Army, sort of a larceny tax.

"The fools," she muttered, including Elar in her thoughts.

When Elar caught Brac and Koru using the Source Gate, he had failed to have them executed. She wondered offhand what sort of accommodations Elar had made with them.

"Now their stupidity might have some use," she said aloud, running her finger along her lower lip.

The technician knew better than to interrupt a superior, especially one of the Command Council members from the Sixth Level. He ignored her words.

San muttered, "I'll have those two find out just what Val is doing." Val was too dense to suspect anything, though Kester was another matter. But Val hated him and was probably setting him up for a fall should Val's plans fail. But Kester would side with her in any action, since he wanted a crack at the longevity virus.

~ * ~

April 22, 1861(Universe 1)

Desiree relaxed in her chair, turned the paper, and read an article dealing with secession. "It occurs to me that compromise would do more for us than war."

Harriette walked to the cushioned window seat and began to sketch the garden. "Maybe, but we seem to be following a different path."

Desiree did not reply. The darkness that had gripped her mind for the past few days had begun to ebb. *Maybe Lincoln will take actions to stop this coming conflict.* "Maybe he's doing it now, and I sense this," she whispered to herself.

A short article caught her eye with the headline, 'Strange Happening.' "Listen to this. It seems that Mr. Wilson, you remember him? That man who owns that farm on the edge of town."

"Yes," Harriette said. "Has he lost another cow?"

"No, he was opening his barn when this stranger darted from it." Desiree stopped as she finished the paragraph. "The stranger was dressed all in black with an emblem on the breast of his coat."

Harriette asked. "What sort of emblem?"

"A metallic, black circle trimmed in blood red, with a red inverted triangle in the center and…"

When Desiree said nothing else, Harriette looked up from her work. "Desiree?"

"Harriette, ring for Millie."

Harriette was on her feet. She quickly moved to Desiree's side. "What is it? You look as if you have seen one of the White House spirits."

"I need to lie down." Desiree's stomach churned; her head felt light. She knew it was due to the description she had read aloud, but could not in the least understand why.

~ * ~

April 23, 1961(Universe 0)

The hall before the Lincoln bedroom was filled with equipment and ISIR personnel. Gray Eagle glanced at his watch. It was 2:30 a.m. His head felt as if it were stuffed with wool and his body ached from leaning against the wall several feet away from the door to the Lincoln bedroom. The three hour time difference between coasts was playing havoc with his metabolism.

After Roger and Amber discovered the hanger manager's body, Beaumont had hustled all of them into one limousine and left Stein to deal with the police. Stein arrived at the hotel several hours later, having driven the car with the equipment in it.

Gray Eagle shifted as he recalled Barstead's pacing until the car arrived. There was a lot of money invested in that equipment. When Stein finally entered the hotel, he explained to the group that the coroner believed the man had died of a massive heart attack. On the surface, Beaumont appeared inclined to dismiss the story told by Amber and Roger. He discounted the claim of seeing a man in the corridor, a man who had then simply disappeared. But Gray Eagle sensed the agent was far more disturbed about it than he let anyone know.

A sudden movement by Rierdon alerted Gray Eagle and he shifted to a less cramped position. Both Amber and Roger were asleep on the floor, while Barstead sat opposite him, eyelids closed. Reed finished pouring coffee from a Thermos and handed the cup to Margaret.

"I'm going to check the infrared camera again." Rierdon walked to the tripod holding a camera Barstead had designed. It was smaller than most such cameras and it had an insulated unit to keep the film cool. The black and white infrared film had a habit of fogging if it got too warm, even if it was loaded in a changing bag. The new film was a design by one of the ISIR biochemists.

"You've checked it twice before," Margaret grumbled. "It works the same as it did on our last dig. Only conditions are better here."

Barstead's eyes flew open. "Something's happening."

"What is it?" Rierdon looked up from the camera.

"My God, it's pegging the needle."

"What is?" Gray Eagle asked, leaning toward Barstead.

"I don't know. It's the magnetic field indicator." Barstead supported the heavy instrument on his lap, staring at the analog meter indicating field strength in Gauss.

"Maybe someone turned on a motor," Gray Eagle suggested, even as he felt a stirring in the region of his solar plexus. Something was happening. His gaze strayed to the door to the Lincoln Bedroom.

As Beaumont had described, a spinning cloud of vapor-mist appeared in the center of the door, followed by the region of darkness the agent had described in detail. A surge of energy plowed into Gray Eagle, pinning him against the wall.

President Lincoln stood before the scientists. Everyone but Gray Eagle got to their feet. Amber, wide-awake, reached out a hand to her mentor. Gray Eagle took it, and using the wall as support, rose. His eyes strayed past Lincoln to Rierdon standing beside the activated camera. The anthropologist was biting bloodless lips while his right hand clung to the tripod.

Beaumont was on his feet facing the specter.

"Mr. Beaumont, isn't it enough that you and your fellows plague me? Must you bring others into my home as well?"

Gray Eagle's breath caught in his throat. The voice sounded high-pitched, not at all like the voice he would expect from Lincoln. He remembered Barstead saying that Lincoln really spoke in a somewhat squeaky voice and most people didn't know this. If this were a hoax, the perpetrator had taken great pains to be historically accurate.

"Sir, these are scientists," Beaumont gestured to the people in the hall. "They've come to try and determine what's going on."

"Scientists," the president said, glancing at the assemblage, his gaze resting first on Margaret then on Amber. "I've seen many women at the lectures on science I've attended, though none dressed such as you."

Gray Eagle listened as the agent introduced the people from ISIR as if he were speaking with someone other than the image of a dead president. As Beaumont spoke, Gray Eagle sensed no death in that hallway. Whatever fronted them was very much alive and that, of course, was impossible.

Barstead, oblivious to everyone, walked directly before Lincoln and lifted the meter he carried toward the vapor. He quickly withdrew the meter, using the attached strap across his shoulder to help support the instrument.

"Sir, what is that?" Lincoln asked.

"It's a magnetic field indicator and it's off the scale. Whatever is going on, it's real enough to affect the meter."

Lincoln smiled at Beaumont. "Sir, your own scientist has confirmed my existence."

A pink flush crept along Beaumont's cheeks. "Dr. Barstead, are you telling me this is real?" Barstead nodded. "Whatever *this* is."

"I find it delightful to discover that I'm real," Lincoln quipped. "Since I have been telling Mr. Beaumont that I'm not a ghost. And now, I believe, neither is he, nor any of you."

Barstead looked at Lincoln. "I don't understand."

"This man," Lincoln indicated the agent. "His friends and others have been appearing in my office since I took up residence in the White House. I thought all of you ghosts at first, but I have come to think otherwise. Now so do you."

During the conversation, Gray Eagle reached into his medicine pouch and removed the pebble he carried. He glanced quickly at the pebble before covering it with his hand. In the instant he had stared at it, the pebble turned translucent and pinpoints of red sparked in its depths.

"We're appearing in your office?" Barstead asked.

Lincoln nodded.

Gray Eagle looked at Lincoln, growing more distinct and solid as the conversation continued. *This must not be allowed to happen in this manner*, a voice whispered in Gray Eagle's head. He had no idea what the words meant, and his next movements were involuntary. He completed them before he was aware he had lifted the stone he held cupped in his hand.

When Gray Eagle stopped the action, Lincoln began to fade, the vapor collapsing into a pinpoint of white light before winking out of existence.

Beaumont jerked toward Gray Eagle. “What is that thing?”

“A Shaman’s Stone,” Gray Eagle gave the name Two Feathers had given him. “It’s a way to another Arrow of Time.” Two Feathers had told him that as well, but had failed to explain what it meant.

“What the hell does that mean?” Beaumont growled. He made a gesture as if to brush away his words. “It doesn’t matter. That stone made the ghost go away.”

Gray Eagle detected both relief and loss in the comment. “It’s just a concretion of quartz,” he lied.

“Gray Eagle’s right,” Barstead quickly added. “The field strength was dropping even as we spoke with the specter, or whatever it was. Gray Eagle is a Shaman as well as an engineer. Shamans are supposed to get ghosts to go to wherever it is ghosts go.”

Gray Eagle said, “At least the specter is gone for now.”

“Will it stay away?” Beaumont demanded.

Gray Eagle asked. “Do you want it to?”

Beaumont’s face took on a hard expression. “Of course I do. That’s why I brought you here.”

Rierdon, somewhat recovered, stepped away from the camera. "Ghosts usually have some focus in a haunting. Let's see if we can discover it. If we can, getting rid of the focus will usually get rid of the ghost."

"The house could be the focus," Margaret suggested.

Rierdon shook his head. "No, I think something else is the focus. Let's study what we've recorded and see what we can come up with."

Gray Eagle was grateful when Beaumont agreed. Everyone was exhausted and morning would give a different light on the subject. He shoved the stone into his pouch, but suddenly felt none of them would escape that easily.

Stein approached. "How'd it go?" he asked, as he prepared to relieve Beaumont. "You people finished?"

"It's disappeared for now," Beaumont said.

Rierdon began to dismantle the camera and tripod. "I wish we had someone on this who knew a lot about the Civil War. That's not my specialty."

"Cc, if it isn't dead at least five hundred years, you're not interested." Margaret offered him a cup of coffee, but he declined.

"Hey, what about your sister?" Stein glanced at Beaumont. Beaumont shook his head. "Don't say no, Arthur. She's helped us before and is good at keeping quiet. Besides, Lincoln is right up her alley."

"Your sister's a Civil War expert?" Barstead asked.

Beaumont gritted his teeth and nodded.

Stein explained. "She has a Ph.D. in history with a specialty in the Civil War and military history. She teaches as an adjunct professor at Georgetown. Mary Frances Beaumont, good looker too, but I'm married."

Gray Eagle sensed Beaumont wanted to wring Stein's neck. "Perhaps she could give us some information on the White House at the time Lincoln was living in it."

"That's what we need to know," Rierdon affirmed.

"Call her, Arthur. I'll take care of the paperwork myself," Stein offered.

Beaumont had backed against the wall during the conversation. He looked at the people around him, sighed and nodded. "I'll call her tomorrow, I mean today." He took Stein by the arm and said to the scientists, "Would you excuse us for a moment?" The two agents walked away from the ISIR team.

"Whew!" Barstead made a pretense of wiping his brow. "I hope he bought that stuff about a focus."

Rierdon said, "It's not stuff. There is a focus in a haunting."

"This isn't any haunting," Barstead insisted. "Whatever is happening, it's real, too real. And I haven't the slightest idea how to proceed."

"Maybe this historian can be of some help," Gray Eagle offered. "If we knew more about that time period, we might be able to come up with something."

"Come up with what?"

Gray Eagle sighed. "I don't know, but whatever's happening here lies in that time, as well as ours."

"You mean we've discovered a doorway to the past?" Rierdon asked.

Gray Eagle shook his head. "No."

"Then what is it?" Rierdon demanded.

Gray Eagle shrugged.

~ * ~

April 23, 1861(Universe 1)

Colonel Val, mission commander for the exploitation / invasion mission A-26-5225, pounded on his desk. His watery blue eyes glared at Lieutenant Wes, his lover.

"I can't believe that damned Bechter told you to get lost."

"Sir, he said he would not cooperate with us anymore." Wes shifted as he reported his encounter.

"Bechter was one of Hazen's operatives during World War II in that universe. He owes us his life. We got him away from the Nazis."

"He refused to help, sir. What are your orders?"

"Kill the son of a bitch before he gets to those stupid scientists."

Wes nodded. "I doubt he can do any damage."

"You're in no position to make such a statement, you fool. Now get out of here and get rid of that idiot. Do him like you did that man who almost caught you at the hanger when you were following the scientists. Give me an oral report. And try not to hide in any barns when you return. You made the papers."

Wes nodded, saluted, and left the secure room in the basement of the Embassy Club. Val watched the door close with a mixture of fury and fear. San was sniffing around again. He knew it. He had to cover his tracks. The two universes, the one he was in, and the buffer 1961 universe, were fast approaching the phenomenon of temporal resonance.

No one alive in the Khysid Army had ever seen such a phenomenon. As far as Val knew, it was merely a theoretical curiosity, but no more. Val had appropriated Hazen's software programs when he had discovered the Micro Ds Pettigrew had salvaged after killing the late Supreme Commander. Those programs had enabled Val to hide his plans for escape from the Khysid Army.

The programs had also allowed him to cover up the massive perturbations building up in the two universes. These appeared as coincidences for certain inhabitants. But the perturbations had grown into what was known as a cascade. Long before this happened, the army should have abandoned both universes, waiting until the perturbations died down before returning. Otherwise, instabilities might occur in the Source Gate being used to create the portals for transfer between universes. The problem was that no one in the army but Val knew of the disturbances.

He had tried to enlist Bechter's aid in deflecting the scientists from ghost hunting. The infrastructure for the Source Gate San wanted established in the secure room of the Embassy Club, was setting up a disturbance between the two White Houses. If he didn't stop the mess soon, slip-throughs would occur. There was no way Val could explain that to San, or hide it from her either.

But Bechter had told him to get lost. He would no longer cooperate with the Khysid Army. Val frowned. The man must be suicidal. Such a refusal was an automatic death sentence.

~ * ~

April 23, 1961(Universe 0)

Amber stepped from the elevator of the DC Hilton onto a carpet of rich paisley hues. The lobby walls, a subtle matching print to the carpet, were decorated with elegant nineteenth century paintings of country scenes. The lobby desk and all the pillars were constructed from marble, and crystal chandeliers hung suspended from the high ceilings.

"I don't see Beaumont's sister anywhere." She scanned the islands of comfortable chairs and loveseats located throughout the lobby. Scattered knots of guest and conference attendees sat discussing topics of mutual interest. Waitresses passed among them taking orders or delivering drinks.

"She'll be here," Roger insisted. "From what Cc said, I gather she's really anxious to get involved in this investigation."

"Oh?" Amber raised an eyebrow. Roger was like a brother to her and the pair had shared many adventures at ISIR. "Did Cc tell you this?"

She shifted in the low heeled pumps she was forced to wear on these occasions. Amber hated wearing anything but slacks. She felt that her straight skirt and long sleeve blouse restricted her movements. She carried a leather purse that fit comfortably over her shoulder since her clothing allowed no room for needed items.

Roger shook his head. "No, Margaret did. She said Beaumont didn't want his sister involved and his sister was a bit peeved when she found out."

"I don't blame her." Amber continued to scan the lobby for someone appearing to be lost. "I know what it's like to be shunted aside."

Roger shot a quick look at her. "You take it so well."

"I don't take it; I just ignore it, and fly right past." She made a waving motion with her hand.

Amber watched a woman enter through the revolving door. "This whole thing with the ghost gives me a funny feeling."

"Never thought I'd see Lincoln in my lifetime," Roger said.

"If it *is* Lincoln."

Amber shivered. The ghost felt real even to Gray Eagle, from the way he had reacted. She hadn't missed the change in the pebble he carried when he held it out to the ghost. She wished they knew what the pebble he carried really was.

The woman she had been watching stepped into the lobby and glanced around. She was about an inch taller than Amber, but her relationship to Beaumont was obvious in her shoulder-length auburn hair. She was a refined image of the agent, dressed in a beige silk suit, accented by a strand of pearls.

"I bet that's Dr. Beaumont." Amber touched Roger on the shoulder, directing his attention to the woman standing just to the right of the revolving door. "Let's go rescue her."

Amber walked up to the woman as Roger followed. "Excuse me. Are you Dr. Beaumont?"

Mary Frances nodded. "Yes, I'm to meet someone."

"Well, we've been sent to find you and bring you to the others." Amber made the introductions and gestured to the hallway to the left. "They're in the hospitality room adjoining the main ballroom. It's next to the pool."

Mary Frances smiled. "Is my brother here?"

"No, but the others are anxious to meet you and talk about the White House of 1861. I understand you're an expert." Amber started in the direction of the ballroom, forcing Mary Frances and Roger to accompany her.

Mary Frances adjusted her handbag, removed her gloves, and unbuttoned her suit jacket as she walked beside Amber. "Arthur didn't tell me much about the sightings. But then he never tells me much of anything."

A smile played on Amber's lips. She wondered if she had found an older kindred spirit. "An occupational hazard?"

"You're quite right in that," Mary Frances replied as she slowed her pace.

There were five women seated behind the registration table. Two were speaking with some of the guests. Roger walked to the table and made inquiries, while Amber and Mary Frances waited by the entrance to the ballroom.

"I didn't realize there were so many women physicists," Mary Frances remarked.

"Those are the wives, or secretaries of the men registered for the conference. I don't think the Plasma Physics Society has any women as members."

"You're not a member?" Mary Frances asked. "But of course not, you're too young." She placed her hand to her lips. "I'm sorry. I didn't mean anything by that."

Amber nodded. "I get that all the time, especially when I fly."

"You're a pilot?" Mary Frances swung to face the young woman. "So am I. I learned to fly two years ago. Are you rated on instruments yet?"

"Yes. I flew ISIR's plane cross country. Of course I had help from Roger and Gray Eagle. Your brother didn't say you flew."

"Arthur worries about me. That's why I never have any fun, well at least any that I can tell him about."

Amber laughed. She would have to steal a few moments with this woman and learn more about her. She seemed more interesting than her stolid and duty-bound brother and she was a fellow pilot.

Roger left the table and came to Mary Frances, offering her a nametag. "Dr. Barstead registered you as a member of the institute so you don't have to pay the conference fee."

"Thanks." Mary Frances took the tag and secured it to her suit. She followed Amber and Roger through the ballroom into the adjoining hospitality suite.

A massive table dominated one end of the room, presided over by an ice sculpture meant to be an eagle, but melting into the vague outlines of a vulture. The table was burdened with canapés and trays of cheeses and fruits. An open bar stood to the right of the food, hosting an equal number of drinkers as eaters.

"I haven't had lunch yet." Mary Frances eyed the table.

"You'll have time to eat. The waitresses bring the food around," Amber explained. "The ISIR people are in the corner. I'll introduce you." She gestured to a grouping of chairs surrounding a low coffee table piled with glasses, plates and papers.

Amber brought Mary Frances to the others and made the introductions. Barstead gestured for the historian to sit beside him and glanced at Amber. He lifted a manila folder, offering it to her.

"I hate to impose, but would you and Roger take this to Dr. Bechter? He's out by the pool."

"What is it?" Roger asked, shooting a glance at Amber.

Barstead cleared his throat. "It's Stan's paper. He forgot to give it to Hans."

Damn, Amber thought. *He's keeping us out of it again.* Aloud she said, "Sure, don't say anything important until we get back." She took the folder and started toward the doors to the pool, Roger trailing behind her. "Weber forgot, my foot," she muttered. "Julian forgot to give it to Dr. Bechter, or it's a ruse to get rid of us."

Roger hurried to keep up with her. "Julian has been forgetting a lot of things lately, especially where Weber is concerned. You think he plans to get rid of the man?"

"Not yet." She shoved open the glass doors with more force than she intended. "It's not hunting season."

She stormed across the flagstone patio toward a table with a blue and white striped umbrella at its center. Sitting beside the table was an older man sipping coffee. He glanced up at the determined young woman coming his way. When he realized he was her destination, he stood.

"May I be of service?" he asked in a thick, German accent.

Amber stopped as she reached the table. "Dr. Bechter?"

He nodded.

"Dr. Barstead asked me to give this to you." She handed him the folder.

Bechter took it. "You are from ISIR?"

"Yes." Amber made the introductions.

"How do you do," Bechter said, gesturing for them to sit. "I gather this is Dr. Weber's paper, no?"

"Yes," Amber said, taking a seat across from Bechter. Roger sat next to her.

Bechter summoned a waitress, requesting some refreshments for his guests. After the woman left, he said. "I agreed to read this. Do you know Dr. Weber well?"

Amber and Roger exchanged glances. The physicist laughed in a deep baritone. He placed the folder on the table and covered it with one hand.

"Dr. Weber is with ISIR," Amber said. Her face felt warm from embarrassment at her obvious dislike of Weber. Bechter seemed to be amused by her reaction. He smiled, accenting the wrinkles on his weathered face. His gray hair was mussed, much like Einstein used to wear his. And like Einstein, Bechter was a theoretical physicist, one of the best.

"I see you know him well," Bechter chuckled. "Stan is a good scientist, even brilliant some times, but he is too full of himself."

Amber tried not to laugh, but the observation was too good to let pass. The waitress arrived with a tray of fruits and drinks, and the three took helpings of everything.

"How did you meet Dr. Weber?" Amber asked between bites of a strawberry.

"I was working on revising a monograph by an old friend, Marie Hasselbach. I needed someone with expertise in magnetic theory and Stan agreed to help me. But," Bechter stopped, his attention focused for a minute on something at the other end of the pool.

"I guess that was before Dr. Weber came to ISIR," Roger said, attempting to continue the stalled conversation.

Bechter gave a quick shake of his head. "Marie and I were friends. She and her lover were part of the underground in Germany during the Second World War. He was killed, and she captured and executed."

Amber stopped eating. "I'm sorry. That was a very bad time."

"Yes, made more so by the…"

The ensuing silence made Amber nervous. "I don't think I ever heard of this Marie Hasselbach." Amber wondered about Bechter's sudden lapses of attention. He radiated anxiety despite his outward calm, but she couldn't locate the cause.

"She was the daughter of Baron Hasselbach and an American woman. Her mother had some African blood and the Nazis, well their attitude toward genetic purity is well known."

"She wasn't killed because she was in the underground?" Amber wondered why Bechter was telling them the story.

"No, her lover protected her. My dear, would you mind if I give you something?"

"I don't understand." Amber sensed a wave of fear coming from Bechter. It was almost as if the past were overlapping the present and he was being hunted. An icy tendril of fear crawled along her spine.

Bechter reached into his coat pocket and removed a thin, printed volume bound in blue leather about the size of a small paperback novel. He placed it beneath the folder before him. He shoved the folder across the table to Amber. The action was so practiced and smooth, that had she not been paying attention, she would have missed it. She didn't miss the implication or the pleading look in the scientist's eyes.

"I'll see that Dr. Weber gets this."

"No, give it to Julian," Bechter said. "I think I have overstayed my welcome. Please excuse me."

He rose, lifted the briefcase on the chair next to him and strode away from the hospitality suite toward the rooms. Amber and Roger exchanged surprised glances. Bechter hurriedly cut across the patio behind the diving board at the deep end of the pool where a swimmer was preparing to dive.

Suddenly Bechter looked at the massive hedge screening the pool. His mouth moved as if he were addressing someone. He leaned forward, clutched his chest, and stumbled away. His briefcase fell from his hand as he dropped backward into the pool. Several bathers screamed and laughed at what appeared to be a comic dive by a fully clothed guest.

Amber jumped to her feet. "Help him!"

Roger shoved aside his chair and raced toward the end of the pool. “Get him out!” he shouted. “He’s had a heart attack!”

The man on the diving board leaped into the pool and caught hold of Bechter’s jacket, dragging the unconscious scientist to the surface. Two others pulled the body from the pool while a third began artificial respiration.

Chaos swarmed around Amber, distracting everyone from the table where she still waited. Cautiously she slipped the book from beneath the folder and secured it under her arm. She took advantage of the confusion around the pool to dart into one of the outdoor changing rooms. Once inside, she shoved the narrow volume into the purse she carried, barely managing to snap the closure.

Amber stepped from the changing room to find Roger hurrying toward her, his face creased in a puzzled frown at her actions. She glanced at the table and shivered. The folder was gone.

Four

No pattern is ever lost.
Codex of Flowering Butterfly

June 30, 1861(Universe 1)

Desiree brushed her hands against the dark green apron tied over her working dress. Again she attacked the stubborn weed threatening to ruin the beauty of an otherwise flawless herb garden. It finally yielded its thick snakelike roots, oozing from the moist soil without further struggle. She tossed it into a wooden bucket set to the side of the garden for just that purpose.

Desiree placed her hand against the small of her back and stretched. Louis had never allowed her the pleasure of a garden she could tend for herself.

"Refined ladies do no such thing," she mocked his words.

Refined ladies also did not tend ailing husbands soiling themselves, but then Desiree knew she had never wanted to be a refined lady. Harriette was another matter entirely. Sitting on a swing supported beneath a lush grape arbor, her young charge was sketching the garden with a proficiency that amazed Desiree.

"Maybe we should go to Paris," Desiree remarked casually, dropping the tool she had been using. It struck the ground near her feet. "You say that at least once a week." Harriette looked up from her drawing. "I wish you wouldn't worry so about me. I can take care of myself."

"I mean to see that you receive an education, as India Hereford is."

The Herefords were old friends of Desiree's. Louis had done business with them before his death. They lived in Boston where Samuel Hereford ran a fleet of ships. Hereford's ships carried Bouchard cotton to mills both in the northeast and in England.

It had pleased Desiree when the Herefords had accepted Harriette. Their daughter India and Harriette had become close friends. India was bound for the Women's Medical College, but Harriette's education was another matter. Where could she send Harriette? She knew that Harriette did not wish to leave her.

"Oh!" Harriette jumped from her seat. "I think it's raining."

Desiree glanced at the sky, noting the massive thunderheads forming above them. *When had this happened?* She had felt nothing about the coming weather change. Several fat drops of rain struck her on the face, forcing her into action. She retrieved her tool and the bucket and raced for the door to the out kitchen. Harriette was holding it open for her.

Lightning struck with the force of a whip, a jagged streak suspended between sky and ground. The following thunder rolled across the house, shaking it with the power of an earthquake.

"My God," Desiree whispered. The old chestnut tree at the end of the garden toppled, split by the strike. Rain pelted the ground in a torrent. Desiree looked at the tree and sadness welled up inside her. "It's gone, all gone."

"It's just a tree. Mr. Wilson will be happy to chop it for us. We can use the wood this winter."

"Harriette, look!" Desiree pointed beyond to the sky, visible between the remains of the split tree.

An arc of green light flared on the eastern horizon, pulsating with fury, as if it were the reflection of something burning just over the hill. Desiree realized it was in the direction of Washington. Suddenly an image of such horror washed over her that she turned and vomited the contents of her stomach, falling to her knees on the packed earth entrance to the out kitchen.

"Desiree!" Harriette dropped her sketch pad and knelt beside her "Millie!" she screamed. "Help me!"

"I'll be fine," Desiree insisted, now that the image had mercifully vanished, leaving nothing but a sour stomach as a residue.

Harriette clung to her. "This is why you cannot send me away. You need me to take care of you."

"Nonsense," Desiree replied, in spite of her wish to hold onto Harriette, to protect her.

"You should have listened to Ruby Blackhawk. She wanted to help you…"

Desiree glanced at the concerned face before her. "With my gift? Ruby helped me with Louis. That was enough."

Millie, their maid, came through the door wiping her hands on a linen towel. "Mrs. Bouchard, what is it?"

"Her time of month," Harriette improvised, helping Desiree to her feet.

Millie nodded sagely. "I'll make you one of those teas," she offered, with the familiarity of one stricken with the same complaint. The two women helped Desiree into the house, leaving behind the fallen sketch pad, rain smearing and distorting the charcoal image of the garden.

~ * ~

June 30, 1961 (Universe 0)

Mary Frances Beaumont studied the pile of notes filling the table she used as a desk. Her brother had been happy when she accepted a temporary position with ISIR and returned with the scientists to California in late April. He was especially happy to be rid of Amber and Roger. Bodies always seemed to turn up when they were around.

Dr. Bechter's death had been ruled a massive heart attack, just like the death of the hangar manager. She learned about the latter incident from Amber, not her brother. With her scholar's mind, she easily concluded that two similar deaths in unusual circumstances meant something more than coincidence. But the released autopsy results had suggested natural causes as the reasons for both deaths.

The shattering ringing of the phone jarred her from her reverie. She reached for the receiver. “Hello.”

“I’m glad you’re in.”

“Arthur, what have you been up to? I’m having fun here. I might even stay.”

“I haven’t been able to get hold of Barstead. Where is he?” Her brother was all business.

Mary Frances tensed. “They’re doing some sort of test at the opposite end of institute land and have only a radio for contact with the main buildings. Why?”

“Get them. Tell them there’s a plane on its way for the team.”

“Why?”

Beaumont added, “You too. The specter is back in full force, and the president’s had me block off the area around the Lincoln bedroom. It’s damned inconvenient for Kennedy and his family.”

“What happened? I thought Gray Eagle got rid of the thing.”

Beaumont made a snorting sound. “So did I. But that Shaman Stone of his didn’t keep that ghost down for long. Worse still, we’ve got this greenish light that keeps appearing on the horizon.”

“The Aurora?”

"No." Beaumont's reply was clipped. "Crazy people seem to think space invaders are coming. One nut wrote a letter to the paper insisting the light meant contact by aliens because it keeps appearing near the building housing the National Geographic Society."

"That's where I'd go if I were a space alien."

"This isn't funny," her brother sighed. "I still can't explain those two dead men."

"What dead men?"

"Bechter and the hanger manager."

"I thought their deaths were natural?"

Beaumont cleared his throat. "Each man's heart had some scarring that looked like the tissue was burned."

When her brother stopped abruptly, Mary Frances realized he had not meant to reveal what he knew. "Like an electrocution?"

"Not quite. Pathologist wasn't sure."

Arthur must want the ISIR people very badly for him to reveal to her what he had. "I'll get on the radio. Give me the details of the plane sent for us and I'll have Julian call."

"Thanks, you're a lifesaver."

Mary Frances pulled a sheet of paper to her, took a pen, and began to write down the information as her brother dictated it to her. Her mind churned with the words he had spoken a few minutes earlier. The deaths of the men had not been natural. Something had killed them and no one knew what or how.

She wondered if she should mention the book Bechter had given Amber. She was still amazed that neither Roger nor Amber had spoken a word about having the book until they reached California. Her brother would be furious when he learned about it. So she decided not to tell him.

~ * ~

July 31, 1961(Universe 0)

Gray Eagle sat alone at a table situated behind the last row of seats in the modified transport. It was an old cargo carrier, but it had been refurbished to a comfort level that spoke of uses far beyond simple cargo. Gray Eagle wondered what special branch of Military Intelligence owned the plane.

Beaumont had said something about working as a liaison group with a General Croll. Gray Eagle did not know Croll, nor had he any contacts within the military to give him some hints as to the man and his character. He looked up to see Amber walking toward him along the aisle of passenger seats, Roger trailing behind her.

"The pilot said no civilians in the cockpit." Amber bit off the sentence, her face giving the appearance of someone who had eaten a lemon. "He let you in the cockpit."

"I was with the Flying Tigers. He wanted to know a bit about the war," Gray Eagle explained.

Amber took one of the seats opposite Gray Eagle, swiveling it around before she plopped into it. It was a task anyone had to perform, since the supports for the four seats at the table were bolted to the floor.

“How did the experiment go? You didn’t say anything when you and Julian got back.”

Roger added, “Weber seemed upset.”

Gray Eagle allowed a smirk to appear at the corner of his mouth. “Yes, he was, because the experiment worked. He predicted it wouldn’t.”

Amber’s face creased in a broad smile. “Good! But does that mean what was in the book is real? The theory is so weird.”

Gray Eagle shook his head. “It only means that the first parts of the equations have a physical basis and the magnetic field studies confirm them. As to the ghost, well…”

“But is it a ghost?” Amber rubbed the edge of the table.

“It depends on whether or not Marie Hasselbach’s theory is correct. Her theory might well explain what’s been happening, but it’s beyond anything any of us has seen.”

Weber gruffly interrupted. “The fact that the book Hans gave you offers a theory about alternate universes does not mean the theory is accurate. And one measly little experiment is hardly confirmation of anything.” He turned in his seat and stared at the trio around the table. Then he turned back to the tablet he held, scribbling additional notes in absent fury.

Barstead and the others quietly left their seats. Barstead took the empty chair and Rierdon, Reed and Margaret found places on either side of the aisle.

"Why did Hans give the book to you?" Barstead asked her for the fifth time.

She shrugged. "As I said, I think he was being followed and he wanted us to have it, or at least you. If I'd told Beaumont, or that police officer when we were still in DC, we wouldn't have it…they would."

"Quite right," Mary Frances remarked as she exited the bathroom. "Arthur would have kept it from us even if it had no bearing on this ghost."

"It does," Amber insisted. "But it's far ahead of our present science."

Much too far, Gray Eagle thought, suspecting what Two Feathers had meant about an 'Arrow of Time'. He remembered when the realization had first struck, how it had frightened him, even as the wonder of the possibility filled him with delight.

"According to this little treatise," Barstead tapped the book in his pocket. It rarely left his person. "When everything began, multiple universes were formed. But beyond that, some of the math is not recognizable to me or anyone at the institute."

Rierdon shook his head. "It's as if Marie Hasselbach read this somewhere. She couldn't have developed this."

"Read it where?" Margaret Aksawan asked. "Her father was an archaeologist studying the Mayas."

"You ever read any of Baron Hasselbach's work?" Rierdon asked.

She shook her head. "No, I gather it was considered outlandish, almost fiction."

"Science fiction," Rierdon snorted.

"So is this," Amber said. "Except your experiment showed the first part of her theory about magnetic effects was real. Even Dr. Weber suggested that you check for magnetic fields associated with the ghost when we went to DC."

Weber offered an obscenity as a comment, but the others politely ignored him.

"From what I have been able to decipher, history and physics are intertwined."

"It makes no sense," Rierdon added.

"To us," Margaret chuckled.

"Yes," Gray Eagle nodded. "But someone took time to create this book, and some of the material in it actually gives physical results."

"If this theory has any truth to it, then the Lincoln at the White House is real," Barstead offered. "Not our Lincoln, but another Lincoln."

"Is he destined to be assassinated by John Wilkes Booth in a few years?" Mary Frances clutched the manuscript she had been working on at Barstead's request. It was a detailed day-to-day compendium of civil war events. She had begun it at Georgetown and continued it when she was offered the facilities at ISIR.

"Speculation is that there are multiple possibilities for each historical event and each of these gives rise to an alternate universe," Barstead continued. "But the Hasselbach manuscript claims this is too simple and that things are far more complicated."

"The original speculation is complicated enough," Roger grumbled.

Barstead patted him on the shoulder. "True, but this theory suggests that the universes that came into existence encompass these possible changes along a simultaneous continuum."

"Must you discuss this?" Weber interrupted. "I agreed to come along for the ride and because I want to see how the new designs perform. I didn't agree to listen to all this hocus-pocus."

Gray Eagle knew he was referring to the special magnetic field meters Barstead and others had constructed. Weber cared little about any proof of some theory he considered worthless, but the equipment was another matter. If it worked, his studies on magnetic confinement of plasmas would ratchet up several notches in the scientific community. Gray Eagle saw the gleam of a Nobel Prize in Weber's sight.

"Sometimes I think he complains too much," Margaret observed.

Gray Eagle wondered about the comment. She was an astute judge of character, and Weber did ask to come along. He wondered if Weber had his own agenda, one that did not include Lincoln, Beaumont or ISIR.

"We've agreed to keep this to ourselves for now," Barstead reminded his audience. "We've planned on a private motel, rental cars and keeping a distance from both your brother and General Croll."

“Then what?” Reed, silent until now, asked in a quiet voice.

“First, we deal with whatever is going on in the White House. But I want us to set up in the Fairfax Inn. I’ve made arrangements there,” Barstead explained.

Beyond that, Gray Eagle knew, they had made no other plans. Everything depended on taking readings within the White House. Those results would determine the next step and the solutions of the next series of equations, the ones his mind had not wanted him to solve at the very beginning.

~ * ~

July 1, 1861(Universe 1)

San, standing in the secure room in the Embassy Club, watched as the Jewel was positioned in its fiber-optic cradle and made ready for use as the heart of a Source Gate. With Val dead because of his attempts to cover up his meddling, and Kester recovering from his injuries, the Command Council of the Sixth Level was finally taking notice of her suggestions. Even General Sig, a man she greatly admired, listened attentively when she offered advice. It was easy, she thought, to be better than members of the Command Council when it came to analysis. Most of them hadn’t done any real work for years.

“Watch,” she cautioned an overzealous technician. “That Jewel is in near mint condition.” It wasn't really that intact, but the more the people under her command thought so, the more care they would take in their work.

Once the Source Gate was activated, the perturbations between the White House in this universe and the one in the buffer universe would cease. The buffer universe was necessary since the portals created by the Source Gate could open only between contiguous spaces in each universe. Proximity portals were the only kind the Khysid Army was able to create.

The same held for the Jumpers, a loose confederation of scavengers from a universe the Khysid Army had attempted to invade before she was born. They had no Jewels, only simple devices known as Rings that drew off the energy of Khysid Source Gates or such gates as the Khysid Army had abandoned when they were no longer functional.

"Now," San ordered, and the technician ran the first set of diagnostics before final power-up. At least Val had done her one final favor. He had rid her of Hans Bechter, one of Hazen's plants in the buffer universe. Just in time to stop the scientists from messing around the White House of that universe.

~ * ~

July 2, 1961(Universe 0)

The ISIR team arrived to a packed city and Barstead had his people set up in the Fairfax Inn over Beaumont's protests.

"You should stay in a safe house," Beaumont insisted, pacing the floor of Barstead's room. It was the agent's second trip to the Inn.

"I told you," Barstead fumbled with one of the new field meters as he spoke. "I don't want people bothering us. No one knows why we're here. Besides, we have to wait until the ghost reappears."

"Will it?"

"I don't know. We can only assume it will. It has before."

"What about your equipment?" Beaumont gestured to the instruments and cameras crowding the motel room.

"It'll be fine," Barstead replied. "Just let us know when the ghost comes back."

"The government is footing the bill," the agent grinned. "You can live in comfort at the Hilton if you wish."

"This place is quite comfortable. It even has a pool."

Beaumont grimaced at the mention of the pool. "I let you see copies of the autopsy report over my superior's protest. Just get them back to me ASAP."

"Will do," Barstead told the agent.

"I'll be back. Maybe take my sister to dinner." He smiled and left the room.

Barstead looked at the closing door. "She won't tell you anything either," he chuckled.

He returned his gaze to the room, delighted with the Fairfax Inn's décor. The room offered two double beds and also a sleeper couch flanked by two comfortable chairs, a coffee table, and a small desk. The colors were muted blues and greens. Each morning the housekeeper left a vase of real flowers on the coffee table and chocolates on the pillow each evening.

Rierdon opened the door from his adjoining suite and stepped into Barstead's room. "Is he finally gone?"

Barstead nodded. "The others ready?"

"They should be here soon. You think this is a good idea?"

Barstead shrugged. "We can't just sit around here playing cards and watching television even if it's at government expense. Our brains will rot."

"That's for sure, if we keep watching that swill served up on television," Reed slipped into the room from the suite he shared with Rierdon. He glanced at the hefty television set placed on the dresser directly before the bed.

Rierdon laughed. "Radio is gone forever, Walt."

Ignoring the jibe, Reed said. "Julian, I saw that agent leaving your room. He worried about the lack of a ghost?"

"I think poor Arthur worries about everything. I also suspect he's grown fond of Lincoln."

Rierdon plopped onto the bed, bouncing to test its firmness. "You've got to admit any Lincoln would be seductive. Think what he did for this country."

Barstead thumbed the power switch on the meter he was adjusting. "Well, if what we know, so far, of the Hasselbach theory is true, let's hope this Lincoln gets to do the same for his country as well."

Rierdon stopped bouncing. “Hey! We could stop Booth from killing him.”

“What?” Reed asked.

“What difference would it make? It doesn’t affect us. But think of it, a Lincoln living on after the war, none of the horror of reconstruction.”

Reed sobered. “We haven’t even taken our first reading and you’re already altering someone else’s history.”

“Why not?” Rierdon repeated. “What harm will it do?”

~ * ~

July 5, 1861(Universe 1)

Harriette shoved her lace petticoat with the pink embroidered flowers on the hem, into her travel valise. “Maybe I should have asked Ruby Blackhawk what to do about Desiree myself,” she muttered as she packed.

The situation was deteriorating around them and Desiree had suddenly conceived the idea of traveling to Washington. She had even asked Mrs. Wyckworth about hiring a driver should a train not be available. Mrs. Wyckworth had asked Joseph Patton, a freedman working for her, if he knew of anyone. Before he could find someone, Desiree had secured train tickets.

Now that they were going to Washington, Patton was able to recommend a driver working in the city, one Peter Former. He had been sent a telegram and would be waiting for them at the station.

"It's because of what she saw a few days ago," Harriette muttered. "I wish she would speak of these things to me."

"Miss Harriette," Millie said, standing by the open door. "Mrs. Bouchard is ready."

"I'll be down in a moment," Harriette replied. *Even if I don't want to go to Washington.*

~ * ~

July 15, 1961(Universe 0)

"We've found nothing except that magnetic anomaly near the National Geographic building." Gray Eagle recited the results of the clandestine survey of Washington. He noticed Barstead was frowning.

"What do you suggest next?" Rierdon sipped his cup of coffee.

The soggy remains of a pizza sat on the table in the suite Barstead had reserved for himself and shared with Gray Eagle and the mounds of equipment from ISIR.

Amber wiped her mouth with a paper napkin. "Didn't you say you wanted to look at places outside of Washington?"

"Right." Barstead smiled at her. "Mary Frances, what action is happening now? I mean was happening on this date in the Civil War?"

"If you want big," Rierdon said, "try Manassas… that was in July."

Mary Frances interrupted. "Battle of Bull Run or Manassas, depending on your partisan leanings. Happened July twenty-first, 1861."

"That gives us six days. Time enough to send for Chen and Marie Lui, maybe Steven, and Lucinda. We can use extra help to check out a larger area. Let Mark, Paul, and Kit fly in some of the Merlins. I don't like being stranded here without our own planes."

Gray Eagle choked on his slice of pizza. That was the first time he'd ever heard Barstead want to have ISIR planes as a possible backup.

"You okay, Gray Eagle?" Barstead asked.

"Yes," Gray Eagle croaked, washing the food down with a Pepsi. "You're worried?"

"Let's say that I'm uncomfortable," Barstead replied. "The fact that the ghost disappeared and has not returned."

"I don't know about you, but I've had it being cooped up in this place. I'm returning to the institute on the next plane," Weber announced.

"When did you make the arrangements?" Barstead asked, just a hint of anger in his voice. Gray Eagle caught it, though Weber was oblivious.

"This morning."

"I see. You didn't consult me?"

"You have no need of me. The instruments were all I cared about, anyway."

Barstead stood. "Would you excuse us?" he said to those present. Taking Weber by the sleeve, he walked the man to the door, opened it, and left the room.

The people in the room said nothing, but a few minutes later Barstead returned. "I told Stan that if he leaves, he's gone from ISIR when his contract ends this October."

Amber smiled. Gray Eagle caught her delight and mirrored it with his own.

“It’s about time, Julian,” Margaret clapped her hands. “You’ve even saved his life. One more week with him and Arthur Beaumont would have had another dead body and a whole room of suspects.”

~ * ~

Weber gritted his teeth as he stormed toward his room. It mattered little to him that Barstead wanted him gone. ISIR had been a mistake. He had known that the moment he’d set foot in the institute. No one there was serious about research. Why, not only did Gray Eagle design airplanes, but he also built radio-controlled models as if he were a child. The fool could have had his own company, but no, he puttered around, playing Shaman.

Weber had reached the door to his room when a dark green car with military insignia pulled up beside him. The back window was rolled down.

“Dr. Stan Weber?”

“Yes. Who are you?”

“General Croll,” the man in the crisp uniform replied. “I’d like to speak with you. Seems Beaumont is getting nowhere with ISIR people. I’ve seen your file and I gather you are a reasonable man.”

Weber grinned, thoughts of revenge replacing the annoyance of a moment ago. “Of course,” he smiled. “How may I be of assistance?”

Five

Information is not knowledge.
Codex of Flowering Butterfly

July 21, 1861

With her first step onto the crowded platform at the Washington train station, Desiree sensed the deadly heartbeat beneath the capitol pulse in her veins. Whatever the malignant thing was, it lay somewhere near the Washington house let to her by friends, the Cohens. They had left the city, concerned because the Union and Confederate armies were massing close by.

After locating their driver, Peter Former, Desiree and Harriette had driven to the Cohens' house. They discovered that only the butler, maid, and cook remained, having nowhere else to go. The Cohens had left a note and their regards for Desiree.

But the urge that had been a mere goad in Frederick now become a raging obsession in Washington. Desiree insisted that Peter drive her around the city until she located the source of her disquiet. It was a tall, lavishly appointed house known as the Embassy Club. She called to Peter to stop the carriage.

"What is that place?" she asked, studying the building separated from the street by a brick driveway.

"It's the Embassy Club, Mrs. Bouchard, a private club for gentlemen." Peter's tone conveyed disapproval. "The Club is highly regarded. Many government officials are members."

"But not highly regarded by you?"

Peter half turned to face his employer. "The club has a somewhat unsavory reputation."

Desiree nodded, understanding what Peter would not say openly. The place was an expensive brothel.

"It's there," she whispered to herself. The throbbing beat in her head, keeping time with her pulse, confirmed that the source of the image she had seen in Frederick was real and hidden beneath the structure before her. But what was it? Her mind reached and grasped at nothing.

"Take me back to the house," she ordered.

Once she had found what had driven her to the city, she was unable to escape. All rail lines had been taken over by the government, adding to the confusion and anxiety that gripped Washington. The armies were massing at Manassas Junction, a railroad interchange not far from the city.

But on July twenty-one as the armies approached, a festive mood prevailed. Hundreds of citizens entered carriages, driving the short distance to watch the battle everyone knew was about to begin. Desiree felt that she too had to see this sight, though why, she could not say. Harriette tried to persuade her to remain in the house, but finally gave in to Desiree's determination.

Early that morning, Peter brought his carriage to the house. Desiree and Harriette climbed into it for the short ride to Manassas Junction. She took no picnic lunch, for unlike the others, she did not plan to be a spectator at the battle. Instead she took medicine and bandages, suspecting they would be of more use.

Peter told her of a back road, less congested than the main one and she agreed to the detour. But five miles from their destination, the carriage developed trouble when its front wheel struck a large stone, damaging the wheel.

~ * ~

Desiree and Harriette had been sitting for two hours in a shady grove on the side of the road while Peter attempted to repair the wheel with the tools he had borrowed from an empty farmhouse several yards from where they had stopped. The two horses were tied to a bush near the wagon, munching placidly as Peter worked.

Desiree fanned herself, feeling the heat of the day press on her and wishing the pump at the farmhouse was working. Peter had tossed his dark coat aside along with his red vest. The sleeves of his modest shirt were rolled to his elbows, sweat staining his shirt and face.

"When will you finish, Peter?"

"It's taking longer than I thought. Now a spoke is loose," he explained.

Desiree wished she had taken food and more water than the small amount stored in her nearly empty canteen. The few carriages using the shortcut had long since passed. No one had come by recently to disturb the quiet summer day. Suddenly the horses reared, fighting at the reins securing them to the bush. Desiree twisted around to see the source of the animal's panic. Peter stopped his work, his head jerked up and he listened.

She listened too and heard it. Fear clutched at her throat as she thought that the throbbing she had sensed with her mind had come alive. It sounded like rolling thunder in the distance, but the day was fair and hot.

"What is that?" Harriette got to her feet. "I see no clouds."

Desiree rose. "Peter?"

He raised his hand for silence.

Harriette grabbed her arm. "What is it?"

"Guns," she said, remembering the militia events she and Louis attended before he was too weak to do more than lie in bed and give orders.

"Artillery!" Peter shouted.

~ * ~

July 21, 1961(Universe 1)

Barstead decided it was better for his teams to find private locations for taking any readings during the centennial ceremonies of the battle of Manassas. With people congested around the Visitor's Center, teams would have time to survey the area and return to the motel without having to explain their presence to ogling tourists.

On July nineteen, Barstead had established a grid on a topographical map of the area and asked for volunteers. Amber had agreed to go with Mary Frances while Roger and Gray Eagle took another section. Rierdon and Margaret took a third. Reed remained with Barstead to shuttle the extra ISIR personnel to the Fairfax Inn. It had taken longer than Barstead had anticipated for the people he requested from ISIR to arrive in Washington.

~ * ~

Mary Frances drove the rental Ford along a country lane to a cutoff not indicated on the road map Amber was holding. The blue and white Ford bumped over the packed dirt road leading to an abandoned farm.

"This place was just sold," Mary Frances said while pulling the car beneath the outstretched branches of a large maple tree. "A few months ago, to be exact. Guess it will be developed into housing." She gazed across the field and sighed.

Amber opened the door and stepped onto the remains of a road leading to the old farm house, merely a pile of rotting timbers situated on a small rise to her left. She reached for the heavy instrument in the back seat of the car.

"Want me to carry it?" Mary Frances offered.

"No, I'm stronger than I look." Amber hefted the field meter's strap over her shoulder and slammed the door. "But I'd appreciate it if you'd take the clipboard."

"Sure thing." Mary Frances pocketed the car keys and walked to Amber. She took the clipboard and pen. "You just tell me what to write."

"We should find a spot." Amber glanced around.

The field beside the road was thick with the remnants of grain from previous plantings. Yellow daisies winked brown eyes at the newcomers with every gust of wind, while blue chicory dotted the field. Tall stands of Lamb's ear and islands of thorny blackberries were testimony to the fact the farm had been long abandoned.

Birds nestled in the thick overgrowth, taking to the air as Mary Frances started across the field. "That stone bridge," she pointed to the structure. "It was here at the time of the battle. Maybe that would be the place to start."

She had no idea what sort of readings they would get, but at least she knew what had happened a hundred years ago on this place. Amber agreed and followed the historian through the thigh-high grass.

"Good thing you suggested we wear slacks." Mary Frances pushed aside the thorny fingers of an errant blackberry bush.

As Amber passed the same bush, she plucked a handful of the warm, ripe fruit, cramming it into her mouth. Mary Frances also grabbed a handful of the fruit. The sweet taste of blackberries picked fresh from the bush was beyond compare.

"Here we are," she said, reaching the gnarled, exposed root of a dead tree. "Some of these trees are over a hundred years old."

"They were here during the battle?"

"And the confusion that followed when the roads to Washington were clogged with civilians trying to escape."

"Why did anyone want to go see a battle?" Amber lifted the instrument, opened the leather case and turned the dial to 'power on' mode.

"Because everyone believed the battle would be over quickly, and each side thought the other would not fight."

"That was a mistake," Amber said, moving toward the stone bridge.

"Be careful," Mary Frances called. "There's a small stream bed under that bridge. See the cattails? There might not be water at this time of year, but there may be a pool of mud."

"I'll watch, but I seem to be getting a reading."

Lifting the clipboard, Mary Frances asked, "What is it?" When there was no reply, she took two steps in Amber's direction. "The magnetic field," she prompted.

"It's off the scale," Amber called. "All around this bridge… it's off the scale."

Mary Frances watched Amber gingerly step through the lush grasses rooted in the mud of the stream bank. A flicker of something appeared in her peripheral vision and Mary Frances turned to focus on it.

~ * ~

July 21, 1861(Universe 1)

The sound of gunfire erupted just beyond the farmhouse to Desiree's left. A bullet whizzed by, striking the tree beside Harriette. The horses, frightened by the strange missile, broke free of the bush, and galloped along the dirt road in the opposite direction from the noise.

"Peter!" Desiree shouted. "Go after them!"

Peter had stopped his work and was racing after his team, calling to them to stop. "Take shelter beneath the bridge," he shouted back to Desiree. "Wait for me there."

She seized Harriette's arm and tugged the young woman across the dirt road into the planted field. Their skirts snagged against the grain and Desiree released Harriette to deal with the caged crinoline that was the height of fashion, but then a deterrent to safety.

"Under the bridge," Desiree pointed to the destination she felt offered the safest hiding place. Harriette stumbled and Desiree stopped to help her. As she turned, she saw several men in Union uniforms racing along the road, one of them throwing aside his musket so he could run faster.

A massive fist of fear gripped her stomach. Desiree helped Harriette to stand and turned her back to her. "Undo my petticoat," she ordered. "Then I will undo yours."

"The men," Harriette said.

"They're not interested in us, but in escape. If we don't get out of these petticoats we will never make it to safety."

Her words were swallowed by a concussion as one of the artillery rounds struck nearby. Both women were knocked to the ground. Desiree rolled on her side and managed to stand, dragging Harriette to her feet.

"Now!" she ordered, lifting her overskirt and the lacy over petticoat with it. "Untie the thing."

Harriette worked with trembling fingers to untie the caged crinoline, stepping back as it collapsed in a pile at Desiree's feet.

"Now yours," Desiree ordered, and Harriette turned her back on Desiree. As Desiree undid the construction, she was glad both she and Harriette wore loose corsets, being thin and having no desire to pinch their waists. It made untying the petticoat easier.

Their skirts dragged on the ground, but movement became less restricted. As a second round struck at a distance, the women sought the safety of the arched bridge.

The area beneath it was muddy, but screened from the road by a massive stand of cattails. Once beneath the bridge, Desiree's breathing slowed, though her heart still pounded in her ears.

"Horses," Harriette said. "I hear horses on the bridge.

Without thinking, Desiree fled her cover, turned and glanced at the bridge, calling. "Peter, thank God you found…" The sentence died in her throat.

Two men sat on jet black horses watching the confusion of fleeing troops on the road before the farmhouse. One man with fair blond hair held a thin flat object in his hand. The second, a man with dark hair, held a compact object he seemed to be watching.

"Brac, what do you think about this spot for recording some of the retreat?"

"Well, what have we here?" Brac said, looking over the side of the bridge.

Koru stopped his work with the camera and glanced at Desiree. “Tasty little thing, isn’t she?”

Brac slid from his horse in one smooth, graceful movement. He looped the reins of the animal around one of the decorative projections on the bridge. “You thinking what I’m thinking?”

“Yes, check out the buffer. We can bring back the body when we finish.”

Desiree felt the strength melt from her knees as the description of the stranger in the paper came back to her. Both men were in black clothes, though neither wore a coat. Instead they seemed to be dressed in military tunics, with upright collars and cuffs of red design. A red inverted triangle filled the front of their tunic and on the left breast each wore a metallic black circle with a red perimeter.

Harriette glanced at Desiree, opened her mouth to speak, but Desiree made a keep quiet gesture. It was in vain, for Brac climbed to the ground, jumping the last few feet to land before Harriette.

“Another one,” he shouted. “Come down here and keep them company until I get back.”

Koru rode his horse from the bridge, dismounted, and walked to Desiree. “Hurry, you know I don’t like to be kept waiting. Now if you ladies would just get under that bridge for a moment until Brac checks the area.”

Koru shoved Desiree beneath the bridge. Desiree pulled Harriette against her shoulder as she compared the men before her to the ones she had seen in New Orleans: men who had spent their lives and fortunes in dissipated living. But there was no comparison. The two before her were a hundred times worse.

~ * ~

July 21, 1961(Universe0)

Mary Frances gasped as if a man dressed in a black uniform seemed to appear out of thin air just to the side of the bridge. His attention was for Amber studying her meter, only ten feet from him.

The man removed a gun from the holster at his side. Mary Frances shook off her shock and shouted, "Amber, watch out!"

The man's glance slid from Amber to her then back to Amber. The action caused him to hesitate for a second. Amber closed the distance between them, striking his wrist with a fast choppy movement. The gun flew from his hand, his face a mask of surprise.

"Amber!" Mary Frances felt rooted to the spot, watching the spectacle unfold.

Amber took a second step, pivoted, and aimed a kick at the stranger's groin. Overbalanced by the heavy instrument she carried, her kick was not delivered with full force and she slid to the ground.

The stranger was between Amber and the safety of the car. He was still doubled over and a stream of profanity issued from between his clenched teeth. He took a deep breath, drew himself erect, and lunged at Amber. She did a side step, pivoted, and raced for the bridge, drawing him after her and away from Mary Frances.

"Not that way!"

"Run for help!" Amber shouted.

But Mary Frances could only watch in open-mouthed awe as Amber climbed to the top of the crumbling structure, the man following her. The sides of the bridge had long fallen away, giving a complete view of the fight. Amber was trying to buy time for Mary Frances, but she refused to abandon the young woman.

The pair reached the top of the bridge when the man pivoted and threw a kick at Amber's head. She spun away with a fluid, dance-like motion. But her opponent was larger, heavier, and from what Mary Frances had just witnessed, equally skilled.

He completed his failed attack, moving into a combat stance. Amber did nothing of the sort, merely stood by the break in the side of the bridge, watching the man like a trapped rabbit. He struck. Just before he reached her, she whirled aside. He made a desperate motion to regain his balance, as Amber brought the full force of the field meter against the back of his neck. He pitched forward, dropping from the bridge to the ground. The body lay still amid the crumpled cattails.

A thin rectangular object slipped from the man's tunic as the body struck. Amber watched as several strings of numbers appeared on a smoky square face. Then they were gone. She quickly climbed to the ground and approached the body.

She knelt, felt for a pulse and glanced at Mary Frances. "He's dead."

"Dead?" Mary Frances felt remote as she said the word.

"He had a gun," Amber reminded Mary Frances as she lifted the rectangular object.

"Yes." Mary Frances, released from indecision, turned toward the spot where she had first seen the stranger. There, she saw it glinting in the sun. If there were others like this man around, the gun would serve as protection. Mary Frances made her way to the shiny object, lifted it and held it in her hand.

It was a semiautomatic, but the make was unknown to her. Her brother had taught her how to shoot and she kept a .38 in her apartment. She glanced at Amber and the object she held.

"What is that thing you're holding?"

"I don't know. It looks like one of those newly introduced calculators, but this is so thin and light. And I don't see any function buttons on it."

Mary Frances scrunched her forehead, before remembering the object Amber had compared to the device she held. *Amber is correct*, she thought, the one she held was too thin.

"Powering down," the object said.

"No, don't do that," Amber replied, wondering if someone was at the other end. "I think it talks."

"What the hell is it?" Mary Frances shuddered. She had reached the body and the man at her feet was indeed dead. What would she tell her brother?

Amber was studying the icons on the backlit screen. Power, control menu, continuous, portal, the words made sense, but how was it operated?

"I think you touch the screen or speak to it," Amber said. "Let's see what portal does."

"No don't," Mary Frances shouted, suddenly aware of the press of wind near the small bridge.

Amber touched the screen. Several feet from them a portion of the air turned translucent, opaque, then the consistency of water. A crimson point appeared and expanded into a small hemispheric opening.

Mary Frances placed her hand over her mouth. She dropped to her knees. A whimper escaped her lips. Amber, already kneeling, lifted the device, and the hemisphere moved with it. She lowered the device, touched the continuous icon and the dark hemisphere instantly cleared.

"It's like looking at a three dimensional movie," Amber whispered.

Before them, displayed in the outlines of the hemisphere, was the stone bridge, the same bridge, but as it might have looked a hundred years ago.

"My God," Mary Frances whispered.

Two women crouched beneath that other bridge. They were muddy and frightened. One woman was white and the other a light skinned black woman. Their clothing was that worn by women in the 1860s, but the man standing before them was dressed similar to the dead man at Mary Frances' feet.

His body jerked and he swung around to stare at them. Mary Frances saw that he held a strange gun against the palm of his hand. He took several steps, crossing the portal and stopping before Amber.

"Get down," Mary Frances ordered.

Amber hugged the ground as Mary Frances fired two shots at the man. He dropped to his knees. His mouth opened in surprise before he sank to the ground. His gun slipped toward the portal entrance. Amber stood, moved around the body, and reached through the portal to pick up the gun the man had been carrying. She pulled her arm back, rubbing it as if she had been stung.

"It prickles."

The sound of distant gunfire came from the portal opening. Mary Frances watched the older woman release the younger, crawl from beneath the bridge, and approach the opening.

"Who are you?" the woman asked in a husky voice. "What are you?"

Amber looked up at her, suddenly realizing what she was seeing. "I'm Amber Valic, and this is Mary Frances Beaumont."

"I am Desiree Bouchard and this is my ward, Harriette. What is this thing before us?"

"A portal," Amber answered. "Oh my God, the Hasselbach manuscript is right. This thing made a portal. How does it do that?"

Mary Frances swallowed her fear. "We didn't construct that thing."

"Did you kill those men?" Desiree asked.

Amber nodded.

"Do not feel any remorse," Desiree cautioned. "They were truly evil and had such designs upon us that I hesitate to speak of."

"The bodies, Amber, help me with the bodies." Mary Frances reached out and began to drag the dead man nearest her toward the opening. "What happens if you let go of that thing you are using?"

"I think the portal stays open until I close it." Amber's voice was shaky. She pulled the man Mary Frances had shot to the portal and rolled his body through it.

Mary Frances looked to Desiree. "I will drag this body to the opening, please pull it through. It must not be found here." Desiree understood. She hiked her skirts around her waist. Avoiding the man

Amber had rolled across, she pulled the body Mary Frances dragged to her into her universe. Mary Frances tore the scarf from her hair and wiped the grip and barrel of the gun she had used. Wrapping it in the scarf, she tossed it onto one of the dead bodies.

"What did you do that for?" Amber asked.

"To get rid of fingerprints," Mary Frances said.

"Who's going to look for fingerprints in 1861?"

"Have you come to help us?" Desiree asked.

"Help you?" Amber looked puzzled. "But you're at war."

"Not just war. Something lies beneath the streets of Washington. It is a malignant thing that came to us and is not meant to be."

"What?"

"Desiree, I hear horses. Could that be Peter?" Harriette asked nervously.

"I live in Frederick, Maryland," Desiree said. "On State Street. Now we must escape."

"Go north and west," Mary Frances advised. "That should take you out of the thick of the battle."

"Thank you, Mary Frances. Come when you can, please!"

"Shut that damn thing off," Mary Frances whispered to Amber.

"It's not a television, there's no off button," Amber said. She touched the menu icon and after a minute figured out how to close the portal. "Power down," she said to the object and the screen went blank. She had discovered a button on the side of the object that turned it on.

"Oh my God, oh my God, it's real."

Amber touched her on the shoulder. “I know,” she breathed, more in wonder than in fear. “It’s real. This thing I’m holding responds to my voice, maybe to any voice. If I had something like this, I’d sure make it more secure.”

Mary Frances looked into the young woman’s eyes, and said, “Hasn’t it occurred to you that we didn’t make the device you just used? And we killed two of the people who owned it.”

Amber’s mouth formed a silent ‘O.’ The same fear in Mary Frances’ eyes was mirrored in her own.

~ * ~

July 21, 1861(Universe 1)

“What happened?” Harriette demanded in a trembling voice. “First the two women appeared in that strange opening, now they’re gone.”

“I don’t know.” Desiree glanced at the bodies in the muddy creek bed. She snatched the scarf, wound around the gun and tucked it into the pocket of her skirt.

“The gun?”

“It’s best we go unarmed,” Desiree said.

“How can you say that after what just happened?”

“Come, we must get out of here.” Desiree looked around, spotting Peter about a hundred yards away. The road was clogged with people and carriages. “We have no time to think about the strange happening,” she counseled.

Peter was hurrying toward them with the horses. Desiree and Harriette moved to meet him, leaving the bodies hidden in the stream bed, screened by cattails.

"Thank God, you found horses. Harriette and I will ride together." Desiree took the reins of one horse.

"It will have to be bareback," he gasped, winded by his chase. "I could find no discarded saddles."

"No matter, I have ridden so as a child." But the reins of the horse were suddenly pulled from her grasp. A man shoved her aside and she stumbled to the ground.

Harriette lifted her skirts and kicked the man in the pants as he turned to mount. He swung around, his hand raised, and she kicked him in the groin with the point of her shoe.

"Mount," she called to Desiree. The man dropped to his knees in pain, his face ashen. Peter shoved him aside and aided Desiree to mount. Peter lifted Harriette behind her, swung onto the other horse and urged them away from the insanity spilling from the road into the field.

Desiree remembered only snatches of the ride through clots of civilians fighting for any means of escape. Soldiers seemed to come from nowhere only to be left behind by their hasty retreat. Gunfire cloaked the area in smoke. After a time they came to a hedgerow. Peter found a path through it. On the opposite side of the hedgerow, they were alone. Peter insisted they walk the horses for a time.

She felt her heartbeat finally returning to normal after the second time they walked the horses. The sun was lower in the sky, but the air still held the oppressive heat of mid-day. She had no idea where they were as they exited from a bridle path through a stand of woods and onto a dirt road.

When Peter called a halt, Desiree glanced along the road to see the dust from several horses. As the army patrol rode toward them, Desiree felt her heart racing again. *At least*, she thought, *they are not dressed in black.* The riders grew closer and she could see they were dressed in gray.

~ * ~

July 21, 1961(Universe 0)

Gray Eagle jumped from his chair at the pounding on the door to his room. It sounded as if someone were trying to break it down. "What is that?"

"Sounds like a raid," Barstead said. He opened the door to find Amber and Mary Frances standing there.

The two shoved past him. "Shut the damn door," Mary Frances shouted.

Barstead blinked at the force of her words, but closed the door. "What's happened?" Amber's clothing was torn; weeds clung to her short, chestnut hair. Mary Frances was so white Barstead thought she would faint."

"The Hasselbach theory is real," Mary Frances gasped in a voice filled with exhaustion and terror.

Barstead frowned and looked at the instrument Amber carried. The leather case was open and the glass covering the meter was shattered. "What happened to the field meter?"

"I killed somebody with it."

Gray Eagle swung to face her, phone in hand. "You did what?"

"This guy appeared out of nowhere. He tried to kill us and I hit him with the field meter. The other man tried to shoot me, but Mary Frances shot him."

Barstead's head was spinning with the strange recital of facts. "Slow down," he ordered. "Tell me what happened."

"Here," Amber pulled from her pocket the device she had taken from the dead man. She placed it on the table along with the gun she had retrieved.

"What are those?" Barstead demanded.

"That thing is some kind of a gun," Amber said in a shaky voice. "The other thing makes an opening between universes."

"Where did you get these?" Barstead demanded.

"Haven't you been listening? We killed the owners and took them," Mary Frances blurted.

Six

Knowledge is always dearly bought.
Codex of Flowering Butterfly

July 21, 1861(Universe 1)

Desiree's horse danced nervously as the riders approached. She counted five men, including the young officer at their head. He rode his horse opposite hers, stopped, and offered her a casual salute.

"I am Lieutenant Elliot Marsden," he said. "I have the pleasure of addressing?"

Up close the officer looked even younger to Desiree. "I am Mrs. Desiree Bouchard, my ward Harriette rides behind me. This man is my driver, Peter Former."

"Your driver?" Elliot said. "I see no carriage."

"Lost, sir, in the mayhem behind us."

"Your husband?"

"My husband is dead these past two years."

Elliot smiled at the attractive, if disheveled, woman before him. "I am indeed sorry to hear that.

But a lovely person such as you should not be riding over battlefields."

Desiree threw back her shoulders. "Don't patronize me, Lieutenant. I'm probably old enough to be your mother."

The sergeant behind Elliot snickered, but Elliot ignored him. "You're much too young. May I ask where you are bound?"

"As far from this disaster as possible," she retorted, just a bit pleased with the compliment from the handsome young officer. "I live in Frederick, Maryland."

"Quite a distance to ride." He urged his horse beside hers, removed his canteen, and offered it to her.

She took it, saying. "Thank you, sir. We lost our water."

"If you continue on this road, about a mile along you will come to a crossroads. The right fork will take you to Buttermilk Falls. It's a small hamlet and you will be able to find shelter for the evening." He paused for a moment. "Where in Frederick do you live?"

"On State Street," she replied. "Thank you for your assistance."

He inclined his head to her, just brushing the brim of his hat. Desiree urged her horse along the road, Peter following. She was wearing enough jewelry to get them back to Frederick and grateful the young officer had behaved in a civilized manner. She shot a quick glance back at the patrol to see the young man still watching her. She knew they would meet again.

~ * ~

Elliot waited until the party was out of sight before turning to his sergeant. “She’s a clever woman. Did you notice the women removed their hoops?”

Sergeant Gage spat tobacco onto the road. “She could hardly do otherwise if she plans to ride all the way to Frederick.”

Elliot glanced along the road, urged his horse toward a section of the wood, and spied the bridle path. He wondered if the Bouchard woman was a Yankee spy. But her accent was anything but northern. “They came along that path. Let’s just ride in that direction for a bit and see where it leads.”

Gage and the others followed Elliot into the woods along the path Desiree and her companions had taken. The trail was still fresh. After a time, they arrived at the field with the stone bridge. The field was quiet, empty of all but the traces left by the passage of terrified citizens and fleeing soldiers.

Elliot rode toward the bridge, hoping there was water in what appeared to be the remains of a muddy stream. He cursed his gallantry in giving away his canteen for he was now thirsty and embarrassed to ask his sergeant for water. He caught the buzzing noise of several flies and reined in his horse.

Gage rode next to him. “Dead, over there, looks like two of them.”

The patrol dismounted and one of the men held the horses while the other four cautiously made their way to the bodies lying in the mud.

"Sergeant, search the area."

Gage motioned for the two men with him and they began a search of the weeds. Elliot moved closer to the bodies. He stared at the object beside the body nearest him. It appeared to be a gun unlike any he had ever seen.

He crossed to the body and retrieved the object. While he turned the gun in his hand, Gage knelt to examine the bodies.

"One's been shot, the other got his neck broke," Gage announced.

"Sergeant, we found two ladies' hoops in the weeds," one of the men called.

Elliot heard the whoops of laughter as the men trotted to him, displaying the soiled hoops like trophies of war. "No need to drag them back. Leave them," he ordered.

"But Lieutenant?" one of the men protested.

"I said leave them," Elliot snapped. "We've got a bigger problem here. What do you make of the uniforms, Sergeant?"

"Was about to ask you that myself, sir. I've never seen the like."

Elliot squinted at the unfamiliar tunic and insignia; if what the uniform sported was even an insignia. He memorized what he was seeing. "Could they be observers? I know the British and French have sent observers to both armies."

Gage shook his head. “Neither’s got a rank, ‘cept for those little triangles on the collar. Should we take the bodies with us?”

“No, leave the bodies for the burial detail. But this gun, what the…?”

Gage looked up at his superior. “Sir?”

“What the hell is this?” Elliot said, holding the magazine that he had inadvertently extracted from the gun. He held the container on edge, seeing the bullets placed inside it. “What is this?”

Gage stood. “What is what?”

“This,” he handed the magazine to Gage.

Gage took the object, examining it in detail. “Got a number seventeen on the base. You don’t suppose that guy was shot with this gun?”

“Watch, Gage.” Elliot took the magazine from the sergeant, shoved it into the grip, and held out the gun for Gage to see.

The sergeant whistled, shoved back his hat, and swore. “Well, if that don’t beat all. What kind of gun is that?”

Elliott shrugged. “More important, Sergeant, why was it left behind? The person who shot him must have left it.”

“Mrs. Bouchard?” Gage jerked his thumb over his shoulder.

“That makes even less sense. But I bet she knows what happened here. Let’s mount and take this back to Captain Archibald.”

“Maybe we ought to take this to that Colonel Crittenden, the one in charge of intelligence?”

Elliott bit his lip. Crittenden's reputation was well known. He was considered fair, but not a man to cross. However, Gage was right about Crittenden being head of intelligence gathering. Elliot shoved the gun into the belt around his narrow waist.

"Let's mount," he ordered. He would take Gage's suggestion. The gun would go directly to Crittenden.

~ * ~

San paced the secure room beneath the Embassy Club, repeatedly smacking her fist into her hand. Had Brac and Koru not been found dead, she would have killed them. It was fortunate for her Kester was such a stickler for details. His insistence that teams taking footage of the battle be checked every two hours became the salvation of the Khysid Army. *Well, almost the salvation*. Brac's transfer device and EM Stinger were still missing.

"I think I have it now," Lieutenant Wes said. "The signal was really corrupted from the mud."

"The mud saved the camera when it fell from the horse," San replied. "What about the video?"

"The first part was easily regenerated, but the stuff recorded after it fell from the horse into the mud is only audio. Bad audio at that, since the camera's mike was damaged when it struck."

"Start when that moron lost the camera," she ordered.

The fool had left the camera on automatic when he carelessly slung the strap over his saddle. The camera had kept recording until the horse reared and the camera had flown into the mud.

Images of a road filled the screen, vibrating with the movement of the horse as it paced nervously amid the tall grasses. The audio was crisp. Since the bridge was within Confederate lines, San assumed the sound of artillery in the background belonged to Rebel forces. Suddenly, the camera took on a more jerky movement flying through the air as the horse reared. She saw the blur of vegetation and for a split second the unmistakable image of an open portal with two women from an alternate universe briefly visible.

"The audio?"

"The best we can reconstruct." He entered a command into the console.

San listened to brief snatches of words, nothing making much sense. Fortunately, the camera had been hidden from all but the most determined hunter. A Rebel patrol was riding away when the bodies were located by a Khysid patrol. The Confederates had not discovered the camera in the mud.

"Turn it off," San grumbled. "I can't make any sense of it. You have a location for the transfer device?"

Kester said as he entered the room. "The last one we were able to pinpoint came from Washington in the buffer universe." He saluted San.

"Well, Colonel, since we know the Rebel patrol didn't take it, who did? I presume it didn't walk to Washington from Manassas on its own?"

"I believe the scientists took it."

"What!" San felt her throat close. "Get it back," she croaked.

"As soon as I can locate it," Kester said. "But there seems to be a problem."

"What problem?"

"Something is shielding it from our efforts to activate the embedded tracer."

"That's not possible," she said.

The only thing that could shield the transfer device's locator sensor was a Jewel. The scientists in the buffer universe couldn't possibly understand the transfer device, let alone reverse engineer it. Nor could they have found an abandoned Source Gate and a Jewel.

"Locate them, especially the ones who were involved in taking the transfer device and the EM stinger. Kill them and get that damn equipment back. If you can't get it, destroy it."

"Yes sir," Kester replied. "It's as good as done."

~ * ~

July 22, 1861(Universe 1)

Elliot found Colonel Crittenden sitting at a writing desk before his tent, sipping coffee and occasionally dipping his pen in the inkwell to write. Crittenden glanced up, his hazel eyes narrowing as Elliot approached.

Elliott saw the slight frown on the man's clean-shaven face. He knew Crittenden was highly regarded in the Confederate Army and that he had served with the Union Army in the New Mexico Territory before the war. It surprised Elliot that the man was so well groomed, his uniform immaculately tailored, his boots almost glove soft. He seemed more attired for a salon than a battlefield. Elliot doubted this was an affectation. He suspected Crittenden's appearance was calculated for effect.

The young officer made a self-conscious attempt to straighten his wrinkled jacket before saluting. "You sent for me, sir?"

"Yes." Crittenden motioned for Elliott to bring one of the camp stools to the rough, wooden table. "You best sit to hear this."

Elliott obeyed, sitting opposite Crittenden.

"Had you not brought the gun to me personally and told me your story sober, I would think you given to drink. Especially yesterday, as many were celebrating the victory over the Federals."

"I don't drink, Colonel," Elliot replied far too quickly. "At least not to excess. What I told you was the truth."

Crittenden sighed. "I know, son."

Elliot sensed something besides the gun on the mind of the officer before him. "Sir, I have a feeling the woman I met on the road knows something about this."

"Yes, Lieutenant, so do I." Crittenden pulled a wad of telegrams to him. "But let's deal with you first. I found out a bit about you. Seems you attended Virginia Military Institute and I think you know General Jackson."

Elliot colored slightly, remembering his encounters with the officer he considered a martinet. “Yes sir. People are calling him Stonewall now.” Truth was that he was always as hardheaded as a stone wall and not as understanding.

The corners of Crittenden’s mouth lifted in a smile. “In any case, I’ve had you transferred to my command, you and what’s left of the Company you were in charge of.”

Elliot’s brown eyes widened, giving him an owl-like appearance. “So fast?” he muttered running his hand through his curly brown hair.

“I have contacts among influential people.”

“Sorry sir. I didn’t mean anything by the comment.”

Crittenden nodded. “But that gun is the real problem and it’s not the only such item I have seen that is extraordinary.”

Elliot’s face took on a deeper puzzled expression. “Sir, I don’t understand.”

“One of the things I learned about you is that you keep your own counsel. I have need of that now and I want your solemn word you will say nothing to anyone of what I am about to tell you.”

“I will say nothing, sir, but why tell me?” Elliot winced at his slip. He had never quite mastered the art of addressing his superiors without saying the wrong thing.

“Have you a difficulty with this, Lieutenant?”

“No, Colonel. But when I remove my foot from my mouth, I will apologize.”

Crittenden laughed heartily. "You are a scamp and a prankster from what I have been given to understand. But you will play no pranks under my command."

Elliott nodded his agreement. "What do you wish me to do, sir?"

"I want you to go to Frederick and speak with Mrs. Bouchard. She is the only person who may be able to shed light on a puzzle that began before the war."

Crittenden had Elliot's interest. "Before the war? There were other such guns?"

"Maybe, though this one does not seem to be rigged to explode as did the one in Richmond."

Elliot's mouth dropped open. He shivered at the thought that he might have been carrying exploding munitions.

Crittenden explained. "After Virginia seceded, a friend and informant was meant to be killed, but the man who was to do the deed was himself shot. The soldier who witnessed the gun the assassin planned to use described it to me. Its description matches the gun you brought in yesterday."

Elliot said. "You said it exploded?"

Crittenden nodded. "Yes, when a curious agent tried to use it."

Another tremor passed through Elliot. "This one, I took out the magazine that holds the rounds. It didn't explode."

"The gun you found wasn't meant to," Crittenden replied; though he said nothing more about how he knew this fact.

"Sir, if I go to Frederick, I'll encounter Union troops. That part of Maryland is still in Union hands."

Crittenden nodded. "You will have to go as a civilian. You must know that the penalty for an officer caught in civilian clothes is death as a spy. I can't say it any cleaner than that."

Elliot bit his lips as he thought. He did not relish being out of uniform and behind enemy lines. Still, what little Crittenden had told him had piqued his curiosity, as had the gun.

"I think this Mrs. Bouchard will keep my identity secret," Elliot said aloud. "But how can I get to Frederick?"

"You will agree to this?" Crittenden asked.

"Yes sir."

"Then listen to what I have to tell you."

Crittenden outlined his plan and explained about the secure houses and taverns Elliot could use if the need arose. Elliot was amazed at the network of informants Crittenden had established and their reliability. He would have a shadow group of men and women he could count on should he get into trouble. When Crittenden finished, Elliot asked a few questions and left to make the arrangements.

After Elliot was out of sight, an officer walked up to Crittenden. Crittenden rose and saluted the man. "He's just as you said he would be, General."

Jackson looked in the direction Elliot had taken. "I hope he's of more use to you than he was to me. He's lethal around artillery. That's why he ended up in the cavalry. Even there, I think he's of more use to the enemy."

"I sense, General, that Lieutenant Marsden has just found his place in this war."

Jackson glanced at Crittenden, but said nothing.

~ * ~

July 22, 1961(Universe 0)

Amber took the twin engine Merlin to an altitude of 6,000 feet and leveled off, heading west from National Airport. Mary Frances sat next to her, hands clasped firmly in her lap, watching the clouds on her right. Gray Eagle had insisted all Merlins of his design be equipped with seat belts such as the larger commercial planes used. Mary Frances' was still belted across her lap. Behind Amber sat Barstead, Roger, and Gray Eagle. The plane held four in comfort, five in relative ease, and six if needed.

"No one has found us so far," Amber said into the quiet cabin.

"No one had better," Barstead grumbled. "Whatever this thing is, it's beyond any engineering I've seen." His hands closed possessively on the locked metal box holding the transfer device and gun.

"I wonder what the gun does besides fire electromagnetic radiation." Roger looked at Barstead.

Barstead had fired the gun in a small field on the outskirts of the Inn, but nothing happened. Using the magnetic field meters, Gray Eagle had been able to determine the gun had actually fired a pulse of electromagnetic radiation in the radio spectrum. The label on the gun said EM Stinger, Special Police Edition, manufactured by EM Engineering in California. But no such company existed in California, nor did the technology to manufacture the palm-sized device.

Reed speculated that if the pulse hit someone at a high intensity and close range, the damage he had read about in the pathology reports could be inflicted. After Amber demonstrated the transfer device, no one asked where the technology had come from. They knew.

"The other team members will follow us," Gray Eagle shot a look at Barstead. "Julian, there are three of us who can fly this plane."

"Four. I'll give you a hand," Mary Frances offered, the first words she had said since they left the airport. "As long as it doesn't take too much time to get used to."

Gray Eagle said, "It's a piece of cake."

"I've been thinking about that string of numbers you see each time you open a portal using that device. I think they represent a location," Amber suggested.

"You're right," Barstead agreed. "But the portals seem irregular and sometimes we can't open one. There is an image that acts as a tuning control." Roger asked, "How can such a little thing have enough energy to open a portal to another universe?"

"I doubt it does," Barstead replied.

Gray Eagle shifted until he found a more comfortable position. "Then where does it get the energy?"

"Damned if I know," Barstead answered. "But I sure intend to find out. I can't even imagine what the device that feeds this thing looks like."

"Where's it located?" Roger asked.

Barstead shrugged. "I don't know, but it seemed to be associated with DC."

"The woman said the malignant thing is in her Capitol." Mary Frances reminded them of the Desiree's words.

"Makes sense, since we found a rough distance beyond which we could get nothing to happen. But where there's one energy source, there must be others."

"Maybe that tuning control inputs the co-ordinates for such a power source." Amber squinted at something at the two o'clock position before her.

"Once we're safely at ISIR, I plan to find out." Barstead was thrown against Roger as the Merlin executed a quick turn.

"What the hell?" Gray Eagle braced himself against the side of the cabin.

"Put on the seat belts," Amber ordered, struggling with her own. "And pick up anything loose in the cabin."

"I see him," Mary Frances shouted. "It's that vintage fighter from National, the one that almost hit us as we took off. The pilot's crazy."

Fear grabbed at Amber's stomach as she watched the P-40 that dwarfed the Merlin she was flying. The pilot wasn't crazy. He was determined to kill them.

"He's after us." She climbed away from the oncoming plane. It passed close to her, the backwash shaking the little aircraft. "Gray Eagle, does he still have his guns?"

"No." Gray Eagle swallowed his fear. "They've been removed. It's not legal to keep them operational."

"Thank God," Mary Frances whispered.

"Amber, what hell are you doing?" Gray Eagle shouted.

Amber dove at the P-40, passing just over the top of the pilot's canopy. The fighter banked away from her. She hoped that the pilot was surprised the tiny passenger craft would turn and buzz him.

"This is neither the time nor the place to play chicken!" Barstead's hold on the box was so tight that the bones of his hands were outlined by the bloodless flesh covering them.

Amber did a loop, Gray Eagle shouting that it was a useless maneuver. "He's trying to rattle you, force you to lose control!"

"I know, but he's in trouble. He has his landing gear down."

"Stupid man," Gray Eagle grunted. "He must know that. The controls will tell him if the plane doesn't. He'll have to wind them up by hand if he plans to fly back to National."

"He's not going to get the chance," she said.

The Merlin dove toward the ground, while Mary Frances closed her eyes and gripped the side of the cabin. "Find a place to land," she whispered.

"Not till I shake our pursuer," Amber vowed.

Her mouth was dry and her stomach felt as if it held a hundred butterflies. But she knew the pilot of the P-40 had made a serious error in ignoring the landing gear. Gray Eagle had told her about the old P-40s, how the landing gear sometimes stuck and how a pilot ignored the problem to his detriment. Now if she could only entice the pilot chasing her to follow her across the fields below.

~ * ~

Wes didn't like the P-40, preferring the Messerschmitt he'd been trained in not that long ago. Still, it would serve its purpose, though he was somewhat unfamiliar with its controls. After forcing the passenger plane and its occupants out of the sky, he planned to ditch the P-40 and parachute to safety. He calculated he could cripple the little passenger plane by clipping its rudder with his wing without too much damage to the fighter he flew.

But he had not counted on an aggressive pilot at the stick. His memory served up an image of a young woman looking all of fourteen as the pilot, not the older Sioux who had experience with fighters. If that were so, she was more skilled than he had counted on, for she actually attacked him.

"What's she doing?" he said, as he watched the small plane dive toward a field of grain. He wondered if she were planning to land. If so, he had overestimated her. She would wreck in that hilly field. It was a pity; he was having so much fun.

He started after her, knowing he could easily catch the small, slower plane. But she was flying erratically and for a moment he thought the plane damaged. Then he realized with a thrill of delight that she was trying to evade him. He wished the plane he had stolen had guns. He imagined the helpless quarry in his sights, blossoming into a fireball before plummeting to its death.

Wes was overtaking the Merlin, smiling as he thought about what he would do when he caught up with it. His eyes widened as he suddenly saw the steel ropes a split second before he reached them. Suspended between the towers were high-tension lines. Wes pulled the stick into his lap, even as he knew it was too late.

~ * ~

"What are you doing?" Gray Eagle demanded of Amber.

"Shaking the tail," she replied.

Gray Eagle's mouth opened as he saw the lacy steel towers, thick ropes of power lines strung between them. He knew what she meant to do.

"Now it's his problem," Amber said forcing the Merlin into a steep climb as it skimmed the power lines.

The nose of the P-40 followed her too late as its landing gear caught in the power cables, snapping them. One cable whipped upward, flailing the wing, forcing the pilot to lose control. The plane banked to the left, the wing crumpling as the forward motion of the plane drove the fuselage into the earth.

Amber stopped climbing and leveled the plane as the P-40 did a cartwheel. The nose and shattered propeller caught against some rocky projection. What was left of the plane came to rest on its back and a small fire could be seen next to the aircraft, followed shortly by an explosion that rumbled through the wheat field setting the ripening grain on fire.

"Climb!" Gray Eagle ordered. "Don't hang around to get clobbered by the debris!"

Amber nosed the plane skyward, smiling at the orders from her mentor. They were probably already at a sufficient altitude so that the debris wouldn't hit them. Her hand slid on the stick and she noticed that her palms were wet. So was her blouse. She brushed away a thin sheen of sweat from her forehead as the realization of what had just happened settled in. Her stomach clenched and she tasted her breakfast.

"Where are we?" Barstead croaked out the first coherent words he could manage.

"Somewhere in Maryland," Amber whispered. "Mary Frances, would you look at the maps?"

Mary Frances licked her lips as she lifted the packet used for navigation. "Call a Mayday."

"No!" Barstead yelped. "Get out of here. Head north."

"There's been an accident," Amber insisted, even as she changed her heading.

"That was no accident," Gray Eagle rubbed his temples. He found his body hurt in several places where he had been banged against the cabin wall despite the belt securing him to the seat.

"What's our location?" Mary Frances leaned toward Amber, map in hand.

Amber glanced at the chart and the notes she had scribbled beside it. "There, over Sharpsburg."

"Oh, my God," Mary Frances whispered. "Antietam."

"North, change course and head for Pittsburgh. Call Allegheny and tell them you have an engine problem."

"What?" Amber glanced at her fuel gauge.

"Is there enough fuel?" Gray Eagle asked, observing her movements.

"Yes," she replied. "But there are several small airports along the way where we can refuel."

"Why Pittsburgh?" Gray Eagle asked.

"Gordo's there," Barstead replied.

"When did you find that out?"

"Two weeks ago," Barstead confessed. "He sent a note. He was hunting up old friends. Has a nice airplane repair business at the airport, doing quite well."

"Why drag him into this?" Gray Eagle protested.

"Carnegie Tech," Barstead said. "They're the closest engineering school, plus there are research labs in the city. We can't go back to California. We'll endanger everyone."

Amber suggested. "We could tell the government, Mr. Beaumont."

"No!" Mary Frances was emphatic. "They'd take that device and we would never see it again."

Amber suspected the historian's interest in the portal opener was more than simply scientific.

"Gordo is good at keeping secrets; besides, no one will find us for a while and we need time to understand this thing."

Barstead's voice held a proprietary tone that Amber understood. What he carried was bigger than the discovery of either nuclear fission or fusion. What he held could change the world.

Seven

When outnumbered use the environment to equalize the odds.
Codex of Flowering Butterfly

July 22, 1861(Universe 1)

Seated in his private room at the Embassy Club, Kester listened with disgust to the report given him by a nervous subordinate. He fumed as the officer recited his tale of Wes' death. Kester had commanded Wes to kill the scientists, but the idiot had chosen to go after a few of them by playing the hotshot pilot in a vintage P-40. Wes probably took too long to locate the group bound for California and was unable to kill them before they left. In fact, Kester thought, Wes had been taking too many liberties lately. He suspected Wes of using what he knew about the Micro D Reader as leverage for future perks. Kester's brows knitted into a frown.

"Thought he had the better of me," Kester mused aloud.

"Sir?" the officer asked, shifting slightly from one foot to the other.

"Leave the report and get out of here," Kester ordered.

Wes had constructed a Micro D reader for Kester after Val's death. Kester knew that the technology from a backwater universe had never been used by the army. If you possessed it, you did so for reasons that had nothing to do with the army. Val had used the technology because he had been hiding extensive databases of material belonging to Elias Hazen, the late Supreme Commander of the Khysid Army. Kester suspected the databases Val had concealed had come from the Army's Deep Archives. When Val died, Kester appropriated the databases, but Val's reader had been destroyed.

Kester knew that the present Supreme Commander, Brie, did not have the encryption key for the Deep Archives. That had died with Hazen. If Brie knew that Kester had material from the Deep Archives, Kester's life would end before Brie snapped his fingers. In that case, Wes' death was no loss. There was no one left to blackmail him. No one who knew about the reader and the databases it contained.

"Now what?" Kester said to the empty room as he drummed his fingers on the cherry writing desk. He had to trace the scientists and get rid of them. But not before he used one of the secret programs Val discovered. Kester didn't like the feel of what was happening. What should have been simple was growing more complicated by the moment. His gut told him another cascade was brewing. He wondered why San hadn't caught it.

Captain Rort was prowling about in the area of Pittsburgh in a universe adjacent to the 1961 buffer universe, searching for some signal from the tracer embedded in the transfer device stolen by the scientists. At least, Kester sighed, he had learned they were in Pittsburgh.

An officer knocked, then opened the door to his room and interrupted his thoughts. "Colonel."

"What is it?"

"Your plant from the White House is here. He says it's urgent."

"I forgot about him," Kester grumbled. "I'll be downstairs in a minute. Stick him in one of the private parlors."

~ * ~

July 22, 1961(Universe 0)

Gordo was delighted when the little Merlin touched down at Allegheny Airport. He had it brought to his hangar so his mechanics could give it a thorough check. He was still clucking over the design when Barstead insisted they go to his place. There was something he needed to tell the man. Gordo sensed intrigue and quickly whisked them to his apartment house in Shadyside. He lived on the top floor of the old Victorian structure on Beacon Alley, a narrow turnoff from Center Avenue. Four houses sat on the dead-end lane and his was the last. Gordo's house was a gaudy confection with turrets and curved porches and painted pink and lilac. The main tower, on the east side of the house, served as Gordo's library. Among the breaks in the bookcases that covered the second and third floors of the tower, were framed photographs of vintage planes.

Gordo plopped down on a soft, brown leather chair across from Barstead. "How do you like the place?"

"You've done well for yourself," Barstead agreed, still gripping the box containing the device that had nearly cost their lives.

Gordo watched Barstead's grip on the box wondering what it held that his friend felt was so precious that he would not place it on the table before him. "I've got ads in the papers to rent out the bottom floor. Got a thriving business, but you know what? I'm bored."

Gray Eagle choked on the Coca-Cola he was sipping. Gordo shot a surprised glance in his direction. His eyes narrowed.

"What's cooking with you people?" There was more to this meeting than simply a chance to renew old acquaintances.

"How would you like to be let in on a little secret?" Barstead offered.

Amber piped, "Little?"

"Shush," Barstead ordered, as Gordo glanced in her direction. "You got room for a larger team from ISIR?"

A conspiratorial smile crept across Gordo's pleasant face. "You bet I do. I'll pull the rental ads in the newspapers. This house was built in 1882 when one of the old coal barons razed an older tenement. His heirs squabbled over their inheritance and it was finally sold for taxes. This place will hold a good twenty people if you don't mind doubling up to sleep."

"We don't mind in the least," Gray Eagle said.

Gordo sighed. "It's like old times. But what's happened? You didn't just drop in for a visit if you're looking for a place to crash."

Barstead told him while Gray Eagle got Gordo another Rolling Rock. "Oh," moaned Gordo as he heard the story of the attempt on their life over Maryland. "That plane belonged to Rich Marsden. He's an old friend. I've known him since Korea. He has lots of family money, lumber and all. Family is from Georgia."

"What's he doing with the old planes?" Gray Eagle asked.

"Flies them, loves them, and even restores them. I recommended a mechanic when his got sick before the air show. He wanted me." Gordo placed the empty beer bottle on the coffee table next to the other two. "His great-grandfather was in the Civil War."

Barstead ignored the comment. "We have to study the device in this box. I've been tinkering with it and I think I've located a power source that will let us open a portal here."

He placed the box on the table, opened it, and removed the transfer device. He showed it briefly to Gordo.

"Julian, this is weird." Gordo stared at the object. He felt cold inside. "I don't believe that little thing can open anything."

"I'll give you a demonstration."

Gordo shrugged. "I believe you were almost killed, but a way to cross between alternate universes, even their existence?"

Barstead thumbed the device and power hummed through it, though not as strongly as it had in Washington. He aimed the device in the direction of Gordo's kitchen. Again, the air turned opaque, the consistency of water, and a pinpoint of crimson fire appeared in the center of the dark mass. The point burned outward into a hemispherical opening.

Where Gordo's kitchen had been, a mean little space, stark and dingy appeared. A cold fireplace outlined in grimy tiles dominated the center of the portal.

"Turn it off!" Gordo covered his face. "My God, that's the tenement in this place before this house was built. Julian, when I said it was like old times, the Civil War was not what I had in mind."

"We must learn about this." Barstead powered down the device. "Can we count on you?"

Gordo's head bobbed. "I wish I knew what I was in for."

"Now I need to use your phone and get the others here from Washington."

~ * ~

July 31, 1861(Universe 1)

Crittenden approached his regimental surgeon, Major Virgil Wescott from Winchester, Virginia. The tall, stocky man was standing beside a shed washing his hands in a metal basin. He chewed with determination on a cigar that had long ceased to burn. It stood out against his full red beard, the counterpart to his head of red hair.

Wescott looked toward Crittenden. “Well, sir, you’ve got another mystery on your hands.”

“What is it this time?”

Wescott rolled his sleeves to his wrists, quickly fastening the shirt cuffs. He lifted his coat from a tree stump and motioned Crittenden into the shed where he had been working. The shed served as a surgery, though it had seen very little use since Manassas. The noon sun filtered in where boards had been removed from the roof. Crittenden saw two bodies lying beneath linen shrouds on the tables used for surgery. Several flies had begun to gather around them.

“What happened, a skirmish?” Crittenden asked, sniffing the acrid odor of blood.

Wescott beckoned Crittenden to one of the bodies and the men stood opposite one another. “This man was tortured. He bled to death.”

Crittenden’s eyes narrowed. “What are you talking about?”

Wescott sucked on his dead cigar. A look of distaste flitted across his face. “Actually, both men were tortured. You can see the marks where this one was tied."

The surgeon pulled back the sheet from the body and Crittenden stared at the contorted face that had not relaxed, even in death. The eyes were closed, but the face was a pulp of battered flesh. The wrists were rubbed raw where the man had fought against his bonds. But his fingers were broken and two were missing.

"Who is he?"

"Courier from Richmond." Wescott gestured to a pile of items in one corner of the room. "All his belongings are there, including the dispatches he was carrying."

Crittenden and Wescott looked at one another. "I can't believe Union soldiers would do this. And why leave the dispatches?"

Wescott covered the dead Confederate and moved to the second body. Crittenden followed. The surgeon removed the shroud.

"If they did that to one of ours, they also did it to one of their own."

Crittenden looked at the body of a Union officer. "Who is he?"

"Special courier for Major General John Dix out of Baltimore. Had his dispatches as well. He must have tried to escape for he was shot in the back. I dug out two bullets in rather good condition."

Wescott took the bullets from his pocket and held them in a shaft of sunlight. Crittenden noted the bullets had been wiped clean. The tips were slightly distorted, but they were just like the bullets he had extracted from that strange magazine that supplied ammunition to the gun Elliott Marsden had discovered.

"Exactly the same," Wescott spoke Crittenden's thoughts.

"Where were these bodies found?"

"In a sutler's shack about ten miles from here. Found by Sergeant Gage, the one who came with the young lieutenant you sent off to Frederick."

"Virgil, what the hell is happening?"

"You're asking me?" The surgeon placed his hand over his chest. "I got two dead soldiers, one from each side. Nothing missing, both tortured and for what? One of them shot with the same kind of ammunition that young lieutenant found."

"Exactly," Crittenden said.

"I don't follow you, sir."

"Both men were tortured for nothing? Nothing was taken."

"Well, not their dispatches."

"Unless they were carrying something else, other than dispatches."

"What?"

Crittenden bit his lip. "Damn, but I bet Baxter has a hand in this. Something is going on in Richmond."

"Then it's going on in Washington too." Wescott gestured to the dead Union officer.

"Have that sergeant bury these men," Crittenden ordered. "Find coffins, keep the bodies wrapped in shrouds, give them full military honors, but plant them fast."

Wescott started to speak, but was interrupted by a soldier with a message for Crittenden. Elliott Marsden had returned. Crittenden left the surgeon and hurried to his tent to find a haggard Elliott waiting for him.

"You see fighting on your way back?" Crittenden motioned for Elliott to sit on one of the wooden stools.

"No, sir, but the area around Frederick is crawling with Union patrols."

Elliott explained that Mrs. Bouchard was in Harrisburg and would be there until the last week in August. He did learn than Colonel Holland was in charge of Fredrick and his assistant was Major Mobrey.

"Seems the colonel likes the bottle and this Major Mobrey is doing all the work of command," Elliot continued. He had used the disguise of a lumber baron from Georgia since his father did own a lumber mill. But there was little more he could offer by way of information.

Crittenden nodded. "You see that lovely lady standing by the steps to the cabin?" Crittenden pointed out a petite woman about his age, with brown hair, near the cabin he was using as his headquarters.

"Yes, sir."

"That, son, is my wife. If you go to her and tell you who you are and ask her kindly, I think she'll give you some breakfast."

"That's very generous of you, sir. With your permission, I would like to wash first."

Crittenden nodded.

Elliot stood. "Have you any idea where Sergeant Gage set up the tents?"

"Yours is in that row." Crittenden pointed to a line of tents several yards from the one he was using for his official duties. Crittenden liked to work outside when the weather permitted.

"Thank you, sir." Elliott turned to go, hesitated, and faced Crittenden. "Sir, when the end of August arrives, I would like to return to Frederick."

"You shall have that chance, Lieutenant."

Crittenden watched Elliot hurry in the direction of his tent. A sinking feeling tugged at the pit of Crittenden's stomach. Ben Mobrey was in Frederick. He had known it, of course, known that Mobrey would do for the Union what he was doing for the Confederacy. But until Elliot had said the name, he had managed to keep the man he considered a younger brother from his thoughts.

Mobrey had been his second in command at Fort Randolph in the New Mexico Territory. Ben and Zoë and their children had been like family. No, Crittenden amended that thought. They *were* family. He had to get word to Mobrey about the dead courier. The informant he was using at Danver Falls might be able to get a message through to Frederick.

Crittenden had no doubt that the people from the Triangle Club were behind the deaths of the couriers. Now they were fielding an army, but how and why?

The dead couriers were carrying something those men like Kester, a club member, wanted badly enough to torture and kill for. What was it? Crittenden drummed his fingers on the table. He'd had a run-in with Kester before the war. The man had been behind the Triangle Club that had a base in Richmond. Crittenden's friend, Trevor Towsen, had destroyed the Cloisters, the club's Richmond brothel, but not the club.

Kester and his colleagues were behind the violence, behind the strange guns and the watch Towsen had rescued from the steamboat Chesapeake before the boat was blown apart. Crittenden carried the watch in his pocket. It kept perfect time and had what appeared to be shadows for hands. But Crittenden had never been able to puzzle out exactly what Kester and the others were up to.

"If I were in their boots, what would I be worried about?" Crittenden muttered to himself. His intuition provided the answer. "Cessation of hostilities." Crittenden didn't know whether he wanted to strangle Baxter or congratulate him.

He knew in his inner heart someone had gotten to Lincoln with the evidence about the Triangle Club, or with something similar. The presidents were trying to communicate and Kester and his minions knew it. Crittenden opened his portable writing desk and removed a sheet of paper. As he prepared the pen and ink, he thought about what to write. First to Mobrey, in the code they both knew.

He had used it before to communicate with his friend. Then to Baxter, in the code he had devised for that purpose after Baxter had learned Crittenden had a knack for creating ciphers.

~ * ~

August 26, 1961(Universe 0)

The ISIR scientists settled in at Gordo's. The others arrived from Washington a few days later, buying two used station wagons for the trip. They left the two remaining planes at National Airport as decoys for their unknown pursuers.

Though the ISIR scientists were eventually able to master the use of the transfer device, they understood little about its construction. Gray Eagle insisted he be present when it was used, for he sensed that the shaman stone he carried in some manner obstructed the original owners from finding the device.

"I'd put in some type of circuit to trace this little gizmo if it were mine," Rierdon had said when he arrived. "Bet they did too. I hope Gray Eagle's right about that stone of his."

He proved to be, for no more attacks were directed at the ISIR people. Barstead's next step was to locate universes technologically in advance of their own. He found three twenty-first century universes and one early twenty-second century universe. Security in the latter proved too difficult to circumvent for the present, but the first three offered possibilities.

The device allowed a visual mode and the scientists studied the universes, finally feeling secure enough to lift some computer equipment.

"To think I've become a thief," Barstead muttered as Rierdon shoved several boxes into Gordo's living room.

"What else can we do? When we find some usable money, I'll pay them back. Right now we're playing catch-up and we're not going do it in this universe." Barstead knew Rierdon was right. Even, as it turned out, prophetic, for on one of the trips to a 2045 Pittsburgh, Rierdon was forced to hide in an abandoned building. Crawling through an escape hole, he discovered the skeleton of a previous inhabitant wedged between the walls along with a cache of precious stones. Rierdon took them and used them as payment when he pilfered what ISIR needed.

But biological minefields awaited them. Crossing into another universe was not a simple matter. When the first volunteers returned sick with a raging infection, the scientists learned that common viruses and bacteria were not identical among the universes. A person would eventually pick up immunity, if he or she lived long enough, but the discovery of an IE (immune enhancing) drug in the 2045 universe bought them the necessary adaptation time.

So they worked and studied as the clock ticked away time they did not have. It was a race to understand what they had discovered and it was one they were losing. Barstead needed Weber's skills. Soon he'd have to make the call he dreaded.

~ * ~

August 27, 1961

"It's a call for you, Dr. Weber," one of the ISIR technicians said.

Weber, miffed at being interrupted, and more miffed that Barstead and the others were somewhere in the East doing God knows what, stormed to the phone.

"Dr. Weber?"

Weber recognized the voice. "General Croll?"

"Doctor, I understand Barstead and his team are in Pittsburgh. Have they contacted you?"

Weber let a smile play on his lips. Barstead might keep his location secret from the rest of ISIR, but not from Croll. "No, he hasn't."

"When he does, would you be willing to join him? You remember what we discussed at the Fairfax Inn?"

"I certainly do. I'll make it a point to join him. How do you want me to contact you?"

"Go into town this evening. Stop at the Sand Crab Restaurant for supper. Mr. Carter will meet you. He'll tell you what you need to know."

"Say seven?"

"Seven it is."

Weber replaced the receiver and smiled. Now all he need do was wait for a call from Barstead. His mind offered up a delicious bonus. He would ask Mark Bouchard to use one of the Merlins to fly him to Pittsburgh when the time came. If Croll arrested the ISIR people, Mark would be present. It was his snipe at Barstead for appointing Alyssia Bouchard as acting director instead of him.

~ * ~

August 31, 1961

Weber's arrival stirred only discord among team members. By the end of the week, everyone was angry with him. He was, however, making headway using one of the new tablet computers. That is, once Amber and Roger had taught him the basics. At first he was shocked by what Barstead revealed, but after a few days acted as if he had known all along that the Hasselbach manuscript was accurate.

Weber's analysis suggested what Barstead and the others had already. The transfer device merely funneled energy from a source. But even with what Weber had learned about the device, he could not locate this source.

"The energy source we're using isn't as strong as the one in Washington," Barstead said, staring at the set of equations on a monitor.

Weber hunched his shoulders, annoyed at Barstead's peering at his work. "It has to be in a space contiguous with this one. That much I can determine. But I just can't seem to get a handle on which universe holds the source."

Amber, listening to the discussion, said, "I set up the regression sequence to find that universe."

Weber made a dismissive gesture with his hand. "Why don't you and the other kids go for ice cream? I thought Gray Eagle was taking you for an outing."

Barstead stepped between Amber and Weber. “Go ahead,” he whispered. “I’ll be in the living room.”

Amber huffed to the library door, opened it, and let it slam shut as she stormed to the hallway where Gray Eagle and Roger were waiting.

“Is Julian coming?” Gray Eagle asked.

“No, he’s staying here. Weber says to take us for an outing,” she mimicked in a sing song voice. “I’d like to take him for an outing.”

“We’ll stop at that little ice cream store in Shadyside. Get us away from the place for a while,” Gray Eagle suggested.

~ * ~

They left the house, walking the length of the road to Center Avenue. From there it was a short walk to Shadyside, fast becoming a trendy neighborhood. Gray Eagle mused that Gordo’s purchase of the house had been fortunate. In time he would be able to rent out apartments for quite a bit of money.

“The others are away shopping for what we need,” Gray Eagle reminded them. “I’m surprised you didn’t want to see this mall in Monroeville.”

“I don’t like leaving Weber alone with that device,” Amber said.

“Julian is there. No one will use it until I get back.”

“Weber took my data this morning. I tried to tell Julian, but he wouldn’t listen to me.”

Gray Eagle stopped walking. “What data?”

“I did this common fit analysis using the sequences of numbers that identify a universe location. I know the sequence translates into a five dimensional plot.”

“And?” Gray Eagle prompted.

“I figured if I could match them with the second string of data that appears when we activate the energy source, we could locate the source, or at least project a possible location.”

“What do you mean Weber took your data?”

“He took it from the tablet computer I was using. I saw him do it.” Amber continued a few paces. She stopped. Gray Eagle was no longer with her. She turned to see Gray Eagle running in the opposite direction, oblivious to the curious stares of the people he passed.

Roger grabbed Amber’s arm. “I bet Weber has located the energy source.”

“And Gray Eagle thinks he’s going to use the transfer device to find it,” she said, hurrying after Roger.

~ * ~

With Barstead safely out of the way in the living room, Weber made his move. This morning he had checked Amber’s work. His blood pressure had hit a new high when he discovered the analysis had worked. He had taken the data from her computer by memory module, erasing any trace of it, and transferred it to Barstead’s computer.

With a bit of judicious tweaking, he had the location of the source of energy for the transfer device. Now, with everyone gone, and Barstead occupied, Weber went to the locked cabinet where the transfer device was kept. Using the keys he had stolen from Barstead, he opened the cabinet, removed the device and walked to the center of the room.

He activated it, punched in the co-ordinates, and opened a portal to the energy source the device he held was using. Before him was a dimly lit room that was carved from the rock of a cave. In the center of the room stood a circular console supported on a central pillar. Directly above the console, a weak sphere pulsated as it was held suspended in a cradle what appeared to be optical fiber ropes. Each of the five ropes was as thick as Weber's forearm.

Lights winked across the console and the sphere responded by a slight increase in pulsation. Awe filled Weber as he stared at the device. For all his training and his vaunted arrogance, he had not the least idea how it operated. Since he had not pressed the continuous icon, the portal retreated before him as he walked toward the console. He reached out a trembling hand to touch it.

"Let it alone, vermin," a voice behind him hissed.

Weber jumped at the words, the transfer device dropping from his hand into the alternate universe. The portal winked out of existence.

"No! No!" Weber moaned.

"Shut up!"

Weber spun to face the intruder. "Who the hell are you?"

The man was dressed in a black uniform decorated by a red inverted triangle on his chest. "You led me on quite a hunt, but prowling around the contiguous space to this Pittsburgh was worth it." He removed a gun from the holster at his side.

"How did you get here?"

"In the same manner that you opened a portal to that Source Gate." The man aimed his gun at Weber.

"Did you manufacture the devices?" Weber wet his lips.

"It's of no concern to you."

"I can be of help to you," Weber offered. "I'm a well known physicist."

"You," the man looked at Weber as if he were viewing a cockroach. "You are of little importance and so ignorant as to be of no help to anyone."

"If you kill me, someone will hear." Weber gritted his teeth. *How dare the oaf before him call him ignorant?*

"I don't plan to kill you here," the man said. He opened a portal to Weber's left and the dim room was again visible. "I plan to kill you there. Let the others think you absconded with the device. That should keep them busy." The man made a gesture with his gun.

Weber took a step backward as the door to the room flew open, striking the uniformed man in the back. He pitched forward and Weber raced to catch the transfer device before it struck the ground. The stranger rolled to his feet, kicking at Weber, but missing his neck.

The man spun toward the door and faced Gray Eagle. A shot passed through the stranger's head and he dropped to the floor. Gray Eagle stood just inside the room holding Mary Frances' .38.

"Put down the transfer device," he ordered Weber. "You were not to use it unless I was present."

"I found the source of the energy." Weber pointed to the still open portal.

"Like hell you did," Gray Eagle muttered. "I said put it down."

Weber placed the device he held on the table beside the computer. Gray Eagle stared at him, then at a second transfer device on the rocky floor of the room where the softly pulsating sphere lived.

Weber followed his gaze. "I can explain," he offered, wetting his lips.

"Let's hear it," Gray Eagle demanded.

~ * ~

"Rich Marsden has a farm in Bennett, Virginia," Gordo called into the living room. He replaced the phone on the wall. "He can't wait to meet us."

"I can wait to meet him," Barstead mumbled.

"It's our only choice," Gray Eagle reminded Barstead. "We've got the stuff from that thing called a Source Gate. We know now what we didn't before." Gray Eagle stopped and glanced out the window. He could see the tall oak tree shading Gordo's yard.

They knew exactly how far from understanding the transfer device they had been. By some miracle, the Source Gate, abandoned in a sixteenth century universe, held the key to understanding its construction. Embedded in the console were memory modules with diagnostics for the transfer device, as well as the entire schematic for the Source Gate. Other modules contained instructions on its use. But there were no data on the sphere, referred to in the memory modules as a Mind Jewel.

No one could understand why the Source Gate had been abandoned, except that the energy it assembled, the word still had an odd ring in Gray Eagle's mind, was less than some rated number in the instructions. In other parts of the house, ISIR team members were packing again, this time to travel south to Richard Marsden's farm. Marsden was the owner of the downed P-40.

"This is too weird." Amber came into the living room holding a Coke "You know where Bennett is located?"

"No." Barstead gently placed the second transfer device into the box he had carried from the Fairfax Inn.

"It's about twenty miles south of Appomattox."

Rierdon plopped into the brown, leather chair. "From Antietam to Appomattox in two months. Gotta be a record."

"That's not funny, Cc," Mary Frances cautioned, then asked Gray Eagle, "What did you do with the dead body?"

"I put it in the room in that tenement house."

Mary Frances protested. "But that's in the universe Mrs. Bouchard comes from."

"Whoops," Amber chuckled. "At least we'll be out of Pittsburgh."

"What about you, Gordo?" Gray Eagle asked.

"I'm coming with you," Gordo told them. "I had Al take over the business for now. He wants to buy it anyway."

Barstead glanced up at his friend. "Don't burn your bridges yet."

"You did that when Amber brought you the transfer device. I did that when I let you use my place. And I suspect Rich Marsden is about to do that, but he doesn't know it yet."

Barstead sighed. "Well, as soon as everyone is ready, we'd better get on the road."

~ * ~

August 31, 1861 (Universe 1)

Rose Callahan returned home to her one-room apartment after a long, hot day at the tiny shop where she worked selling dry goods. The stairs seemed clammy and dusty and she yearned for the cooler weather. It was eight in the evening as she turned the key and opened her door.

Enough light filtered through the dirt-encrusted window to outline a black pile of what to her appeared as a heap of discarded clothing huddled against the fireplace. She knew she had left nothing there. She reached out a hand and touched the mass. A dead man rolled onto his back, his opaque, unseeing eyes staring at her in silent accusation at disturbing his rest.

Eight

Every event in Physical Reality was first a pattern
in another Reality
Codex of Flowering Butterfly

September 7, 1861(Universe 1)

Crittenden stared at the article in his recent copy of the *Richmond Dispatch.* The story from Pittsburgh had been sent by telegraph to other newspapers and had been printed because of its unusual content. A young woman had found a dead man in her tenement room. The man was clothed in a black military uniform that had a red inverted triangle on the chest. On the left breast of the uniform was a metallic black circle outlined in red.

"So, they have come out into the open again," Crittenden whispered.

The paper's description of the uniform matched what Elliott had seen on the bodies he had found near the stone bridge at Manassas. Since the bodies had worn similar uniforms, Crittenden reasoned they had to be related.

The newspaper story explained that the body in Pittsburgh had disappeared from the morgue, along with the uniform and the strange gun found with it. The gun's description matched that of the gun Elliott had brought to him.

As Crittenden sat waiting for Elliott, he wondered who had killed the man and dumped the body in that tenement. He speculated that the people who had killed the man were not the same ones who had removed the body from the morgue. Had they been, the body would not have been left where it was first found and neither would the gun.

"There are other players in this mystery game," Crittenden mused. "I wonder just who they are and which side they intend to support."

Because the Confederate Army was still encamped around Manassas, Crittenden had time to sift through the reports he had requested from his informants. Crittenden had learned Mobrey, under Holland's orders, was collecting reports on the deaths of eight couriers. There was also a report of civilians being killed. It was the one report Crittenden had difficulty reading.

The recent news around camp was that Lee had been promoted to full general and was in Western Virginia. Baxter, civilian head of Confederate Intelligence, was still in Richmond and no one was admitting to anything. It was time, Crittenden thought, to get some answers.

Elliott interrupted Crittenden's musings. The young officer saluted. "You sent for me, sir?"

"Yes, Lieutenant. I want you to return to Frederick. I've learned that Mrs. Bouchard is home. This time, you are going through the network of sympathizers."

"Sir, I went by rail before."

"Hush up a minute, son. There is more danger than you realize in this trip."

"Sir?"

Crittenden offered Elliott a summary of what he had learned. "You have to really blend in with the civilians. It's your only chance. Your enemy may not be the Union soldiers. In fact they may be of some help."

"Who are those men in the strange uniforms?"

"I wish I knew," Crittenden admitted. "But keep your eyes open and listen for anything you can about them. Especially what Mobrey has discovered."

Crittenden outlined his plan and Elliott listened carefully. When the young officer left, Crittenden stood and stretched his frame. He was grateful that Jackson had agreed to have Elliott transferred from his command. The young man was the least military soldier Crittenden had ever seen. That fact would be to Elliott's advantage.

~ * ~

September 8, 1861(Universe 1)

"I see, Colonel, that you have yet to find the scientists." General Sig spoke as he studied the display of data filling the large screen projected on the wall of the secure room of the Embassy Club. "I want no interference with the invasion. The

Command Council is busy finalizing plans."

"Sir, the scientists left Pittsburgh a week ago and have not used a transfer device since Rort discovered them. He was one of my best operatives. We found him dead in the Pittsburgh of this universe. I know a portal was opened between the sixteenth century universe and Pittsburgh in the 1961 buffer universe and it was kept open for some time."

"No other Source Gate near that area?" Sig clasped his hands behind his back. He was taller than Kester, with blue eyes and light brown hair. His face held a tiny scar on the right cheek, one he refused to have regenerated. It was a badge of honor for him.

Kester's dark eyes, flecked with green, watched his superior. "Sir, that Source Gate was minimally operational. But it's down."

Sig looked at his subordinate. "Have you any idea why?"

Kester squirmed beneath that gaze. He had several ideas why, each more unpalatable than the one before it. "I've no evidence as to what happened, sir. Just that particular Source Gate is no longer functioning."

"That's happened before when the abandoned gates finally crash."

"Perhaps this one did the same from overuse by the scientists? It'll take time to send in a team to investigate."

"Why was Rort killed? What happened to his transfer device?"

Kester felt the world caving in around him. "I suspect the scientists killed him. He was shot with a .38. We got Rort's body and his gun from the morgue, but he was not carrying his transfer device."

"Where did the scientists go?"

"We're still working on that. I'm trying to trace phone records."

Sig glared at Kester. "You're better than that. What's the holdup?"

"It's a mid-twentieth century universe. They haven't networked their computer systems yet. Hell, they don't even have real computers."

"So somewhere in that twentieth century universe is a group of scientists, bright ones from what your research shows. They have two transfer devices and, until the Source Gate crashed, the chance to run amok through no one knows how many alternate and technologically advanced universes."

"I'm afraid so, sir."

"Unless they can find another abandoned Source Gate, we should be able to locate them. The tracer sensor in Rort's body led you to him. The same type of sensor in the transfer devices the scientists have should lead us to them. San thinks the Source Gate in that sixteenth century universe was shielding the scientists while they were in Pittsburgh."

Kester started at the words. If the Source Gate had shielded them in Pittsburgh, what had shielded them before that? He hadn't been able to find them using the tracer sensor. He'd had to depend on old-fashioned legwork. Kester felt his temper flare. "I'll find them, sir," he vowed.

"No, you've been reassigned to my command," Sig replied.

Kester's mouth dropped open. "But sir, I'm a Mission Specialist."

"Precisely." Sig swung to face him. "The logistics of fielding and army in a mid-nineteenth century universe are complicated. All our resources must come from alternate universes and you are in charge of obtaining them. I'll see you in my headquarters in one hour."

Sig left the room before Kester could offer him a salute. As the door to the secure room closed, Kester smacked a swivel chair with fury, sending it spinning in the process.

"Damn that San!" he shouted. Feelings of betrayal by his former commander welled up like lava from an active volcano. "I'm a field officer, not a desk jockey. Now I've just been turned into a quartermaster."

~ * ~

September 8, 1961(Universe 0)

Marsden's farm was a hundred and fifty acres of rolling land interspersed with woods. The town of Bennett was ten miles northeast of the farm. Roanoke was the largest city to the west and Danville lay to the east of the farm. The area had changed since the Civil War, though it was still mostly farmland.

A small runway had been constructed for Marsden's private plane, a twin engine Cessna. When Barstead learned of the runway, he made plans to bring two of the Merlins to Virginia. But his first task, and that of his colleagues, was to reconstruct the Source Gate they had dismantled and brought to their universe.

The day after they arrived, the scientists were making headway and the Source Gate was already nearing operational status. Marsden was the perfect host, even showing them a secret room to use for their work.

"This farm was part of the Underground Railroad," he explained as he demonstrated how the lever counterweight system opened into a four hundred square foot room. "It was owned by a wealthy Quaker couple. This room is solid."

"How can we compensate you for your generosity?" Barstead asked as he studied the room.

"You can tell me what the hell happened to my plane. And just what is going on."

"Gladly," Barstead chuckled.

"By the way, electricity is a bit iffy in this part of the state," Marsden said as he stared at the boxes of equipment the scientists were unloading in the basement.

Barstead smiled. "Don't worry, Rich. We brought our own power source."

~ * ~

Work progressed smoothly for several days, as the ISIR people hurried to reconstruct a technology that was part science, part alchemy. Marsden was delighted to meet the young pilots and especially delighted to meet Gray Eagle and learn about his time with the Flying Tigers.

During breaks between round-the-clock shifts, Marsden, Gordo, and Gray Eagle would sit in Marsden's study swapping stories about World War II. When that avenue was exhausted, Marsden and Gordo talked about their time in Korea.

Marsden had not been happy since his wife and daughter had been killed in a car accident seven years earlier. Gordo had gotten him through the rough parts and he owed the man his life. Had Gordo not been there to help, Marsden knew he would have killed himself. Letting the ISIR people use his farm was a means to repay Gordo.

But he had some problems with the situation, and alternate universes were not the only part of his disquiet. He had yet to see what the scientists claimed they could do. His greatest concern was the minor slip Barstead had made about General Croll.

~ * ~

Marsden walked down the basement stairs carrying a large coffeepot. There were several outlets in the basement and he often prepared coffee for the scientists. He also prepared meals, directing the younger members of ISIR on the finer points of gourmet cooking. He had a passion for cooking, one his late wife had appreciated, since she had hated to cook.

"Thanks, Rich." Gray Eagle took the thirty-six cup coffeepot from Marsden. "I'll take care of it."

"I need to talk to you and Julian," Marsden said.

Gray Eagle placed the pot on a workbench and plugged it into the outlet. "What's wrong?"

"It's General Croll. Gordo knows some of this, but not all. Don't trust Croll."

Gray Eagle asked, "Why? He's working with Beaumont and the other agents."

"He's working for himself, always has been. And Julian was wise not to tell him what you people found. Avoid contact with that man. He's dangerous. I'm surprised Gordo didn't tell you this before."

Gray Eagle sensed anger bordering on hatred from Marsden and wondered about the man's bias. "Why?"

"Gordo will confirm this. Croll had me kicked out of the Air Force, even though he was in the Army." Marsden held up his hand. "Oh, I was allowed to retire. Anyone with my combat record would be. But Croll wanted me in on some dirty dealings and when I refused, he fabricated evidence against me."

Gray Eagle sensed truth in the words. The anger was for Marsden's loss of privileges in flying the new jets. *So he flies old warbirds instead*, Gray Eagle thought. *That's as close as he can come to his beloved combat planes.*

Aloud, Gray Eagle said, "I'll tell Julian when I see him."

Marsden looked around. "Where is he?"

"On the phone. Alyssia, one of our research physicians, called from ISIR. She's the only one with this phone number. Julian asked her to head ISIR while he's away. Mark's her son. He's one of the pilots in my aerobatics team." Gray Eagle gestured to the young man helping Rierdon.

Marsden raised his eyebrows, but said nothing. "Gotta go back upstairs and see to lunch." He called to Mark. "I'm preparing lunch. Anytime you have a free minute, let's talk about flying."

Mark waved and returned to his work.

~ * ~

"I'll take care of it, Alyssia," Barstead spoke while crossing his fingers. "Just assure the other parents everyone's fine. I'll see about returning to Washington and getting rid of the ghost once and for all. Yes, we know how."

Marsden stood in the hallway between the kitchen and the dining room. Barstead looked up and nodded at the man.

"Just do as I ask," Barstead said. "Institute the security procedures I outlined. Oh yes, it's big." His face took on an amused expression. "Bye, Alyssia."

Barstead replaced the receiver on the cradle. He looked wistfully for a moment at the rotary dial phone and longed for one of the tiny cellular devices he'd seen in other universes. But the infrastructure to support them did not exist in his universe.

"Something up?" Marsden asked.

"Yes. Seems the ghost is back and General Croll has been calling ISIR about our status. I get the feeling he might know where we are."

Barstead did not miss Marsden's reaction. The man gripped the decorative back of a nearby chair, his hand squeezing it so tightly Barstead thought the section of chair might break under the pressure.

"Don't trust Croll," Marsden said through clenched teeth. "I just told Gray Eagle about him."

"Well you can tell me about him over lunch. But you might want to let go of that chair first."

Marsden glanced down, saw what he was doing, and released his grip.

~ * ~

General Croll paced his office at the new underground facility in the Pentagon. He'd had only one contact from Weber and that was garbled and incoherent. The scientist babbled something about alternate universes. *What had the fool been drinking? Couldn't he see this nonsense in the White House was a Soviet plot? They had some new technology probably based on the recently discovered laser devices.*

"And Weber babbles about nonsense." Croll pounded his desk with his fist. Weber was almost as bad as those fools shrieking about flying saucers. Next he would be claiming aliens had landed.

The call to the West Coast should shake the scientists out of Bennett. The fact that Marsden was in on it suggested to Croll that this was some sort of a scam. But his gut told him it had nothing to do with revenge. He was convinced the ISIR people knew about what was happening at the White House and were keeping it secret. He wanted them in DC. He wanted them where he could get his hands on them.

~ * ~

"Julian, I'm just speculating." Gray Eagle took a healthy bite out of his turkey sandwich and chewed, savoring the taste of freshly baked bread. He swallowed. "This thing I carry is a Jewel, one no longer completely operational. I figured that out from the data in the memory modules we took when we found the Source Gate."

"An even bigger mystery is who was Elias Hazen?" Margaret sipped a glass of freshly squeezed lemonade. "That old piece of luggage we found hidden in the pile of rubble in that room with the Source Gate had his name sewn inside it."

"That luggage is what was used about a hundred years ago," Mary Frances offered, munching on a carrot stick.

Gray Eagle continued to eat his sandwich. He thought about the room where the Source Gate was hidden. They had taken everything from it, including the pile of rubbish in the corner, which proved a treasure trove of discarded packaging from several universes. Apparently someone had been using the place intermittently, but why?

The bag with Hazen's name in it had been hidden beneath a pile of rubbish and contained a surprise: four Jewels packed in protective padding, not all the same size and from what the scientists could tell, in varying stages of shut down. The console had memory modules and a removable reader, but there were no instructions accompanying the Jewels.

Rierdon asked Gray Eagle. "Do you think there's a barely functional Jewel in the White House of that 1861 universe and that it's responsible for Lincoln appearing in our universe?"

"That's my guess."

Amber asked, "What are the Jewels and where did they originate?"

"They were probably made by the people who made the transfer devices." Barstead sipped his coffee.

"That one we found in the Source Gate was in a pretty decayed state. Why did they leave the things around?" Amber pressed. "It seems careless."

Gray Eagle had wondered that himself, just as he had wondered how his grandmother had acquired the decayed Jewel he called a Shaman Stone. "Maybe they are the only ones who can use the technology, so they're careless of it?"

"Well," she replied, "it was fortunate for us they were careless and that this Elias Hazen had left extra ones in that trash heap."

"In any case," Marsden interrupted his guest's speculations. "What are your plans in DC?"

"To get to the White House, contact Lincoln, find the decayed Jewel triggering the interaction between the universes, and get rid of it," Barstead explained.

"I'll give you a bit of advice," Marsden said.

"What advice?"

"Get in, get it over with, and get out fast. Don't deal with Croll."

Gray Eagle saw Barstead nod agreement. He knew Barstead planned no interaction with General Croll. Not after Croll's call to ISIR and his not-so-subtle attempt at intimidation. The only thing Gray Eagle regretted was not hearing Alyssia Bouchard telling General Croll to put his threats "where the sun don't shine."

~ * ~

September 9, 1961(Universe 0)

Barstead and his small team arrived in Washington around three in the afternoon. He met Beaumont and explained they had taken rooms at the Fairfax Inn. He would not permit the agent to drive them to the White House, insisting that he and the others bring their own car.

Stein finally intervened, agreeing to the scientists' use of the station wagon, and explaining that he and Beaumont would make the security arrangements.

"Will this put an end to the ghost?" Stein asked.

Barstead nodded. “We think there is something in the Lincoln bedroom that is the focus of the appearances. I’ve redesigned one of my magnetic field meters and will use it to pinpoint the location.”

The truth was that Barstead had found a computerized field meter in a 2020 universe and hidden it inside the old meter that Amber had destroyed. His plan depended on getting Beaumont and the other agents out of the way so he and his colleagues could communicate with Lincoln.

“How will your new meter locate this so-called focus?” Stein asked.

“I want you, Beaumont, and Kraft to take individual meters and station yourselves here.” Barstead pointed out a sketch of the layout of the East Wing. “Take careful readings,” he cautioned, hoping his words were convincing. “But keep this quiet. That’s why you need to do this, not us. You are a familiar sight around the White House.”

“Then what?” Beaumont squinted at the diagram.

“Then we triangulate. Where your field strengths cross ours is where the focus of the problem will be.” Barstead made a gesture with his hands. “When we get rid of the focus, you get rid of the ghost.”

“Good enough,” Beaumont said. He glanced at his repaired watch. “We meet at eight to set up. But Kraft is on another assignment. I’ll see about getting a replacement.”

“We’ll drive to the White House. You just be there to let security know we are legit,” Barstead said. “I don’t relish being shot.”

Stein and Beaumont said good bye and left the suite. When their car drove away, Mary Frances knocked on Barstead's door. The others soon crowded in as well.

"Did he buy it?" Reed asked Barstead.

Barstead shrugged. "I think so. We need to keep him out of the way long enough to talk with Lincoln. Lincoln's got to know what we know. If this Mrs. Bouchard is right, Lincoln is sitting on a Source Gate probably in the space contiguous with the National Geographic Society building in this universe. He also has a decayed Jewel in the White House."

Gray Eagle nodded. "We found the largest anomaly in our universe near the National Geographic building the last time we were in DC."

Barstead rubbed his weary face with his hands. He wished the evening were over and his team back in Bennett. In truth, he wished he and the others were back in California. But he had the feeling this was never to be.

~ * ~

Beaumont and Stein were trapped behind a slow moving truck and their return was taking longer than they had anticipated.

"Take the next road," Beaumont told Stein. "I know a way around this mess."

Stein laughed. "So you live. Thought you died. You haven't said a word since we left."

Beaumont rubbed his temples. “You know, I think they’re hiding something. My own sister is in on it as well.”

Stein signaled right and made the turn. “You think they don’t know what there’re doing and don’t want to admit it?”

“I think they know exactly what they’re doing and don’t want to tell us. Can’t blame them if Croll is on their back.”

“You tell Croll they arrived?”

Beaumont let a smile play on his lips. “No. The man’s tied up in some secret meetings. No need to bother him.”

Stein chuckled. “My sentiments as well. What about Kraft?”

“He’s shadowing the president in New York. Maybe when Kennedy gets back, the ghost will be gone.”

“And things will be back to normal?”

Beaumont shook his head. “Things will never be normal again.”

~ * ~

September 10, 1961(Universe 0)

Barstead and the team were ready by two in the morning. The agent helping Beaumont was in the Rose Garden, Stein was in the Treaty Room, and Beaumont was in the second floor reception room. He stood in the middle of the room holding a heavy instrument, waiting for something to happen. The dial on the meter flickered now and then and he dutifully recorded the readings. He wanted to be in the hallway with the scientists but could not discount that his readings might be important. So he fumed, but remained where he was.

Ten minutes after two, the vapor appeared. Barstead's new computerized equipment followed the magnetic anomaly, displaying its outlines in three dimensions on the screen of the hand-held magnetometer. Barstead was as elated with the equipment as he was with the return of the specter.

Barstead met Lincoln's gaze and raised his finger to his lips. "Sir, we haven't much time and a great deal to tell you."

Lincoln nodded his agreement. "What is it?"

"You are quite real," Barstead held up his hand to stem any comment from Lincoln. "And in great danger."

"The war," Lincoln conceded.

"That too. Sir, in your Washington, there is a device buried beneath your city. Show him the map, Cc." Barstead stepped aside.

Rierdon unfolded a map of the Washington of Lincoln's time. A red dot indicated the location of the Source Gate."

"What is buried there?" Lincoln demanded. "Confederate guns?"

"No," Barstead replied. "The Confederates have nothing to do with this thing. It's a Source Gate, a way to cross between one universe and another."

Lincoln rubbed his head. "I have had so little sleep and now what you tell me makes my head ache."

Reed stepped between Rierdon and Barstead. He carried a new magnetic imager and passed it over the specter. It gave him a steady reading, despite the more intense magnetic fields swirling in the area of the hallway.

"Stop that." Barstead forced the instrument away from Lincoln.

"I've got some sleep medication he can take. It isn't habit forming," Reed said.

Barstead smacked his hand on his forehead. "We don't have time."

Reed opened the soft-sided medical kit he had appropriated from the 2050 universe. He reached in and removed a plastic vial containing tiny pink pills. Reed tossed the vial at the mist and the vial slipped through, dropping at Lincoln's feet.

"Take one at bedtime as needed," Reed ordered. "No alcohol with them. And keep that plastic out of sight."

"President Lincoln, do you have something purchased recently that has a piece of crystal in it that looks like this?" Barstead motioned for Gray Eagle to display his Shaman Stone.

Lincoln squinted at the object with recognition. "Indeed I do. It is in the headboard of my bed. Mary bought the headboard the week we moved into the White House."

"Get the crystal out of the headboard and get rid of it," Barstead ordered. "It's the focus of these interactions in the White House."

"I am not certain I want these interactions, as you call them, to stop," Lincoln said.

"They must, sir, otherwise both our universes are in danger," Barstead insisted.

"I shall do so on one condition," Lincoln demanded. "I want your word that you will help me with this terrible war. And I insist on additional proof that what you say is so."

Barstead was taken aback by Lincoln's adamant demand. "What can we do?"

"You, sir, are the scientist. You will think of something."

"As to proof," Barstead shrugged.

"Wait," Mary Frances said. "Desiree Bouchard lives on State Street in Frederick, Maryland in your universe. My scarf was left in your universe at Manassas. She may even have it. If not, she will remember what happened. Contact her, and she will verify our story. My name is Mary Frances Beaumont."

Lincoln smiled at Mary Frances. "Are you related to the agent who was so gallant in my defense the last time? The one whose handkerchief I have?"

Mary Frances nodded. "I'm his sister."

"Then I shall do as you ask, though I neither understand nor like what you have told me." He looked to Barstead. "Your word, sir, and that of your colleagues. Your help with this war."

Barstead's jaw opened, his mind raced with the request. "I, well, yes."

"We'll do what we can," Margaret said. "Company coming, Julian."

"Sir, I must ask you to leave."

"I will do so when I am ready." Lincoln grew annoyed.

"Gray Eagle," Barstead called. "Sorry, Mr. President. You'll do so now."

Gray Eagle lifted his Shaman Stone and oriented it toward the president. The vapor dissipated.

"Of all the impertinent—" Lincoln never finished his sentence.

~ * ~

It was a soft melody of aching sweetness. The song brought with it images of long forgotten-memories. Amber jerked awake, but the song was still in her head. She glanced at the clock. It was two forty-five. She slipped into her shoes, took her robe, and left the room she was sharing with Mary Frances, who was unfortunately in Washington and so Amber could not waken her to ask if she too heard the music.

Amber stepped into the hall and quietly closed the door.

"So you heard it too," Roger said.

She jumped, placing her hand on her chest. "You scared me. Where's it coming from?"

Roger looked at the stairs. "I think the basement."

The pair walked down the stairs lit by a series of night-lights and made their way to the basement. Amber pressed the lever to the secret room and the counterweight opened the stone door. She stepped into the room, touching the switch for the newly installed lighting. The small basement room was flooded with light.

"There," she whispered, pointing to the glass case holding the Jewel they had taken from the Source Gate and the four they had discovered hidden beneath the trash. The Jewel from the Source Gate was pulsating. Amber walked to the case, lifted the lid, and reached for the Jewel. Roger grabbed her arms.

"It could be radioactive," he warned.

"We checked before. And if it is now, we're already dead. But I don't think this is radiation, at least not the decay from a nucleus. The Jewel is the source of the song."

She pulled away from Roger and lifted the device. It was as if a light, fragrant breeze caressed her mind. Color swirled around her. Song, light, images she could make no sense of filled her being.

"I am a Mind Jewel," the device sang to her and she knew Roger heard the song as well. "I have been used to draw energy from the Void, but that is not my purpose. It is a perversion." "What is your purpose?" Amber thought.

"You will come to understand in time," the Jewel sang. "I know you must use me so, but be aware there is another way to create portals."

"How?" Amber thought.

"This is how." The Jewel sang into her mind and Roger's mind the equations and techniques to create a crystal that drew energy from the Void, just as did the Jewel. It sang to them of where and how to obtain what they needed to grow such a replacement.

"I don't understand. The people who use you, why can't they do what you've just told us? Why use Jewels?" Amber asked.

"They have forgotten what has been revealed to you and none of the Jewels will ever tell them."

"But why tell us?" Amber asked.

The Jewel sang a song of happiness and release. "Because you are the long awaited ones, the Light Dancers. You will free us, you will free everyone." And the Jewel fell silent.

Nine

Only the truly wise profit from other's mistakes
Codex of Flowering Butterfly

September 12, 1861(Universe 1)

Lincoln woke refreshed, the way he always felt after coming to a critical decision and sleeping well. The sleep was due to the tablets Dr. Reed had slipped through the mist. On Thursday he had taken a few private minutes and pried from the headboard of his bed the object Barstead had insisted he remove.

Now as he walked along the Potomac with McBride, Lincoln threw the thing into the water.

"What was that, sir?" McBride asked.

"Something I have been meaning to discard," Lincoln said. "I want you to do two things for me, Nathan."

"Anything, Mr. President."

"I want you to go through the intelligence reports and find any reference to, well, something that does not seem to be due to action by either army."

McBride stopped walking. “Such as?”

“That I cannot help you with.” Lincoln noted McBride’s expression, but ignored it. The men continued walking. “The second thing I want you to do is to find me someone known to you. Someone you personally trust, who can do a very special mission for me. This person should be well versed in the sciences.”

“The sciences?” McBride again stopped walking. Lincoln continued s few paces before turning to look at the man Pinkerton had suggested as a personal bodyguard. Lincoln was very fond of McBride and he knew the man held him in high regard.

“Yes. It is important.”

“Sir.” McBride cleared his throat. A faint pink flush crept to his cheeks and he tugged absently at his silk tie, fasted in an elaborate bow. “You haven’t been seeing them again, have you?” He let his words drift off, ducking his head from Lincoln’s gaze.

Lincoln chuckled. “Nathan, you’re the best diplomat I have ever met. Come, man, out with it. Have I been seeing ghosts?”

“Sir?”

“You bet I have. Only they are not ghosts and I am quite sane. Find me the man I asked for and do it soon. As to my other request, I trust your fine mind to see the answer when you read the reports.”

McBride gave his head a quick shake as if to dislodge some errant thought. “I will do as you request, sir.”

~ * ~

September 13, 1961(Universe 0)

Croll glared at Major Landers. “What do you mean, the scientists left town? I told you to find some way to detain them.”

“They were here and gone before I could do so,” Landers confessed. “Dr. Weber was unable to contact us. He can’t use the phone in Marsden’s house and with one of the cars gone, he’s had trouble getting into Bennett.”

“So, because of this little mix-up we lost the scientists?”

“But Weber sent a report, but it’s crazy.” Landers offered his superior an envelope.

Croll pulled his chair around and faced the carved wooden desk he had recently purchased for his office. The three pages he withdrew from the envelope were covered with neat, legible writing. Croll read the contents twice. He looked up at Landers, still standing before his desk.

“Is Weber kidding?”

Landers shrugged. “I have no idea, sir. It sounds so farfetched, yet he swears he will be able to get us proof.”

“I want a team watching those scientists when they leave Marsden’s house. I want them shadowed every step of the way. I don’t know what’s going on in that house, but Weber isn’t the only way I plan to find out.”

~ * ~

September 14, 1861(Universe 1)

"So couriers from both sides were killed by some sort of outlaw gang dressed in black uniforms?" Lincoln dropped the written report McBride had given him onto his desk. "But to have killed that poor woman in such a disgusting manner." Lincoln felt his stomach turn as he remembered the words describing the fate of several civilians ambushed in Maryland. "Anything else?"

McBride shook his head. "Except to ask how you knew something was going on?"

"A lucky guess."

"Divine intervention?" McBride cocked an eyebrow.

Lincoln chuckled. "Keep that to yourself," he ordered. "Now this man you found for me."

"Lieutenant Penfield is waiting outside, Mr. President." McBride seemed pleased with his choice. "He's a second lieutenant from an artillery company, the Tenth New York Volunteers. He's the son of a good friend and has been studying science at Harvard for three years."

"Well, show him in." Lincoln rubbed his hands together. "I am quite eager to meet him."

McBride left the office for a few minutes and returned with a young officer in a dress uniform, complete with sword. Lincoln's eyes widened at the sight of the handsome young man, far younger than he had imagined. *When had this boy gone off to college*?

"Mr. President, may I present Lieutenant Joshua Penfield."

Joshua saluted Lincoln and stood at rigid attention. The officer's anxiety made Lincoln uncomfortable. He was used to a more relaxed atmosphere and wondered if Joshua planned to spend the entire interview standing at attention.

"I am pleased to meet you, Lieutenant Penfield."

Joshua wet his lips and nodded. Lincoln chose a comfortable chair. He gestured to the chair opposite him. "Please sit, Lieutenant, I don't bite."

He waited until Joshua complied, sitting opposite him but in an attitude of attention. He suddenly wondered if the officer was old enough to shave. But if McBride considered him a candidate for what Lincoln had in mind, he must have the resources to carry out the mission.

"Lieutenant Penfield, I understand you were at Harvard?"

Joshua relaxed just a little. "Yes, Mr. President. I was admitted at sixteen and have been studying mathematics and natural philosophy."

"Well, Joshua. May I call you Joshua?"

The officer nodded rapidly. Lincoln bit back a smile. Joshua was frightened of him and it suddenly occurred to Lincoln why. The young man thought he was in serious trouble. McBride would have told him nothing, as Lincoln had requested.

"Son, I need help from someone who is bright, which Nathan obviously thinks you are. Someone versed in the sciences, which you have to be after three years at Harvard." Lincoln saw the glimmer of surprise in Joshua's stare.

"Mr. President, I will give you whatever help I can," Joshua replied, his voice just breaking the level of a whisper.

"Good. The task I have for you is not an easy one. I will tell you what I want you to do, but I cannot tell you why. If you are successful, you will tell me why I sent you."

Joshua gave a quick shake of his head. "Sir, I, well, whatever you wish, Mr. President."

Lincoln chuckled. "I know the request seems strange, but I also need someone who is clever and discreet."

"He is that," McBride vouched for Joshua. "Don't underestimate this one, sir. He's been a handful since he started to walk. I can testify to that. His family and mine are good friends."

Lincoln shot a glance at Joshua. The young officer looked as if he were about to choke. "I believe you, Nathan. Lieutenant, I'll give you a chance to make up your own mind. I will tell you what I wish and if you feel you cannot do this thing, you may leave, and it will be as if this meeting did not take place."

"I understand, Mr. President," Joshua said. "I will have forgotten whatever words you speak."

Nathan was right, Lincoln thought. There was a depth to the young officer before him that was not visible from surface appearances. Lincoln folded his hands in his lap.

"Listen carefully, for not even Nathan yet knows this task. In Frederick, Maryland lives a woman, Desiree Bouchard. Her house is on State Street. You are to go to her and ask her about a woman she met, a Mary Frances Beaumont."

Joshua nodded, committing the facts to memory. Lincoln watched curiosity spin a web of interest across the young man's face.

"Ask her what she knows about the danger facing the nation and if she remembers the scarf Mary Frances left with her."

Lincoln finished speaking and looked from Joshua to McBride. McBride's face was screwed into a perplexed frown, but Joshua seemed to accept what Lincoln had said.

"I will do this task, sir," the young officer said in a firmer voice. "I have memorized your words."

"Son, this is not a coded message," Lincoln cautioned. "The mission I send you on is very dangerous. You will go to Frederick under the pretense of responding to the claims of Major Mobrey about outlaws. Nathan will give you a way to return a message to me so that no one knows you carry it."

Joshua sat forward in his chair. "May I ask you a question, Mr. President?"

Lincoln nodded.

"Sir, I will do this mission for you, but I fail to see why you need someone versed in the sciences."

McBride shot Joshua a look of disapproval, but Lincoln brushed it aside.

"When you speak with this woman, I think the reason will become clear."

"Yes, Mr. President."

Lincoln stood. Joshua jumped to his feet as if he had been propelled from a cannon.

"Show him the clever pouch you devised, Nathan," Lincoln ordered. McBride nodded and ushered the officer from Lincoln's study.

Lincoln moved to his desk and lifted a report from General Reynolds. Reynolds was in western Virginia and had fought Lee's forces to a standstill in the muddy terrain of Cheat Mountain. Lee had managed to carry out a complicated attack plan and Reynolds was in need of reinforcements. Lincoln crushed the report in his fist.

McClellan knew of Reynolds difficulties, but insisted the men training in Washington were not ready for the field. If Reynolds were forced to withdraw, western Virginia would be firmly in Confederate hands. That might open the way for an invasion force to move on Pittsburgh and the Ohio River.

Lincoln had pried a promise out of the scientists and he was sure they would keep it. Their concern seemed genuine, but he also sensed a naiveté about them. Wherever they came from, he was dead, or at least the agent claimed so. Felled by an assassin, the man had said. Well, he wasn't dead here and he had no plans in that direction. He did have plans that included the scientists and he couldn't wait until they arrived. He knew in his heart they would come.

~ * ~

September 14, 1961(Universe 0)

Gray Eagle sat in Marsden's kitchen looking through the screen door and listening to Barstead and Weber talk as they stood on the flagstone patio. Smoke from the grill drifted skyward in a straight line. Marsden was planning steaks for supper. Gray Eagle turned to Amber and watched her make a face as Weber offered a new name for the Source Gate.

"A Weber Gate my foot," she muttered. "It was a turnkey operation. Everything we dismantled was in modular form. All we had to do was put it together and turn the key."

"I know," Gray Eagle replied. "But Stan wants the glory."

"What glory?" she demanded. "No one knows about this, maybe no one ever will. The thing is finally operational, but if you want to go to Frederick, you'll have to use whatever is in DC. Frederick is beyond portal range for this energy source."

"Besides, something happened while you were gone," Roger said as he and Amber exchanged glances. "We need to speak with you about it."

"And Julian?"

Amber bit her lip. "Just you for now. I know Julian accepts your Medicine, but I think we'd better talk about this away from the house."

Curiosity prevented Gray Eagle from doing more than nodding. He rose, went to the patio, and told Barstead he was going for a walk with Amber and

Roger. Barstead waved him away and Weber ignored him, still babbling in excited animation about “his” discovery.

Gray Eagle, Amber, and Roger headed away from the house toward a small stand of maple and locust trees. It was hot and still. Insects glided over the wildflowers sprinkled across the grassy path as the trio passed by. The air had a dry, end-of-summer feel. It smelled of late-blooming flowers with just the hint of approaching fall.

The gray, weathered body of a dead tree offered them a seat beneath a canopy of shade. Amber sat on one side of Gray Eagle and Roger sat on the other.

“There’s no easy way to say this.” Amber began her tale of the happenings in the basement while Gray Eagle was away in Washington.

“It sang equations into your head?”

She nodded.

“And you remembered them?”

Roger said. “We put them in Amber’s new tablet computer, along with the notes, and used a spreadsheet to calculate the cost of equipment.”

Gray Eagle mentally shuddered at the proficiency of his students. Three months ago the most complicated computer they had dealt with was a lumbering IBM called a mainframe in some universes. That behemoth required punched cards to program. Today these two were busily using voice and gesture input to create a report on how to construct a crystal replica of the Jewel.

Gray Eagle rubbed his forehead as he spoke. "This is too much."

"It's true," Amber insisted.

"I know it is."

"There's more." She gave him a conspiratorial wink. "Roger, Mark, and Kit were playing around with the data in the memory modules we extracted from the Source Gate."

"But only when Weber was busy creating his version of the gate and felt he had no need for this extraneous data." Roger mimicked Weber's voice with surprising realism.

"And, what did they find?" Gray Eagle prompted.

"That the transfer devices we have are equipped with an embedded tracer sensor. So we, well, appropriated them when Weber told us we were nuts to think that." She smiled at Gray Eagle. "We removed the sensor and destroyed it."

Gray Eagle shot her an annoyed stare. His eyes narrowed. "Are you sure?"

She nodded rapidly. "Yes, we wouldn't do anything to hurt that device. The sensor was easy to remove. It wasn't even integrated into the circuitry, just drawing power from the fuel cell."

"And by the way, one of the devices needed charging, so we did that too," Roger offered.

Gray Eagle gave a large sigh. These two were dangerous. "Don't do anything like that again unless you first tell me or Julian."

Their faces dropped and he felt a pang of guilt. He had not meant to stop their quest for knowledge, only to caution them.

Roger said. "The transfer device still works. We tried it with the Source Gate operational."

"The Source Gate was used?" Gray Eagle demanded.

Amber nodded. "Weber tried it out but didn't go anywhere. He didn't tell anyone either. But we knew because when a Source Gate comes online near the transfer devices, they detect it."

"What Jewel did he insert into the fiber optic cradle?" Gray Eagle asked.

"The one that sang the stuff to us," Roger told him.

"We would like to get the equipment we need to make the crystal," Amber suggested. "It would give us a backup in case the Jewel we're using goes down and the other ones fail to work. The change in circuitry is minor."

Gray Eagle nodded. It was an excellent idea and he wanted to see the report the two had devised. He also wanted to tell Barstead, but away from Weber. His intuition told him Weber was again up to something and he planned to keep an eye on the man. He knew that with the sensor removed from the transfer device, it could be used without the creators detecting it.

"I understand." He stood. "Now let's get back so I can see what you and the others have discovered. I'll see about getting what we need, but I'll do it as my idea."

Amber and Roger nodded their agreement. "We were hoping you'd say that. Weber won't cause any problems if it comes from you."

"I want to see the data on how to build this crystal," Gray Eagle said. "Could we construct our own transfer devices as well?"

The two shrugged.

Stymied at last, he thought, and a smile crossed his face. He'd better hustle if he wanted to catch up with these two. "Download what you have and let me study it. I'll check the spreadsheet to see the cost and location of what we need."

The two hugged him and raced across the field toward the house. He followed at a more leisurely pace. "Damn, I'm good," he said. "I sound like I almost know what I'm doing."

~ * ~

September 16, 1861(Universe 1)

Joshua stepped from the train onto a small wooden platform, glanced around, and spied two soldiers standing beside the entrance to the station. Both were enlisted men and Joshua squinted as he watched them study the civilians passing by.

One of the men looked in his direction, nudged the other, and boldly approached him. He returned their salute.

"Sir?" the older man said in a voice suggesting it would be to Joshua's advantage if he identified himself.

"I'm Lieutenant Penfield. I've been sent in response to Major Mobrey's inquiries about outlaws."

The older man raked Joshua with his gaze and his face took on an expression Joshua recognized. Joshua knew that he could not help looking younger than he was; not that he was exactly old. He straightened a bit so that he at least filled out his five foot, six-inch frame.

"Sir, Major Mobrey is in a house just up the street. You'll see our regimental flags flying from it."

"Thank you, Sergeant," Joshua said, lifting his small bag and trotting off before he could hear the men exchange comments about boy officers. Colonel Holland's headquarters was a former manor house whose occupants had fled when the Union Army arrived. Joshua was ushered into Holland's presence with a minimum of protocol. He saluted Holland and presented the colonel with the letter from Lincoln.

Holland's dark, unfocused eyes slipped from Joshua to the letter held in his outstretched hand. The colonel shifted his portly body in his chair and wiped his right hand over his uniform as if his hand were dirty. He reached out and took the letter.

Joshua stepped back a pace, taking a quick breath. Holland reeked of whiskey. The letter shook in Holland's hand as the officer attempted to make drunken sense of the missive. He finally threw the letter at Mobrey.

"Here, Major, you deal with it," Holland ordered in a thick, slurred voice. He rose to his feet and steadied his body by placing his hands on the desk. After taking a deep breath, Holland walked to the door. He fumbled with the knob, opened the door, and staggered from the room. The door closed behind him.

Joshua turned his attention to Major Mobrey, who was dressed in a clean uniform, his dark hair groomed. His eyes were focused on the letter at his feet as his face took on the expression of someone who has eaten a piece of rotted fruit.

Mobrey picked up the letter and scanned the contents. He looked at the officer standing before him. "Someone has at least read my reports," he said. "But you are not sent for that, are you, Lieutenant?"

Joshua started. This man was astute and probably as clever as McBride. "Sir, I am sent by President Lincoln."

"And," Mobrey said, his eyes never straying from the young officer.

"I see the colonel is suffering from the strain of command."

A look of annoyance crossed Mobrey's face. "You, Lieutenant, are being diplomatic. The colonel is drunk. I doubt he has any idea what's going on and he hasn't for at least a month. Now why are you here?"

Joshua sputtered. "I, well, sir, I am to look into the reports."

Mobrey tried to keep from laughing. "If you wish to do intelligence work, son, you are simply going to have to seem less eager."

Joshua colored at the remark, mentally berating himself for giving away his mission. He had not even met the object of his trip, yet everyone he encountered seemed to know why he was in Frederick.

"Don't be too hard on yourself," Mobrey offered, sitting in the chair Holland had occupied a few moments ago. "Who are you to meet?"

"Sir, I have been sent to look at the reports, but also to speak with a Mrs. Desiree Bouchard."

Mobrey leaned his elbows on Holland's desk and his face took on a predatory look. "Now, we're getting somewhere. I don't know how the president knows something is going on in that house, but I bless him for sending you."

Joshua blinked in surprise.

"Mrs. Bouchard knows everyone on Holland's staff. None of us can discover if she is a Southern sympathizer and what she is up to. But you, son, are another matter. I would give a great deal to get you into that house."

"I, well…" Joshua's mouth parted in awe. "I am supposed to speak with her." He swallowed. "Sir, do you know if she engages in visiting with friends?"

Mobrey bit his lip at the question. Joshua lowered his eyes. He had been raised amid wealth and knew about the custom of paying afternoon visits. It was obvious from Mobrey's expression that the major found his manners amusing.

"Yes, indeed you will do nicely, Lieutenant. Mrs. Bouchard does some little visiting, but receives many callers. She and her ward, Harriette, entertain often."

"Then I shall call upon her tomorrow," Joshua said.

Mobrey raised a curious eyebrow. "How do you plan to convince her to receive you?"

"I shall endeavor to take care of that matter, sir."

Mobrey nodded his approval. "You learn fast, Lieutenant. When you finish your little tea with the lady, I want you to report to me."

"Sir, I am to speak with no one other than the president…" he stopped.

Mobrey nodded. "Whatever your mission from Lincoln, I respect that. But I want to know what you saw in that house, you understand?"

Joshua nodded.

"There are several empty rooms upstairs. Take whatever you need."

Joshua took Mobrey's words as a dismissal. He saluted and left the room. Beside the stairs leading to the second floor was a table. Its surface was covered with a collection of holders and candles. He took a candle, placed it in a holder, and lit the wick from the flame of an oil lamp burning on another table.

Shadow fingers cast by the flickering candle flame reached for Joshua, but he evaded them as he climbed to the second floor. He found a clean, empty room with fresh linen and soap for washing. He also located the privy in the back yard. The pump in the out kitchen supplied him with clear water.

He was served dinner, but no one ate with him. The atmosphere in the house was unusually tense and he decided to retire early. After washing, Joshua slipped into bed and lay staring at the dark ceiling for at least an hour before he fell asleep.

~ * ~

Kester stood in the main parlor of the Embassy Club, sipping a glass of excellent bourbon and wishing he knew what was going on at Command Central. Supreme Commander Brie's recent orders for all his senior field officers to appear before the Council brought tension in the Army to a new level.

The invasion was about to begin, Kester thought. He felt it in the air, a stirring of the atmosphere into action that lifted his dark mood. What would a future living in this universe as a home base bring for him, Kester wondered. He had never known a home of any sort. No one in the Khysid Army had a home, only the mission they were on or the barracks they used between assignments.

His thoughts were interrupted by one of his officers entering the parlor.

"What is it?" Kester muttered.

"Sir, your informant from the White House is here and he says it's urgent. He said he's not going back."

Kester blinked. He had forgotten about the man since being reassigned to General Sig's command. This should be San's problem or at least the problem of the Mission Specialist replacing him in her command. "Show him in," Kester ordered.

But the informant did not wait to be admitted. He burst into the room, shoving aside the officer standing before Kester.

"McBride suspects me," the beet-face man sputtered. "And Lincoln has sent someone to Frederick to find out about your doings there."

Kester's hair stood on end at the blunt recital. It didn't surprise him that McBride was suspicious of the man before him. Dunmore was the most incompetent spy he had ever fielded. What brought Kester's brain to the edge of turmoil was the comment about doings in Frederick. *What doings?*

~ * ~

September 17, 1961(Universe 0)

"Julian, I think the idea of trying to build this backup crystal is a good one." Gray Eagle stood on the patio facing Barstead.

The scientist blew out his breath between pursed lips. "My God, that Jewel, what is it?"

"When we have the luxury of finding out, then we'll study it," Gray Eagle suggested. "For now, what about getting the supplies?"

Barstead nodded. “Let Cc get them for you. He’s becoming quite adept at horse trading.”

“It seems to me he’s trading other than horses.”

“Do what you must. I’ve not told Weber or the others. Only you and I know about what happened to Amber and Roger. But I think it’s time we paid Mrs. Bouchard a visit.”

Gray Eagle pulled a chair to him and sat. “You think that’s wise?”

“I know what’s happening is located in her universe. And I think we are in danger as well.”

“I agree, it’s just that…” Gray Eagle paused and spread his hands.

“We burned our bridges the second time we left California.” Barstead rubbed at the edge of the table as he looked at Gray Eagle. “I’ve asked Mary Frances and Margaret to make us the clothing we need to go to that universe.”

“Who are you planning to take?”

“Mary Frances. She’s got the best insight into how those people might behave and can nudge us in the right direction.”

“Just the two of you?”

Barstead shook his head. “Walt, because we may need a physician, and Amber and Roger.”

Gray Eagle grew rigid. “Why them?”

“Desiree Bouchard met both Mary Frances and Amber at Manassas. She will recognize them. But Roger and Amber are like you in many ways. On this trip, we may need their intuition more than we need their precocious knowledge of this Jewel.”

Gray Eagle looked away from Barstead. “When are you planning to go?”

“In two days. I want you in charge while we’re gone. I want you here with that stone of yours keeping an eye on things, including Weber.”

“You’ll need to find an energy source near Frederick.”

“We can draw on the one in DC of that universe.” Barstead placed his hand on Gray Eagle’s shoulder. “With those sensors gone from the transfer devices, we can slip into that universe and be back before the owners know we used their equipment.”

Butterflies danced in Gray Eagle’s stomach. It was not fear he sensed, but excitement.

Ten

Even the smallest action has unexpected consequences.
Codex of Flowering Butterfly

September 17, 1861(Universe 1)

Joshua baked under the warm September sun as he approached the house on State Street. He tugged at the collar of his dress uniform, wishing he had worn anything but wool. The shade cast by the porch invited him to hurry and he walked to the suggestion of respite, taking the two steps to the door in a single bound. He lifted the polished brass handle and brought it against the door in three rapid strikes.

Footsteps sounded from inside. The door was cracked open. A thin-faced woman offered a tentative smile. She wore a maid's brown dress, white starched apron, and frilly cap. "May I help you, sir?"

"I am Lieutenant Joshua Penfield. I am here to call upon Mrs. Bouchard."

"Is she expecting you?" The maid's fingers gripped the door as if it were a source of protection.

"No, but it's of the utmost importance that I speak with her. I have been sent from Washington."

Two brown eyes flickered at him. "She has another visitor. Perhaps you might call later."

"I cannot do so." Joshua's mind raced to find the words that would gain him entrance to the house. "I bring greetings from a Mary Frances Beaumont, please tell her that."

The maid hesitated, her brows knitting in a frown. She opened the door a bit wider and motioned for Joshua to enter. He stepped inside, removing his campaign cap. The maid pointed to a room to his right and he walked into a tiny receiving parlor. The door was shut behind him but remained so only a few minutes.

"Mrs. Bouchard will see you now. This way please," the maid said as she opened the door to the receiving parlor.

Joshua followed her along the hallway to a set of double doors drawn aside to reveal a spacious parlor. He stepped onto a landing and glanced around. Wine velvet loveseats faced each other across a low table covered with a marble top. The flocked wallpaper was of wine stripes on a cream background.

The room spoke of wealth and taste. Joshua looked to his right and noticed a man his age, dressed in civilian clothes, rise from a chair as he entered. The woman who also rose to greet him was his senior, but she had kept her youthful figure and her looks. He offered her a salute.

"I am Lieutenant Joshua Penfield."

"Please come in, Lieutenant," Desiree said. "I am Mrs. Desiree Bouchard. This is my ward, Harriette, and this is Mr. Elliott Marsden."

Joshua nodded to the attractive, light-skinned Negro sitting on the loveseat. He had seen several Negroes from the South, for his family held abolitionist leanings. But he had never encountered one dressed in an elegant pink afternoon gown and serving tea as a hostess.

"Miss Harriette," he acknowledged her. "Mr. Marsden," he said as he stepped down to the parlor floor and moved to shake hands with Marsden.

As he turned to face Desiree, his gaze rested a moment on a spinet placed before a window. The spinet was open for playing and he wondered if Mrs. Bouchard played it. The table to his left held a porcelain vase filled with late summer flowers, their fragrance just noticeable in the room.

"Please sit and join in our conversation," Desiree commanded with the force of one of Joshua's superiors.

Joshua took a seat next to Elliott while Harriette poured a cup of tea and brought it to him.

"Do you wish cream or sugar, sir?"

"Neither, thank you," Joshua said as he took the delicate cup and matching saucer decorated with blue painted flowers.

"Would you like a pastry?" Harriette asked.

"No, thank you," he said, bewildered at the scene before him. While his eyes took in a perfectly normal afternoon tea, his stomach clenched with unspoken tension. Desiree brushed at her peach afternoon dress, a color that complemented her complexion, and he suspected, had been chosen just for that reason.

"Well, gentlemen, we have had our little greetings. I suggest we now speak plainly to one another."

Joshua choked on his tea. Elliott laughed at the reaction, covering his mouth with his hand. Joshua glanced around for a napkin and Harriette offered him one. He dabbed at his face and uniform.

"Mrs. Bouchard," he gasped, finding that some of the tea still resided in his throat. He coughed.

"Call me Desiree," Desiree said. "I shall call you Joshua. I assume you have no objections?"

If Joshua had any objections, he could not voice them at the moment. He was too intent on catching his breath. Desiree waited patiently until his coughing stopped.

"Mrs. Bouchard?"

Desiree lifted an eyebrow.

Joshua again cleared his throat, his discomfort with addressing Desiree by her first name obvious. He paused. "Desiree. I don't know quite what you mean."

"Why have you come? Who sent you? And how do you know Mary Frances Beaumont?"

Joshua's face took on the color of the pink rose in the vase by the spinet. "I, I," he stumbled. "What I have to say is for you alone."

"What you have to say is to be shared among the four of us, as is what Elliott has to say."

Joshua shot a glance at Elliott and felt sympathy for the expression on the man's face. He knew in that instant Elliott was a Confederate officer. Desiree caught the exchange between the two men.

"You, Joshua, will swear to me on your honor you will take no action against this man," she demanded. "Or I shall tell neither of you anything you came to hear."

Caught between his duty to expose Elliott and his duty to report to Lincoln, Joshua chose the latter. "My word, Desiree."

"Good. Now how did you learn of Miss Beaumont?"

Joshua shook his head. "I was told about her and that you might have her scarf. I am to ask you this and what happened at Manassas."

Desiree sat back against the loveseat and rubbed at her forehead. "Gentlemen, I can scarce believe what happened to me and my ward at Manassas, but it is true. Nor can I believe the malignant thing that rests beneath the streets of Washington."

Both men sat forward on their chairs. They glanced at one another, then at Desiree. Elliott spoke. "I found bodies by the stone bridge at Manassas. The men had with them a handgun such as I had never seen before. The ammunition was contained within a small rectangular magazine that fit in the grip of the gun."

"Sir, you can't be serious," Joshua protested.

"But I am. I handled it. I took it to Colonel Crittenden." Elliott stopped.

"What of you, Joshua?" Desiree prompted.

Joshua shook his head. "What I have told you is all I know. I am only a messenger sent to ask you questions and to return with your answers."

"By whom?"

"I am not at liberty to say."

Desiree accepted the answer, though Joshua suspected she had guessed the identity of the man he represented.

"Harriette, will you please?"

Harriette rose, went to the double doors, and closed them. She returned to her seat beside Desiree.

Desiree clasped her hands in her lap and looked at the two men before her. "I went to the capital because I sensed something dangerous and evil lay there. I later discovered this thing is in a place called the Embassy Club. I believe the club is an expensive brothel."

Joshua's eyebrows lifted at the description. He had known from the beginning that Desiree was a lady without pretense. He had appreciated that in her and now he admired her courage.

"Foolishly I had Peter, my driver, take us to view the battle," she continued her narrative.

Joshua listened to the tale that seemed to belong more to fiction than to the battle that had taken place a few months earlier. His furtive look at Elliott confirmed that the man held a similar opinion.

"So that is how those men died?" Elliott said, after Desiree told them what had happened.

"This gun," Joshua glanced at Elliott. "Where was it manufactured?"

"No one has been able to discover. But I have been told it is unlike anything ever seen by either of us." Elliott cleared his throat, embarrassed by what he had said. "The cartridges were small and the gun operated on a spring mechanism."

"How did you learn of this?" Joshua asked.

"The colonel showed it to me." Elliott again bit his lips. "But what I have learned here far exceeds my capacity to understand. A doorway was formed. Where did this doorway open to?"

Desiree sighed. "To their world, I think. It is so different from our own. The two women wore trousers and the younger held a strange device that was responsible for the opening."

Joshua felt his head about to burst from what he had just learned. Lincoln would be disappointed in him. He understood none of what Desiree had told him. Three years study of science had not prepared him for such a wild tale. Yet he knew she spoke the truth, and urgency burned in his mind. He must get what he had learned to Lincoln.

"Thank you for your hospitality." Joshua stood.

"Before you leave, Joshua, I want your promise that you will return when I send for you," Desiree insisted. "And I must know that the person who sent you believes my words."

"If at all possible, I shall do so," Joshua said.

Desiree nodded. "I will send word to Major Mobrey. I trust him, but not the man commanding this area. The major will see you receive my note."

Joshua nodded. He faced Elliott. "Sir, I have given my word."

Elliott inclined his head but did not rise.

Desiree stood, slipped her arm around the young man's, and ushered him from the parlor along the hall to the door. She opened the door and Joshua stepped onto the porch.

"Those women I saw," Desiree said. "I believe they will try and contact me. When this happens, I shall send you a message."

The door closed, leaving Joshua with a feeling of confusion and fear. Something had happened at Manassas and no science that he knew could explain it. Lincoln had learned of the event and wanted confirmation. Joshua stepped onto the brick driveway and hurried to the wooden sidewalk. Two people, Desiree and Lincoln, had experienced something he could not understand but that he knew in his heart was true.

~ * ~

When Desiree returned to the hallway outside the parlor, Elliott was on his feet preparing to leave. He had heard her comments to Joshua when he had followed them to the landing and into the hall.

"How will I get word to you?" she asked.

"I'll see what the colonel has to say about your story," Elliott replied, sensing urgency in her words. "There are ways to get a message to me, but I dare not reveal them without permission."

Desiree nodded. "Then you contact me."

"Why do you think these women will get in touch with you?"

"They will," Desiree said with fierceness.

"Then I will." Elliott turned and collided with Millie, Desiree's maid.

"Oh, sir, please excuse me," Millie's voice was thick with fear. She had removed her cap and apron. She finished wrapping her shawl around her shoulders. "Mrs. Bouchard, I must leave. May I have my wages?"

"Millie, why are you crying? What has happened?" Desiree took the woman by the arms as Harriette stepped into the hallway.

Elliott watched the maid sniff into a cloth and thrust it into her pocket. She shrugged away Desiree's grip and took a pace backward. She was trembling and fear radiated from her.

"I'm leaving for my sister's in Greencastle. It's these murders. Now I just heard across the way that another young man was found dead. The soldiers think he was a Confederate spy," Millie recited.

Elliott shot a look at Desiree, but her expression was guarded. She said. "Harriette, would you please get my purse? The beaded one I keep on my vanity."

Harriette moved to the stairs, taking them quickly despite the gown she wore. A few minutes later, she returned with Desiree's purse. Desiree handed Millie the coins and a generous gift. She closed the woman's hand around the money when Millie objected.

"Go, Millie, we will be fine."

Millie sniffed, turned, and darted from the house.

"You cannot leave, Elliott," Desiree insisted. "You must stay here, for I fear it is you they seek."

Elliott felt his stomach tighten. "You're right. But my staying here will put you and Harriette in danger."

"We are already in danger. No, you will stay. Joshua will go to Washington and return, for the man who sent him will insist on it."

"If he makes it to Washington," Elliott said with a shudder.

~ * ~

Mobrey was waiting for Joshua in Holland's office. He gestured to the officer to relax. "You will not leave for the Capitol any time soon," Mobrey announced.

"Sir, I have to get word to the President."

"But you needn't necessarily take it yourself," Mobrey explained. "Someone talked too freely in the Potomac Tavern and let slip your name. Now how would they know your name?"

Joshua was stunned, his expression answering Mobrey's question.

"I see. You have no idea what this game may be. I have no idea either, but there is danger in it for you. Have you a way to get your message secretly to Lincoln?"

"Yes, sir, but what I write and how I conceal it is for the President only."

Mobrey nodded. "I shall leave you and make the arrangements. Have the guard before this door summon me when you are finished."

Alone in the room, Joshua removed a silk pouch from his jacket and smoothed it out on the desk. He opened the fabric as he had been shown by McBride and teased from the cord binding two thin sheets of paper. He untwisted them, placing them on the desk next to the pouch. Using Holland's pen and ink, Joshua wrote his terse report. When the ink was completely dry, he again twisted the sheets and inserted them into the area where they masqueraded as the binding for the pouch.

He took a sheet of Holland's stationery and wrote a brief note about finding no outlaws, stuffing it into the pouch as if this were what he had been sent to discover.

Finished, he went to the door and told the guard to summon Mobrey. Mobrey returned, closed the door, and asked, "Have you completed your report?"

"Yes, sir, but I feel my duty…"

"Your duty, son, is to stay alive. I have a man to carry that little bauble to Lincoln. I will even insert a message myself." Mobrey took the pouch, opened it, and looked at the folded sheet of paper. "I see you have anticipated the need for providing fodder for others' eyes."

"I learn quickly." Joshua tried to conceal his grin at having surprised the clever intelligence officer.

"Well, I hope the Confederate officer spying in the area learns quickly as well or that lad is already dead."

"Sir?"

"I have a dead man on my hands and I suspect the outlaws are still searching for someone else." Mobrey stopped at the door. He faced Joshua. "I'll see that your stay is useful, Lieutenant. The room you used last night is still available. Supper is at seven." He left the room.

Joshua stood alone in Holland's office, his mind filled with conflicting thoughts and emotions. Amid the chaos swirling around in his head, one thought was very clear. It was a silent prayer for Elliott's safe return to his own lines.

~ * ~

September 19, 1861

"It's not your job to play spymaster, Kester," General Sig insisted, smacking the desk with his fist.

"Sir, this Lieutenant Penfield was sent by Lincoln to Frederick, Maryland. That point of coalescence Colonel Val discovered was in Frederick. There are Confederate spies in that area as well." He had learned about the perturbations in Frederick from the late Colonel Val just before the man had been killed. San knew about them also, but seemed to be ignoring them.

Sig's lips flattened against his teeth. "Are you stupid, Kester, or merely suicidal? Your task is finished. We have no further need of indigenous informants in this universe. We are about to invade it and sweep their petty war aside."

Kester nodded, but his gut told him the army would ignore the information at its peril. "Sir, I have located…"

"Enough!" Sig made a cutting gesture with his hand. "My men have other tasks to perform and they don't include looking for Union and Confederate spies. You will never again usurp my authority. I have put an end to this search-and-destroy mission. Do you understand?" He shook a finger at Kester.

"Yes, sir." Kester bristled at the reprimand. His temper was so close to the surface that he wondered he did not set off the infrared proximity sensors near the door.

"Get on with your search for the equipment I need," Sig ordered, his temper simmering just below volcanic level.

Kester saluted and stormed from the room. Sig was an excellent field officer, but he had no idea how the simplest of acts could cascade into a dangerous situation. He confronted foes on a battlefield; shadows were not his style.

Even the Command Council seemed oblivious to any perturbations though several major ones were brewing. Kester had seen them. He had calculated them with the programs Elias Hazen had devised and that Val had stolen. The fluctuations were so great that they were impossible to ignore. But that was exactly what the Council was doing. He had no idea why, but he knew it had nothing to do with the coming invasion.

~ * ~

A refreshing change in the weather settled on Washington. The temperature hovered in the upper sixties and the humidity that had ruled the city in the summer was absent. McBride carried the pouch to Lincoln shortly after Pinkerton's man brought it to him. The man had told him that the young officer sent to Frederick was forced to remain there, but had given no reason for the change in plans.

McBride hurried to Lincoln's second-floor study, closed the door behind him, and offered the pouch to the President. The late afternoon sun filtered through the windows reflecting from tiny dust motes dancing in the still air of the study.

"So there is a message." Lincoln took the pouch and placed it on his desk. "Where is Joshua?"

"He was detained, sir. I'm concerned, but I'm given to understand he is still at Colonel Holland's."

Lincoln shot a sidewise glance at McBride before returning his attention to the pouch. He ignored the sheet of paper stored within the body of the pouch. From the ribbing he pulled the twisted sheets containing the report. His hands smoothed the papers on the table and he read what Joshua had written.

So all that the scientists had told him was true, he thought. “He has a fine hand,” Lincoln said at last.

McBride relaxed. “Joshua is quite talented. He plays the piano as well as being gifted in the sciences.”

Lincoln sensed McBride’s fondness for the young officer, rather like that of a second father. “But what he has discovered goes beyond his talents.”

“Mr. President?”

“Read the letter,” Lincoln ordered, handing the sheets to McBride. “Do not fear for my sanity any longer. I can hardly believe I have received corroboration of what I suspected to be true.”

McBride read the sheets and reread them. He returned the papers to Lincoln with shaking hands. “What is happening to us, Mr. President?”

Lincoln leaned back in his chair, stretched out his lanky frame, and rested his feet on a small bench placed beside his chair for that purpose. He pointed to a couch opposite him and waited until McBride sat.

"I will tell you what I know and what I suspect."

McBride listened with a sober expression, his head aching from the bizarre knowledge Lincoln offered him. After Lincoln finished, McBride stood and paced the floor of the study with the attitude of a caged panther.

He stopped. "These scientists, when will they contact you again?"

"Soon, I hope. And it is good that Joshua stayed in Frederick. Send this Colonel Holland a telegram to that effect."

"Sir?"

"Don't you see? If these scientists can't come to Washington, they may try and make contact with Mrs. Bouchard."

"They were in the White House," McBride protested.

"Not this White House," Lincoln corrected. "We but spoke through a mist and Dr. Barstead said another president lived in their White House. I caught tension between the scientists and the agent, Beaumont."

McBride blinked. "She is an agent?"

"No, her brother is the agent who stepped before me to prevent his colleague from shooting at me."

McBride rubbed his temples as if he had a headache. "I'll have my agents watch this Embassy Club."

"Take great care in that area," Lincoln cautioned. He dropped his feet to the floor, reached into his vest, removed a key and stood. After moving to a walnut cabinet set against the wall, he used the key to unlock a small drawer.

McBride watched him in silence. Lincoln withdrew a thick vellum envelope from the drawer and offered it to McBride.

"I had an ulterior motive for wanting to know about the deaths caused by the outlaws. Many men on both sides died to see that at least one of these was delivered."

McBride's hands were icy as he took the envelope. Across the front were written the words, "President A. Lincoln." The seal was already broken and McBride turned over the letter, withdrawing the contents. His eyes took in the new seal of the Confederacy embossed on the stationery. His gaze dropped to the signature: Jefferson Davis, President of the Confederacy. McBride's breath caught in his throat as he read the contents.

"Now you see, Nathan, what I have known for some time. This enmity between the states must cease, for we face an even greater danger."

McBride's mind grasped at the common, nebulous enemy that offered only hints of its presence. "What do you want me to do?"

"Set your men to ferret out what is happening at the Embassy Club and then find what Secretary Seward has kept from me."

"Seward a spy?"

"Seward is not a spy, merely a man who wants his own way. Once you complete these two tasks, return and together we will make plans for the meeting suggested in the letter you hold."

McBride agreed, numbed by the contents of the letter. His beloved country teetered on the brink of oblivion, for only something that catastrophic would drive Lincoln and Davis to a secret meeting.

~ * ~

September 21, 1961(Universe 0)

While Barstead and his team prepared for the trip to Frederick, Gray Eagle used the time and Rierdon's skills, to acquire the equipment he needed to construct the crystals Amber and Roger had designed. Weber ignored him, intent on becoming familiar with the Source Gate and its construction. Gray Eagle's suspicions of Weber turned to alarm when he caught Weber making notes in a private diary.

Barstead left Gray Eagle in charge of the people at the farm and Gray Eagle announced that no one would go into Bennett alone as long as the team was in Frederick. Weber blustered, but the others came to Gray Eagle's defense. Marie and Chen Liu then demanded Weber stop hogging time on the Source Gate and give them a chance to study it. Faced with massive rebellion, Weber agreed. His resentment toward Gray Eagle for orchestrating the situation deepened.

Satisfied that the he had blocked Weber's plans, whatever they were, Gray Eagle set up the growth chamber and the new fuel cell. With the help of

Marie, Rierdon, and Lucinda, he began preparing to grow one of the complex crystals Amber and Roger had designed. The crystal would serve in ISIR's own version of a transfer device. This, he knew, was the first step to really understanding the Source Gate.

As Amber had told him, the modules constituting the recovered gate were a turnkey operation. Once rebuilt, the Source Gate was easy to use but difficult to understand. The technology of 1961 could not reverse engineer it. And there was no technology in any universe he had seen so far that could tell him exactly what the Jewel at the heart of the Source Gate did as it assembled energy from the Void.

~ * ~

Mary Frances and Reed met Barstead, Amber and Roger for dinner the evening of September 20 at a small motel outside of Frederick. Mary Frances had discovered a map of the town from 1861 in the records of a local historical society. While that would help, it had been necessary to find a place to move between the universes and not be exposed, especially since the team members had to wear period clothing.

After a few hours of searching, Barstead had settled on an old springhouse located on an abandoned property not too far from town. There was room to park a car nearby, hidden from view of the road.

At noon on September twenty-one, the team drove to the springhouse and changed into period clothing appropriate for a century earlier. Reed insisted on carrying a medical bag equipped with technology from mode-advanced universes.

Despite practice, Amber found the long skirts and the hoop beneath them, cumbersome. "This is stupid," she muttered, pulling at her jacket.

"Hold still," Mary Frances cautioned as she finished pinning a snood to Amber's short hair. "You must wear this, for your hair is too short for a young woman of that time period."

"You look cute," Roger offered.

"Stick it," Amber returned.

"Watch your words," Mary Frances cautioned. "If you feel like saying something that wouldn't be accepted, try smiling, looking away, anything but stick it."

Amber grimaced.

"Ready, ladies?" Barstead asked. He opened a portal within the dimly lit structure. The two springhouses appeared superimposed on one another as Reed crossed followed by Mary Frances, Amber, and Roger. Barstead flicked the switch on the small torch he held, for Reed had opened the door to the springhouse in the 1861 universe. Barstead stepped through the portal and deactivated the device.

He took a deep breath to hide his excitement and followed the others into the sunlight. The small springhouse was abandoned in the 1861 universe as well, though he knew that in three years it would again serve its purpose for an encampment of Union soldiers. Well, he thought, at least it did where I come from.

Everything before him looked similar to the surroundings of the springhouse in his own universe. But a quarter of a mile beyond the abandoned farm stood the wooden sidewalks and the bustling town of Frederick, Maryland, of a universe a hundred years behind his.

Eleven

Beware even of intended consequences.
Codex of Flowering Butterfly

Universal Time 1.00.09.21.61(Universe 61)

Kester glanced through a foot-thick porthole that lined the biosphere serving as the recreational facility for Command Central. The universe chosen for the honor of housing Command Central was in the throes of another hurricane. The porthole muted the noise generated by the pounding acid-laced rain, but Kester's mind imagined each oily drop sizzling like a steak on a grill.

Life as it was known in other universes was gone here, the world seething beneath a choking cloud of dust spewed by a half dozen super-volcanoes. What had mutated to survive in the sulfur-laden atmosphere was better left in that atmosphere.

Before Kester, a huge English-style garden with topiary hedges, raised flower beds, and tall shade trees ended in a clear lake. The lake was fed by three streams of recycled water, one creating a waterfall with a small cave behind it. Beyond the water was a forest climbing the ridge of a simulated mountain.

The domed structure was large enough to have its own microclimate. Every other afternoon, the computerized weather wizard (CWW) programmed a spring shower to fall for twenty to forty minutes.

Kester ducked behind one of the elaborate hedges as Brie and Elar hurried past, heading for the lake and an afternoon swim. His gaze searched the path until he saw San following. When she was directly opposite him, he called to her, “General San.”

She hesitated, looked around, and slipped behind the hedge to join Kester. Kester raised his hand in a salute, but she stopped him. “What do you want?”

“I must speak with you, General.”

“You’re under Sig’s command, Kester.”

Kester ignored the comment. “There’s a big problem in the universe we are planning to invade. Somehow Lincoln has learned about…”

“About what?” Impatience was a warning thread in her voice.

“I’m not quite sure. I think the Embassy Club. McBride is having it watched. But before that, Lincoln sent some lieutenant to Frederick, Maryland, to visit a woman who lives there.”

San’s delicate brows arched. “Really? The town where Val found that point of coalescence?”

Kester nodded. "I've got just a few more minutes. I'm here delivering some requests from General Sig, but I had to speak with you. I know it's not my place to say this, but we've got to hold off."

"It isn't your place to say that," San replied, her eyes searching out any listening ears.

"I tried to kill the man Lincoln sent, but Sig caught me and put an end to it. I can't prove anything, but I'm convinced something's wrong. We've lost track of the scientists in the buffer universe as well."

"I imagine they returned to their institute," San suggested.

"No. They've ticked off some brass called General Croll. That's as far as I got before I had to stop. All my informants are gone, and the transfer devices are still missing."

"Kester, keep quiet for a while," San advised in a cautious voice. "There are problems, but you're not equipped to deal with them."

"But…"

"Go back to your assignment," San ordered. "Leave the decisions to me." She turned and stormed from Kester toward the lake.

Rebuffed again, Kester wondered if Val had the right idea. Maybe it was time to think about getting away. Maybe Val had left his escape plans in the Micro Ds Kester had yet to decipher.

~ * ~

September 21, 1861(Universe 1)

Barstead felt Mary Frances's cautious hold on his arm as they stepped onto the wooden sidewalks of Frederick. The sidewalks were uneven and not what he had expected. Behind him followed Amber and Roger with Reed between them. The five of them were strangers in town and several people they passed had offered courteous greetings.

Barstead tipped his hat to an approaching man, and the man returned the action.

"Excuse me, sir, "Barstead stopped. "My friends and I are visiting an old acquaintance, Mrs. Bouchard. We are not certain which house is hers."

"My wife and I are friends of Mrs. Bouchard. I am Carl Denton, editor of the *Frederick Herald*. You are?"

"Mr. Barstead and my wife," Barstead introduced Mary Frances, who covered her surprise with a polite smile. "My colleague, Dr. Reed."

"Are these your children?" Denton looked at Amber and Roger.

"My niece and nephew, staying the summer with me in Washington," Barstead lied, recalling his practice from WWII.

"So you are just come for a visit. Well splendid, perhaps Desiree will have a small salon party and we may become better acquainted. I am curious to learn about Washington. Do you know if President Lincoln is feeling better?"

"If you mean what the president has claimed to see in the White House, I can assure you sir, the visitors have departed."

Denton's face took on a predatory cast. "Indeed, we must speak more. I hope you will be staying for some time."

"Just a short visit for now," Barstead replied, realizing he had spoken too freely. "But perhaps later."

"I look forward to our talk, sir. Mrs. Bouchard lives several houses from here. Hers is a two-story brick house with a portico supported by two fluted columns. The only one of its kind in the town."

"Thank you, Mr. Denton," Barstead inclined his head. Denton tipped his hat again and continued walking.

"The first person you speak with is part of the press," Reed hissed from behind Barstead. "Are you nuts?"

"He seemed pleasant enough." Barstead pretended to cough to hide his embarrassment.

"What does your wife think of him?" Amber quipped.

Barstead laughed, covering his mouth with his hand. "Stop it," he ordered between chuckles. "This is serious."

"Let's move," Reed commanded. "This coat I'm wearing is hot."

"Try wearing these stupid petticoats," Amber muttered. "It's like walking with an open parachute on."

Barstead hurried until the party reached the house described by Denton. He stopped, licked his lips, and suddenly wished the house vacant. He squared his shoulders, ignoring the odd look Mary Frances gave him as they walked to the porch. Mary Frances removed her arm from around his, and Barstead climbed the steps. He reached for the brass knocker and struck the door four times. “I hear footsteps,” Barstead whispered, as if the sound of someone inside were unexpected.

The door opened and he faced a young, attractive Negro. He suspected she was Harriette, for she fit the description given him by Amber and Mary Frances. Harriette looked first at Barstead, but her gaze drifted past him to Mary Frances and Amber. Recognition glinted in her eyes.

“You are the women from the battlefield,” Harriette gasped. She turned and fled along the hall without shutting the door.

Mary Frances stepped onto the porch around Barstead and into the house. “Come on,” she encouraged. “This is what we came for.”

Barstead moved into the hallway as if in a dream. Not until this moment had he sensed the impact of what he and the others had accomplished. A scant six months ago he had been listening to Beaumont talk about a ghost in the White House. Now he was moving between universes as if accomplished in the task.

He watched Mary Frances stop and look at a mirror placed beneath a table standing in the hallway. She moved her skirts and Barstead realized it was a piece of furniture called a petticoat table. Since it was difficult to bend dressed in clothing worn by women in this universe, women glanced at such mirrors to see if their petticoats were concealed. He wondered what they did if they discovered an errant piece of lace.

Roger and Amber walked past Barstead, but Reed placed a hand on his shoulder. "Julian, get a grip."

"I have a grip," Barstead muttered and marched along the hall after the others.

The doors to his right were drawn aside and he walked into a silent tableau. Amber, Roger, and Mary Frances were poised on a landing above the parlor. Two women stood opposite them. Harriette held Desiree's arm. Desiree's hands were raised to her mouth, a wet stain visible on the folds of her green silk gown. A broken china cup lay at her feet, the contents soaking into the intricate pattern of the rug.

Behind Desiree a young man with light brown hair and dressed in a suit was standing before a chair that Barstead suspected would bring an antique dealer to tears in his universe. Next to him, a young dark-haired Union officer stood before an identical chair.

"You are real." Desiree lowered her hands, patting Harriette's grasp on her arm.

"Indeed we are," Mary Frances said, stepping to the parlor.

Desiree came to her, reached out a hand, and touched her face. She drew back. "Forgive me such a familiarity, but this is all too hard to comprehend." She whirled around. "Forgive me my manners also, but these gentlemen know about you. They are Lieutenant Elliott Marsden and Lieutenant Joshua Penfield." She returned her gaze to her new guests on the landing. "You must call me Desiree."

Barstead's eyes narrowed as he looked at Elliott. The man was in civilian clothes and he wondered if he were on leave. He suddenly realized how little he actually knew about the daily lives of the people in the room.

"How did you come to us?" Harriette asked.

"By constructing a Source Gate and moving from our universe into yours," Barstead explained. "Well, actually it was not as simple as that."

Mary Frances tapped Barstead on the arm. "Desiree, this is Dr. Julian Barstead, Amber you already know. This is Roger Merit, and Dr. Walter Reed."

"You have come, as I knew you would," Desiree said, drawing Barstead to a seat beside her. "Please, all of you be seated. We have much to discuss."

Harriette picked up the pieces of the broken cup and placed them on a tray sitting on a low marble-top table. Mary Frances and Reed moved to the loveseat opposite Barstead and Desiree, while Elliott and Joshua offered their seats to Amber and Harriette. Roger stood beside the two young men.

"How did you arrive in Frederick, sir?" Elliott, standing behind Amber, asked Barstead. "I know not what this Source Gate is."

"My colleagues and I recovered one and assembled it," Barstead explained. And he knew by Elliot's accent that he was from the South.

"We know what it is and pretty much what it does, but not everything about it."

"You invented this device?" Joshua asked.

"No, we recovered it," Amber said, glancing at him.

"From where, Miss Amber?"

"That's a very long story," Barstead replied. "We have only a short time here, so let me give you a quick explanation."

He launched into an abbreviated version of the events that had brought them to Frederick. The two men asked few questions until he completed his tale.

"You came from California? How did you come so quickly to the East?" Elliott wondered

"We flew," Amber replied.

Joshua looked at her. "In a balloon?"

"No, an airplane." She stopped at the confused look on Joshua's face. "A flying machine."

Elliott moved to Amber's side. "A flying machine? Such a thing is possible?"

"Ever since the Wright brothers flew in 1903."

"But that is in the next century," Harriette gripped her chair.

"All the universes are not at the same place, but we are all at the same point in a timeline," Barstead explained. "Our universe is one hundred years ahead of yours." He suddenly wondered how he could explain what he knew to people with a science so primitive that they did not even know about bacteria.

Desiree interrupted. "Elliott, Joshua, tell them what happened and why you have come."

The men exchanged glances. By unspoken agreement, Joshua began his tale of Lincoln's order that had sent him to Frederick. Then Elliott, with a sheepish expression, explained why he was in Frederick.

"Do your governments know what's happening?" Barstead asked the officers.

"I have no idea what President Lincoln knows, besides what I have transmitted to him," Joshua replied.

"Colonel Crittenden knows something and he's seen a gun similar to the one I found at Manassas. Only the gun found in Richmond was made to explode."

"What's happening to us, Dr. Barstead?" Desiree pleaded.

"Please call me Julian." Barstead patted her hand. "I wish I could tell you, but I really don't know. These men in black uniforms, they have been seen in our universe as well. Amber and Roger saw them at Dulles when we landed."

"Dulles? Landed?" Desiree's face clouded.

"Roger and I flew the flying machine to Dulles airport," Amber explained. "It's a place where you land flying machines and store them."

"You flew the machine, Miss Amber?" Joshua's eyebrows retreated into his curly hair.

Barstead was suddenly aware that the room was growing dark. He saw Harriette rise and move to light oil lamps around the parlor. He pulled his watch from his vest pocket, opened it, and glanced at the time.

"Walt, Mary Frances, we have to get back."

"The time, Julian," Mary Frances stood. "I'd forgotten."

Barstead turned to Desiree. "Is it possible to find an unobtrusive route to the old house at the edge of town?"

"The abandoned one?" Desiree asked.

Barstead nodded.

Desiree looked at Harriette. "First Street?"

"Not the safest of streets."

"I will escort you," Joshua offered, with more curiosity than gallantry. "The patrols will not bother you with an officer along."

"Thank you," Mary Frances said.

"Joshua, you clever man," Elliott chuckled. "You will get to wring more information from them by the time you arrive at your destination."

Joshua offered a hesitant smile. "Thus giving you a chance to leave as quickly as possible."

Elliott sobered. "My thanks," he muttered.

Barstead allowed Desiree to usher her guests from the parlor to the out kitchen and into the garden. Standing by the door, the team said farewell. Joshua started across the garden path, stopped and turned to say good-bye to Elliott. The darkness was splintered by a single shot and Joshua dropped to the ground.

"Down!" Barstead commanded, drawing Mary Frances and Amber with him. Reed and Roger grabbed Desiree and Harriette, but Elliott drew his pistol, aimed at a spot in the bushes, and fired two rounds. The acrid smell of gunpowder covered the porch.

"Julian," Amber whispered. "Did you bring a flashlight?"

Barstead pulled a pocket LED flashlight from his coat and passed it to Amber. She took it, but he cautioned, "Don't, we must not attract attention to ourselves."

Amber returned, "If he's one of those men, he's probably got night vision goggles. He can see us no matter what. We need to wipe out his night vision device."

Barstead heard the rustling in the bushes stop.

"Stay down," Elliott ordered, creeping toward the bushes lining Desiree's backyard.

Reed, paying no attention to Elliott, crawled to Joshua, turned him on his back and examined him in the dark. "We've got to get him inside," he hissed.

Elliott reached his objective, kicked at the bush and stooped. “This one is dead,” he announced.

Reed stood, hurried to Elliott and confirmed the observation. “Give me a hand,” he called to the others. “I must get Joshua into the house.”

Barstead and Roger went to Joshua as Harriette lit an oil lamp and brought it to the door to the out kitchen. Desiree stood, followed by Mary Frances, but Amber moved beside Elliott. She flicked the switch on the flashlight and played bright light over the man at her feet.

“He’s dressed in a uniform and wearing night vision goggles,” she announced. “Elliott, give me a hand.”

“Does he have a transfer device?” Roger called from the doorway as he and Reed carried Joshua inside the house.

“I’d bet on it.” She stooped, frisked the body, and removed a transfer device. It was powered down and she thumbed the power key. “When I open a portal, Elliott, shove the body through it.”

“Miss Amber, what do you…” but the portal opened before him. “My God!”

“Now, roll him across.”

“Roll him where?” Elliott shoved the body to the opening. “Where is that place? It is as dark as here.”

“I don’t know,” she confessed. “It looks unpleasant. Discard the gun too,” she ordered.

“But the gun.”

“Get rid of it. We don’t want it around.”

Elliott tossed the gun onto the body and Amber closed the portal. "Had Joshua but seen that," he blew out his breath. "His stomach would be as knot-tied as mine."

"Let's see what Walt can do for your friend," she glanced at Elliott. The two hurried into the house as Amber shut down the device and shoved it into the pocket of her skirt.

~ * ~

When Amber entered the house, she saw several oil lamps in an adjacent room leaking light into the out kitchen, where Mary Frances helped Desiree with a pack of linen towels. Desiree was lighting a woodstove, and Barstead was pumping water into a large bucket.

Roger entered holding two unlit oil lamps. "These were all I could find," he said to Desiree.

She glanced to the doorway. "Those will do. Bring them to me to light them. We have the candles for the parlor."

Reed said, "Amber, I need that flashlight."

She handed it to him as he left.

"Julian, did you bring a small tool kit?" Amber asked, glancing at the transfer device she had taken from her pocket.

Barstead placed the full bucket of water on the floor. "No, but I have a Swiss Army knife in my pocket."

"Let me use it." Amber held out her hand. "I want to take out the tracer sensor from this transfer device."

"If you don't need me, I'll give Amber a hand," Roger offered.

"Go to it, you two," Barstead ordered.

Suddenly, more shots erupted from the alley where the body had been only moments ago. "What's that?" Amber caught her breath and swung to face the door.

"Stay here," Elliott cautioned. "I'll go. Just take care of Joshua." He slipped from the house before anyone could protest.

Amber glanced at Barstead. "How is Joshua?"

"He's lost a lot of blood. Walt's going to operate."

Amber shuddered. "Here?"

"Walt's brought some of the new equipment, medicine and a portable laser scalpel. Harriette agreed to assist him."

"We shall help Joshua," Desiree told her. "I believe you have a task to perform on that object you are holding."

Amber smiled at her. "Come on, Roger. Let's take the claws from this device so the owners can't locate it."

~ * ~

Amber sat across from Barstead studying the transfer device she held. "How long has Elliott been gone?" she asked Barstead.

Barstead removed his pocket watch, held it near a candleholder with three burning candles, and announced. "It's been about forty minutes."

"The shooting stopped as quickly as it began," Desiree pointed out the obvious. "Why is he not back yet?

Barstead wriggled in his chair. "We have to get out of here. If we were traced this far, they might come back."

"The sensor is out of this device, but I don't think they were after us," Amber said. "And by the way, here's your knife."

"Why do you think you were not the target?" Desiree asked.

Amber searched her mind before replying. "I just sensed it was Joshua, not us, they were after. I think they don't know we're here."

Reed entered the room, rolling down his sleeves. "He'll live. The bullet went through the shoulder but hit nothing vital. He's going to need care and a place to stay for now. Once we move him, he should remain quiet for a day or two at the very least."

"Thank God you were here, Dr. Reed." Desiree sighed. "There is a bedroom upstairs where he may recover. I will let Major Mobrey know and think up some story as to how he was injured."

"I may have one for you." Elliott slipped beside Reed. "I heard what you did for Joshua, Doctor Reed. Thank you."

Reed smiled at the young officer. "I'd worked under worse conditions in Korea. I'd been a doctor only a short time before I volunteered for the army."

"What story?" Amber interrupted the exchange. "You said you had something Desiree might be able to use."

"Yes. There was a fight in the Potomac Tavern and two of the men pulled guns. They fired several shots. Then they raced up the alley behind your house, Desiree, and were caught by a patrol," Elliott explained.

"How clever, Elliot. We will say that poor Joshua was shot during the altercation." Desiree clasped her hands together.

"And convenient," Amber frowned. "Julian, don't you think a lot of this is rather too convenient? Like those synchronistic things Carl Jung talks about in his books. I've been wondering."

"Not now," Barstead brushed aside her comment. "Are you about finished, Walt?" he asked.

"Yes, just need to give Harriette some instructions about using the antibiotics and keeping the wound clean. Clever and brave woman," Reed said. "She didn't flinch during the operation."

"She is indeed brave," Elliott said. "I would rather face a cavalry charge than work with a surgeon."

"If I had to use the medicine of this universe, I'd agree with you," Reed replied. "But I had a little more going for me than ether and a knife."

"Joshua is still asleep," Harriette spoke from behind Reed.

Reed turned. "Good, I need a board of some kind to move him to the bed."

Amber watched as Desiree directed Reed, Barstead, and Roger to the kitchen for an ironing board. The men carried Joshua to the bedroom while Amber and Mary Frances remained in the parlor.

Amber was miffed that Barstead had dismissed her observations. There was something going on beneath the events that seemed to be drawing them into the conflict of this universe. She tasted it with her inner being, as if someone or something had planned the happenings. She had begun to wonder about this after Bechter gave her the book. Why had he brought it to the plasma physics meeting?

The book had provided the one piece of information they had needed to make sense of what was happening at the White House. Did Bechter know what was happening? Did he know about the Source Gates and the people who had manufactured them? Elliott's footsteps in the hallway interrupted her musings.

"Now that Joshua will recover, I must leave. It is not safe for me to remain here."

"What will you tell your commander?" Reed descended the stairs behind him.

"That you, sir, are the finest surgeon I have ever seen and I wish you were attached to his command."

Reed laughed as Desiree, Barstead, Roger, and Harriette followed him to the hallway from the stairs.

"When will you return?" Desiree asked Barstead.

"I can't say. But it will be soon. Walt likes to check on patients and I need to take some readings in this universe." Barstead motioned to his team. "We have to get out of here. We'll chance the walk along First Street."

"It should be safe, sir," Elliott offered. "The patrols are gone for now and the tavern patrons cleared out after the fight."

Elliott escorted Barstead and the others part of the way along First Street before ducking into the shadows and leaving them to complete the journey to the dark springhouse. Once there, Barstead activated the portal, ushering his team safely through to their home universe.

~ * ~

September 21, 1961(Universe 0)

As Barstead deactivated the portal, he heard a yelp from Amber. "What's wrong?"

"Our clothes," she grumbled. "They're wet."

He felt the pile of clothing he had placed on the ledge lining one side of the springhouse. It was soaked. Playing his flashlight over the ceiling, he saw that drops from a recent shower still clung to the cracked boards.

Barstead told the others, "We'd better get to the car and sneak into the motel. I think we can do that."

"First, let's get out of these stupid hoops," Amber suggested. "Otherwise you three will have to sit in the front seat."

Barstead laughed and the men waited outside while Amber and Mary Frances removed their tiered hoops. Barstead took the wet clothes to the trunk of the car and opened the doors. The others followed, squeezing into the car.

"Well, we made it," Barstead sighed. "We made it."

He felt drained but exhilarated and licked his lips as if he had just eaten something tasty. It would take some time, he knew, for the reality of what they had been through to sink in, but it would be something to savor. They had crossed into another universe and made it back. Not even a Nobel Prize could compare to what they had accomplished. Barstead started the car and drove across the bumpy ground to the street leading to the motel.

~ * ~

"How the hell did they get into that shed?" the agent sitting in the dark green car asked his partner.

The man next to him shrugged. "We searched, but all we found was clothes. They've been gone for hours."

"What are we going to tell General Croll?"

"I don't know, but we better think of something. He's not going to believe we lost five people in a tiny springhouse for most of the day."

Twelve

A pattern in any Reality may end as an event in Physical Reality.
Codex of Flowering Butterfly

September 23, 1861(Universe 1)

Elliott inhaled deeply of fall-tinged air. Wood smoke from a dozen cooking fires filled the area before him and mingled with the smell of bacon fat and ham. He wondered where Crittenden had secured the food. A small group of soldiers was picking apples from the over-burdened trees on the hillside about a quarter of a mile from a red brick farmhouse, while others were tending pots of boiling water filled with dirty clothes. Elliott realized the men felt they had time enough to do laundry.

He dismounted and offered the reins of the horse he was riding to one of the men in the search party that had finally located him. Crittenden, ordered by General Johnson to fall back from Manassas to Warrenton, had sent out scouting parties to find

Elliott, an action for which he was grateful enough that he didn't ask to stop and eat.

Crittenden was seated at his table near an open fire. Elliott saw a pot of coffee warming on a grate over the coals. His stomach growled. Ignoring the protest, Elliott hurried to Crittenden, stopped before the table, and saluted.

"Colonel, sorry it took me so long to find your camp."

"I gather my scouts found you." Crittenden continued making notes in a bound leather book. He reached for a rock anchoring a pile of papers, lifted it, and removed the top sheet. Then he replaced the rock. "Why did you stay in Frederick?"

Elliott's gaze took in a tray to Crittenden's right containing freshly baked bread, fruit, and preserves. "I was unable to leave immediately, sir. The men you spoke of were hunting me. They were also hunting a Union officer."

Crittenden casually glanced at the sheet he held. "Yes, a Lieutenant Joshua Penfield, sent by President Lincoln to visit Mrs. Bouchard."

The man has the gift. "Sir, he was sent to discover what I was sent to discover."

"And what did you discover, Lieutenant?"

"That I should have paid more attention to my science classes," Elliott replied, shaking his head. "Lieutenant Penfield probably understood better what the scientists said than did I."

Crittenden straightened in his chair. "The guests that Mrs. Bouchard received were scientists?"

"Your informants are very clever, sir," Elliott chuckled. "But they missed the meat of the situation." He ran his hands over his weary, dusty face. "I guess the best way is just to tell you everything that happened."

Elliott did, explaining nothing unless Crittenden requested him to do so. After he concluded, Crittenden sat chewing the end of his pen, lost in his own thoughts. But Elliott could not keep his eyes from the bread, his stomach reminding him that he had not eaten since noon yesterday.

Crittenden stopped chewing his pen and replaced it in the holder. He lifted the tray of food and placed it opposite his seat. "Have some breakfast, Lieutenant, while we talk more about what you witnessed."

Thank you, Colonel."

Elliott looked at his grimy hands. Crittenden pointed to a basin lying on a stump. Elliott walked to it, filled it with water from a nearby bucket, and washed his hands and face using the cake of soap lying next to the basin. He dumped the water and dried his hands and face on a linen towel hanging on a dead branch protruding from the stump. He poured coffee into one of several cups beside the fire and sat opposite Crittenden.

"These five people you met claim to come from another universe?"

Elliott nodded, slathering preserves on a thick slice of still-warm bread. "That is what this Dr. Barstead said. I don't understand, but I saw Miss

Amber use an instrument she took from the dead man. She caused it to open a hole in the air."

"What?"

"Sir, I can't describe it better than that. It was like a hole in the air. But it went somewhere. And she had me push the dead man across. When I shoved the body through that hole, my hands prickled as if I touched the electric fluid that rides the telegraph wires."

"This young woman, she was also the one who told you of the flying machine?"

Elliott nodded, noticing Crittenden's expression mold into anger.

"Who are they, son?"

"I believe they are who they claim to be. But that they can travel between these, ah, universes, means they have knowledge we don't possess."

Crittenden sat back in his chair. "But for all their knowledge, they have no idea who the men in black uniforms are?"

Elliott nodded, chewing and swallowing a chunk of bread. The taste was exquisite. "They were also victims of these men. I hope that wherever those scientists are, they are safe."

"So do I," Crittenden said. "For now, the regiment is stationed on this farm. General Johnson wants nobody to move, even to give the indication of hostilities."

Elliott stopped chewing. "Why?"

Crittenden looked at him and the young officer colored.

"Sorry, sir, it really isn't my place,"

"I have not been enlightened as to why we are to stay here. Though I am ordered to provide as much information as I can gather."

"I heard the fighting in Western Virginia is at a stalemate." Elliott reached for another thick slice of bread.

"It is. Lee and Reynolds have fought each other to a standstill. What's happening in the Kanawa Valley is little more than tests by each army to learn the strength and determination of the other."

"Sir, if you need any volunteers for scouting," Elliott offered.

"You take a few days' rest," Crittenden ordered. "Then I'll see what use I can make of your clever mind."

Elliott blushed. Jackson had thought him a dolt, certainly not a clever mind. But then Jackson had also given boring lectures on Natural Philosophy. Perhaps, Elliott thought, had someone like Crittenden or Dr. Barstead given the lectures, he might have paid more attention.

"May I find my quarters?" Elliott asked.

Crittenden nodded. "Find Sergeant Gage. He's got your tent and equipment. He takes good care of the men in your company."

Elliott stood, saluted, and hurried toward the sea of tents, newly mushroomed about a hundred yards east of the farmhouse. Crittenden watched him go.

~ * ~

An hour later Captain Hargrove, the new captain of Elliott's company, stood before Crittenden. "You sent for me, sir?"

"I want you to take fifty men, but not Lieutenant Marsden or Sergeant Gage. You are to go to Frederick and wait for the people described on this sheet of paper. When they visit Mrs. Bouchard, you will take them prisoner and bring them to me."

"Yes, sir. What of Mrs. Bouchard?"

"Capture her as well and her young ward. Leave no one in the house in Frederick."

"I understand." The captain hesitated. "Lieutenant Marsden is a capable officer."

"Indeed he is," Crittenden replied. "But he will be a dead one, along with you and the other soldiers, if he goes back. Without him you are just another patrol. With him, those outlaws, or whatever they are, will know you are up to more than scouting."

"I see," Hargrove replied. "Anything else?"

"Yes, Captain. Listen carefully to these orders and follow them, for they might mean the difference between success and failure of your mission."

~ * ~

September 23, 1961(Universe 0)

"So they don't know anything about the owners of these little gizmos." Rierdon tapped the transfer device Amber had taken from the man Elliott had shot.

"Apparently not, but shooting people to steal these is a nasty way to get them," Margaret observed. "And the owners must be pretty miffed by now."

"These people in black uniforms, I wish we knew what they called themselves." Reed drummed his fingers on the table. "Or where they come from."

"Obviously they come from another universe." Rierdon poured coffee into his cup. "When you go back, Margaret and I are going with you. This thing is too dangerous for Roger and Amber."

"No, they did very well," Barstead defended the young pilots. "They go too, or we will never hear the end of it. We must stay for a few days and find a way to get to Washington."

"Yes, Lincoln will want to talk to us," Rierdon said. "If we can pool our information, we may get somewhere."

Barstead asked, "What about Crittenden, this Confederate officer Elliott mentioned? He seems to have seen these twentieth century guns before."

"Once we get to Lincoln, there will be a way to speak with the colonel," Reed suggested. "So far we've got three of these transfer devices."

"Well, actually you have five," Margaret said.

"Five?" Barstead jerked around to face her.

"Remember that little set of plans Gray Eagle was working on, the ones requiring the growth chamber? We were able to construct two new devices. They open only a small portal and let two people cross," she explained.

"So it worked." Barstead chewed on his lip, oblivious to her questioning stare.

She nodded. "But the devices we built have a forty-five minute down time once used."

"What does Stan think of them?" Barstead asked.

"Not much, but then he's enamored of his Weber Gate," Rierdon grumbled. "Gray Eagle is preparing the growth chamber to make a backup Jewel crystal, at least according to his calculations."

"Good, he can stay here and work on it," Barstead replied. "And keep an eye on Stan. How's Rich Marsden taking this?"

"The proverbial duck to water," Rierdon announced with glee. "He's giving up heirlooms for me to use for money. We found an antique mall nearby in a 2018 universe. The stuff goes for a mint there. I convert it into gems when possible and bingo! We've got the money to buy equipment."

"That Ph.D. in anthropology wasn't a waste," Barstead teased.

"Best time I ever spent," Rierdon agreed. "All that cultural nonsense comes in handy when you have to traipse around other universes blending in with the natives."

The group at the table laughed. "We are the natives here," Barstead reminded him.

"Yes." Rierdon rubbed his index finger across his lower lip. "I wonder what's trying to blend in with us?"

~ * ~

Universal time 1.00.09.26.61(Universe 61)

"General San." Brie toyed with the computer he wore around his neck, attached to a gold chain with links the size of his thumb. He used a stylus to trace doodles on the thin screen as he spoke. "You will cease any more action against the inhabitants of that universe until the invasion is under way."

"Does the Supreme Commander know that the level of instability in that universe is at temporal resonance status?" San asked, wishing Brie would sink into the chair he occupied in the domed room of the council chambers.

"Yes." Brie's singsong reply grated on San's nerves. "The Supreme Commander knows. And I just told you to stop."

"Perhaps, sir, you are not really aware…"

"Oh, shut up, San!" Brie shouted. "You're a junior member of this Council and can easily be removed."

San's lips curved in a soft smile. "Only by challenge." The steel in her words raised the tension in the room.

Brie's jaw set and his narrow, piggy eyes glistened like the sheen on a slick olive. "You dare call a challenge. You asshole. You'll die for this." He struck the table with his fist.

"San," Elar's voice was calm. "Do you call a challenge?"

"Yes," she whispered the word she had been waiting to issue as soon as Brie tripped over the subject. "I call a challenge."

"Then it's done." Elar spread his hands on the table. "Your second, Supreme Commander?"

Brie sputtered. "You fool, San, I can choose anyone to represent me. Stop this now and all you will suffer is a loss of rank."

"I name Colonel Kester as my second," San replied.

Elar turned to Brie. "You, Supreme Commander?"

"You, Elar, as my second," Brie snorted. "And General Vrill to represent me."

San's confidence dropped a notch. Vrill had been unexpected. The actions would take him away from his troops readying for invasion. That would anger him and his anger might prove an added weapon.

"Accepted," San replied, keeping up a confidence she did not feel. She would have to kill General Vrill to keep her seat on the Council. If she succeeded, Brie would die as well. A fact she found as tasty as the crabmeat she had consumed for lunch.

"The meeting is over." Brie jumped to his feet and stormed from the room. The other Council members followed. Cal exchanged glances with Elar before she left. San got to her feet.

"I will inform Generals Vrill and Sig," Elar told her.

“Thank you, Council Member Elar.”

“We have the same desire,” Elar said. “And I think we may be of help to one another.”

San raised a delicately manicured finger to her lips. “Oh?”

“No one has ever survived a challenge without help from another Council member,” he told her.

Her brows closed ranks. “What?”

“You want that fool dead, and I want command of the council. I shall see to it we both get what we want. If the price is General Vrill, so be it.”

~ * ~

September 29, 1861(Universe 1)

Lincoln read the letter as McBride paced before his desk. “Nathan, please sit down,” Lincoln requested. “Your pacing is disturbing.”

McBride plopped into a chair but teetered on the edge, his left foot tapping a tattoo. “Is it what you wished, sir?”

Lincoln looked up from the letter, then at McBride’s left foot. “Yes,” he said in a sharp tone, then relented. “Davis has agreed to the terms for the meeting.”

McBride ran his hands through his hair as he sighed. “Thank God. It took no end of careful planning to get this arranged. At least Baxter is someone I know.”

“Can you trust him?” Lincoln asked.

“In this matter, yes. He also sent a letter outlining what he knows about the outlaws.”

Lincoln frowned. “And I have the material from Seward, who was less than gracious when it came to relinquishing it.”

“Oh, and Mr. President…” McBride patted his pockets, removed a letter, and handed it to Lincoln. “It’s from Joshua, I mean Lieutenant Penfield.”

“Is he recovering?” Lincoln asked, aware the officer had been shot in some sort of altercation in an alley.

“As far as I have learned,” McBride replied. “The letter is for you.”

Lincoln nodded, cut open the letter with his penknife and read the contents. Lincoln’s eyes grew wider as he continued to read. He looked at McBride. “Penfield was not shot in some altercation, but injured while escorting the scientists. The scientists went to Frederick. They were the guests Mrs. Bouchard was hosting when the lad was shot.” He handed McBride the sheets.

McBride took the letter, read it, and looked up from the sheets in awe. “You were right.”

Lincoln laughed. “I wish you wouldn’t say it in that tone. You have me sounding as if I were daft until this letter.”

McBride shook his head. “No sir. You’re quite sane. But what Joshua writes, this is unbelievable. The physician operated and gave him something called antibiotics.” McBride sounded out the unfamiliar word. “This medicine prevents infection,” he read from the letter.

"These scientists came to Frederick, I suspect, because they met Mrs. Bouchard at Manassas." Lincoln sat forward in his chair and folded his hands on his desk. "They will return. And when they do, I want Major Mobrey to bring them to Washington."

"Sir, Colonel Holland is in charge." McBride made a face.

"He drinks, from what I have been told, and by you, Nathan," Lincoln reminded McBride.

"He is also a close friend of General McClellan."

Lincoln sat erect. "I don't care if he is the husband of Queen Victoria. I'm president and my order will go to Major Mobrey. And I don't care if he has to kidnap those scientists, I want them here."

McBride was rapidly nodding his head. "Me too," he replied. "I want to see this strange medicine."

"Forget the medicine, Nathan. I want to see the flying machine and this portal the scientists create between what they call universes."

~ * ~

September 29, 1961(Universe 0)

Amber's sleep was restless, but just before dawn she quieted as the dream unfolded. She stood in a cave staring at a large pool of liquid light. Two streams fed the pool, one of clear water, the other of fire. Where the streams met, the liquid light coalesced, filling the rocky basin to an indeterminate depth.

"The light is called the Mirror that Illumines," a voice said.

She spun to face the speaker. "Who are you?"

"I am Eagle-Being," the part-human part-eagle spirit replied.

"I never heard of this Mirror," she gestured to the pool, but did not quite touch the bubbling, frothing mass it contained. She sensed power from the contents and something else, almost as if a memory were trying to surface from the depths of her being.

"It shows much to those who seek the truth, including the future, as it will now show to you." Eagle-Being gestured to the pool. "Gaze into the mirror."

Amber hesitated, but found the urge to look into the depths irresistible. She stared at the liquid light that behaved as if it had a life of its own. The pool quieted, the bubbles disappearing as the surface took on a glass-like quality. An image of a two-story, stately farmhouse appeared. At a distance from the house, apple trees clung to a steep hillside. The tangy odor of ripe fruit drifted across the fields, mingling with smoke from campfires to the left of the farmhouse.

Orderly rows of canvas tents stretched beyond a pond where several white ducks swam, oblivious to the activity around them. Men in gray uniforms carried out a variety of tasks. To the right of the farmhouse was a large, fenced-in field, fallow as if it had not been planted for some time, though it was covered in clover. Several horses were corralled in the field, running freely and enjoying the bounty still available from the late growth. Outside the fence, a row of cannon faced a dirt road running in front of the farm.

It was as if she looked into a three-dimensional television set, but one that showed reality, not a mere image. The scene had a Currier and Ives feel to it: nostalgic and warm, as if it were the past imagined. But this was no painted image to be bought in a store. It was real and it was happening in the present. She grasped the rocks lining the basin edge to still her trembling hands.

The image slowly faded, allowing her time to catch her breath. The mirror returned to its original state. Amber faced Eagle-Being.

"I don't understand," she said. "What was that? It looked like it could be a scene from the universe we visited."

"It is the path you and the others will walk, the path with heart."

Amber sighed. "Where does this path lead?"

"Home."

"That's home?"

"Not quite, but it is a good location. Once you get rid of the horse droppings."

"What?"

Amber awoke and bolted upright. "Horse droppings?" She shook her head to scatter the fragments of questions filling her mind.

Mary Frances turned over in the twin bed opposite hers. “What are you talking about? Horse droppings?”

“I had a weird dream.”

“A smelly one too, if you ask me.” Mary Frances laughed.

“Well, not exactly.” Amber glanced at the clock by her bed. “It’s six. We better move if we plan to pack.” She threw aside the covers and darted for the bathroom.

“We’ve already packed what we will need,” Mary Frances called, snuggling deeper beneath her quilt.

“I have a few more things to stuff into the case,” Amber mumbled, her mouth filled with toothpaste. Such as the new, small transfer device and another pocket flashlight, she thought. She really wanted to take the Palm-Com, but that would be too obvious. She would settle for some extra money and a handful of the gems Rierdon was hoarding.

Amber spat out the toothpaste and rinsed her mouth. She gazed at her reflection in the mirror, suddenly wondering why she had the urge to pack the money and gems. She had not intended that last night. She nodded, as if mentally confirming a new idea. These new items she would carry on her person.

She would add a change of clothes, shoved beneath what Mary Frances insisted would be suitable for a nineteenth-century universe. These clothes would be suitable for a twentieth-century or twenty-first century universe. She knew she would need them.

Amber sighed at the reflection staring from the mirror. There were times when she wished she were not like Gray Eagle. But if that happened, she would no longer be able to exist. For these strange intuitions had become so much a part of her life that there was no life without them. The only problem she could see was that they seemed to have intensified after her encounter with the Mind Jewel.

~ * ~

September 29, 1861(Universe 1)

Each morning since the scientists left, Harriette had stationed drawing equipment before the large window overlooking State Street and the brick path to the house. She sketched and painted, waiting for the return of the strange men and women who filled the house with talk of other places and other times. The operation Dr. Reed had performed on Joshua still burned in her mind.

Harriette was used to helping with medical problems, but nothing she had ever seen, including a difficult birth in the slave quarters on the Bouchard Plantation, had prepared her for that surgery. Each morning she dutifully fed Joshua one of the large yellow pills left by Reed. The young officer healed rapidly.

No infection had set in. None could, she knew, because the pills somehow prevented it. But Dr. Reed had used no knife when he had operated. He had used a strange light and forced her to don a set of glasses as he did, so the light would not hurt her eyes. The wound had cauterized as he worked, the light searing the flesh, sending thin streamers of smelly smoke as proof. Reed had called the thing he used a laser scalpel.

Harriette glanced from the window, but only the usual bustle filled the streets of Frederick, except for the Union soldiers occasionally patrolling near the house. That began this morning and Harriette wondered if Joshua's note to Lincoln had reached the president. Perhaps the patrols too were waiting for the return of the scientists.

Her eyes strayed to the clock on the mantel over the fireplace. It was nearing five. She stopped her work, stood and stretched. It was time to give Joshua another pill. The medicine would be gone with this dose, but she knew the scientists would bring more.

~ * ~

"I will help with the dishes," Joshua insisted. "It's the very least I can do for all you have done for me. I would rather recuperate here than in the barracks."

"I'm delighted to have you here." Desiree beamed at the young man sitting opposite Harriette. "I can cook, you know. It's not just a rumor."

Harriette and Joshua laughed at her. "No, indeed it is not," Joshua agreed. "The meal was excellent. If I remain here for another day, I shall not be able to button my uniform."

Desiree eyed his trim, lean figure. His appetite had been healthy since the day after surgery when he left his bed, insisting on returning to headquarters. Desiree refused and reminded him that she had sent Major Mobrey word about the injury. Mobrey arrived the next day, but Desiree had her charge tucked in bed.

Mobrey agreed to Joshua's recovery in the Bouchard house. Desiree suspected he was pleased with a spy beneath her nose, one she tended as if he were her son.

"Joshua, I…" A rapid knocking at the back door interrupted Desiree's comment.

"Let me," Joshua shoved back his chair, dropped his napkin on the table, and hurried to the kitchen.

"Could they have returned?" Harriette asked.

Desiree heard the sounds of a scuffle. Rising from her seat, she moved around the table toward the tall cherry sideboard covered with the remains of a baked ham, two peach pies, and bread. She pulled open the second drawer where she kept Louis's old pistol.

"Desiree," Harriette shouted.

Desiree turned to face the young woman and froze. Joshua stood gritting his teeth in a mixture of pain and fury. On either side of the Union officer stood two Confederate soldiers. An older man moved from behind Joshua.

He offered Desiree a casual salute. "Excuse me, Mrs. Bouchard, but it has become necessary to occupy your house. I am Captain Hargrove."

Desiree slammed the drawer. “How dare you!”

“I have no choice,” Hargrove said. “I’ve been sent for your guests and they are coming up the walk to your house at this moment.” He smiled at her outrage. “Before we leave with you and your guests, may I prevail on you for a bit of supper for my men?”

~ * ~

Having eluded the Union patrols, Barstead straightened his shoulders, lifted the brass knocker, and struck the door. He waited, but there was no answer. Oil lamps were burning in the windows, which had to mean someone was home.

“Give Desiree and Harriette time,” Mary Frances cautioned. “They may be afraid since the shooting.”

The door opened and Harriette stood in the entrance. She gestured for them to enter and the team piled inside, chatting excitedly, all except Amber. She waited until Harriette closed and locked the front door. The two women exchanged glances and Amber felt her skin crawl.

“Not them?” she mouthed.

Harriette shook her head. “No, but…” Her eyes strayed along the hall toward the opened doors to the parlor.

Amber followed Harriette’s gaze and saw two Confederates, rifles in hand, standing at the end of the hall. “I hope they cleaned that field,” she whispered beneath her breath.

Harriette favored her with a curious stare, but said nothing.

Thirteen

Beware of intended consequences.
Codex of Flowering Butterfly

October 2, 1961 (Universe 1)

"Where are they?" Marsden demanded.

"I wish I knew," Gray Eagle replied. He felt they were safe, but he also sensed danger. The contradiction twisted his stomach but there was nothing he could do about it.

When Barstead did not call and efforts to trace the team failed, Gray Eagle ordered everyone to pack the equipment needed to reconstruct a Source Gate. This included the growth chambers he had purchased to grow the crystals. He had everything loaded into the secret room in Marsden's basement. If they had to transfer to another universe, that could be accomplished without using their Source Gate. His efforts to find all the crystalline materials and powdered metal he needed to grow the substitutes for the Jewel had resulted in his locating an apparently abandoned Source Gate nearby. It was weak but usable and he had originally planned to dismantle and take it once he was finished with his work. It would serve a different purpose now.

Marsden rested the palms of his hands on the kitchen table, supporting his weight on them as he glared at Gray Eagle. The kitchen still smelled of fresh cinnamon buns from last night's supper. "The Maryland State Police traced the rental car to Barstead and called ISIR."

"I know. It took me an hour to convince Alyssia that everyone was safe." Gray Eagle doubted that she had believed him. But the stone he carried whispered no warnings, offering support for his intuitions.

"What if Croll has captured the team?" Marsden removed his hands from the table.

"We don't know that."

"We don't have a clue as to what happened to them. We've got to find out if Croll took them. Croll with that transfer device makes my skin crawl. The man is a damned octopus and you don't know where he is until he strikes."

"That's somewhat of a mixed metaphor," Gray Eagle joked.

"It's not funny," Marsden accused. "You're worried too. You're taking precautions to protect the Source Gate. It's dismantled and stored."

Gray Eagle held up his hand. "What do you suggest?"

"I'm going to DC with Gordo. I have a lot of people who owe me. It's time I called in a few chits."

Gray Eagle sighed, drumming his fingers on the table as he thought. "You sure this won't alert Croll?"

"Hell, he's already alerted, especially if he has them."

"Why haven't we heard if he does have them?"

Marsden shrugged. "I don't know, but I'm going to DC and taking Gordo. I've got a small arsenal in the house if you need to use weapons."

Gray Eagle stopped drumming his fingers. "I'll give you the transfer device I constructed and program it to draw off the Source Gate in the 1861 DC. I'll also program it for the 1861 universe. If you and Gordo have to cross, you can use it. And use these enhancer patches as well."

Marsden held out his hands, shaking his head for emphasis. "I don't like this."

"You have no choice. If Croll goes after you, you have to get away."

"And what if he comes after you and the people here?"

"We'll be ready to go to that universe too. We can't get to the president here, but we can get to Lincoln."

Marsden snorted. "Gray Eagle, you're in southern Virginia. The only president you can get to in that universe is Davis."

Gray Eagle shrugged. "There is always this Confederate colonel Julian spoke about. From what Julian said, the Confederates must have an idea something is going on as well."

"What if they don't care?"

Gray Eagle searched his feelings before answering. "I have a suspicion that sectional hatreds will evaporate if there is a greater danger facing both sides."

Suddenly Marsden brightened. "Wait, this place was a stop on the Underground Railroad. The Quakers who owned the farm will get you north if you have to cross to the 1861 universe."

"It may not come to that," Gray Eagle offered, with a conviction that he did not feel Still he took comfort in Marsden's words. If they had to escape into the 1861 universe, there was a way to Lincoln, even from the heart of Virginia.

~ * ~

October 2, 1861(Universe 1)

General Sig stood before the console of the Source Gate in the secure room beneath the Embassy Club. Now that he had the field command, the room had been reduced to Spartan décor. Gone were the plush chairs and the sectional sofa, items San preferred. The walls were still utilitarian white, the floor black tile, but only the needed electronic equipment filled the room.

His hands clasped behind his back, Sig rocked on the balls of his feet waiting for Kester. He did not wait long.

Kester entered the room and saluted "You sent for me, sir?"

"Yes, Colonel." Sig continued to rock, his back to Kester. "You are relieved from duty and are to report to Command Central."

Kester started. "Sir, I don't understand."

Sig turned to face his subordinate. "General San has called a challenge against the Supreme Commander."

Kester scrunched his forehead tightly, forcing his eyebrows to meet in a single line. "Begging the general's pardon, but what has this to do with me?"

"She's named you as her second."

Kester's brows remained stationary. He had only the vaguest idea what such a challenge entailed. He had what he had worked for, promotion and the longevity virus. Beyond that he had made no other plans except to wear the disk of a general. He suddenly wondered if this would get him that promotion. After all, his previous actions had caused him to jump at least one rank. Maybe he didn't need to look to escape the army.

"That is an honor," Kester offered with a slight hesitation.

Sig cocked an eyebrow. "A dubious one."

"Sir, I've located several old P-40s as you requested. They're in excellent condition, plus fuel and ammunition. Still, jets…"

"Jets require a logistic tail longer than the dog," Sig waved aside Kester's words. "Those planes will do and the Messerschmitts will do even better when the arrangements are finalized."

"My work is documented," Kester explained. "The person taking my place will be able to follow up."

"You're a good officer, Kester. I hate to lose you, which I will do in any case."

Kester felt a thrill bubble in his chest. If San won, she planned to keep him in her command. There was no telling what heights he could reach under those circumstances.

"But if General San loses, I will probably be reassigned to your command again."

Sig frowned. "You jackass. If San loses, she dies, and you die with her."

~ * ~

October 3, 1861

Captain Hargrove watched his captives sitting beside a pool formed by the stream they had crossed the previous evening. The stand of woods bordering the stream on one side was flanked by an open meadow. This morning the area held the smell of early fall. Insects were busy with the remaining flowers, and the stream sang a noisy refrain as it cascaded over the rocks in its path.

The men and women he was escorting to Crittenden were a tough group, including Mrs. Bouchard. Despite the peach silk gown she had insisted on wearing, she rode as if born to the saddle. The same was true for Harriette. But Barstead and the others treated horses as if this mode of transportation were a sport rather than a necessity.

Every one of his captives had insisted on bringing along luggage and, after a tongue-lashing by Mrs. Bouchard, he had reluctantly agreed. She had the same fire and determination as Sergeant Gage, though she was far more attractive.

The women guests of Mrs. Bouchard were different. They were indeed attractive, but they were less concerned about social convention and in some cases ignorant of it. They puzzled Hargrove. Their manner of speech was blunt and after several hours in their presence, he realized this must be how they spoke wherever they originated.

Barstead and Reed had complained about the lack of privacy, except for bodily necessities, and then only one person at a time could attend to their needs. Hargrove had explained to them that Crittenden had ordered this be done. For some reason, his captives seemed to understand and the understanding had made them more compliant. Hargrove brought his wandering thoughts back to the scene before him.

"Just keep that bandaged for another day," Reed said as he finished dressing a deep cut on the hand of one of the soldiers. "You'll be fine. It's a good thing I thought to bring the extra TD patches."

Hargrove slipped from the stump he was using for a seat and came to Reed. "TD patches? I don't understand." Reed had treated Private Suter when the man had received a deep gash while setting up a makeshift shelter for the captives.

Reed looked up at Hargrove. "Trans-dermal patches, Captain. They let medication cross into the body without using a needle and will eventually dissolve. Found them in this 2030 universe. In this case I need them to prevent tetanus. I believe you call it lock-jaw."

The young soldier drew his hand to his chest, his face ashen. "I have the lock-jaw?"

Reed patted Suter on the shoulder. "No, and you're not going to get it. The medication in the patch I placed on your arm will prevent it."

"How is such a thing possible?" Hargrove squatted beside Reed and studied the contents of the bag the physician carried. "I know about the treatment to prevent smallpox, but lock-jaw?"

"And rabies, diphtheria, typhoid, cholera. All the things you have to fear, there are inoculations against." Reed closed his bag.

Hargrove stood, his face taking on a sober expression. "How I wish you had been here two years ago when my daughter died of diphtheria."

Reed pushed himself to his feet, his face also sober. "I wish we had too. Maybe we could have prevented this war."

Hargrove brushed aside the memory of the flaxen-haired child who had died in his arms. "Nothing could have prevented this war. But your medicine might have prevented the death of a loved one." He glanced at the soldier still clutching his hand. "Private Suter, ride ahead and inform the colonel that we will arrive by noon."

Suter stood, saluted, and hurried to his horse. Hargrove turned to Reed, but Reed was staring at the others by the pool.

"We are only a few hours ride from your camp?"

"Yes," Hargrove said. "How is Lieutenant Penfield?"

"His wound is almost healed," Reed explained, brushing the twigs and grass from his pants. "I've given him an additional antibiotic, but that was just a precaution. The microbes here have no resistance yet to antibiotics and I don't want to encourage any."

Hargrove merely shook his head. *These people speak strangely.* "I suspect Major Wescott will want to talk with you. He is the regimental surgeon."

"Ether and laudanum," Reed grimaced. "Have I got a few surprises for him!"

Hargrove called. "Let's mount." His men brought horses for their captives. As they prepared to ride, the people he was shepherding to his superior again filled Hargrove's thoughts.

Crittenden was the finest officer he had ever had the pleasure of serving under. The man was fair, strict without being a martinet, clever, and resourceful. But he wondered if even his foxy minded colonel was ready for the tempestuous group he was bringing to the camp in Warrenton.

~ * ~

Amber dismounted and reached for her luggage attached to the saddle. A soldier quickly came to her assistance, removing the bag and offering to carry it for her until Hargrove ordered him away. Amber took the luggage, trying not to smile at the disappointed soldier.

The entire ride had been that way… the men solicitous of every need she or the other women expressed. It had been amusing at first, even flattering. But it had quickly become tiring as she tried not to hurt anyone's feelings.

Amber moved beside Roger and Mary Frances as the party prepared to walk to the farmhouse. Hargrove and three soldiers escorted them, not that an escort was necessary since there was no place to run.

"Mary Frances." Amber inclined her head toward her friend. "How many men in a regiment?"

"In 1861, anywhere from eight hundred to twelve hundred."

Amber nodded and faced the farmhouse. It was as if she had stepped into the image from her dream. Everything was the same, including the wood smoke and tangy smell of the apples from the orchard on the hill. What her dream had not conveyed was the additional pungent odor from the horse droppings in the field and the less than twentieth century hygiene from the tents beyond the farmhouse.

The party arrived at the porch. Amber watched Hargrove climb the four steps and salute a meticulously groomed officer. She suspected the man was Crittenden. He appeared around

Barstead's age, with slightly graying hair and hazel eyes. But his physical appearance was less imposing than his presence.

Here was someone like Gray Eagle and perhaps as well trained. *What on earth was he doing in the Confederate Army? Who had trained him as a shaman?*

"I must apologize for the way you were brought here," Crittenden said to his captives. "But Lieutenant Marsden has told me about you and the device you possess. Please give it to me."

"What?" Barstead demanded. "Are you crazy? How are we to get home?"

Rierdon grimaced, while Reed merely shook his head. Amber realized the admission was a blunder. Crittenden did also, for he walked to Barstead.

"Doctor, I have no intentions of harming any of you. But we are in grave danger and what you hold is of the same importance to us as it is to you."

"I can't give you the transfer device," Barstead insisted. "It can't leave my person. You don't know how to use it."

"Instruct me then," Crittenden demanded. "I am an engineer."

"Big time do-do," Amber whispered to Roger. He nodded.

Crittenden saw the exchange. He moved away from Barstead and toward the pair standing to the right of the steps. "You are far too young to be scientists." He smiled at them.

Just like a wolf smiling at his dinner. Only this wolf was handsome and there was no darkness in him. She sensed his concern was genuine and went far beyond any duty he was sworn to perform.

"We're the pilots of the flying machines," she replied.

Crittenden's eyes grew wide. "Pilots, yes, Lieutenant Marsden spoke of the flying machines. You are indeed welcome at my camp, and we shall have a long talk about these flying machines."

Joshua, silent through most of the trip, inched to the head of the group, saluted Crittenden, and said. "Sir, I am Lieutenant Joshua Penfield."

Crittenden accepted the courtesy. "Lieutenant Penfield, I believe you know Lieutenant Marsden. You will share his tent."

"Sir?"

"Son, forget about any prisoner exchange. You're remaining here for now, along with everyone else, until I have some answers as to what exactly is going on."

"We'd like the same answers," Reed said.

"Good, then we have much to talk about." Crittenden turned his attention to Barstead. "The device, sir, if you please. Otherwise I will have you forcibly searched."

"No," Barstead replied.

"Sir, you are the acknowledged leader of this group," Crittenden said. "I suspect that for all of you to escape to the place from which you come, you must be together."

Barstead smiled to cover his misgivings about handing over the device. "You are quite clever."

"Only enough to take precautions that you do not escape. But since I cannot commit your party to the care of fifty of my men for much longer, I would prefer the device."

Barstead reached into his pocket, removed the transfer device and handed it to Crittenden. "I ask only that you secure it until we leave, Colonel. And that you do not use it unless one of us skilled in its use is with you."

Crittenden held the unfamiliar object in his hand, examining it with a hungry expression so intense Amber wondered if he would salivate at the sight of one of the aerobatics planes Gray Eagle had designed.

"My word, sir." Crittenden gestured to the door with the device he held. "Now, please come in and refresh yourselves. We will eat soon and my wife Beatrice is anxious to meet you."

Joshua stepped closer to the porch. "Colonel, I must protest. You have taken these innocent people hostage and hold me, a Union officer, as a prisoner without hope of parole."

Crittenden favored the officer with a look he reserved for naughty children. "Behave yourself, son, or you'll get no supper. Now, come inside and get cleaned up so you can eat with us. We have much to discuss and I know you were sent to Frederick by Lincoln."

"But sir?" Joshua's protest was almost a whine.

"You, Lieutenant, are going nowhere but inside to eat, or the guardhouse. Take your pick."

Apparently food held more attraction for Joshua than prison, for he moved up the steps to the porch. Amber and Crittenden's eyes met and she looked away, realizing that like Joshua, they were going nowhere but inside the farmhouse.

~ * ~

October 4, 1861

At seven in the morning, Amber stood on the porch looking for Crittenden. She saw him sitting beneath a canopy several feet from the pond where three ducks squabbled over some errant insect.

"Come on, Roger, let's do a little investigating." She tugged at her reluctant companion. Neither had had breakfast and Amber wanted a cup of coffee. Roger followed her across the grass toward Crittenden.

Before they reached Crittenden, Joshua intercepted them, accompanied by Elliott. "Miss Amber, Roger, I hope you had a pleasant night."

"If you call the lack of indoor plumbing pleasant," Amber muttered, remembering her choice between a chamber pot and an outdoor privy some distance from the house.

Joshua's brow wrinkled. "Indoor plumbing?"

"Yes, water inside and other facilities." She tried to think of a delicate way to put it. Saying crapper or toilet would probably make no sense or offend them.

"You have such where you come from?" Joshua said as he hurriedly buttoned his jacket.

"You missed one, Josh," Elliott whispered to the officer.

Joshua looked down, noticed the error, and remedied the problem.

Amber smiled at him. "Even hot water from water heaters."

"That Bea would like most of all." Crittenden spoke from his seat.

Amber glanced at him. "I don't blame her. Bea told me you must boil water to wash clothes."

"Come." Crittenden gestured to the four standing a few feet from him. "Bea sent enough breakfast for several people, please."

The please came out as an order and the four trooped to Crittenden. When Crittenden pointed out a pile of tin plates, Joshua and Elliot grabbed the same plate, intending to offer it to Amber. But she stepped around them, snatched a plate from the pile, and moved to a table set with apples, cheese, and freshly baked bread. She took a slice, covered it with strawberry preserves, and accepted a cup of coffee from Crittenden.

Joshua and Elliott followed Roger, doing the same as Amber. The group ate breakfast, chatting as if they were on a picnic and not in an army camp somewhere in Virginia in a nineteenth century universe. When they finished breakfast, Crittenden looked at Joshua and Elliott.

"Gentlemen, you are dismissed."

Elliott stood, followed by Joshua.

"I wish to speak to these two alone now."

The two officers saluted, leaving with obvious reluctance.

"I thought soldiers were taught to obey orders instantly." Amber glanced at the retreating forms of the two men.

"They usually do, Amber, but you hold an attraction for them."

She faced Crittenden. "Is it my obvious good looks or my knowledge of flying?"

Crittenden laughed. "Both. And I must confess I have never met a woman as forward as you."

"Sorry, Colonel, but my universe is a century ahead of yours."

"She's forward even for our universe," Roger joked, and she jabbed him with her elbow.

"The tales we shared last night," Crittenden said. "I still find it unbelievable, yet your presence here is proof."

"Have you any idea who the Triangle Club people are? The ones you told us about. They have the ability to make the transfer devices and the Source Gates, but what are their plans?" Amber asked.

She could make little sense of the tale Crittenden had shared with her and the others last night. He had explained that a group called the Triangle Club was responsible for setting up brothels in three cities: Richmond, Washington and Baltimore. Club members and the club's backers were using the brothels as cover for their activities, including murder and edging the North and South toward war.

“I have only suspicions. I know these club members do not favor either North or South.”

As Crittenden spoke, Amber reached into the pocket of her skirt and pulled out a Swiss Army knife. She opened a blade and used it to cut the dark spots from the apple she planned to eat. She realized that Crittenden was watching her in fascination.

He asked. “What is that?”

She looked up at him, aware she was using something not yet invented in his universe. “It’s called a Swiss Army knife, more complicated than your penknives. Julian said we were not to carry ours, but…”

“I know.” she wiped the blade on her handkerchief and offered the knife to Crittenden.

He examined it, his expression again intense and probing. “It even has a magnifier.”

“But it isn’t the top of the line. Those have a compass,” Amber explained. “In some technological advanced universes the knives include computers with GPS input.”

Crittenden handed the knife back to Amber. “Please keep that little gem out of sight of the men, or you will have to fend off more than interest. They will seek to give you anything for it.”

Amber shoved the knife into her pocket. “Colonel, we’ve been gone for some time and Gray Eagle is probably searching for us. Let Julian call him and tell him where we are and that we’re okay.”

“Call him?”

She finished her apple and placed the core on the plate. “Yes, like a telegraph, only you talk on it and the person at the other end of the line hears and answers you.”

“Such a device exists?”

“Yes, it’s called a telephone,” she said.

“In some universes, you don’t even need wires,” Roger added. “You use microwaves to transmit the signal. The phones are so tiny that you can carry them in the palm of your hand or wear then as jewelry.”

“Indeed,” Crittenden said. “Such a call would relieve the anxiety your friends have for your safety?”

“Yes,” Amber said.

“Then come, let’s speak with Dr. Barstead about this matter.”

~ * ~

Barstead agreed to Crittenden’s proposal that he return to his own universe to inform his friends the team was safe, but prisoners at a farm outside of Warrenton. Crittenden insisted he take no one with him, ensuring his return with the transfer device. Rierdon was reluctant to let him go, but Barstead assured him it would only be a matter of a few hours’ work.

Having no map of the twentieth century Warrenton, Barstead rode toward the nineteenth century Warrenton until he located what he considered a suitable site to cross. Hargrove and three men accompanied him.

After a visual scan with the transfer device, Barstead settled on a gas station on the outskirts of Warrenton in the twentieth century universe as the place to make the transfer. A stand of trees existed at the same place in both universes. Hargrove and his men could wait there in the nineteenth century universe until he returned.

Barstead activated the device. “Captain, please don’t be frightened by what you see.”

“I have seen you do that magic before.” Hargrove reminded him about the demonstration given for Crittenden last evening.

“Give me half an hour,” Barstead told the officer. “I need to get through to my friends in Bennett. If the line is busy, I’ll have to try more than once.”

Hargrove simply nodded and had his men take the horses several yards away from Barstead as he opened the portal.

“Half an hour,” Barstead called, stepping through the opening.

~ * ~

October 4, 1961(universe 0)

Once through, Barstead closed the portal and shut down the device, thrusting it into the inside pocket of the tweed jacket he had had the foresight to bring. He ambled down the slope from the woods, crossed the road, and entered the large gas station. The gas station had a general store and restaurant attached to it. He walked into the restaurant and approached the woman behind the counter. She looked up when he asked if he could use a phone. She pointed to the pay phone, made change for his ten-dollar bill, and returned to her magazine.

Barstead shoved the money into the phone and dialed Bennett. When Gray Eagle answered, he gave the number and asked that he immediately call back. Gray Eagle did.

“Where in God’s name are you, Julian?”

“It’s a bit hard to explain, but I’m in a gas station on the outskirts of Warrenton, Virginia.”

“What the hell are you doing there?”

“It’s a long story.” Barstead told him what had happened and the present status of the team.

“That’s crazy,” Gray Eagle replied. “You’ve got to get out of there. Rich and Gordo went to DC. Rich thinks Croll has you.”

“Nope,” Barstead chuckled. “The man who captured us is a lot nicer and a whole lot smarter.” Barstead’s ears suddenly caught the whoosh, whoosh of a helicopter.

“I don’t care if he’s Einstein. You have to get back here.”

“No can do. The others are still at the camp. I’ve got to return. Otherwise they’re marooned in that universe. I’ve got the only transfer device.”

“Amber has another one,” Gray Eagle said, but Barstead did not hear him. His attention was directed toward the far door. Two men had entered the building looking as if they were searching for someone. Barstead knew he was the target of that search.

"Company, gotta go. Call you later." Barstead hung up.

He slipped into the men's room, peeking through the crack in the door until the agents started his way. He locked the door, activated the transfer device, and thumbed the visual mode button. A weathered side of a barn stood in the same space as he occupied. Barstead cut the power and shoved the device into his pocket. He opened the narrow, frosted window, and climbed outside.

He suspected the phone lines to the house in Bennett were tapped the moment her heard the helicopter. From his government work, he knew there was a secret CIA base near Warrenton. The men from the helicopter were probably military intelligence. That meant Croll had just heard what he had told Gray Eagle and had radioed his men in the area. Croll must have some base nearby to get a helicopter to arrive as quickly as it had.

Barstead stood looking around for some haven. He was afraid to open the portal. He peeked around the side of the building and saw a truck parked beside the station, the motor on, the man finishing a Pepsi.

"Can I go now?" the driver asked one of the agents.

The man nodded, replaced the canvas cover on the truck's bed, and walked away. Barstead moved to the truck, crawled beneath the canvas, and waited. The driver slammed the door and drove off, Barstead jostling around in the bed of the truck.

He swore for not simply opening the portal and stepping across once he was out of the bathroom. Now he was bumping along the road at fifty miles per hour and could not open a portal. The scientists had learned that limitation shortly after they learned the portals they created were only proximity portals.

Movement through a portal was dependent in a complex manner upon the momentum of an object. The heavy truck he was in at its present velocity probably exceeded the safety limit for any portal he might create. When that limit was exceeded, the portal collapsed, trapping whatever was inside it in the Void. Neither he nor the truck driver would appreciate such a fate.

Fourteen

The essence of each spirit is unique.
Codex of Flowering Butterfly

October 4, 1861 (Universe 1)

Dusk coated the sky and shadows raced across the land as Hargrove waited patiently in the copse of trees for Barstead's return. His eyes grew tired staring at the weathered old barn occupying the spot where Barstead had opened a hole between the universes. Finally, he had ordered his men to remain the night and had hurried back to camp.

Crittenden was speaking with Major Wescott when Hargrove found him. "Sir, Dr. Barstead has not returned. He said he would be no more than half an hour."

Crittenden leaned against the fence, crossed his arms over his chest, and sighed. "I did not think him the type to maroon his friends."

"He's not, sir," Hargrove insisted. "He had no intention of remaining in his, his, universe." Hargrove finally recalled the term Barstead had used. "I brought him and the others to camp. I've seen how they acted with one another."

"You feel that something has gone wrong?"

"Yes sir. As we searched for a place for him to use, he spoke of a General Croll. He said the friend who allowed them to use his house felt this man a threat."

Crittenden sighed, glancing at the final retreat of daylight. Lantern lights sprang up amid the tents as if a hundred fireflies filled the area. Crittenden slowly shook his head. "He spoke to me also of the man, Croll, as someone to beware of. If I have sent him into the clutches of that man, I am to blame."

"Alex, we can't be sure he's a prisoner in his own," Wescott turned to Hargrove, barely visible in the darkness. "What did he call it?"

"Universe," Hargrove answered.

"True," Crittenden agreed. "Now I must tell the others about his absence and the danger he no doubt faces."

~ * ~

October 5, 1961 (Universe 0)

Rich Marsden combed DC, visiting several of his friends and former colleagues. Two of the men owed their lives to him and with their help he learned that Croll had tapped the lines to the house in Bennett. But Croll didn't have Barstead.

"He ordered round the clock surveillance on you and your friends," the man told Marsden. He glanced around the stairwell. "He sent a 'copter to pick up some man outside of Warrenton, Virginia."

"Who?" Marsden felt his flesh prickle.

"Don't know, but the guy got away. Croll nearly had a stroke." The man again glanced around the stairwell. "I've got to go. Good luck."

"Thanks." Marsden watched his friend climb the two flights to the ground floor and disappear through the doorway. Marsden opened the door to the garage level and darted toward the rental car where Gordo waited.

He slipped into the passenger seat. "Let's get out of here."

Gordo started the car, drove to the exit, and paid the parking fee. As he stopped, waiting for traffic to thin, he said. "I called Gray Eagle while you were conferring with your friend."

Marsden jerked his head toward Gordo. "The damned phone lines are tapped."

Gordo made a right turn. "The guy you spoke with. Did he tell you that?"

"That and the fact that Croll sent a 'copter and two of his thugs to pick up someone outside of Warrenton."

"It had to be Julian." Gordo made a second right. He chuckled. "If it weren't for the fact that we are in big time trouble, this whole thing would be funny. A Confederate cavalry patrol was waiting for Julian and the others in Frederick. They were taken to a camp west of Warrenton. The guy that kidnapped them is Colonel Alex Crittenden."

"What was Julian doing outside of Warrenton in this universe?"

"Calling to let everyone know what had happened. This colonel let him go, provided he came right back."

"He didn't go back and Croll doesn't have him."

Gordo whipped the car left, crossing in front of a truck. The driver blew an angry horn, followed by muttered curses and hand signals.

Marsden clutched at the armrest. "You're acting as if you're trying to lose someone."

"I am. We're being followed by a green Chevy. You got any ideas what to do?"

Marsden grunted. "I have one I don't like." He looked around for something familiar. Seeing where they were, he ordered Gordo to pull into the next gas station and fill the tank.

As the attendant pumped gas, Marsden whispered to Gordo. "Tell him to forget checking the oil and cleaning the windows."

Marsden left the car and went to the trunk. Using the spare key, he opened it and removed the luggage and a small canvas bag containing two semiautomatic Ruger handguns and several boxes of ammunition. He took out the guns, casually thrusting the remaining items in the back of the car before he returned to the passenger seat.

After Gordo paid for the gas, he looked at Marsden. "What next?"

"Take route twenty-nine west," Marsden ordered. "We'll hit two-eleven near Warrenton. The road is being widened into a four-lane highway, but it's the old road to New Market. It would still be the same road in that 1861 universe.

Gordo headed west. "You aren't thinking about?"

"Transfer, just temporarily." Marsden shivered as the car left DC. "I have no intention of being involved in any Civil War. But we can't let Croll get us while we carry this device."

"We could lose the tail," Gordo advised.

"We are going to do just that." Marsden leaned his head against the seat as Gordo drove.

~ * ~

Near Warrenton the weather changed abruptly, becoming foggy and wet, the rain falling in oily threads. The fog was a shroud over the countryside, smearing the outlines of trees and buildings.

They entered route two-eleven where the traffic was sparse, but the fog denser. After they left Warrenton, Marsden began to count the miles. He spied a collection of trucks, cranes and other construction equipment.

"Pull into the field," he ordered Gordo. "When you get out, take the bag and gun on your side of the back seat. I'll do the same." Marsden was holding the transfer device in the palm of his hand, the only thing separating them from Croll's men behind them.

"Then what?" Gordo asked, pulling into the muddy field.

"I'll open the portal and you go through. I'll follow. Leave the car running. That will give them pause and time enough for us to escape."

Gordo grunted. "I don't like this."

"Now," Marsden ordered.

Gordo slammed the car into park, pulled on the emergency brake, and jumped from the driver's seat. He opened the back door, dragged out his luggage and the gun. Marsden was doing the same on the other side of the car. Gordo dashed after Marsden, rain dripping from his nose, insinuating itself beneath his raincoat.

"Stop!"

The order came from behind them. Marsden thumbed the open button and the portal sprang to life as it had in Bennett. "Get!" he shouted.

Gordo ran through, turned and faced Marsden. "Hurry!" he begged, as the man behind Marsden leveled his gun,, steadying it with his left hand.

Marsden pressed the continuous button and dove through the opening. The man fired.

"No!" Gordo screamed as the portal winked out of existence. He blinked. "You shut the damned thing down in time."

Marsden rose to his feet and turned to face the space where the portal had been. He shut the power to the device he held and shivered. "I didn't close the portal."

"What closed it?"

"The bullets. Remember what Gray Eagle told us about driving fast through portals. Only walk through them because momentum above a certain value can make a portal collapse?"

Gordo nodded. "Thank God it didn't collapse on you."

~ * ~

October 5, 1861(Universe 1)

Marsden thrust the device into his pocket with shaking hands. The relationship between mass and velocity when moving through a portal was something Gray Eagle had drummed into him when he gave Marsden the device. The relationship was so complicated that momentum simply didn't describe it and Marsden hadn't bothered to pay much attention to the intricacies of the subject. He wondered how close he had come to being trapped in the portal. He shoved aside the thought.

The frosty bite in the air and the absence of rain claimed his attention. They stood on soil covered with blunted remains of harvested field corn. Before them was a fence fronting a winding dirt road.

"My God, we're here," Marsden gasped, staring at the ground, then the fence.

"I don't want to be here long," Gordo grumbled. "What's our next move?"

They quickly applied the enhancer patches as Marsden held up his hand.

"Horses," he said.

A mounted patrol rode into view headed by an officer, a captain by the bars he wore. Marsden's lips compressed into a thin line. He did not relish this encounter.

"Shit," he whispered. The men were Confederate soldiers. "From a cold war to a hot one in two easy minutes." Marsden shivered at the strangeness of his surroundings.

"Any other bright ideas?" Gordo quipped. "I mean besides name, rank, and serial number."

"They didn't have serial numbers," Marsden said. "Don't have," he amended.

The officer at the head of the patrol stopped before the fence. He casually brushed his hat. "I'm Captain Hargrove. I believe you must be friends of Dr. Barstead, for I watched you come to us in the same manner that he left us. Did he send you?"

Marsden felt his mind spin at the question. The soldier was not surprised by his use of the transfer device. "No, we were in trouble and had to get away fast." He stopped. "How did you find us?"

"We have been waiting here hoping for Dr. Barstead to return." Hargrove pointed out a copse of trees just above the cornfield.

"We were looking for him until we were followed."

"You are, sir?" Hargove asked.

"I'm Colonel Richard Marsden and this is Gordon Sykes." Marsden thought giving his former rank might assure him some formal recognition in this universe.

"Sir, you are the man Dr. Barstead spoke of as lending out your house to him."

Gordo snorted. "Julian blabs a lot. It still surprises me he ever did intelligence work in WWII."

"You will please come with me," Captain Hargrove said, ignoring Gordo's remark. "Curruthers, give the colonel your horse and double up with Lassiter. Jones, have Mr. Sykes ride with you."

The two men identified by Hargrove rode before the fence. One dismounted and offered the reins of his horse to Marsden. Marsden walked across the dry stubble and climbed the fence followed by Gordo. He took the reins.

"But first, sir, the guns you carry. I assume both of you are armed."

Marsden looked at the officer. "It's one nasty weapon," Marsden said, removing his gun from the pocket of his raincoat. Gordo followed suit.

Hargrove looked at the guns, ejected the magazines, and tucked them into a haversack slung across his saddle.

"Wait," Marsden held up his hand. "You've seen something like those guns before."

Hargrove nodded. "Colonel Crittenden has such a weapon."

"Then you better remember to remove the round in the chamber." Marsden walked to the officer. "Please, allow me." Taking each gun, he removed the chambered round.

"I did not know," Hargrove said.

"No, but you learn fast." Marsden mounted the horse, suddenly feeling better about being in Hargrove's universe. "We know that Colonel Crittenden has our friends, so let's meet this clever superior of yours."

The patrol rode toward the camp.

~ * ~

Twenty minutes later, Marsden saw the farmhouse and the sea of tents spreading out on the field east of the house. Some distance from the house was one of the largest barns he had ever seen. He estimated it was at least three stories, with a stone foundation. About an eighth of a mile from this barn he could see another smaller barn-like structure tucked into a contented section of the hillside.

One of the soldiers held Marsden's horse as he dismounted. Gordo came to him, carrying his luggage and the bag with the ammunition for the guns. Apparently Hargrove did not realize they had brought extra ammunition.

Marsden and Gordo followed Hargrove across well-cropped grass, kept so by several active goats, and three fat sheep. Ducks swam in a pond fronted by a small open tent with a canvas canopy designed to offer protection for the user. Beneath the canopy sat a man Marsden suspected was Crittenden.

Hargrove approached the officer, saluted and gave a quick report. As he spoke, Crittenden shot a glance at Marsden and Gordo. Marsden grew uncomfortable as Crittenden continued to stare at him, almost in recognition.

"Their guns, Colonel." Hargrove offered the two guns to Crittenden along with the clip and the extra bullet Marsden had removed. Hargrove explained about the bullet.

Crittenden looked at Marsden. "Colonel Marsden, I am Colonel Crittenden."

Marsden nodded. "Mr. Gorden Sykes," Marsden introduced Gordo.

"I prefer Gordo," Gordo explained.

"Then I shall call you that," Crittenden said. He held out his hand to Marsden, but the action was not meant as a greeting. "The device that allowed you to come to us. Give it to me, sir."

Marsden balked. "No way."

"Do it of your free will, or I shall have it taken from you by force," Crittenden ordered.

Marsden grunted. He took his time removing the device and handing it to Crittenden. Crittenden's eyes narrowed as he examined it. He looked at Marsden.

"This, sir, is unlike the one used by Dr. Barstead."

Marsden read the accusation in the words. *This is one sharp man.* "It's a transfer device, but not as complicated as the one Julian carried. Gray Eagle manufactured this one. We took the other from those men in the black uniforms."

Crittenden accepted the explanation. He gestured to the farmhouse. "Please come with me. Your friends are there and anxious for whatever news you bring. Have you heard from Dr. Barstead?"

Marsden fell in step with Crittenden. "No, Colonel. But Gordo phoned Gray Eagle and learned Julian called them. Julian broke off communications when he sensed trouble."

Crittenden asked. "Was he captured by this man he said was not to be trusted?"

Marsden smiled. "No, Croll didn't get him. He sent a 'copter to Warrenton to pick up Julian, but somehow Julian gave him the slip."

"What is a 'copter?"

"Helicopter," Gordo explained. "Whirley Bird," he made a whistling noise and moved his finger in a circle.

Marsden saw Gordo frown when Crittenden stared at him as if Gordo were slightly mad. "Gordo, he has no idea. It's a machine that flies, not a fixed wing, but a rotor."

"A flying machine, such as the young pilots Amber and Roger told me of?"

"Yes, but not an airplane. This one…" Marsden stopped. "It's a bit more complicated to explain."

"I have time to hear of it." Crittenden resumed walking to the house. "And I am very interested to learn of this new type of flying machine."

"Well, Gordo will be happy to explain it to you, in all the aerodynamic detail you desire."

~ * ~

Marsden accepted a second cup of coffee from Crittenden's wife, Bea, and another helping of apple pie. Bea was a gracious hostess, considering she had a house full of strange scientists and now two more added to the milieu. Marsden observed that she was about Amber's height, slender, but determined. Her hair, like Crittenden's, held threads of gray, but her eyes were the blue-green color of the sea he had seen years ago in the South Pacific. She was aided by Margaret Aksawan and Mary Frances, who refused to let Bea cater to this crowd of colleagues.

While Marsden found the pie delicious, the revelation of an Elliott Marsden within Crittenden's ranks shocked him.

Elliot Marsden was the name of his great grandfather who had fought with the Fifth Virginia Cavalry. He had joined the army just after he had graduated from Virginia Military Institute. Marsden knew that the young lieutenant in Crittenden's command was not part of his family line, but the resemblance between them must be there, for Crittenden had seen it.

"Which explained why he stared at me when we met," Marsden muttered between bites of his slice of pie.

"What?" Margaret, sitting beside him on the sofa, glanced at him.

"Nothing, just wondering about all this." Marsden attacked his pie with more vigor. I didn't realize you had gone with them," he said. "I thought that you were still in Bennett."

Margaret shook her head. "Julian wanted another anthropologist along."

"What of this man, Gray Eagle, and the others with him?" Crittenden asked. "He needs to be contacted and told he is in danger."

"Gray Eagle broke down the Source Gate and the other equipment and has it stored in the hidden room. He found an abandoned Source gate he can use to transfer if he needs to do so."

"When did this happen?" Reed demanded.

"When we didn't hear from you and Alyssia called. The Maryland State Police had contacted her about your rental car."

Roger slipped into the room and took a seat beside Rierdon. Marsden caught the entrance and wondered where he had been and where Amber was. He had not seen her for the last hour and a half.

"What does Gray Eagle intend to do?" Rierdon leaned forward, resting his arms on his knees.

Marsden looked at the man. "Cross to this universe and ask the Quaker couple who own the house to get him and the equipment north to DC."

Desiree gasped, raising her hand to her throat. "No, no. He must not go to Washington, that thing is there beneath the Embassy Club."

Crittenden nodded. "Desiree is correct. Gray Eagle and the others must come here where they can be protected."

"Someone should tell him that." Marsden looked at Reed, then at Crittenden.

Crittenden shook his head. "I cannot permit any of you to leave for now. You have no idea which danger is the greater: General Croll or these men in black uniforms."

Margaret lifted her head, glanced around and asked. "Where's Amber?"

Bea said. "She wanted to sit on the back porch, but I did not see her when I went to the kitchen a few minutes ago."

"Roger, where is Amber?" Margaret asked.

Roger shrugged, but his action did not fool Crittenden. The officer glared at the young pilot. "Where is she?"

Roger bit his lower lip. "It's kinda hard to explain."

"Why not try?" Crittenden suggested with the hint of a threat.

Roger colored and dropped his gaze to the floor. "We decided not to tell you until she was gone." He looked at Crittenden with a pleading stare. "She insisted and well, I went along with her."

"What are you talking about, son?" Crittenden demanded.

"She went to our universe to call Gray Eagle and tell him about Rich and Gordo," Roger confessed.

"What!" Crittenden jumped to his feet. The chair he was using toppled to the floor. "I have the only transfer device and that I took from Colonel Marsden."

Roger's blush deepened and he stood, moving behind Rierdon. "We had another."

Margaret blurted. "What do you mean you had another device?"

"The two Gray Eagle made, remember? Well we took one. It's like the one he gave Rich. But it only lets two people cross and has a down time of forty-five minutes before it's fully charged again."

"Does she not realize the danger all of you, all of us face?" Crittenden thundered.

Roger nodded.

"Then I fail to understand her reasoning, or yours for that matter."

Roger spread his hands. "We have to warn Gray Eagle. She'll be back, I know she will."

"How long has she been gone?" Margaret demanded.

"About an hour," Roger explained. "She had to change clothes. After she finished calling, she was going to go to a small strip mall called Seven Stars not far from here, but in a 1987 universe."

"Why?" Marsden shuddered. "That's not very clever. Why not just come back?"

Roger shook his head. "No, we decided that there are things we need. She plans to do some shopping."

"Shopping?" Crittenden rubbed his face with his hands. "This General Croll almost killed your friends and is still hunting for Dr. Barstead. God knows what those others are up to and Amber is going shopping?"

Marsden watched Crittenden. The man was angry, but he sensed amusement beneath the anger and just a tinge of admiration for the young woman who had given him the slip. Marsden doubted that once Amber returned, if she returned, Crittenden would ever underestimate her again. For that matter, Marsden thought, neither would he.

"We have to find her," Reed demanded.

Crittenden blew out his breath. "No, I cannot let anyone go after her. We don't know where she is and you have told me the device you used does not allow one to see without opening a portal."

"But Colonel," Reed protested. "She could be in danger."

"Not if she makes it to the 1987 universe," Roger offered. "No one knows her there."

"Son, you were not listening to me," Crittenden reprimanded the young man. "I told you the man you fear in your universe is not the only danger. What of those others? What if they go after her? They are not confined to a single universe as is your General Croll."

Roger paled. "I didn't think about that."

Crittenden sighed. "I hope Amber did. Now if you will excuse me, I must make arrangements for your comfort for the evening. Roger, you will share a tent with Penfield and Marsden."

Marsden looked at Crittenden. "Penfield… oh, the young man sent by Lincoln."

"Yes, but I meant Elliott Marsden, sir. I want the three of them together, so I can keep an eye on them."

And separated from Amber, Marsden thought, who seems to be the instigator of your problems. He offered a silent prayer that she had the resources to deal with any problems she was facing. It was going to be a very tense time until she returned.

~ * ~

October 5, 1987 (Universe 8)

The plastic bags cut into her wrists as Amber crouched beneath an outcropping in the dark woods behind the parking lot of the Seven Stars Mall. She pulled her woolen sweater closer, shivering in the damp, and not a little from fear. Out there, in the woods beyond where she hid, were two men dressed in black uniforms. Somehow they had tracked her to the mall in the 1987 universe.

She gazed at the rain-drenched woods, praying the storm was enough to deter the men. Lightning cut a sudden path through the twilight with a purple zigzag, turning the darkness into day for a split second. Thunder rolled over the small rock shelter, followed by a massive downpour. Hail bounced before her, turning the ground white.

A second bolt split a tree about thirty yards from Amber and she held her breath, her stomach a mass of knotted muscle. The burning wood from the tree sent streamers of smoke through the gloom, the smell mingling with the dead leaves and moisture-soaked earth.

Still crouching, Amber distributed items from one of the bags she carried among the others. She smoothed out the empty bag and sat on it, massaging her cramped leg muscles. There was no way she could open a portal and return until the storm left the area. The electromagnetic fields generated by the storm interfered with the operation of the transfer device.

She reached out with her mind and sensed the men were no longer hunting her. Relaxing, she used the flashlight attached to her Swiss Army knife to illuminate the outcropping. It was too wet to build a fire and probably not a wise idea. She rummaged through the bags until she located the Polar Fleece pullover she had found on sale. Tearing off her damp sweater, she donned the warm top, and hugged her arms about her until she stopped shaking from cold and fear.

She smiled as she remembered the man at the rather seedy coin and pawnshop just outside the mall. He had given her several hundred dollars for a few of the diamonds she carried. She knew they were worth five times that amount, but quietly took the money. His dishonesty was evident to her when she had entered the shop. He was probably a fence. The man would not call the police and the money had bought what she needed.

Now she would have to spend a cold, wet night in a rock shelter, a quarter mile from a mall in a 1987 universe. She wondered how Crittenden was taking her absence. She wondered what he would do when she returned.

Fifteen

Observe nature closely, for omens in nature hold immediate significance.
Codex of Flowering Butterfly

October 6, 1961(Universe 0)

Croll insisted on being present when his men raided Marsden's house. He knew about the secret room in the basement and suspected that the scientists would hide there. It pleased him to imagine finding Marsden and the others crouched in the room, frightened of his armed soldiers, willing to negotiate at any price. The image gave him a boost of energy.

"Let's scare the hell out of them." He ordered his men to storm the house.

He had expected no one in the upper part of the house and followed his men to the basement and waited until his experts in sabotage located the room. They declared it clean after a short inspection.

"Open it," Croll ordered. The door swung upward and Croll stared into a dark empty room. He stepped inside, found the dangling chain, and pulled the light on. The room was still empty but the walls bore evidence of having held additional wiring.

"Where are they?" Kraft demanded. "You said they would hide in this room."

Croll's lips flattened against his teeth. "Tear the damn house apart! They have to be here. No one left even after the last phone call."

"What about a tunnel?" Kraft pounded on the walls but they were solid.

Croll brushed aside the remark. "There's no tunnel; there's only this room." He held out his hand, pointing at the room, accusing it of complicity in hiding the scientists.

"What do we do now?" Kraft muttered. He was working closely with Croll, despite warnings from Beaumont and Stein. The ghost was gone and Kennedy no longer cared about the matter. But Croll did. He wanted the scientists. So did Kraft.

"Sir," one of his men came up to him. "There's no one in the house."

"I can just guess where they went," Croll sighed. "It's how they got to their destination I want to know about. Keep a watch on this place," he ordered.

"What next?" Kraft smacked the wall.

Croll took Kraft by the arm and drew him away from the others. "We go back to DC. I want to listen to those tapes from the phone tap again. "

"But if everyone went to that universe…" Kraft lowered his voice at a gesture from Croll. "How are we going to get to them?"

A sly smile spread across Croll's face. "I've got a mole with them. He'll get to us when he can."

"Is Weber trustworthy?" Kraft glanced at the soldiers ripping through Marsden's belongings.

"No, but he wants what I want and is prepared to do anything to get it."

~ * ~

October 6, 1861(Universe 1)

Gray Eagle felt for the release. He pulled it and the door swung upward, giving air and space. But the door opened into darkness. He switched on his high-beam flashlight and painted the walls, ceiling, and floor of the basement with light.

"Where are we?" asked Karen 'Kit' Jackson, another of the young pilots.

"In the 1861 universe," Gray Eagle whispered as he felt the hard-packed earthen floor. The stairs were absent, replaced by a ladder-like construction. "Stay put," he ordered.

He moved silently across the dirt floor, climbed the ladder, and touched the door to the ground floor. The door gave, swinging open a fraction. Light spilled onto the narrow landing where he stood. He flipped the switch on his flashlight.

With his eye to the opening, he saw a man and women in plain clothing sitting at a table eating breakfast. Gray Eagle shifted his head to get a better view, but his abrupt movement forced the door to swing open. The man heard the door and turned to see the cause. His eyes widened and his mouth opened. He half rose from his seat.

"Who are you?"

Gray Eagle stepped into the kitchen. "We are no threat to you, but are in need of assistance."

"Sir, my wife and I are simple people. We have little. Take what you wish and leave us unharmed."

Gray Eagle shook his head. "I have no intention of harming you. But my friends and I need your help."

"Friends?" The man tilted his head to one side, as his wife stood and moved beside him.

"In the basement, in your secret room."

"People in my basement?" The man gasped. "But how did you get into the room? We have no…" his voice trailed off.

"We're not escaped slaves," Gray Eagle assured the man. "It's very difficult for me to explain." He rummaged in his coat pocket and removed a gold nugget and a diamond. "Please accept these for your help."

The farmer and his wife stared at the objects Gray Eagle deposited on the table. Gray Eagle reasoned that thieves would hardly offer gold and gems for services. The farmer looked at Gray Eagle for further explanation.

"I need you to send a telegram for me. Is there a place near here where you can do so?"

"Yes," the woman answered. "In Bennett there is a telegraph office."

"I'll write out the telegram. Please send it to Colonel Alex Crittenden. He's stationed outside of Warrenton, Virginia."

The man asked. "He is in the army?"

"Yes, and there's a very great danger to both sides in this war. I must reach him immediately."

The man relaxed and his wife, though still hesitant, gestured to the table. "Please share our meal."

"That's kind of you, but I have ten other people with me plus a truck load, I mean a wagon load, of equipment."

"In my basement," the man started, arching backward at the revelation. "But how did you get there?"

"We walked across," Gray Eagle said.

"Across what?" the man asked.

"A bridge between universes," Gray Eagle explained to the bewildered couple.

~ * ~

It was ten in the morning before the weather cleared and Amber felt safe to open a portal. It took longer than she had expected to cart her booty the two miles to Crittenden's camp. A half mile from the camp she encountered Hargrove. Though he tried to seem angry, she noted he could not hide his relief.

He dismounted. "Everyone has been worried about you, Miss Amber."

She cocked her head to one side. “Is the colonel mad?”

“Seething.” Hargrove chuckled. “I’ll take those,” he offered and she handed him the bags. “What is this material?” Hargrove felt the plastic of the bags.

“It’s called plastic. Good thing it’s waterproof. I had to spend the night in a rock shelter.”

“Hadley, take these to Dr. Aksawan at the farmhouse,” Hargrove ordered a young man with carrot-red hair and a face full of freckles. “And mind that you not look at the contents.”

“Yes, sir,” Hadley replied.

“Not that one.” Amber grabbed a blue plastic bag from the depths of one of the white ones. “It’s a gift.”

Hargrove lifted her onto his horse and climbed into the saddle behind her. “This will be faster than walking.”

As the party trotted into camp, Amber asked. “Do you think Colonel Crittenden will respond to a bribe?”

Hargrove shook his head. “No, but you can try.”

Crittenden, Wescott, and Reed were standing before the pond when Hargrove rode into camp. He dismounted, lifted Amber from his horse, and brought her to Crittenden. Reed moved away from the others and hugged her.

“Are you hurt? Did you get cut or scratched?” He babbled. “I’ve got more of the immune enhancer in my bag.”

“I’m fine.” She stepped away from him.

"What are you wearing?" Reed asked, rubbing the material of the dark blue polar fleece shirt.

"It's a new synthetic material I picked up in that 1987 universe. It's light and warm."

"Doctor Reed, Major Wescott. Would you excuse us?" Crittenden interrupted.

"Come on, Amber," Reed coaxed, holding out his hand.

"Hargrove," Crittenden ordered. "Take Dr. Reed to the farmhouse."

"I won't go," Reed blustered.

"Don't worry," Amber assured him. "I'll be along in a minute."

Hargrove took Reed by the arm, tugging when he proved reluctant to hurry. Wescott offered Crittenden a casual salute and jogged after Reed and Hargrove.

Amber looked at Crittenden. "Do you still shoot people for desertion?"

"You have to be in the army first in order to desert. Technically you are my prisoner and have a right to escape. That you came back is another matter." He smiled at her. "Have you had breakfast?"

"No, but I could use some coffee."

He gestured toward the canopy and the pair sat opposite one another while Crittenden poured her a cup of hot coffee. Amber placed the plastic bag on the table between them and cupped her hands around the coffee for a moment before sipping it.

"What is that?" Crittenden asked, inclining his head to the curious object.

"A bribe for you," she joked. "Both Roger and I think you should have one too." She handed the package to Crittenden.

Crittenden rubbed the material of the bag between his fingers before dipping into it to find the contents. He removed a box with a diagram of an object he had seen Amber use the day after she came to camp. Printed beneath the image were the words Swiss Army Knife.

"You know you are in deep trouble," Crittenden shook the box at Amber. "Do you know the penalty for trying to bribe an officer?"

"I was hoping for a hot bath and a change of clothes, but I'll settle for a cup of coffee."

Crittenden opened the box. "You had us worried. When you finish your coffee, I want that transfer device you are carrying."

"I figured you might." She reached into her pocket and handed it to him.

"What did you do when you were gone?" he asked. The words were casual, but Amber sensed a probing behind them.

"I called Gray Eagle and told him where we were. He said Julian had already called him, but he didn't know where Julian was. He also said Rich and Gordo went to DC, but they hadn't called back either. I told him they were with us."

"What else did you talk about?" Crittenden opened the compass on the knife and studied it.

"I told him to cross into this universe and send you a telegram and that you would be able to help him." She looked at Crittenden. "Will you help him and the others?"

That had been her real fear. Gray Eagle and her friends were in southern Virginia. She needed someone with Crittenden's authority to get them and their equipment safely north.

Crittenden reached across the table and patted her hand. "I've already done so. I received the telegram an hour ago and have sent a reply. I've also contacted General Lee about seeing your friends have unrestricted access to the trains."

"If Julian is still free, he will try and go back to the institute."

"Has he the funds to travel there?"

"He might call Alyssia. She could wire him money, maybe even a plane ticket, depending on where he is." That worried her. "We'll have to cross to call ISIR and find out."

Crittenden shook his head. "Not yet. Why did you not return last night?"

She sighed. "Two of those men were following me. I had to hide from them. They were in the mall in that 1987 universe. I don't know how they found me. The transfer device we made had no tracer sensor." She shoved her cup away and thought out loud. "It must generate some sort of a signal that can be picked up. But how come the other one doesn't when the tracer is removed?" She shrugged away the thought for the time being and looked at

Crittenden. “How soon can Gray Eagle and the others get here?”

“General Lee is already taking care of the matter since he is in command of the army. He is making the arrangements and providing an escort. But your friends will have to come by train and the gauges of the rail lines are different in that part of the state. It will require several trains and transfers.”

Amber looked at Crittenden. “The gauges of the rails are different?”

Crittenden nodded.

“General Lee is in charge of your army? But that isn’t supposed to happen until next year. What happened to General Johnson?”

It was Crittenden’s turn to look puzzled. “General Johnson was wounded in an artillery accident in August. Lee has commanded the army since. He is on his way to Manassas and I will be meeting him there shortly. I have much to tell him about you and the others.”

“Wait a minute.” Amber shook her head. “Why is he going to Manassas? Has fighting started again?”

“On the contrary, both sides have ceased hostilities and talks have begun under a flag of truce.”

“Who ordered the talks?”

“Both presidents,” Crittenden told her. “Yes, to answer your question, there is more to it than simply my report of you and the others. The presidents recognize that the strange men we have been dealing with are a danger to both sides.”

Amber rubbed her face with her hands, stood, and asked. “I’d like to go and get something to eat.”

“Certainly,” Crittenden stood, accidentally brushing a sheet of paper that fell to the ground.

Amber picked it up and offered it to Crittenden, but snatched it away as he reached for it. “What is this?” she gaped at the sketch on the sheet of paper. The location was written on the bottom was Zeller Farm.

“It’s something from one of my informants,” Crittenden said in a stern voice. “Give it to me, please.”

“No,” she replied.

“What do you mean no?” Crittenden raised his voice.

She looked at him. “This thing that looks like a road.”

He caught the tension in her voice. “It is a road leading nowhere with another at an angle to it. Both are being macadamized.”

“What you mean by macadamized?” She offered the sheet to Crittenden.

“A careful way to make a road,” he replied. “You layer decreasing sized stones in place and the road is smooth. It takes time and money. Why Zeller does this on his farm, I have no idea.”

“Look at the marking.” Amber pointed to the sheet. Crittenden squinted at the markings sketched by his informant and looked at her for enlightenment.

"In my universe, you don't put those on a roadway; you put those on a runway."

"A what?"

"A landing field, an airport, a place where you plan to land airplanes, flying machines. Ask Rich and Gordo. They'll tell you. Someone is constructing a landing field on that farm."

Crittenden's face took on a hard expression. "A place to land flying machines?"

Amber felt the cold eat its way beneath her polar fleece shirt as she realized the implications of what she just told Crittenden. "Yes. A place to land flying machines."

~ * ~

Universal Time 1.0.10.8.61(Universe 61)

Kester lounged in a brocade chair with his feet plopped on a matching stool. His eyes took in the furnishings of his assigned quarters at Command Central. He held a glass of fine French brandy, the aroma tweaking his nose each time he lifted the glass. The baroque table before the sofa opposite him was covered with a platter of delicacies, brought to the room by one of the many indentured servants the army used for the comfort of its officers.

"One continual last meal," Kester muttered, wondering if getting drunk was his only way out. He had yet to meet with San and still could not comprehend that, as a second, he would die if San lost the challenge. Nor had he any idea when the challenge would begin or what it entailed.

He sipped more of the brandy and glanced at the kitchen area of his quarters, where the man assigned to him worked at preparing a noon meal. "Leave it," Kester called.

The servant came to Kester. "Sir?"

"Leave the food and me for now," Kester ordered. "I wish to be alone."

"Are you displeased with me, sir?"

Kester sighed. "No, just get out of here for now. Come back to prepare supper."

The servant nodded. He returned to the kitchen to put away the food before he left Kester alone in his quarters.

Kester rose, walked to a blank wall and pressed the controls to his right. The wall cleared, turning into a window with a view of the biosphere. He stared at the lake, the woods, and the imported animal life that gave the biosphere an aura of a natural organic space.

"What was that young woman doing in that 1987 universe?" Kester wondered aloud. His men, he had discovered, were still loyal to him. They had sent him a duplicate of the report they'd sent to San. The only reason his men had been alerted to the young pilot was that the energy signal from her transfer device looked similar to that from one of the Jumper's Rings.

He wondered if the scientists had recently developed as crude a Para-temporal technology as the Jumper's Guild possessed, but quickly discounted it. The Khysid scientists and technicians had never been able to duplicate either the Jewels or the Rings, despite having access to both. If the army couldn't replicate the devices with all the knowledge they possessed, then no second rate group of scientists from a technologically limited alternate universe could construct a Ring transfer device from scratch.

"The scientists must have damaged the transfer devices when they removed the tracing sensor," Kester said to the window.

He knew they had learned how to remove the sensor. *Otherwise, why couldn't he locate the devices?* The idea bothered him and he quickly shoved it from his mind. The appearance of the young woman in the 1987 universe meant that meant the scientists were still in Virginia in some universe.

His thoughts were interrupted by a knock and Kester hurried to the door. He pressed the visual mode on the accessory panel and saw General San. He quickly deactivated the sonic stingers and opened the door.

"Please come in, General." Kester gestured with his brandy glass.

"Have you forgotten all military protocol?" She glared at him.

"No, but I thought that being your second, and in line to die might give me a few perks." He watched her cross the threshold and stare at the vision of the biosphere presented by the transparent wall space.

"You needn't worry." Her voice was cool and deliberate. "I have no intentions of dying. That will save your life as well. Only the Supreme Commander may send someone in his or her place to face a challenge. I alone will face General Vrill."

Kester released the door. It closed with a soft click. "I see."

San swung to face him. "I doubt it. We have a bigger problem right now, one that has delayed the challenge."

"Oh?" Kester cocked an eyebrow.

"Yes. The armies in the 1861 universe have called a truce and are beginning negotiations."

Kester's mind reeled at the news. "That's not part of the standard historical sequence. That universe is so close to the standard sequence, they should be duking it out in the West."

"They aren't duking it out, as you put it, anywhere." San moved to the brandy decanter and poured a glass for herself before Kester could offer to do so for her.

"What's happened?"

"Remember those perturbations you were worried about?" San took a healthy swig of the brandy.

"Yes?"

"They've cascaded. Like the old saw, one more drop to set the cup overflowing. Now we have a flood on our hands."

"Then we back off for the time being."

"No." San toyed with the glass she held. "We escalate. Those planes Sig wanted for reconnaissance? Well, they will serve a different purpose. You see, when the Command Council realized what was happening, we sent ultimatums to both presidents."

"What?"

"The ultimatums had been prepared for use down the road, after much of the war got under way and we got good footage of the carnage. But now we can't afford to wait."

"You sent ultimatums?"

"Yes and both presidents refused us and are pressing on with this stupid meeting at Manassas."

Kester walked to the table to refill his brandy snifter. "I don't understand. What difference would it make to wait for a year or two? Our technology is superior to theirs."

"The difference is that the Jewels are decaying."

"They do so each time a Source Gate is used." Kester stared at his superior. "Every officer learns that in basic."

"True, but now, for some reason, the rate of decay has increased."

"Why?"

San shrugged. "Unknown. So you see, if we want that universe and want the Army in one place so we have the luxury of trying again to replicate the Jewels, we don't have much time. We need to take that universe by any means possible."

~ * ~

October 8, 1861(Universe 1)

As Major Percival Robbins studied the drawings, his face contorted in a look of perplexed wonder. Crittenden was at Manassas meeting with General Lee and his last order had been to take anything out of the ordinary to Colonel Marsden.

Robbins walked to the farmhouse where most of the scientists were staying, though their friends had yet to arrive on the special train sent to retrieve them. Marsden and Gordo were standing outside gazing at the fenced-in field and talking with considerable animation when Robbins interrupted them.

"Colonel Marsden, Colonel Crittenden said that if his informant sent anything I considered extraordinary, I was to let you see it."

Marsden stared at the officer. He knew Crittenden had come to depend on Rierdon, Reed, and Margaret for information about the alternate universes. He half expected Robbins to go to them with anything that might pertain to the men everyone feared, but whose name no one yet knew.

"Is this from the informant near the Zeller farm?"

Robbins nodded.

"Now what?" Gordo asked. "Are they building another landing field?"

Marsden unfolded the sheet of paper and stared at the image the woman had captured on the sheet. He knew the informant was a woman, but he had no idea she was an excellent artist. Only an artist could capture the essence of the machine she had painstakingly depicted.

"You look like you've eaten a rotten apple," Gordo joked.

"A barrel of them." Marsden passed the sheet to Gordo.

"My God! It's your plane."

"No," Marsden corrected. "Mine is, or rather was, a Warhawk. That one is a Kitty Hawk, a slightly different model. See the numbers and the markings? And there are seven planes on that landing field."

Gordo looked at Marsden. "These people have balloons. Their artillery can't shoot down a P-40. Hell, a blimp would be a disaster to them."

Marsden saw the anguished look on Robbins's face. "Can you get a message to Crittenden?"

"Yes, of course, Colonel. That machine." Robbins touched the paper. "It is what you meant by a flying machine?"

"Oh yes it's a flying machine designed for war and that field has seven of them. Look here." Marsden pointed out the projections on the wings. "Those are guns and the planes can be fitted with bombs as well."

He saw a hint of understanding dawn in Robbins's eyes. Robbins tore the paper from Marsden's hand and raced for the telegraph line recently set up at the farmhouse.

"Why a P-40?" Gordo asked.

"Probably surplus in the universe from which they got it."

"But there were better WW II planes."

"True and I know of places where there are still functional P-51s and a few P-38s."

Gordo snorted. "Why not a jet? Remember that F-126 all-purpose job we saw in that 2030 universe."

"You try servicing that baby here. You need more mechanics and parts than this whole world could contribute, and you need robots. If I were planning an invasion of this universe and I wanted air superiority, I'd pick those WW II fighters."

"You could take these people out with a Sopwith Camel," Gordo protested.

Marsden shook his head. "No, too close to some of the weaponry they can field. Those old P-40s were sturdy and they could land on a cratered runway and not bat a prop."

"Yeah, provided you didn't tip them."

"This choice tells me something… logistics of economy."

"What?"

"If you were planning an invasion and you had to truck in all your supplies through portals from an alternate universe, you'd pick the most economical way to field an army. Jets are not just overkill here. They're a logistics nightmare, especially where fuel is concerned."

Gordo rubbed his jaw. "Yeah, with those new ones, why you have to sweep the damned runway to keep stuff from being sucked into the engines." Then he blinked. "Invasion? What do you mean invasion?"

"My gut tells me that those men we've been seeing are the tip of an iceberg. And the iceberg is the invasion army."

"You think the Union and Confederacy know that?"

Marsden nodded. "I think they've guessed it, especially Lincoln and Crittenden."

Gordo grabbed Marsden's arm. "Is our universe next?"

Marsden shrugged and blew out his breath. "The Zeller Farm is near Danver Falls, which is a housing development near Herndon in our universe. I remember when it was built."

Gordo favored Marsden with a curious stare. "What's going on in your head?"

"The informant says the field is not closely guarded."

"Why guard the planes? No one here can operate them."

Marsden smiled. "Not true, my friend. What say we do a little midnight raiding?"

"Are you crazy? How are we going to do that?"

"With the help of two very clever and quite good young pilots."

Sixteen

Symbols are rich in meaning and a key to activating the Realities.

Codex of Flowering Butterfly

October 8, 1975(Universe 8)

Sweat trickled along Barstead's chest while his collar hugged his neck as if it were a large boa constrictor. The sick feeling in his stomach told him that his recent move had been a stupid one, but the only one possible under the circumstances.

Crouched behind a dumpster in an alley in the Pittsburgh of a 1975 universe, Barstead fumbled with the transfer device, praying he could locate the co-ordinates for his home universe.

After the driver stopped the truck Barstead had hidden in when he escaped from Croll's men, Barstead had crawled from the bed and hitched a ride to Baltimore. He made a quick call to Gray Eagle to let him know he was fine. Always one step ahead of Croll, he managed a circuitous route to Pittsburgh. Once there, he took a taxi to Gordo's house. Barstead still had the key Gordo had given him when they first arrived. He knew Gordo always kept large sums of cash on hand and hadn't taken much with him when they left for Bennett. Barstead had located the money, taken a shower, found some clothing that would fit, and had a good night's sleep.

Well, almost a good night's sleep, for he had been awakened at two by the sound of someone forcing the door on the apartment. Barstead wiped his face with his sleeve as he recalled his narrow escape from Croll's men. He was glad he had slept in his clothes.

His recent escape, more panicked than reasoned, had ended as a hasty dash through a portal into a universe where there were riots in Pittsburgh. His mind served up images of race riots in other cities in other universes, but this was like being in a war zone. The National Guard was patrolling the streets and the city was under martial law. His ears caught the unmistakable sound of a truck rumbling along Grant Street. He winced as he heard it stop, his hand trembling while he punched in another variation of the code. The green gleam of the small light told him he'd found the co-ordinates he was seeking. He never looked, simply activated the portal.

"You in the alley…come out, reaching for the sky!"

"Bull," Barstead muttered.

The portal stabilized and he rolled through as shots struck the spot where he had been a moment ago, missing both him and the portal.

~ * ~

October 8, 1961(Universe 0)

Barstead cut power to the device and the portal winked out of existence.

"Hey, Pop, you sick?" A young police officer called from the entrance to the alley.

Barstead jumped up amid the collection of garbage, surprised he was able to look somewhat relaxed and coherent. "I simply felt sick to my stomach, Officer. I think it was something I ate."

"There are public restrooms two blocks down from here," the man told him.

"Thank you, Officer." Barstead ran his hand through his hair. "I think I'll take advantage of them." He hurried off before the man could question him further. When he found a small coffee shop, he ducked inside to find the men's room. After a few minutes he emerged, looking less like he had spent the night on the streets.

"You want breakfast?" the surly waitress asked.

"I'd just like coffee and toast."

Barstead pulled a crumpled five from his pocket. "After breakfast, what remains is yours."

She sauntered toward the counter with a cup and a steaming pot of coffee. After she poured the aromatic liquid, Barstead inhaled the steam. He had not realized how stiff and cold he was until this moment. Tension gripped all his muscles, forcing them to ache as if he had run ten miles.

The waitress set a plate of fresh toast before him and scooped up the five before he had a chance to order more. "I'll be back with the coffee refills."

Barstead ignored her, his mind churning with his next task. He needed to let Alyssia know he was coming to California. Croll was probably watching them and calling her would be a stupid move. He needed an ally outside of ISIR. His mind presented him with Sam Preston.

Barstead summoned the waitress and had her change another five. He went to the pay phone, dialed the operator, and got Sam's number. While the phone rang, Barstead thought about Preston. The man had recently left ISIR to start his own airplane repair business.

"Sam and Gordo would get along fine," he mused.

"Preston here," the voice sounded tired and annoyed.

"Sam, it's Julian."

"Who?"

Barstead frowned, wondering if he had the correct Sam Preston. "Sam, it's me… Julian Barstead."

"Julian?" the fatigue vanished. "How are you? Boy it's good to hear your voice again."

"Why, what's wrong?"

"This business is not what I thought it would be. I miss you guys. You, Gray Eagle, even the little hellcats he trained."

A smile crept across Barstead's face. He stood straighter than he had for the past five days. "Sam, I need your help. This is big, about the biggest thing I've ever seen."

"Really?" eagerness tinged the voice. "Can it use a good mechanic and one super manager? Connie and I are about to sell the business."

"We can use all the help we can get and it's dangerous."

The operator chimed in, "Please deposit a dollar and fifty cents."

Barstead fed the machine. "Sam?"

"I'm still here."

"Listen and do what I say. But be really careful, I've got some army brass hunting me."

"I'll take care of it," Preston replied.

Barstead's mind presented him with an image of Preston licking his lips at the thought of tangling with some officious general. He'd been kicked out of the service for telling off some idiot captain in Korea. Preston had been right. The officer had later died, along with too many of his men.

When Barstead finished, he replaced the receiver, grabbed his last slice of toast, and headed for the bus terminal. Preston might not like the brass he had to deal with in this universe, but he knew Preston would help him and especially Crittenden. After all, Preston originally hailed from Virginia.

~ * ~

October 9, 1861(Universe 1)

"Last time I listened to one of your ideas, it got me into the Civil War," Gordo said, crouching closer to the ground.

Marsden played the light from his small flashlight on the dial of his watch. “You’re still in the Civil War and about to take it to new heights.”

“Very funny,” Gordo sniffed. “I can fly one of those planes. We don’t need the kids.”

“We need the kids because you are going to Crittenden and tell him what we’ve done and what we suspect. The kids will be safe. His informant said the planes were unguarded.”

“That worries me,” Gordo muttered. “Maybe there’re booby traps.”

“That’s why we need Walt’s medical scanner. It can detect any electromagnetic anomaly.”

“I’d feel better if we went alone.” Gordo was interrupted by footsteps.

“Just us,” Amber whispered. “We got the scanner and both transfer devices.”

“We can take care of ourselves,” Roger reminded Gordo.

“This isn’t a game,” the mechanic cautioned. “This is for real. One mistake and we‘ll all be dead.”

“What choice do we have?” Amber countered. “It would take hours to explain and Major Robins and Walt and Cc. would nix it anyway.”

“Check to see if the construction has gotten this far,” Marsden ordered.

“With these devices I can only open this portal for us to cross. They have no visual capabilities.”

“Oh shit, I forgot,” Marsden grunted. “Let’s cross. The longer we hide, the better chance we have of one of the sentries spotting us.”

Amber teamed with Marsden, Roger with Gordo. She and Roger opened a portal and the two pairs crossed. When the portals were deactivated, Amber looked around.

"I don't see any construction. Now what?"

"We take a car," Marsden replied.

"It's one in the morning. Where are we going to get a car?" Gordo snorted.

Marsden pointed at the twin headlights cutting a slow path along route two eleven. "Amber, stand on the edge of the road and wave at the car."

She glanced along the empty pavement at the approaching vehicle. "You want me to flag down a car? I don't look like a commando."

"If you looked like a commando, the driver wouldn't stop. Look panicked."

"That's not hard to do."

Marsden, Gordo, and Roger slipped into the dried shrubs lining the roadway, while Amber stood at the side, waving at the car. The driver slowed as his headlights caught a slender, young woman frantically hailing him.

He stopped, slipped the car into park, and opened the passenger side. "What's the matter, honey? You shouldn't be out here by yourself this time of night."

"I've got a problem, mister. I need a ride." *It a good thing this isn't a twenty-first century universe or this guy could be dangerous.*

"Just hop in and…" the man stopped as the driver's door was opened and Marsden placed a gun to his head.

"We need your car, sir. It's a matter of national security. Now if you would just get out."

The driver complied, shaking as he stared at the four people surrounding his car. "Here, take my money," he reached for his wallet.

"No, you'll need it to get home." Marsden motioned with his gun and the man moved to the side of the road.

Amber and Roger climbed into the back of the four-door sedan, while Gordo slipped into the passenger seat. Marsden crawled behind the wheel. The car sped away.

"What's this national security?" Amber piped from the back seat.

"Well, I could hardly tell the man we were planning on stealing three P-40s for General Lee."

"We better steal them fast. Once that guy gets to a phone and reports his car stolen, we'll be in big trouble." Gordo folded his arms across his chest.

"True, but I want to make one stop before we go back to that universe. I want to change license plates to buy Gordo some time. He's going to have to get to Manassas after we reach the field."

"The devices have a forty-five minute down time. We'll need to use both for the three of us to cross," Roger reminded Marsden.

"I know," Marsden replied. "But we got problems, too. Just because that woman informant didn't see human sentries doesn't mean the airfield is safe. I hope that little medical imager does the trick."

"It will have to," Amber replied.

Marsden knew she was correct. It would have to work, or they wouldn't be flying P-40s into Crittenden's camp. They wouldn't be flying them anywhere. It took longer than Marsden had expected for them to make it to the Danver Falls housing development. The sprawling residential suburb offered few places to hide and a large number of noisy dogs. Marsden finally located the contiguous area to the airfield in the 1861 universe. It turned out to be a secluded playground. He parked the car.

"Remember, Gordo. Get to Manassas with the car first. Otherwise, you are in no man's land."Gordo nodded. "I hate to leave you here."

"There's no other way. We knew this before we left. "The group exited the car. Gordo opened a portal, and Marsden crossed. Amber and Roger crossed using the transfer device they possessed and both portals winked out of existence, Amber pocketing one device, Gordo the other. Gordo was left to find an all night gas station and drive alone to Manassas.

~ * ~

October 9, 1861(Universe 1)

The field was dark, but the planes were silhouetted against the star-filled sky. Amber felt the dew collected on the wet grass dampen her tennis shoes and wished she had thought to buy a pair she had seen in the Seven Stars mall. There such shoes were called sneakers.

“See anything?”

She jumped at the sound of Marsden’s whispered question. “No, the device registers blank. I wish we had those night vision glasses.”

Marsden squinted at the dark blobs against the horizon. “Once Gray Eagle gets to the camp and sets up the Source Gate, we can get what we need.”

“How will we find Crittenden’s camp?” Roger’s voice was barely audible. “There’s no maps, no airports to call.”

“Dead reckoning,” Marsden said. “You must have learned that.”

“True.” Amber studied the dial, seeing a tiny blip appear on the screen. “But I never expected to use it to find a Confederate camp.”

Marsden’s ears caught the strain in her voice. “What is it?”

“There’s something coming, close to the ground, over there.” She pointed to the eastern end of the field.

She heard the rustle of the dried brush as the machine scuttled toward them. “Roger, you think that adjusted medical laser will take out the thing?”

“It had better.” Roger stood. He had one of Reed’s portable laser scalpels and adjusted it to a wide beam, lethal setting.

The mechanical guard drew closer and Amber thought it looked like a horseshoe crab.

The squeaky machine announced. “Stay where you are while I summon help. Move and you will be…” The voice stopped abruptly, replaced by the acrid smell of burning electronics.

"Well, it works," Roger grunted. "You think there are any more of those things?"

"Yeah," Marsden replied. "Let's get into the planes before another one finds us."

Amber and Roger followed Marsden onto the runway. The macadamized runway felt rough to Amber, but was not as gravely as she had expected. They chose the first three planes and removed the chocks from the wheels. The planes were not tied down. Marsden demonstrated how to get into the aircraft. Amber and Roger selected their respective planes and crawled inside. Once in the cockpit, they sat and waited, studying the controls until it was light enough to take off.

The smell, the sensation of power, the weight of the fighter, seemed to envelop Amber. There was no comparison to the other planes she had flown. Those were meant to dance in the sky. This one was meant to kill. While Amber used her penlight to study the controls, she felt the sensation of butterflies in her solar plexus. She glanced out the cockpit and noticed several ground-hugging shapes spill onto the runway and scurry toward the planes. The miniature army, sniffing for intruders, massed around the planes she, Roger, and Marsden occupied.

She saw a thin sliver of pink cut the horizon and the sky begin to lighten. It was almost dawn. She knew they needed to get airborne before the machines radioed for help. Amber used her penlight to search the survival kit Marsden had told her the planes carried.

Her hand closed on the kit and she tugged it open without removing it from the straps that held the container securely to the cockpit side. She had them… flares. Amber pulled out two of the flares, opened the canopy, and lit the flares. She tossed them at the massed army of machines. The flares were phosphorous, bright and nasty and if the machines depended on infrared, the light from the flares would saturate their sensors.

A few minutes later, other flares appeared around Roger's plane then Marsden's, following her example. The machines scuttled around, running into each other, and she knew her guess was correct. She heard the motor on Marsden's plane engage as it roared to life. She closed her canopy, sinking into the unfamiliar seat and buckling the harness that secured her to it. There was no time for further study of the controls; she would have to depend on the diagrams Marsden had drawn back at camp and that she and Roger had memorized. They had to take off and fly to Crittenden's camp, like the crow flies, Marsden had said. If they failed, they would not eat crow; they would be the food for the carrion feeder.

~ * ~

October 9, 1961 (Universe 0)

Gordo was lost, driving along unfamiliar roads and detours shoved in place by builders anxious to complete the new housing developments mushrooming around the battlefield park. Dawn inched across the eastern horizon when Gordo heard the first pulse of a siren. The police car pulled in behind him, blue and red lights flashing as it tailed the sedan he was driving.

"Now what?" Gordo wondered aloud. He could not be captured, but if he ran, the police would follow. Worse, he was almost out of gas. He floored the accelerator and the car leaped ahead.

The state trooper, surprised by the action, took a few seconds to accelerate after his quarry. That gave Gordo the time he needed. He cut a sharp right and drove the car into a tangle of brush. He slammed the car into park and jumped from it without cutting the motor.

His plan was to run into the woods that fanned out behind the brush. He started through the thick vegetation, but his foot touched empty space and he tumbled into a narrow gorge. He rolled to a stop, the transfer device slipping from his hand. A thick patch of thorny, dried blackberry canes immediately swallowed the device.

"Oh shit!" Gordo cursed, prying the canes aside, his fingertips just brushing the device. His ears caught the sound of the patrol car stopping and the static of a radio.

"You down there, are you hurt?"

Gordo pried apart more canes. He could almost touch it. His fingers poked at the object, pushing it further out of his reach.

"Damn," he swore.

"You, down there, answer me!" the trooper shouted, but his voice was drowned out by the sound of the sedan Gordo had abandoned. The gear had slipped and the car had started over the incline. Weeds and vines clung to it with dried fingers but failed to stop the progress.

Gordo looked up at the sound and saw the blue sedan creeping toward him, gaining momentum as it plowed through the brush. He forgot about the thorns and hurled his body over the springy blackberry canes. He grabbed the transfer device and fumbled for the activation switch.

The warning words of the trooper were garbled by Gordo's pulse throbbing in his ears. "Open, open," he thumbed the switch with slippery hands.

The portal appeared, as the car reached him. Gordo jumped through the opening, fell on his back and stared at the sedan speeding toward him. As it reached the mouth of the portal, it was swallowed when the portal collapsed into a black maw. The device abruptly powered down.

~ * ~

October 9, 1861(Universe 1)

Gordo lay back against a mass of dried leaves panting and staring at gray light filtering through the orange-gold canopy above him. Sweat traced an icy finger along his back. He swallowed air for a moment, gulping as a drowning man does. His mind served up an image of the portal winking out of existence when the bullets went through it in the cornfield. But what he had just witnessed left him dizzy. The Void had eaten the sedan. Where had the car gone? Maybe to the safe place everyone put things they can never later find, or perhaps where socks go that disappeared from a dryer.

"I'd hate to have to explain what just happened to my insurance company."

Gordo shook aside the bizarre thoughts as his pulse slowed and his breathing steadied. Blood trickled from the cuts on his hands. He shoved the transfer device into his pocket and removed a handkerchief. Dabbing at his wounds, he lay still, gazing again at the canopy of leaves, thinking about his narrow escape.

They had taken no first aid kit in case anyone was hurt, though Reed had given them an enhancer patch when they first arrived. In fact, he mused, he and Marsden had thought about little except stealing the planes. So intent was Gordo on reviewing what he and the others had planned, that he did not hear the approach of the soldier until the man spoke.

"Get up." The order came from a young soldier in gray.

Gordo glanced to his right to find he was staring down the barrel of a very large rifled musket. He came close to having an accident.

"Get up." The soldier motioned with the musket. "You ain't armed and you can't be tryin' to sneak into camp. I heard you clean across the woods."

Gordo got slowly to his feet. "I lost my way. I'm here to speak with Colonel Crittenden; he's head of intelligence."

"You best see Lieutenant Taylor first." The young man motioned with his musket.

Gordo moved through the woods, stumbling in the wan morning light. He reached an encampment that was part of a larger one filling the meadow before him with tents and huts. Taylor asked him if he was an informant for Crittenden and Gordo replied that he was. He had important information for Crittenden, so important that he had to bring it to the colonel in person.

Taylor accepted the story and ushered Gordo through the maze of regiments encamped on the open field. It was dawn when they reached the area used as headquarters by General Lee. Taylor asked about Crittenden and was directed to a small clearing where Crittenden leaned against a tree drinking coffee.

The expression on Crittenden's face was a mixture of shock and anxiety. He tossed away the dregs of coffee in the cup he held and stood away from the tree.

"What are *you* doing here?" Crittenden's eyes took in the twentieth century clothing Gordo was wearing. His expression hardened. "Now what have you been up to?"

Gordo cleared his throat. "Did you receive a telegram from Major Robbins?"

Crittenden nodded, and motioned for Taylor to leave. The lieutenant saluted and walked away. "Yes, it said something about flying machines on the Zeller farm."

Gordo bit his lips. This was not going to be easy. "Well, we went after three of them. See, the way Rich and I figure, those people are coming,"

"You did what?" Crittenden's face grew crimson.

"We went after them."

"Who?"

"Rich, me, Amber, and Roger."

Crittenden made a vacant gesture. "How? Why?"

"Well, how takes a bit, but the why I was about to tell you. There are seven of those planes on that field and they are fighters, as well as able to carry a payload of bombs."

Crittenden rubbed his temples. "Taking those machines will alert the people at that farm."

Gordo frowned, sensing something was amiss. "Colonel, you don't understand. Those planes are armed. They're not going to be used for reconnaissance. They're ready for combat."

"You don't realize what you have done." Crittenden covered his face with his hands for a moment before looking at Gordo.

"We've just saved your bacon," Gordo explained. "Now you have three planes, or will have as soon as Rich and the two kids get them to your camp."

Crittenden thundered. "You're taking those flying machines to my camp!"

Crittenden's outcry had the effect of stopping all action within fifty feet. It also drew the attention of another officer standing about twenty yards away. The man hurried toward Crittenden.

"Alex, what's happened?" he asked.

Gordo turned to the newcomer and the color left his face. He had seen the image of the man in the history texts of his universe, only the image was of an older, worn version. The man before him still had dark hair, his eyes were clear, his posture straight. He glanced from Crittenden to Gordo.

"This is Gordon Sykes, General," Crittenden introduced Gordo. "Gordo, this is General Lee, commander of the army."

"You look better than you did in my universe," Gordo said without thinking, still unprepared for both the man and the meeting.

"Mr. Sykes?" Lee inclined his head a fraction.

"Of course, in my universe you're dead, so you can't help but look better here," Gordo observed. He saw the expression in Lee's eyes and realized the man was gauging his sanity. Apparently he found it wanting.

"Colonel?" Lee turned to Crittenden for an explanation.

"Mr. Sykes is one of the scientists I told you about. Their universe is somewhat more advanced historically than ours."

Lee rubbed his temple in confusion. "I remember your tale. But what is the problem now?"

"Mr. Sykes and his friends have just stolen three…" Crittenden did not finish.

Gordo heard it too, the sound of propellers cutting through the morning air. He looked toward the planes, flying in an echelon formation as if the three had done this before.

"They're using this camp as a benchmark," Gordo said. He stole a glance at the two officers, but both men had fixed their gaze on the planes.

Gordo heard a horse whinny, the sound of a cup being dropped, the rustle of leaves as an early morning breeze teased life into the woods surrounding the field. He looked around to see everyone staring at the sky, mouths opened in horror or awe, he couldn't tell which.

The planes were visible for only a few seconds before they headed toward the south and Crittenden's camp.

"The fence," Gordo said. "Colonel, you've got to telegraph Major Robbins and have your men removed that fence around the field where you sometimes keep the horses."

Crittenden looked at Gordo. "Why?"

"They need a place to land and Rich will choose the field. It's flat and the ground isn't rutted."

Lee ignored Gordo for the moment. "Those," he took a deep breath. "Those machines are what you were telling me about?"

Crittenden nodded. "But I had no idea they were so big, so powerful."

"They're only P-40s." Gordo stopped. To these people, he thought, they're a disaster.

Lee took a deep breath. "You and your friends have no idea what you have done," he said.

"Though seeing what I just have tells me it would not have mattered in the long run."

Gordo looked from Lee to Crittenden. "I don't understand."

"He has more than upset plans," Crittenden said to Lee.

"True, but with such as that…" Lee gestured to the sky.

"Gordo, you said something about bombs," Crittenden asked.

Gordo's face pinched into a frown. "Yes, they carry bombs, why?"

Lee answered "Three days hence, both President Davis and President Lincoln will meet on this field under a flag of truce. We are charged with their protection, as will be General Wilcox of the Union Army."

"You can't protect them against an airplane." Gordo stopped as he realized what the men implied. "Oh my God, you were keeping this secret from everyone. We took the planes; we tipped your hand."

Lee nodded. "Yes, but I would not waste time in recriminations, Mr. Sykes. Seeing those flying machines tells me there was little we could have done to protect anyone."

"But those people at the farm have only four planes left," Gordo insisted. "Rich could take them out single handed." Gordo stopped. "Why are the presidents meeting like this?"

"Come with us, Mr. Sykes," Lee insisted, taking Gordo by the arm. "It's time you learned about the very great danger facing all of us."

"Rich was right," Gordo said as he walked with Lee.

"This man you spoke of as stealing those flying machines?"

"Rich Marsden," Gordo explained. "He must have known or must have guessed."

"Guessed what?" Lee stopped walking.

Gordo took a deep breath. "This universe is about to be invaded."

~ * ~

Sig, standing in the secure room of the Embassy Club, stared at the computer screen, his eyes bulging as he read the terse message. Three planes were gone and no one knew how. Dozens of security robots had damaged sensors and one robot had been fried by electromagnetic radiation.

"Damn," he swore. "We've been depending on those mechanical security robots." He was partly to blame, he knew. This challenge between San and Brie had usurped all plans for the invasion. Orders had become haphazard and General Vrill was busy in talks with Brie.

"Get me planes to replace the ones we lost," Sig ordered his Chief of Staff.

"Sir, who stole those planes? No one in this universe can fly."

"Colonel Tam, the scientists are responsible. The planes went south, which means they are with the Confederates."

"What about Davis? We knew Lincoln would reject our offer."

"So did Davis. Their 'honor their countries' honor' be damned." Sig swore. Neither president seemed to get the irony of their own enslavement when both side still held slaves. But they had refused to surrender.

"The presidents are going to meet at Manassas and we are going to take them out and much of their armies, leaving both nations leaderless and in confusion."

"The army isn't ready for invasion yet," Colonel Tam protested. "If the scientists took the planes, can they use them?"

Sig drew his index finger across his lower lip. "As far as I know, only this retired Air Force officer would be able to do so, he and this Gray Eagle. The others are mere children."

"They stole three of our planes," Tam again reminded her superior.

"Yes, and they have just upped the odds." Sig grinned. "They come after us, we'll destroy them and that will leave no one to help this universe." *As if those petty scientists could have been of any help in the first place.*

"Three replacement P-40s," Tam said.

Sig nodded. If Brie, Vrill, and the Command Council wanted to waste time on some stupid challenge, let them, Sig thought. A simple display of air power will drive all hope from the inhabitants of this universe. In the confusion that follows, we will sweep both armies aside and take what we want.

Seventeen

Never shove someone off the fence unless you know on which side they will fall.
Codex of Flowering Butterfly

October 10, 1861 (Universe1)

"Where is Gray Eagle?" Marsden demanded.

Crittenden's face was drawn and Marsden realized the man was tired. Crittenden had arrived by train that morning along with Gordo. His arrival was not as spectacular as Marsden's the previous day. Marsden was grateful Crittenden telegraphed Robbins to remove the fences and horses from the field. Now if he had only remembered to remove the horse manure, but one does have to deal with a learning curve.

Crittenden sat at the sturdy wooden kitchen table nursing a cup of coffee. "I don't know where they are. There was some difficulty with the trains near Petersburg and that's the last I heard from their escort."

Marsden accepted a cup of coffee from Bea. He stared at the dark liquid in the blue-spattered tin cup. “Look, Alex. If we can get Gray Eagle here, he and I can fly the planes.”

“But Gray Eagle is in Petersburg and it may take two days before he can arrive.”Crittenden sighed.

Marsden shook his head as Gordo, Amber, and Roger came into the room. “Get a message to Gray Eagle. Tell him to get here by any means possible. He’s got that transfer device. He can cross, get a car, and drive here faster in some other universe than he can get here by train in this one.”

“The planes are in good condition.” Gordo slumped into the chair next to Crittenden. “I had some of your artillery people help me remove the bombs. Hope you don’t mind, Colonel.”

Crittenden stared at Gordo. “Mind? I don’t even understand.”

“Less load with the bombs gone,” Amber explained. “The planes will fly faster, use a bit less fuel.”

“We can go with you,” Roger told Marsden. “We got them here and we know how to fly them.”

Marsden swung to face Roger. “You’ve never flown in combat. Your trip here is your only experience in a fighter. Gray Eagle flew P-40s in combat.”

“He’s not here and we are,” Amber reminded Marsden. “Besides, we’ve done aerobatics in planes modeled after P-51s.”

“We can practice,” Roger suggested.

"No you can't." Marsden slammed his cup on the table, coffee splashing onto the clean surface. He felt his temper rise, goaded by fear of their suggestions. "We don't have any more fuel but what the planes already have. We don't have any more bullets either."

"Maybe you can take out three planes, or four planes," Amber interrupted. "But what if there are more? Can you take out seven or eight?"

"Can you?" Marsden countered.

Crittenden intervened. "I'll have Robbins contact Gray Eagle with your suggestion."

"It's my fault," Marsden grimaced. He wondered if his reckless act was due more to his love of flying, than to his fear that this universe was being invaded and that his might be next. "Maybe it's because I see myself as the world's oldest fighter pilot."

"In this universe, you're the world's only fighter pilot, besides Gray Eagle." Amber patted him on the arm.

"It's no one's fault," Crittenden said. "Those people who are about to invade us have a name. They call themselves Khysids."

"Khysids?" Marsden stared at Crittenden. "Where did you learn that?"

"From the ultimatum they sent to President Davis," Crittenden replied. "I presume they also sent one to President Lincoln. It's rather an ironic message."

"I don't understand." Marsden took a rag from Bea and wiped the coffee from beneath his cup.

"You were correct about an invasion." Crittenden looked at Marsden. "The ultimatum told us to lay down our arms and become servants of the Khysids, or die like the vermin we are."

"So that's why you were at the camp, why the presidents are meeting," Amber said. "Makes a somewhat moot point of the slavery issue, doesn't it?"

Crittenden nodded. "Indeed, these Khysids have turned the war on its ear."

"What about our universe?" Amber wondered.

Marsden looked at her, seeing the pain and fear in her eyes. She was right. If these people fell, his universe could be next. Then another and another; the feared domino effect that had governed western policy since the Korean War was being played out on a much larger scale.

Marsden came to a decision. "I'll brief you and Roger as if you were going to accompany me."

Gordo jumped to his feet. "No! They're just kids."

"So were the men who flew in the war you and Rich fought. They were our age," she gestured to Roger and herself.

"I'll brief you as if you were going to accompany me," Marsden started over again, his mind presenting him various options as he spoke. "Have Robbins set up a telegraph line close to the field where we put the planes. If Gray Eagle gets here in time, there will be no problem."

"If he doesn't, then what?" Crittenden stared at Marsden.

"I want to know the number of planes that take off from that Zeller farm. If there are four, I can handle them. If there are more, then I will need help."

"And if you don't have Gray Eagle?" Crittenden looked at the two young people standing next to Marsden.

"I'll teach you some tricks that may be of use." Marsden looked first at Amber, then at Roger.

He lied about being able to handle four planes. He had no idea about the capability of the fighters he was going against. He tried to convince himself that Amber and Roger had already flown fighters with which they were unfamiliar. They had gotten the planes to camp, landed in a field that was less than desirable, and did it as if they were comfortable with the P-40.

But that had been level flight, not the stomach-twisting confrontations of aerial combat. Still they had flow aerobatics. If they worked in tandem, flew as a team, that would almost be the same as two against one. Their salvation might lie in their knowledge of aerobatics.

"It may work," Marsden said aloud, aware that everyone was staring at him.

"And if it doesn't?" Gordo countered.

Marsden slowly shook his head. “It has to, Gordo. There are no options.”

~ * ~

It was evening when the telegraph operator at the Petersburg station received the message. He handed it over to the young corporal assigned to the task of decoding messages. But the man could make no sense of it and it fit none of the ciphers in use. He took it to his superior.

“What does it say?” Lieutenant Zimmer glared at the soldier.

“It reads, ‘Gray Eagle, transfer, get a car and drive to Crittenden’s camp at Warrenton. We need you to fly a P dash 40.”

Zimmer held up his hand. “Enough, Sands, now what does it really say?”

“But sir, that’s just it. That’s what it says.”

“Shit.” Zimmer spat tobacco juice into a spittoon, narrowly missing the edge. “Major Harker forgot to give us the new cipher book. Now how are we supposed to interpret this?”

Sands shrugged. “But this Gray Eagle, he’s with that party General Lee was having escorted to Warrenton.”

“Send the message to Lee at Manassas. Maybe he can make sense of it. That Colonel Crittenden will be there in any case.”

Zimmer saluted and left his superior’s office, wondering just what sort of nonsense espionage was up to this time.

~ * ~

October 10, 1861

"Sir, we've intercepted a telegraph message to General Lee," the officer said as he saluted Sig.

Sig looked up from his work. He leaned back against the chair, and sighed. "Is it important?"

So many of the messages from that simple technology were intercepted that his office was filled with their junk. Power leeches placed on the various wires used the current to download and translate the simple codes. The results were radioed to nearby transceivers.

The officer said, "Oh yes, sir. This one is directed to one of those scientists. Someone called Gray Eagle."

Sig snatched the thin computer from the officer. A narrow smile etched across his lips as he read the contents. "So this Air Force colonel is alone." He grinned. "How many planes do we have?"

"Seven," the officer replied. "We should have ten more by next week."

"Seven will do nicely, give the boys and girls practice against him before they get rid of him." Sig rose. "Make sure they bomb the field first."

The officer saluted and hurried away.

~ * ~

October 12, 1861

As if in answer to Marsden's unspoken prayer, the weather was crisp, cool and clear. The sky was a deep, blue pool and ribbed clouds were all that remained of the cold front. Marsden, Amber, and Roger stood beside the airplanes on a cleared section of the field serving as a runway.

Marsden felt the tremor of excitement in his stomach that he always felt before combat. He briefed Roger and Amber as thoroughly as he could. He had them go through the motions of charging and clearing the guns, should they jam. But for all the things he could tell them, he could not explain what it would be like to go up against planes in a fight, especially without any previous experience.

The P-40s were armored and had self-sealing tanks. Still, neither of the young pilots had combat training in such planes. He could only pray that their training in aerobatics gave them the confidence to handle the fighters and the edge to defeat them.

Reed, Rierdon, and the others had been furious with him for agreeing to let Amber and Roger fly. But he really had no choice. Today, on that field in Manassas, both presidents would sit down for an historic meeting. The results would determine the fate of this universe and maybe that of others as well. And out there hid a nebulous army called the Khysids. Their purpose was invasion and their intentions were to kill the men meeting on that field.

Marsden heard the click of keys echo from the new location of the telegraph line, just fifty feet from his plane. He wanted to keep the engines running, but they had to conserve fuel. They would have to start, take to the skies, and race the planes from the Zeller Farm to Manassas.

The operator, stopped, took a brush and painted a number on the sheet as the prearranged signal. Marsden glanced at the number and his heart sank. His only thought as he climbed into his plane was that at least they carried parachutes.

~ * ~

Gray Eagle galloped ahead, having taken Hargrove's horse at the captain's insistence. The garbled message about the P-40 had gotten to him as the train arrived in Warrenton. His stomach twisted with fear, his mind serving up the vision he had experienced on that runway in California so many months ago.

He urged the horse, digging his heels into its side, angry that he had to treat the animal so, but there was little time. The fencing for the farm came into view, stopping abruptly where it had been removed to accommodate the planes. He saw the tents, the farmhouse, the horses tethered far from the landing field.

His horse shied and he fought it for control as the sound of airplane motors thundered across the tops of the trees. He glanced up at the three P-40s taking to the sky, swallowing his scream with their roar. Three of them, with white blotches on their wings, flew toward Manassas. He knew then what he had not known in that vision: the reason for the hastily painted splotches. They were going against planes with the same markings and the paint was to identify them as friendly. And he also knew the name of the third pilot: Colonel Richard Marsden.

~ * ~

The formal greetings completed, the two presidents seated across from one another began discussions. Crittenden's neck muscles ached from the tension surrounding the field as he glanced at the presidents. Lee and Wilcox stood to on the left of both presidents of the small platform, decorated with red, white, and blue bunting, watching the drama unfold. Lincoln was animated while Davis remained detached.

Crittenden stood to the right of the platform several yards from a telegraph station manned by operators from both sides. He removed his watch, glanced at it, and frowned. It read ten-thirty. His intuition told him something was very wrong. He felt a sudden tap on his shoulder and an officer handed him a message.

He read the words, 'Nothing yet,' and the notation Rhea always used to indicate it was her message. It was absolutely wrong, he thought. This was not from Rhea, his informant. Something had happened.

"Who sent this?" His sharp demand startled the officer.

"It came from Grover's Mill, sir."

"Send this to my camp, The Zeller Farm, when and how many?"

"Yes, sir."

"Now, Lieutenant, and fast!"

As the officer scurried away, Crittenden caught Lee and Wilcox staring at him, but he ignored them for the moment. His attention was focused on the telegraph station. His stomach twisted with fear as he sensed the danger growing around him. His eyes scanned the field for some sort of protection when, not if, they had to take cover.

Major Benjamin Mobrey crossed from the cluster of Union officers standing beside the telegraph station to his old commander.

"Alex, is something wrong?"

Crittenden swung to face Mobrey and smiled. "Ben, it's so good to see you again."

"Good to see you too."

He took Mobrey by the arm and tugged him a few steps away from everyone. "Something is drastically wrong, I can sense it." He felt Mobrey's body stiffen in his grasp. Mobrey knew about his intuition.

"Is Lincoln in danger?"

"We're all in danger." Crittenden looked up as the lieutenant approached him, holding out a slip of paper. Crittenden tore the paper from his hand and read the message: Zeller Farm, they're off, 10:15, seven."

Mobrey glance over Crittenden's shoulder at the message. "What does it mean?"

Crittenden's eyes scanned the horizon for the planes, while his ears strained to hear the distant humming he associated with the machines. There, he thought, not quite, but my mind tells me they are near.

He turned to Mobrey. "Get them out of that damned area and into," he glanced around. "There, over there toward that old stone millrace. The flying machines are coming!"

Wilcox darted to the edge of the raised platform, Lee close behind. He glared at Crittenden. "What the hell's the matter?"

Crittenden pointed to the horizon. "That!" he shouted. The sound was muffled and distant, but Crittenden knew it was only a matter of a few moments before the planes were above them.

"Get the presidents to that stone millrace, toward that depression in the wooded area. It's a natural trench." He briefly wondered what good a trench would be since the pilots of the planes should be able to see them from their position above the field.

Wilcox started down the two steps, glanced at the sky and froze for a second. "My God!"

"Edmund," Lee called, ushering the two presidents toward the steps.

Wilcox grabbed Lincoln by the arm and rushed him across the field while his staff followed. Lee did the same for Davis.

"The millrace!" Crittenden shouted, urging everyone to take cover, what little cover was available. He dragged Mobrey with him, throwing the man onto the ground and dropping beside him as the first bomb slammed into the platform. It tore the meeting area apart, leaving a small crater behind. Debris rained on Crittenden and Mobrey.

Crittenden stood, dragging Mobrey with him. "Quickly, get the hell off the field," he ordered and the two ran for the protection of the clogged millrace.

The millrace had been hollowed out of native stone, thick and deep. It angled off to the side, offering some protection to anyone hiding within it. Trees grew around the long abandoned mill, rooted in the tough soil, and filling the area. Crittenden glanced toward the telegraph station, where officers and men from both sides, clustered in a tight mass; both flags held by standard bearers were dangerously visible.

What are they doing? His breath caught in his throat as the second bomb struck almost on top of the mass, destroying the cluster as the previous bomb had destroyed the platform. And Crittenden understood. The two companies were the ceremonial companies for each president. They were acting as if the presidents were with them, not hiding in the millrace.

Segments of bodies flew in all directions, but Crittenden forced himself to watch. Tears slid along his cheeks at the sight. He knew in his heart that after that scene, the men in both armies would never again fight one another. He prayed the presidents knew it, too.

His ears caught the sound of more planes as Mobrey dragged him from his exposed position deeper into the congested area around the millrace. Bombs rained on the field and on the men who had not been able to find cover. One dropped within a dozen yards of the millrace.

Just as quickly as it began, the bombing stopped. Crittenden rose, moved from his cover, and stared at the sky. Mobrey shouted to him to get back, but he couldn't. Something was happening in the sky above Manassas. The flying machines were shooting at one another.

~ * ~

Amber watched the people on the field scattering like blue and gray ants. Horses fled as segments of the field erupted, spewing earth skyward like miniature volcanoes. The planes from the Zeller farm had broken formation and were swarming around the field at a low altitude.

She heard Marsden's voice in her ears. "Keep together. You will do better as two against one, copy?"

"Copy?" she answered, smiling as she remembered Roger insisting on using that word rather than Roger.

"Break!" Marsden called and he was gone. In fact, she realized, the sky was empty.

She'd lost sight of Marsden's plane and could not see Roger anywhere. Then she saw Marsden diving toward a P-40 flying across the field strafing the men huddled on the ground. She banked right, coming in behind what she thought was Marsden's plane, when she realized Roger's plane was in front of her.

"How does anyone keep track of the action?" she said, frustrated by the confusion. She climbed away from the pair, knowing that this was not a movie. This was real, maybe too real and she had no idea what she was doing. Only Marsden seemed to know.

Her stomach twisted as she realized how stupid she and Roger had been to think their training in aerobatics was preparation for this melee. But her mind cautioned that they were in it and their training was all they had.

She saw a P-40 cartwheel across the field and her heart sank, until she realized it carried no white paint on its wing. Someone had shot it from the sky, but she had no idea who was responsible. There was no chatter in her earphones; the air was silent. She heard only the roar of her own motor.

Suddenly a plane popped up before her, directly in her path. She jumped in shock while her mind registered it was an enemy plane. She charged her guns and got the enemy within her optical sight before she was conscious of her actions. Amber fired a burst at the plane. Her eyes caught the tracer rounds that seemed to move in slow motion reaching out like fiery bolts toward the tail of the enemy plane. The tracers were followed by the armor piercing and exploding rounds that tore into the aircraft. Oily smoke billowed from the stricken fighter. She was close enough to see the smoke fill the cockpit as the fighter began a death spiral.

"Pull up!" Marsden's voice echoed in her ears. "Don't hang around to watch!"

"Yes, copy," she gasped, climbing away from the dying aircraft. She frantically looked around for more, but saw nothing. "Where is everyone?"

"Watch for them, keep alert. We've taken out two," Marsden ordered. "Nice job," he complimented.

The acrid smell of the gun's exhaust filled her cockpit. Her hands were sweaty on the stick and the plane suddenly felt like a tank. She remembered what Gray Eagle had told them when he had trained them in aerobatics. Extend yourself into the plane as if it were part of your being. It was not simply his training as a shaman that had taught him this, but his time in Japan after the war. It was a belief in the Martial Arts that a warrior who became one with her weapon was unbeatable.

~ * ~

Roger banked away from fire directed toward him that seemed to come out of nowhere. Where was Amber? Where was Marsden? He had lost the colonel after their first pass across the field. He heard the exchange between Amber and Marsden, for the channels were open. Gordo had switched frequencies so that the Khysids could not hear them. But Roger wished for the multi-channel devices he had seen in the 2014 universe. That way he could hear the Khysids as well.

He wished for a wingman also, or wingperson as the politically correct universes would call them. At this moment, he wished for anyone as he twisted and turned in his seat to see what was happening around him. One of the planes from the Zeller farm dove at him, but he saw it in time and climbed away. The two planes passed within inches of each other, the enemy plane recovering for another try.

Calling on his training in precision flight, Roger imagined the plane that had attacked him was part of his team. He turned and stuck to it with the tenacity of super glue. The enemy pilot tried to shake him as the two planes began a macabre dance across the sky.

Roger charged his gun, dropped back and fired as the pair dove toward the ground. He pulled out of the dive, but his quarry continued into the ground exploding in a massive fireball. Roger climbed then leveled off. He twisted in his seat to see what was happening. "Colonel Marsden, do you copy? Amber, do you copy?" There was no reply. "Please," he begged.

"Where is everyone?" Amber's voice spread relief through Roger.

"Beats the hell out of me? I just shot down one of the planes."

"Good." Marsden's voice filled his earphones. "That makes four, I took out two. There are three more at two o'clock."

Roger was then aware of another plane on his right.

"Roger, the two of us can get that straggler," Amber suggested.

"Together, like that clever little maneuver we used to do in the air shows."

"Copy, Roger!" she called and they pursued the retreating planes.

~ * ~

"No, wait," Marsden ordered. He was behind them, his hands clutching the stick as if it were a lifeline and he could reel them in. "Let the bastards go!" he shouted, realizing that cursing was as much a part of combat as dying.

Before his eyes, his two protégés took out a third plane and the remaining P-40s were retreating as if the devil were on their tails. They'd downed five planes, more than he could have hoped for and better than he had imagined.

"Hey you two!" he called. "Let's go home, copy?" He did a snap roll and Amber and Roger copied his movements, regaining formation as easily as if they had done it a thousand times. *It was a good thing,* he thought, *they were not as cocky as most of the pilots he'd trained. Just wait till they see the holes in their planes. Thank God nothing important had been hit. Thank God for self-sealing tanks.*

~ * ~

"Alex," Mobrey was beside Crittenden, tugging at the sleeve of his uniform. "I have never seen the like."

"Nor have I." Crittenden wet his lips, as he sought to keep a pair of planes in sight of his field glasses. "My God, what a sight!"

"Alex. May I?" Lee stepped beside him.

Crittenden looked away, realized what Lee wanted, and offered him the field glasses. Wilcox was standing next to Lee. Crittenden looked over his shoulder to the men huddled in the millrace.

They were standing, forming a protective shield around the presidents. But Lincoln was trying to extricate himself from the mass despite the protest of Nathan McBride.

Crittenden smiled in spite of what had happened. He suspected Lincoln's attempted destination was the field glasses Lee had just offered to Wilcox.

The three remaining Khysid planes dashed northeast, but were pursued. One was shot from the sky before the pursuers regained the formation they had used when they had approached the fight. The three planes rotated about their axis and sped south toward his camp. Crittenden let out his breath in a slow sigh.

"You are Colonel Alex Crittenden?" The voice startled Crittenden and he jumped. He turned to face Lincoln.

"Yes, Mr. President."

"And those flying machines, I understand they are returning to your camp?"

"Yes sir. The scientists are there also," he confessed.

Lincoln nodded. "Will they help us in our fight against the Khysids?"

Crittenden nodded. "That is their intention, sir."

"I've finished speaking with Mr. Davis and we agree. Can you get us more?"

"More what, Mr. President?"

"More flying machines and people to fly them. More of whatever we need to prosecute this war?"

Crittenden smiled at Lincoln. “That, sir, is my intention.”

He glanced at Mobrey staring in awe at Lincoln, and Crittenden felt the tension slide from his mind. Lincoln had said the magic words, he thought. He had included both the Union and Confederacy against the Khysids. Crittenden knew Lincoln was the bridge that would span the two sides. That had been his intentions when he was elected. Crittenden sensed that a common enemy would create a tighter bond than glue.

Eighteen

A cascade once started cannot be reversed.
Codex of Flowering Butterfly

Universal Time 1.00.10.14.61 (Universe 61)

Sig's hand trembled as he read the display on the computer sheet. The contents showed a copy of a dispatch from Lee's headquarters. The computer reproduced whatever was sent to it or scanned by it, so the dispatch Sig read was in Lee's handwriting.

Rage filled his chest, spilling over into a tantrum. He threw a container of memory modules across the quarters he occupied at Command Central.

"First they steal my planes. Then they dare take out my planes. Now this!" he smacked the computer sheet. As reason slowly returned, he let his mind dwell on different possible actions the two armies might take. An alliance against the Khysids was not one he had imagined, but then neither had his superiors.

He stormed from his quarters to the seclusion room where San and Vrill were preparing for the challenge. Sentries jumped aside as he entered the staging area, fearing to be dragged along in the wake of his rage. Sig planted his palm on the control panel and muttered.

"Access code ninety-one, twenty-three, thirty - six emergency."

The door split, allowing Sig entrance into the chamber. Muted light greeted him; an aura of comfort and peace reigned inside. Colors of serenity in variations of purple, lilac and rose were reflected in the cushioned mats and recessed seating. A crystal fountain offset to one side of the round, domed room bled water over stones with a soothing gurgle.

San and Vrill were deep in meditation. Jolted by Sig's entrance into the chamber, they glared at him as he approached. The soft ambiance of the room did nothing to cool his temper.

"This challenge has got to stop!" he roared, throwing the thin sheet computer at Vrill. "You can stop this. You head the field army."

Vrill ducked the incoming missile. "I can stop nothing. A challenge has been called and it has to be completed."

"Those scientists stole three of my planes and used them to take out five of my fighters over Manassas. Both presidents are still alive and pissed as hell. That," Sig pointed to the sheet computer on the floor before San, "indicates the two armies are cooperating."

"It's unimportant," San offered. "The standard historical sequence for that universe is dead. We will invade it."

"If you live, San," Vrill smacked his lips as if he tasted some delicious treat.

"I'll live," San countered.

"Well, I'm not waiting for this challenge to be completed." Sig folded his arms across his chest. "That computer I tossed in your direction holds a copy of a dispatch sent by Lee. It's an order to cease all hostilities and offer any help to the Union Army that it needs against us."

"Sig, you have my orders." Vrill unwound from his meditative posture and stood. "Now carry them out."

"If I wait to send the preliminary invasion force across, it will give the scientists time to prepare."

Vrill clenched his fists. "Prepare what, you idiot? They have only two transfer devices."

"As far as we know," Sig retorted.

Vrill ignored the words. "They know nothing important about the Source Gates, nothing about the Jewels. What the hell can they prepare?"

Sig dropped his hands to his side. "They stole three of my planes."

"That's because you depended on mechanical sentries. Use human sentries from now on and the mechanical as an adjunct. The challenge will begin in a few days and you will attend. After I get rid of this," Vrill gestured to San. "I'll demand a seat on the Council: hers in fact."

"General," Sig protested. "Don't underestimate the people in that universe."

"They're vermin. You'll do as you're ordered, or I'll have you shot for insubordination. Now get the hell out of here!"

Vrill returned to his seat opposite San. Sig clenched and unclenched his fists in impotent fury before storming from the room.

~ * ~

October 14, 1861(Universe 1)

A raw wind drove sheets of rain across the countryside, beating against the windows of the farmhouse. Clumps of leaves, the color of mud, were torn from the trees with each rush of wind. Ignoring the gale, Marsden lifted a tray of cinnamon buns from the wood stove using a folded towel and dropped them on a wooden cutting board on the table. He tilted the baking sheet, forcing the buns onto a serving platter.

"Not every pilot bakes as well as you do." Amber plucked one of the hot buns onto her plate.

"Have to keep up your strength," Marsden countered, placing the empty sheet onto the stove.

He sat opposite Roger and Amber, while Bea came to the table and poured coffee for them. She placed the pot onto the wooden cutting board and sat beside Marsden. The others in the house were still asleep, exhausted from the trip from Bennett, plus a late-night strategy session.

Bea smiled at Marsden. “Pierre used to cook for us when we were at Trevor’s house in Richmond. I do miss him. He is an excellent cook.”

“We need a cook and that’s not your job, even if your cooking is great. You have a house full of people and we should pitch in and help.”

“You are a gem,” Bea said as she smiled at him.

Amber studied the screen on her computer Gray Eagle brought when he and the others arrived. Marsden saw her intense stare and suspected she was glad to have it back.

“Rich’s right about getting help,” Amber mumbled, her mouth filled with the breakfast bun. She swallowed. “Access next file,” she told the computer.

Marsden stared at the rattling windowpanes over the cup of coffee he held. Yesterday he, Gordo and several of the men managed to tie down the P-40s against the storm that came up quickly from the southeast. They needed accurate weather forecasting, and a hanger, more fuel, more ammunition, just about more of everything.

Amber turned the computer screen so he could see it. “These universes are where we found the items Gray Eagle brought from Bennett, including this computer.”

A list of unfamiliar numbers appeared on the screen in some sort of database readout. Marsden squinted at the results. He shrugged.

“Cc seems good at scrounging,” he said.

Amber laughed. “He’s in his element when it comes to getting things.”

Roger nodded. “I guess a degree in anthropology has its uses.”

“Logistics and support of an army being among them,” Marsden said. He changed the subject. “You two were good at Manassas,” he said for the second time. It still amazed him that the pair before him had succeeded, especially since they were untrained in any form of aerial combat. Well, he couldn’t say that anymore after what had happened in the sky over Manassas.

“It wasn’t as easy as we expected,” Amber confessed. “It seemed so simple in the movies.”

“They make it seem simple.” Marsden took a folded towel, lifted the pot and poured more coffee into his cup. “But your instincts are good and your training served you better than I’d hoped.”

Amber smiled at him. “I’m glad we didn’t disappoint you. You were really worried about us.”

“I had reason to be worried.”

She nodded. “Now that we know how to use the planes, well,” she traced out an imaginary line on the table. “We can fly again. But we need better planes, faster, and more maneuverable ones like a P-51 or a Spitfire.”

Marsden nodded. “Been thinking about that. The P-51s are possible, but it will be a bit tricky to get a Spitfire on this side of the Atlantic.”

“A Spitfire?” Crittenden said, standing in the doorway. “Is that the name of one of your flying machines or your pilots?”

"Alex." Bea's face broke into a smile. She jumped from her chair and raced to him. They embraced.

Crittenden dropped the saddlebags he carried in his right hand so he could hold his wife. Marsden saw water drip from the oilcloth coat Crittenden was wearing. Bea stood away from him, her dress and apron wet.

"Sit, please and tell us what happened," Marsden suggested. He caught Bea's odd look at her husband and stared closely at Crittenden as the man removed his wet coat. Crittenden was wearing a different insignia, a wreath enclosing a gold star on each collar.

"I see that you've been promoted," Marsden said. "I gather that insignia is a general's rank?"

"Yes," Crittenden said. "Thanks to you three and what you did. But this is only the beginning." He accepted a cup of coffee from his wife and a cinnamon bun from Amber. "I have something for the three of you and the others from your universe."

Marsden saw the gleam in Crittenden's eyes, and felt his own breath catch in his throat.

"What?"

Crittenden reached into one of his saddlebags and removed a packet of official documents. Marsden noted the folded papers had names written on them. Two seals covered each document. Crittenden offered a document to Marsden.

Marsden accepted the paper with his name, Colonel Richard Marsden, written across the front.

He broke the dual seals and read the document. He reread the document before setting back in his chair.

"I don't know what to say."

"I'm hoping you will say yes," Crittenden replied.

Marsden knew if he accepted the offer, he would never again return to his own universe. But he had already committed himself to these people when he convinced the others to steal the planes. Even before, his mind cautioned, when you let the ISIR people use your house.

"What is it?" Amber's curiosity was such he thought she would reach across the table and snatch the paper from his hand.

"It's a commission in the army," Marsden replied.

"Which army?" she asked.

"Both," Crittenden said. "The two countries will combine their armies under the joint commands of Generals Lee and McClellan."

"McClellan?" Marsden made a face.

Crittenden stared at him. "So, your McClellan had a dubious reputation as well."

Marsden forced a wry smiled. "He could train an army, but using it was another matter."

"Well, Lee preferred Wilcox, but he was not given a voice in the matter. Lincoln had others to appease for now."

"President Lincoln didn't go back to Washington, did he?" Roger asked.

"I'm afraid so. And we did try to persuade him to go to another northern city. But he wanted to avoid panic as he began the evacuation of the Union capital."

"The Khysids have a base in the Embassy Club. They'll see the people leaving," Amber protested. "They'll come after them, won't they?"

Crittenden shrugged. "We have no idea exactly what the Khysids will do. In the meantime," he offered Amber and Roger each a sheet from the packet.

"What are these?" Amber took the folded and sealed sheet and placed it before her.

"It's uncommon, but not without precedent to have women in the army," Crittenden explained. "Lincoln insisted these be given to all the pilots and a commission as well. You two will not start on the bottom rung as I did."

Marsden looked up from his commission. "What?"

"They are given commissions as first lieutenants. That was also at Lincoln's insistence. He convinced Davis to sign the commissions, too."

"Just shows how desperate you are," Marsden said.

Crittenden rubbed his chin. "Oh, I don't know. I will be in command, so that finally gives me…"

"Some real clout with us," Amber muttered.

Crittenden, Bea, and Marsden laughed. Crittenden removed a velvet-covered box from his saddlebag and offered it to Marsden. Marsden accepted the box, opened it, and stared at the insignia it contained.

"Those were my colonel's insignia. I want you to wear them."

Marsden answered, choking back his emotions. "I'd be honored, sir."

"I need to see some of you in the parlor in an hour." Crittenden removed his watch from his pocket and stared at the face. "For now, I must speak with Lieutenant Penfield."

"Will he be sent back to Washington?" Roger asked.

Crittenden gave an abrupt shake of his head. "No, he'll remain with my command. By the way, you will form the core of the Air Cavalry. I hope you like the name. We could think of no other." He stood, glanced at his wife, and said. "Bea, please come with me. This talk with Joshua will take some of your skills as well."

Marsden was on his feet. "What happened?"

"Joshua's parents and young sister were dragged from their carriage as they drove to their hotel in Washington. They were shot and left to die in the street. The act was most likely in revenge for Joshua's work for Lincoln. A note was left indicating such death is to be the fate of all who offer aid to the Khysid's enemies."

Amber raised her hand to her mouth. Marsden saw tears in her eyes and felt the hot grief in his chest as well. It was unfair, but war was always unfair. His heart raced as he pondered the implication of the note.

He knew in his innermost being that the word ‘all’ applied to ISIR personnel. Barstead had to be located and the others in California had to be alerted.

“I have a letter from Nathan McBride for Joshua. Only McBride’s duty to President Lincoln kept him from delivering the message. He blames himself, for he sought out Joshua and asked for his help.”

Marsden shook his head. “No, he’s not to blame, those Khysids are. Reprisals are a way of instilling terror in a civilian populace. ”

“Did this tactic work in your universe?”

Marsden shrugged. “Not always, for civilian resistance continued till the end of the war.”

“Remember, one hour, and see that Rierdon, Reed, Margaret, Gray Eagle, Gordo, and Mary Frances are also there.” Crittenden looked at Amber and Roger. “You two as well.”

Amber and Roger stood. “Yes sir,” they said in unison.

“Well, at least you seem to know something about military protocol.” Crittenden grinned at the pair.

“Not really, General,” Amber replied. “But we can wing it.”

Marsden groaned and exchanged glances with Crittenden, only to find the officer’s eyes filled with laughter.

~ * ~

The clock on the mantel showed it was nearing eight. Crittenden had yet to return from speaking with Joshua. Margaret and Mary Frances sat beside one another on the sofa while Desiree sat on one of the wooden chairs with a needlepoint seat. Her presence had not been requested, but she was there anyway. Reed paced away his annoyance with the situation. He glanced at Gray Eagle sitting next to Roger and Amber, discussing their actions over Manassas.

Marsden heard the door to the house open and bounce against the wall. The sound of someone running along the hall sent a shock wave through him. He jumped to his feet as Joshua raced into the room. The young man's face was wet, his eyes red-rimmed, his mouth a thin line.

"Colonel Marsden." He saluted Marsden.

Marsden stared at Joshua. "Lieutenant?"

"I want to learn to fly those machines," Joshua shouted. "I want to get the people who did this to my family. Fanny was only twelve."

"I understand your feelings," Marsden said. He was faced with a new recruit to his Air Cavalry. "But revenge is a poor motive."

"I can control my emotions, sir," Joshua insisted. "I have spent three years at Harvard studying Natural Philosophy, sir. I have some background."

Probably all of it wrong, Marsden thought. Before he could answer, Elliott raced into the room, coming up behind Joshua.

"Colonel, if you accept Joshua, you have to accept me."

"I suppose you spent your time at VMI studying Natural Philosophy?"

"Heavens no, I had General Jackson as a teacher. He would put an insomniac to sleep."

Marsden laughed as Joshua glared at Elliott. "I remember Jackson's history, or rather the history of the Jackson of my universe. Let Dr. Reed give you both a physical, see what shape you're in. If you pass, Gray Eagle and I will begin to teach you how to fly."

Gray Eagle choked on the coffee Margaret had just given him. He coughed, sputtered, and tried to clear his throat. "How are we going to do that?"

"One of those Merlin's ISIR personnel flew to DC has dual controls. Amber told me about it. We'll need it to teach the soldiers how to fly. How long before you get that Source Gate up and running?"

Gray Eagle stood, dabbing the coffee from his sweater with his handkerchief. He had yet to open his mouth to answer when Crittenden entered the room.

"Yes, Major Gray Eagle," Crittenden said. "How long before you get that Source Gate up and running?"

Marsden beamed with delight. He had just acquired a second in command.

~ * ~

October 18, 1961 (Universe 0)

Barstead sat in his office with about twenty ISIR staff surrounding him. They were hunched forward in chairs, perched on his desk or leaning against the wall. He placed the transfer device on his desk.

"Satisfied?" he asked after his demonstration.

Alyssia bit her lower lip. "Yes, but what are we to do now? Croll has people watching the institute. I'm certain he knows you're in California, if not here at ISIR. He's already bugged Sam and Connie's house."

"That's fine by us." Connie stubbed out her cigarette. "We don't speak at home. Probably drives him crazy. Don't do anything else either for now. If that SOB wants his jollies as a voyeur, he's going to have to get them elsewhere."

"We have to get out of here," Barstead explained. "Croll won't stop at simple intimidation."

"You're right," Alyssia agreed. "But where can we go?"

"To the Warrenton of that universe," Barstead offered.

"We can't get involved in that war," she protested.

"We're already involved. We can't go to Croll and we'll never get to Kennedy. Those Khysids are a danger to us as well. Rich will call any minute. He said he would call back." Barstead knew he needed the call he was waiting for to prove what he said.

"I wondered how he managed to find a phone?" Alyssia asked. "But the demonstration you did with that device convinces me."

"Even if we could get to that universe, how can we get back east?" Sam protested. "If it's 1861 there, we're going to need a wagon train. They don't have the Trans-Pacific railroad yet."

The ringing phone interrupted Barstead's answer. "Hello!" he shouted into the receiver.

"I can hear you, Julian," Marsden replied. "No need to shout. I'm in your universe."

"Does Croll know where you are?"

"No, and he's occupied right now with a message from the president."

"How do you know that?" Barstead demanded.

"I sent it," Marsden replied. "Now listen carefully. You have that speaker arrangement I asked you to construct?"

"Yes, everyone can hear you."

Marsden cleared his throat. "Good. Now our universe is in as much danger as the 1861 universe is. We'll have the Source Gate up and running in a few days, but you will have to get to us using that weak source you discovered."

"How are we to get to you?" Barstead protested.

"Cc is taking care of the arrangements now. I'm giving you the co-ordinates of the universe you will use to get here. It's 1974 there. Cc is arranging for tickets to get everyone east, but in groups of 30 to 40 as if you were doing a tour."

"I've got over three hundred people here."

"You can do it. You are going to end up in that 1974 universe in a section of West Virginia."

"Rich, this device is running out of power. I have no way to recharge it," Barstead told Marsden.

"We'll come get you once you arrive at the destination Cc has chosen. And a warning, you don't have much time to do this. We suspect the

Khysids will come after you as a reprisal for what we did at Manassas."

Barstead's brow puckered. "What did you do at Manassas?"

Marsden ignored the second question. "They recently killed Lieutenant Penfield's family. Like any thug, they use reprisals. You people will be next."

Barstead felt his chest tighten. Not only had they to deal with Croll, but now ISIR had to deal with an army, one with a technology superior to their own. He'd have to convince the others of this fact, convince them to walk from the only home they knew into a war zone. Convince them to leave what they thought of as security for an uncertain future. But if they stayed in this universe, they had no future.

"Well, at least we will have an army to protect us," he muttered.

"You will have two armies. The North and South have joined together to fight the Khysids. They need our help and we now need theirs."

"I understand," Barstead replied. "What do you want us to do?" He listened as he watched the others in the room take in Marsden's directions. Some seemed resigned, but many were excited, though a few were still in varying stages of disbelief. But Sam and Connie beamed at the prospect.

~ * ~

October 20, 1861(Universe 1)

Gray Eagle had commandeered what the men called the stone barn, fighting Rierdon for a section to use as housing for the Source Gate. Rierdon had already divided the barn into various sections as storage areas for the supplies he planned to obtain from other universes. The barn, about thirty yards west of the house, was quite large. The dimensions were at least one hundred and twenty by one hundred feet. A sturdy three-story structure including a stone basement, it had begun life as a distillery before being converted to a barn two years earlier. Not all of it had been used to house farm equipment and animals.

With the help of local stone masons and carpenters, Gray Eagle and Rierdon had an enclosure for the Source Gate constructed on the barn's lowest floor. The large, open space was divided into three rooms and the Source Gate placed in the smallest of the three. This was to ensure security.

Rierdon, using the transfer device and drawing on the energy of the Source Gate in Washington, had been able to procure fuel cells, specialized wiring, cables and heating and ventilation equipment. As the carpenters and masons worked, Gray Eagle and the others reassembled their own Source Gate.

Weber offered some assistance, but spent his time grumbling about being required to live in a tent, while the women had the run of the farmhouse. He wanted indoor plumbing, but was forced to settle for composting toilets in a bathroom installed in the barn.

"We need other things just now, Stan." Reed tried his hand at placating the irascible scientist.

"We will never be clean again," Weber growled as he washed his face with cold water.

"Oh yes we will," Reed insisted. "We'll soon have a water tower and heaters. Alex showed us where the spring that feeds the pond originates. We'll have what we need, including washers and dryers for clothes. If I have to practice medicine here, it's going to be at least twenty-first century medicine with twenty-first century equipment."

"Just keep Amber away from the transfer devices," Weber snorted. His stomach ached with revenge each time he saw her use the equipment.

"Alex is seeing to that," Reed assured him. "Besides, the others from ISIR will be here soon."

Weber dried his hands on a pink terry cloth towel from a batch Rierdon had gotten at a discount mart in a 1978 universe. "How do you know they will come? Not everyone wants to play Boy Scout."

Reed frowned. "In case you haven't heard, we don't have much choice. The Khysids killed Joshua's family and left that threatening note. It was meant for us. The ISIR people are next. Remember that Khysid in Pittsburgh?"

Weber shuddered. "Yes."

"He called you vermin. Seems I heard that kind of thinking before. People you consider vermin you get rid of."

Reed slapped his towel onto the wash stand before the tent he shared with Weber and stormed toward the small brick barn. It had been constructed as part of the original farmstead and was about a few hundred yards from the house and distillery barn. The structure was in the process of being refitted as a hospital where Reed was teaching volunteer physicians the rudiments of modern medicine.

Weber watched Reed's form as the physician hurried away. He finished wiping his hands and carefully folded the towel he had used. Despite Reed's warning, he didn't think Crittenden or anyone in this universe capable of defending him against the Khysids. But Croll and his troops were.

Tomorrow he would play the petulant scientist, insisting that he be given a cot in the building that housed the Source Gate. Since he had seen the security installed, he knew how to circumvent it. He would contact Croll and give him a communicator created by the Gray Eagle, but not a transfer device. By the time he finished with Croll, the general would be doing his bidding.

Let the ISIR people come east, he welcomed that. Once Croll set up the action Weber intended, Weber knew he would take every transfer device and Jewel they had in this universe and maroon the scientists. If the Khysids wanted reprisals, he would give the Khysids the opportunity and the time to take all the revenge they desired.

~ * ~

Universal Time 1.00.10.29.61 (Universe 61)

"Colonel Kester," Brie summoned. Kester, dressed in training fatigues, approached and accepted an EM-Stinger redesigned to give varying degrees of disabling charge. The red line indicated the final, lethal setting.

"Supreme Commander," Kester said with a salute. He stepped back.

Elar directed Kester to stand to one side. He offered Brie an EM-Stinger and waited until Brie took a position opposite Kester.

Kester felt his palms sweating as he recalled the directions drummed into his head from yesterday's briefing. He was to act as San's second. If San died in the fight, so did he, killed by a shot from Elar who was serving as Combat Master. Brie had announced he would be Vrill's second.

Elar took a position in the red circle to Kester's left at an end point in the elliptical fighting arena. This marked the safety zone and no one was permitted into the circle but Elar. The elliptical combat area was mirrored in the elliptical combat arena. Surrounding Kester and the others were officers from the Sixth Level as well as all Command Council Members. Kester's stomach did a flip when he heard the trumpets announcing the beginning of the challenge.

The lighting in the surrounding arena dimmed as San and Vrill in combat armor stepped into their respective red circles opposite Elar. To Kester, San had always loomed large as a superior officer. But dressed in black armor, her face hidden behind a shield, she looked less intimidating when compared to the bulk that was Vrill.

"You know the rules of the challenge," Elar's voice rang out in the arena. "You will fight to the death. Any show of cowardice and the fight will be stopped, the coward and his or her second executed. Is that understood?"

The helmeted figures nodded at Elar. Cal stepped forward. She handed Elar a tapered black wand topped with a red glass sphere. Kester was at a loss as to the purpose of the device. The sphere looked like a Jewel.

"This Jewel will be destroyed when one of you dies," Elar said.

A collective gasp escaped the officers and council members assembled in the viewing section of the arena. Hushed voices became a background murmuring.

Kester jerked erect. That statement made no sense. *If the cache of Jewels was decaying, why destroy one when a combatant died? Why destroy a Jewel at all?*

"That is how it is written in the Deep Archives." Elar's words offered an answer to Kester's unspoken question, and put an end to the whispering by the audience. "We must proceed as it is written. Let the combat begin."

As they had been instructed, San and Vrill stepped from their respective circles into the area designated for combat. Before San could turn and salute Vrill, he used the steel rod he carried to aim a vicious blow at her mid-section. She ducked, but he caught her on the right side.

Kester sucked in his breath. He scanned the arena, noting the possible exists. Through his mind flashed several escape plans. He wondered if he could take out both Elar and Brie before he fled the arena.

Nineteen

The forms may change, but the spirit remains.
Codex of Flowering Butterfly

October 29, 1861(Universe 1)

Two P-40 Kittyhawks flew side by side toward the Zeller Farm. Gray Eagle found his memories of the old plane returning as he flew. He wished Marsden had stolen a better version of the P-40, but knew these were what the Khysids had stored on the field, which Marsden insisted on calling Zeller Field.

Crittenden's informant, Rhea Benton, and the couple she had been staying with had managed to escape the massacre at Grover's Mills conducted by a Khysid squad after she'd sent her telegram.

"And so it begins," Gray Eagle's soft voice filled the cockpit.

"What begins?" Marsden's sharp call burst into Gray Eagle's headset.

"Just my ramblings. It's been a long time since I took to the sky to fight an enemy."

"Keep alert, Medicine Man," Marsden cautioned his friend. "Nothing can happen to either of us; there's too much at stake."

"I know," Gray Eagle replied.

"I don't just mean this universe. Anything happens to us and Amber and Roger are in charge of the squadron. You don't want that, do you?"

Gray Eagle laughed, the joke relaxing him. He adjusted the new headset he wore. Rierdon had managed to locate them and Gordo, Roger and Amber had adapted the electronics in the P-40s to accept the new solid state equipment. Gordo was working on a state of the art display for the pilots.

Rierdon had found a source for several vintage P-51s and was busy negotiating a purchase. Gray Eagle prayed that he and Marsden got back in time to ferry the planes across. God only knew what Amber and the others would do with the fighters before someone stopped them. Simulators may be adequate for beginners, but sooner or later you have to take the stick. He just wanted them to wait until he and Marsden got back. Crittenden needed both planes and pilots in one piece. Besides, finding and storing fuel was a major problem.

"Get the camera ready." Marsden's voice jerked Gray Eagle from his reverie. "We're approaching the field."

"One pass at twelve hundred feet as we agreed?" Gray Eagle asked for confirmation.

"Copy, one pass, oh damn," Marsden growled.

"What?" Gray Eagle wondered if the new digital cameras on Marsden's plane were acting up. Rierdon had insisted the equipment, installed on the belly of the P-40s, would produce better records than adapting the old gun cameras to the newer electronics. But as Gray Eagle looked at the red light on his instrument panel, he realized it was not the digital recorders. It was the mini-radar detector fastened to the instrument panel.

"They imported radar."

"I should have known. Best be ready for a fight."

Gray Eagle followed Marsden as his new commander began a pass over the field. He saw the radar tower, the dish, and several nasty looking devices surrounding the runways. The objects were unfamiliar, but by their structure he suspected a new form of anti-aircraft gun. Gray Eagle braced for fire, an involuntary memory from the war he had never been able to discard. But their planes flew unmolested.

His inner sense hummed, alerted by some vague malaise he could not pinpoint. Danger loomed around him, but he sensed it was not for the P-40s. As he and Marsden finished the pass across Zeller Field, Gray Eagle felt chilled. He sensed that no one was there: the field was empty for the moment. But the chill was not for that realization. His eyes caught sight of what his mind had sensed a few moments ago.

"Let's get out of here," he called to Marsden.

"Copy, Medicine Man. It's homeward bound." Marsden climbed, and Gray Eagle followed. Once they were at ten thousand feet, Gray Eagle switched on his oxygen mask.

"Did you see them?" Gray Eagle asked.

"Yeah."

"I hope Rierdon got those P-51s. I'd like a few Thunderbolts too. But I'd settle for at least two trainers, maybe an AT-6."

"The others can train in the P-40s," Gray Eagle suggested. "But you're right about anyone from this universe. Once we get them able to fly, they will need some sort of trainer."

"Yeah, and we may not have the time we need to really prepare them," Marsden grunted.

"Where do you suppose the Khysids got Messerschmitts on this side of the Atlantic?"

"Damned if I know. But I wonder if whoever had those BF109s would be willing to part with a couple."

"What are German WW II planes doing in this hemisphere? I doubt the Khysids went to some universe and transported them across the Atlantic. That's a big investment."

"Good question," Marsden returned. "I suggest that when we get home, we try and find out."

Gray Eagle felt a knot of fear grow in his stomach at the thought of the new planes sitting on the runways at Zeller Field. It was not simply the presence of the German fighters that disturbed him, but the absence of any Spitfires, or P-51s.

~ * ~

Universal Time 1.00.10.29.61(Universe 61)

San rolled away from the slicing blow aimed at her head, jumping to her feet as she fielded several jabs at her chest. Vrill was alternating both ends of the steel rod issued as the combat weapon of Brie's choice. Topped by a steel arrow-like point at one end and a slicing scalpel blade at the other, the weapon had the reputation of cutting through the special armor worn by both combatants.

Another blow was aimed at her head, but San ducked aside in time, tripping Vrill with the arrow end of her rod. He fell forward and recovered with an awkward roll. When he faced her, her mind tasted his rage and loathing for her. She knew he hated anything he considered weak and he had a special dislike of women officers. San wondered where that had originated, since he had been raised in the coed training pens. It had to be the two years he spent in that 1940 universe.

Vrill attacked again, and San jumped aside, aiming a blow at his crotch. She missed, but he managed to pierce through the armor covering her upper arm. She felt blood seeping from the gash. Her breath came in gasps and she was forced to depend on her reflexes rather than upper body strength and mass.

Her peripheral vision offered an image of Elar licking his lips. He was up to something, she was certain of that. In that certainty, she knew, he had no intention of helping her win as he had originally suggested. She doubted he cared who won, though he did want rid of Brie. *Will he kill Brie and blame it on Kester if I die?*

San parried another blow, before self-preservation instincts took hold. She spun away from a second blow aimed by Vrill, coming up behind him and dragging the cutting edge of her weapon over the armor on his leg. He roared like a wounded T-Rex.

Vrill staggered and lunged for her, and she backed away, tripping herself with her rod. She could almost hear him laughing as he came in for the kill. He pinned her right leg to the ground with his foot, lifted his face shield, and smiled.

She knew he would be unable to resist having her see his face as she died. The next series of actions seemed to take place in slow motion. Using his greater strength, he drove the arrow point toward her chest. San had to wait for the right moment, for she would have only a second to strike. She grasped her rod in both hands and swung from her side as she brought the arrow point against his throat. Pain seared through her confined knee and leg, but she held the rod until Vrill's forward motion drove her weapon through his neck, severing his spinal cord.

Vrill seemed to hang suspended on the rod for a second before he pitched to the side, just missing San. Now that her leg was free, she reached for it to see how badly she was injured. The pain burned as if she had placed her knee against a hot iron.

Oblivious to the commotion in the arena, San took Vrill's discarded rod, and used it to stand.

"No!" Brie screamed. He aimed the EM-Stinger he held at San, despite his being too far away from her for an effective shot.

"Stop or I'll shoot," Kester ordered. For a split second, Brie glared at him.

San supported her body on both legs despite the throbbing pain in her knee. Her right hand lifted the rod and she took several steps, swinging it in an arc. She bit her lips to shut out the screaming pain in her knee and complete the forward motion of throwing the rod like a spear. The steel missile reached Brie a second before he realized what she was doing. It was too late and his scream ended in a bloody gurgle as the rod tore through his chest. Brie staggered backward under the force of the impact, blood frothing from his lips. He fell to the floor and died.

Kester lowered his EM-Stinger.

Elar let out his breath, pointed the Jewel tipped rod toward San, and announced. "You, General San, are the winner. Vrill's command is yours. The seat you held is yours."

"No thanks to you," San muttered through lips torn and bloodied from biting against the pain in her leg. "I'm injured," she said in a sharp voice.

"Medics!" Elar called. A medical team hurried to San and removed her armor. Kester followed them.

"You won, General."

"You damn idiot, why didn't you fire at Brie?" she berated him.

Kester's eyebrows met in a frown. "I was told not to by Council Member Elar. He said I could fire only if Vrill showed cowardice, not Brie."

San winced as the medics removed her leg armor. They immobilized her leg and ordered a carrier while one placed a TD opiate patch on her neck.

"I should have known," she muttered.

Cal moved to Elar. "The Jewel," she indicated the rod Elar carried.

"Take it back to storage," he said.

"What? A Jewel is destroyed with the death in a challenge."

"Take it back," he ordered over her protest. "The cache of Jewels is decaying. We can't afford to waste one on some stupid tradition." He looked at the men and women in the gallery of the arena. Raising his voice he said. "As soon as General San is treated, the Command Council will meet to declare a new Supreme Commander."

"Get me functional," San ordered the medics as she was lifted onto the carrier. "I'll begin therapy later."

"You may need surgery," a female medic said.

"Then see it's arranged, but after the Council meeting." The medic nodded.

Elar called to San. "General, you are now in command of the Field Army. Have you any orders for General Sig?"

Sig stood as San twisted on the litter to better see him. "Yes, as soon as you receive word about the new Supreme Commander, you will take out Washington in that Universe. We've already wasted too much time."

~ * ~

October 29, 1861(Universe 1)

Amber stood beside the steps to the farmhouse porch and tugged her uniform in place. She was wearing one of the Union uniforms sent to the camp from extras General Wilcox had at his disposal.

"Good thing most of these men aren't big," she said aloud.

It didn't really seem to matter who wore what color at this point, only that the men in the regiment commented on women in trousers. Marsden had put a stop to that a day ago when he had addressed the men and women in camp at Crittenden's urging.

Marsden explained that the goal was to win this war against the Khysids, not snipe at what people wore. Only an idiot, he had said, would fly a combat plane in a dress. Since Crittenden agreed, the men said little more. She knew some still didn't care for the idea of women in pants or as officers. The idea of Negro officers was even more unpalatable, but she knew they would eventually have to swallow it if they chose to live.

Amber adjusted the small drive attached to her computer. Since the reader was a simpler form of technology, she had had to make an adapter for her computer to accept the data. Crittenden would be able to see the reconnaissance images as soon as Gray Eagle and Marsden returned.

Rierdon was busy importing as much technology as he could to make the new air base comfortable and useful for those in residence.

So far he had managed to install bathing areas, better toilet facilities, and fuel cells to power electric lighting. He was working on importing hangers for the airfield. Plans were being made to bring across earth moving equipment and synthetic materials to construct real runways and additional fuel for the planes.

Wilcox had sent Crittenden a team of engineers and Lee had dispatched another team. Both teams consisted of volunteers for the air base. Eager volunteers, from what she could see of their recent actions. Gordo was given a commission as major, over his extensive protests, but in the end, he agreed to help train the engineers and use them where he could.

The air was warm for late October, the sky clear and blue. It was the perfect weather for flying. Marsden and Gray Eagle should get excellent images even if they had to fight.

Amber shoved the computer into the small leather carrying case and placed the strap over her shoulder. Crittenden was still working beneath the canopy while Rierdon was having the receiving parlor remodeled into an office for the general. She knew Rierdon was almost finished. At the moment, he was choosing the palette of colors for the paint, drapes, and furniture. She laughed at the thought. This was a military base, not an interior design school, but Rierdon could not be dissuaded once he got hold of an idea.

"Wait." Weber strode toward her, holding out his hands in a demanding gesture. "I want that computer."

"Sorry, Dr. Weber, General Crittenden is expecting some data and he needs it for the readout."

"Listen, you little bitch, that computer's mine."

Amber cocked her head to one side. "Actually it's mine. I found it. I bought it. You have other computer equipment."

"I said give it to me," he demanded, taking a threatening step in her direction.

She backed away from him. He had been after her computer for two days ever since he moved to the basement of the distillery barn. She had protested when he moved from the tent, her intuition registering alarm. But Marsden had told her it was best to let Weber have his way. Having his way was one thing, but she suspected he was doing something beyond the plans for the base.

"Sorry, I have to go." She turned to go.

Weber grabbed her by the wrist, pulled her around, and smacked her across the face. She was stunned by the blow, then outraged. Weber raised his hand to deliver another, but was prevented. Amber circled her hand around his wrist, but did not withdraw it from Weber's grasp. Instead she clasped Weber's wrist with hers, secured her grip with her left hand, and locked Weber's arm. She leaned forward, driving him to his knees.

Crittenden had seen Weber hit Amber, as had both Joshua and Elliott. The three men ran to her defense only to find Weber was the one needing defending.

"Let me go, damn you," Weber moaned.

Amber released her hold and Weber got to his feet, rubbing his arm and shoulder.

Crittenden looked from the scientist to Amber, and demanded. "What's going on?"

"He struck me." Amber glared at Weber. She noted Joshua and Elliott were making some sort of saluting hand signals. She ignored them.

Crittenden cleared his throat. He cast an amused look at Amber and a sterner look at Weber. "Dr. Weber, what have you to say? I saw you hit Lieutenant Amber."

"I don't like it when subordinates refuse to obey my commands." Weber locked eyes with Crittenden. "Surely you've disciplined your men in the same fashion."

Crittenden's handsome face contorted with anger. "I do not brutalize those I command, sir. And Lieutenant Amber is not your subordinate. I will not tolerate such behavior in my camp. Is that understood?"

A spasm passed through Weber's body. Amber sensed rage in the scientist. He glared at her and the three men before him before storming from the area.

"What did he want?" Crittenden asked her.

"He wanted my computer. It's not his and besides, it's fixed for you to use to review the data from Gray Eagle and Marsden." Her ears caught the sound of the planes.

"Bring the computer to my table," Crittenden ordered. "I want to see how it operates." He strode away as Joshua and Elliott stood at attention and saluted him.

"Amber, you are supposed to salute the man. He's a general, I mean, my God, you must even salute a captain," Elliott said.

"Oh?" Amber watched Crittenden resume his seat. "I really don't understand all this stuff about military protocol."

"We will be happy to teach you." The two men replied, exchanging glances.

"Just so that's all you two have in mind," she returned.

Elliott cleared his throat, the noise drowned out by the two P-40s coming in for a landing. She noted that the gleam in the eyes of both men was for the planes.

"I'll teach you to fly, or at least what you need for the ground school, if you two show me what I have to know about this saluting stuff," she offered.

"It's a deal, Miss, I mean Lieutenant Amber," Joshua said.

Amber shrugged. She watched Marsden and Gray Eagle climb from the planes. An engineer scooted beneath each plane and removed the digital recorders, offering one to each to pilot.

~ * ~

The Palm-Com sat on the table Crittenden used as a desk. The computer screen was expanded to full size and the image of the runway on Zeller Field sharp and precise.

"Those are Messerschmitts." Marsden explained about the unfamiliar planes.

"With German markings." Amber ran the index finger of her right hand over her lower lip. "They look relatively new. Where did they come from?"

Marsden shrugged. "We need to discover that fact pronto. And we need something more than P-40s if we are going up against those babies. I hope Cc is finished with your office, sir."

Crittenden leaned back in his chair. "Yes, he just completed it. I think the office will be, as you say, a real experience."

"He's put the best equipment in it for you," Amber said. "Even one of these computers."

Crittenden lifted an eyebrow. "Indeed?"

She nodded. "I fed the computer some instructional programs so you will have no trouble learning to use it."

Marsden gritted his teeth, but Gray Eagle covered his mouth with his hand. "Sir, about the planes on the Zeller Field. There are ten P-40 Kittyhawks, but three Messerschmitts. I want those P-51s. I've taken out Messerschmitts in P-51s and I'd rather have my pilots flying the best."

"Why not jets?" Amber asked.

Marsden shook his head. "Too costly for maintenance, repair, and supply. These old WW II planes are better and can do the job here just as well. I think that's why the Khysids have not imported jets."

"Didn't the Germans make a jet?"

"Yes, the Me262. But it had lots of problems. It was vulnerable during takeoff and landing and it had only about twenty minutes of fuel. We had the Y-80 at the end of the war." Marsden studied the image on the screen. "I think the Khysids take whatever technology is available and adapt it to their use. Planning an invasion will mean committing lots of resources to this universe."

"Indeed it will." Crittenden resumed his study of the image of the planes. "And since none of it can be manufactured here, all of it must be imported by both them and us. Makes for a very interesting supply line, doesn't it?"

"With any Source Gates as targets," Gray Eagle suggested. "I presume you want intelligence on these Khysids and their actions in other universes?"

Crittenden nodded. "It appears that we will have to rethink espionage as well as combat tactics."

Marsden looked at his new commander. "This is one sharp cookie," he muttered. "Makes me glad it was he who kidnapped us and not McClellan."

"Colonel?" Crittenden glanced at Marsden.

"What's our next move?" Marsden asked.

Crittenden looked at Amber. "Just what sort of defense did you use against Weber?"

"It's something I learned in the Martial Arts. Chen and Marie Lui are instructors in the technique," she explained. "It's a form of unarmed combat."

"Then that is our next move," Crittenden replied to Marsden's question. "If a woman as slight as Amber can render a man Weber's size helpless with a single hold, I want my troops taught that method."

~ * ~

October 29, 1961(Universe 0)

The discussions at ISIR were heated, but Croll's final phone call of intimidation was enough to tip the balance of opinion. Barstead prepared the first group to leave, including among the evacuees not only technical and medical personnel, but also the parents of the young men and women in the 1861 Warrenton. However, Alyssia Bouchard insisted on remaining with Barstead and leaving with the last group.

Several more groups left before Barstead received a call from Rierdon.

"We have the first batch and they're at Winchester." Rierdon's voice rang with excitement. "The second group is coming in now and the others should be arriving at their destination in the 1974 universe any time."

"I thought we were to go to Warrenton?"

"No, Warrenton is housing the air base, Julian. Word from Lincoln is that he agrees with Lee in putting us up in Western Virginia. I think they eventually want to move us to some remote location in southwest Pennsylvania."

Barstead strained to remember what the United States looked like at the dawn of the Civil War. His memory of history failed him. "Why some remote location?"

Rierdon gave a snort. "They have no major highways, no rapid means of transport except steam engines. The Khysids are as confined by that universe's infrastructure as are we. Putting us in a remote location insures our safety."

"How many Jewels do we have?" Barstead rubbed his forehead as he strained to remember the cache they had located in the alternate universe while they were staying with Gordo.

"Four, one is being used right now. There are three remaining and Gray Eagle is manufacturing what he claims is a similar type crystal."

"Who's helping Gray Eagle?"

"Amber and Roger, when they are not bothering Rich and Gordo about the P-51s."

"The next to the last group is ready to leave," Barstead assured Rierdon. "They should be on their way in a few minutes. Alyssia, Sam, Connie, I will be the last."

"Good, I'll breathe easier knowing you're out of there and away from the Khysids."

"Not just the Khysid threat," Barstead stopped. The door to his office slammed against the wall and an irate Beaumont stormed inside.

"Julian, where the hell is my sister? Croll has

some stupid story about her being captured by the Confederate army. First Lincoln's ghost, now Confederates. Just what the hell is going on?"

"It's Beaumont, Cc," Barstead muttered into the phone. "Call back later." He replaced the receiver.

Beaumont marched to the desk, leaned across it, and barked. "There is no later, Julian. Croll and his men are surrounding the place. He sent me in to negotiate."

Barstead jumped to his feet. "I haven't time to explain, Mr. Beaumont, but we are in serious trouble."

"No kidding?"

"Not just from Croll."

Beaumont jerked erect. "What do you mean, not just from Croll?"

"Remember the hanger manager and Dr. Bechter? They were killed by members of an army called the Khysids."

Beaumont gave a rapid shake of his head as if the words added a second layer of confusion to his brain. "Army? I don't understand."

Before Barstead could explain, Connie burst into the office. She glanced at Beaumont, but ignored the man. Barstead saw she was breathing rapidly. The sleeves of her pink blouse were rolled to her elbows and several thick strands of her blond hair had escaped the confines of her ponytail.

"Connie, what happened?" Barstead asked while Beaumont turned toward the woman.

"We got the last group through, but something is wrong with the device. We can't keep a portal open for more than a few seconds."

Barstead swore beneath his breath. The transfer device was almost drained of power.

"Through where?" Beaumont demanded.

Barstead waved away the question as he moved around his desk. "I've got an idea that may work. But we can't wait. We'll have to go now."

Beaumont looked at him, then at Connie. "Wherever you're going, I'm going too, especially if Mary Frances is there. Besides, Croll has given you only two hours before he storms this place."

"Some negotiator you are," Barstead snorted as he left the room.

Twenty

When the ingathering begins, no action in any Reality will stop it.
Codex of Flowering Butterfly

November 1, 1861(Universe 1)

Amber dreamed she saw a valley that continued beyond a sparkling river. On the opposite side, the valley sloped upward to a forest where spring was beginning its slow march to the summit. She gazed at the river threading a sinuous path along the valley floor. The place seemed familiar, but she knew she had never seen it in her waking life.

Eagle-Being walked up the gentle slope from the river's edge carrying a shield. Amber cocked her head to one side as she studied the round shield. It was divided into two sections by an S shaped line, much like the line for the Eastern yin-yang symbol. But slightly below the center on the shield was the symbol for infinity, a horizontal figure eight. It was gray on the blue side of the shield and blue on the gray side. Perched above the symbol was a stylized jaguar with wings.

Amber inclined her head toward the shield. “What is that?”

The spirit presented the shield to her. “Wear this symbol on your uniforms, for it is an image of a hidden Reality. When the time comes, it will announce to those who will ally with you that you too are Light Dancers.”

The dream faded and Amber woke into the cool darkness of the bedroom she shared with Harriette and Kit. She lay still for a few minutes thinking about the dream and its meaning. Such dreams were not uncommon to her, but Eagle Being was a spirit teacher for Gray Eagle. A fact he had shared with the pilots he trained. This was the second time she had dreamed about Eagle-Being.

Amber lay for a moment, savoring the warmth. The small heater, powered by an internal fuel cell, kept the room at a comfortable 70° F. There were several touch lights scattered around the room, but Amber decided not to awaken anyone by using them.

She reached for her watch resting on the table beside the bed. Three small single beds had been placed in the third-floor room that had been used by the servants of the farm family prior to becoming Crittenden’s headquarters.

Amber held the watch and pressed the button for the time. The digital readout told her it was 5:30 a.m. Since the days were growing shorter and with the new lighting, people were working later. Crittenden had the camp bugler sound reveille at 6:00 rather than 5:00 a.m.

She slipped from her bed, went to the newly installed bathroom, and dressed. It was a real joy to finally have a form of indoor plumbing, even if it was limited to a simple composting toilet and cold water. Finished, she left the room and made her way to the main floor. Breakfast smells drifted from the kitchen, promising a hearty morning meal.

Mary Frances, Margaret, Desiree and Bea were busy preparing food for the scientists and pilots. Amber wondered where Crittenden was, since he and Marsden were always early risers.

"Need any help?" she offered.

"No, we can handle this. We finally have two microwaves." Margaret grinned with pleasure. "Never thought I'd like to use the things to cook, but these imports are a delight."

"Pierre will either love them or hate them when he arrives," Bea chuckled. "I will wager he will hate them. He prefers an open flame."

"Then we'll see to it he has access to gas." Mary Frances plopped a fresh loaf from the bread maker onto a plate. "These little kitchen appliances are great when you have a group to feed. We set three last night, and behold: fresh bread in the morning."

Bea shook her head. "I never thought to see such machines. Rich had Alex in the kitchen last night explaining the finer points of bread making."

"Was he interested?" Amber took a seat at the table after she poured a cup of coffee from the fifty-cup coffeemaker.

"No, he rather prefers the computer and flying machines."

"It's better that way," Amber chuckled. "It keeps him out from under your feet."

Bea laughed and poured herself a cup of coffee. She joined Amber at the table. "True, the man is all thumbs in the kitchen. But he loves the fuel cells and this wiring that brings the electric fluid to all these devices."

"Electric fluid?" Amber said. "It really isn't a fluid."

"I know," Bea sipped her coffee. "But some things are hard to forget. I suppose in a few months we shall be speaking of such machines as if they were devices we grew up with."

Amber shook her head. "Even we didn't grow up with some of these." She rubbed her forehead with her hands.

"Does your head ache?" Bea touched the young woman's hair.

"No, I had this weird dream. It was about a symbol shown to me on a shield. I was told that we are told to wear it on our uniforms for our allies, whoever they may be."

Bea sat erect. "Allies?"

"Yes, but Eagle-Being never said who they were."

Bea raised her hands to her mouth.

"Bea, what is it?" Desiree asked.

"Amber, you said this person in your dream was Eagle-Being?"

Amber nodded. “I dreamed of him and of this camp before General Crittenden had Captain Hargrove come for us.”

Bea rose and went to a heavy butcher-block table squeezed beside the new wooden table holding the bread machines. She lifted a small pad and pen Margaret kept there and brought it to Amber.

“Draw for me the symbol you saw in the dream.”

Desiree moved beside Bea. She whispered, “Have you seen this spirit before?”

The two women exchanged glances. “Yes,” Bea answered, patting Desiree’s arm. “It is a comfort to have someone like you here.”

Desiree nodded and glanced at Amber sketching on the paper Bea had given her.

“I’m not as good at drawing as Harriette is, but the jaguar had a sort of Aztec look. I’ll see if I can show you what the symbol looked like.”

As she finished, the sound of a bugle tore through the morning stillness. Amber dropped the pen, glanced at her watch and stood. The call the bugler was playing was not something she had heard while at camp and not the usual notes she associated with reveille. But the sound had an ominous feel to it. She knew it meant danger.

“What is he playing?”

Bea started at the first notes. “It’s called ‘Boots and Saddles.’ He’s calling the Cavalry to mount.”

Amber felt her stomach flip. It was not Hargrove and his men the bugle was summoning, but Marsden and his pilots. The call was repeated twice more before the door to the farmhouse burst open and Marsden raced inside.

He stopped at the entrance to the kitchen. “Get everyone up; we have big trouble.”

Amber raced from the kitchen to call Kit as Gray Eagle, Roger, and Mark entered the house. Margaret darted to the entrance to the kitchen.

“What’s happened?”

“Alex just received a telegram from Lee. Washington is under attack. Wilcox managed to get a message to Lee.”

“Wilcox? Where’s McClellan?” she demanded.

Marsden shrugged. “I don’t know. Maybe he already went with the part of the Union government that moved to Philadelphia.”

Desiree came to stand beside Bea. “What about Lincoln?”

“From what Alex tells me, Lincoln wanted to stay until the end. Wilcox will guard him with his life. So will Nathan McBride.”

“What can you do with the planes?” Margaret asked.

Marsden blew out his breath between clenched teeth and looked at Gray Eagle. “Offer whatever aid we can, especially if the Khysids are flying in support of their ground troops. We’ll take the two P-51s. Remember those Messerschmitts?”

Crittenden poked his way inside the crowded hall until Gray Eagle and Roger realized he was there and moved aside.

"Sorry, General, we didn't know it was you," Gray Eagle apologized.

Crittenden waved aside the apology. "Baltimore has also fallen," he announced, gesturing to the crumpled piece of paper he held in his hand.

"Baltimore? Wasn't that the home of another of those clubs you told us of?"

"Yes, but the city was in Union hands until today." Crittenden looked at the people crowded in the hallway and at Amber, Kit, and Harriette just entering it. "I don't know what the situation is, or where Lincoln is, even why it was Wilcox who sent the message to Lee."

"We'll assess the situation when we get there," Marsden said.

Amber watched Crittenden sigh. "Buy Wilcox the time he needs."

"Sir?" Marsden asked.

"The time to save the eastern part of the Union army."

~ * ~

When Bea returned to the kitchen to clean the table, she saw the sketch Amber had almost completed. As she lifted the sheet of paper and peered at the drawing, her hands trembled and she felt someone cover them with his.

"Bea, what is it?" Crittenden asked his wife.

"Oh Alex, look," she said as she handed him the paper.

"Where did you get this?"

“Amber drew it.” She told him about the dream Amber had had. “The jaguar is almost identical to that slate tablet Trevor has in his house. Remember? The one he bought from the Baldwin Gallery.”

Crittenden gave a slow nod. “Yes. The tablet his late friend had given the jeweler in payment for his debts. I wonder why this image comes to Amber.”

“Gray Eagle spoke of his time with an air company called the Flying Tigers,” Bea reminded her husband, though she knew he remembered the tales. “This is a winged jaguar.”

“Let me ask Margaret or Cc.”

“Has Cc joined the army?” Bea asked.

“Today.” Crittenden kissed his wife on the cheek. “I need these people under my command. I can’t have them running off on any tangent that pleases them.”

“You think being in charge will stop them?” she teased.

Crittenden laughed. “No, but it will at least give them pause, and me a breathing space.”

~ * ~

Sig was receiving tactical reports from his field commanders. The secure room bustled with an energy he hadn’t felt since before Brie’s death. The latest report told him of Lincoln’s escape. That was something he hadn’t expected. The president had fled the White House hours before the first shock troops crossed into his universe.

"Where is he?" Sig wondered aloud. He knew McClellan was badly wounded and had been taken away. Sig didn't care, since the level of medicine in this universe all but assured McCellan's death.

Sig waited until the first of his planes arrived above the Capitol. He suspected the pilots from that field in Warrenton would come after his, but he had better intelligence on the command at Warrenton. They had nothing to match the Messerschmitts and he knew a P-40 against a Messerschmitt was history.

~ * ~

"I see them." Marsden heard Amber's voice in his headset. His planes were operating on an open channel so that anyone speaking was heard by everyone else. This required real discipline so that not everyone spoke at once.

Beneath them, on the outskirts of the Union capital, Marsden saw a quagmire of people, smoke, broken carriages, wagons, and horses. It looked like a sea of civilians and soldiers running in a general northeast direction, though some were scattering south. Behind them was an organized army of dark uniformed troops. Masses of people were dropping at random near the front. Marsden's stomach sank. Khysid soldiers were shooting into the retreating chaos.

Ahead Khysid P-40s were dropping payloads into the crowd. He called into this microphone. "Get them!"

His seven planes broke formation to pursue the enemy. Acquiring the additional P-40s had been simple for Marsden since there was a repository of planes in eastern Virginia in a 1947 universe. Even acquiring the two P-51s he and Gray Eagle were flying had been relatively easy. But they were better planes and the owners of the plane repository had been rather reluctant to part with them.

Tackling one of the Messerschmitts was far less dangerous in the plane he was flying than in one of the hefty P-40s. Marsden had been determined to get the better fighters for his squadrons along with the needed spare parts.

"One's on your tail, Rich!" Gray Eagle called Marsden's wandering attention back to the fight. Marsden cursed, reddening at his lapse of attention.

His ears caught the gunfire behind him while tracer bullets spun ribbon trails to either side of his plane. He climbed as a P-40 spiraled to its death beneath him. "Got the SOB!" Gray Eagle called.

"Score one for you, Medicine Man," Marsden answered. "A big thanks."

"Your turn, I got a Messerschmitt on my tail."

Marsden banked left, saw the action, and dived after the plane pursuing Gray Eagle's P-51.

~ * ~

Wilcox looked up from the spreading carnage that had become a disorganized rout. It was far worse than Manassas. There had been a semblance of control there. But just as at Manassas, civilians and soldiers were intermingled here. With McBride's help, Wilcox had gotten Lincoln and the remainder of his cabinet out of Washington by a secret route. By then, their train was heading for Harrisburg.

"All I have to do now is save the civilians and what is left of the army," Wilcox grunted. "My army," he amended.

McClellan had been wounded a few hours ago and word had come that all command was transferred to Wilcox, the only ranking officer above colonel alive on the field. The Khysids had decimated the officers of command rank.

His mind replayed the horror of the last four hours; hours that had seemed like days. Around 1:30 in the morning, the Khysid troops had erupted from the Embassy Club, killing everything in sight. Their soldiers carried rifles that fired so many rounds at a time that Wilcox's men had been helpless to stop them,

But Wilcox knew he was fighting men and as he later realized, women. They could die. It was just necessary to get out of the reach of the guns they carried. Not an easy task, since the guns had a long range and required no reloading after firing. When General Stuart, his second in command, was killed, Wilcox ordered all his troops away from direct confrontation. He made them fight building to building, using the structures in Washington for cover. He had been able to save the remaining men and force the civilians they were screening out of the city.

Shortly before dawn, the Khysids began throwing grenades more powerful than anything the Union army possessed. They were also using a long-distance shell he could not identify. But the building-to-building fighting had bought the Union army time. Wilcox had sensed the Khysids had not expected the type of resistance they were encountering. It had taken them time to change tactics. Wilcox made a mental note of that observation.

But Washington was in flames and its defenders dead or dying, clogging its streets with their bodies. The gaslights of the city had cast an eerie pall on the battle just before the gas lines were severed.

When Wilcox reached the outskirts of the city, the bombing started. The flying machines came, taking huge chunks out of his forces. By some miracle, he found a still-operating telegraph line. The lines to Warrenton were down, so he sent a message to Lee encamped near Winchester.

The Confederate army had moved from its Manassas encampment after the meeting between the Presidents. This was at McClellan's insistence after Wilcox had returned with Lincoln. Wilcox had objected, but his objections were ignored. It was McClellan who had ridden through the city as conquering hero.

"At least you were right, Little Mac," Wilcox muttered. "But for the wrong reason. You spared Lee's army this." He glanced skyward at the sound of additional planes and saw P-40s with white star markings on their wings.

Crittenden's flying machines were arriving, as Lee had promised they would. He had learned that the planes were flying lower than usual. That was the reason he and the others had seen them in combat. He didn't really understand and didn't care. Att this moment, Wilcox could have embraced Crittenden. *Bless the man for capturing those scientists*, he thought. The bombing and strafing subsided as the Air Cavalry engaged the Khysid planes.

Now he had time to try to organize what remained of his army and force the civilians to move west or anywhere beyond the reach of the Khysids. A silent grief welled up in his chest, his eyes stung with tears as he watched the smoke on the horizon. The capital was gone and he could not recover the dead or dying.

He glanced up at the sky and watched the Khysid planes retreating, after being mauled by the Air Cavalry. His heart did a flip in his chest. Only one of the strange new Khysid planes remained undamaged. The other Khysid planes were similar to those flown by Crittenden's pilots except for the black markings on their wings. He wondered if a pilot ever went among the enemy arrayed as the proverbial wolf in sheep's clothing.

Wilcox looked around for anyone he could use. He saw one of the young telegraph operators from the White House sitting on top of an overturned wagon. The boy cupped his dirty face in his hands while his body shook.

"You, son," Wilcox shouted. He was rewarded when the boy looked up at him. "Fourteen if he's a day," Wilcox grunted. "Lad, find a mirror and get it at the right angle to use the sun. You know code?"

The boy's head bounced rapidly. "Yes sir. What do you want sent?"

"The mirrors will reflect the sunlight."

"I know that," the boy pouted.

Wilcox smiled. *The kid had courage.* "Signal those flying machines with the stars on the wings. They're ours. Tell them to kill the enemy on the ground."

The boy scampered through the remains of the overturned wagon until he found a large mirror he could manipulate easily. He waited until one of the machines flew in his direction and, using the sun's reflection, he signaled the aircraft.

~ * ~

"Rich, that's code." Amber banked away from the flashes of light. "Something about killing the ground."

"The enemy on the ground," Gray Eagle added. "Wilcox wants a strafing run."

"It's Mark, Colonel," Mark Bouchard called. "I'm watching troops coming from the north, looks like another army."

"Baltimore," Marsden swore into the open channel. "Medicine Man, take two pilots and do what you can against the new troops. The rest of us will try and clean up here."

"I hope they don't have any hand held missiles," Amber interjected.

"Doesn't look like it," Marsden replied. But he made a mental note to have Rierdon track down such equipment.

~ * ~

Wilcox had assembled a disparate staff of officers from different regiments. Colonel Bristow was the highest-ranking officer among them, Major Embry next. Bristow stood in his stirrups, field glasses in hand, watching the flying machines.

"General Wilcox, why are three of the machines going north?"

Wilcox uttered a stream of profanity, most of it swallowed by the roar of the descending P-40s as they began a strafing run against the Khysid troops. He was sitting on his horse on a small rise that projected him above the flood of soldiers and civilians.

"Baltimore fell!" he shouted to Bristow. "I bet those bastards have sent in reinforcements from the north. How the hell can we fight this battle on two fronts? We can't even fight it on one?"

Wilcox felt his control slipping as fear gnawed at his stomach. *Nothing he could do.* But he vowed that would not stop him from trying.

"Your orders, sir?" Captain Fritz Gruber, a grizzled German immigrant, asked.

"Colonel Parker is on our northern flank. Find him. Tell him that troops are coming from Baltimore and to get ready for them."

Gruber saluted. He directed his horse through the mass of people, fighting off those who attempted to pull him from his mount. Wilcox watched his progress with satisfaction. A small voice inside whispered to him that they were going to make it. It was irrational, he knew, but the thought gave him courage and comfort.

He stood in his stirrups and waved his hat at the young telegraph operator standing on the overturned wagon. "Embry, go fetch the lad. We can't leave him there and may need his help again."

~ * ~

Gray Eagle took Amber and Mark, leaving Marsden with four planes. Below him the periphery of the mass exodus was ringed with stragglers, both soldier and civilian. The people running north were headed directly for the approaching army, but it was a strange army. The lead troops appeared to be a disorganized gang and the main body of troops marched behind them. Gray Eagle saw, with some satisfaction, that the Khysid troops had no mechanized transport.

"Let's get them," he ordered and the three planes screamed toward the approaching menace, strafing the ground troops. The planes had made three passes when Gray Eagle heard the distress call.

"I'm hit!" Amber screamed into the radio.

"How bad?" Gray Eagle fought his stomach for control. He knew they were vulnerable. The fact was something he had managed to shove aside until he heard her words.

"I'm losing fuel, but I can still control the plane," she continued. Her labored breathing sounded loud in his headset. "But I'm bleeding and can't tell how badly I'm wounded."

"Get out of here, now!" Gray Eagle saw the tracer bullets erupt from nowhere.

"One on your tail," Mark's voice held a thread of fear.

"Mayday! Mayday! Mayday!" Gray Eagle called. "Rich, we're under attack!"

"Copy," the word sounded reassuring.

"Amber, get out of here, now!" Gray Eagle shouted.

"Copy," she called.

Gray Eagle offered up several prayers that she be unmolested by the Khysid planes. He intended to do something about that by making himself a target. He climbed, as he realized that the Messerschmitt had already found him.

~ * ~

Wilcox saw the planes that started the strafing run leave and fly north. He needed no field glasses to see the planes coming from the direction of Zeller Field.

"Damn," he swore. His saw a lone plane flying south towards Warrenton, a small banner of smoke trailing from the engine. His mind hoped the pilot had some way to escape the machine besides crashing. He had seen no such escapes at Manassas or here. The enemy planes had been blown apart in the air or had crashed to a fiery death on the ground. He offered a silent prayer for the pilot of the stricken plane.

"General Wilcox." Major Embry rode to the small rise. "Sir, look," he pointed in the direction of Washington.

Wilcox saw space between the end of the retreat and what had been the press of the Khysid soldiers. Whatever the pilots had done, it had bought him more time. His eyes scanned the area to his left, and what he would later deem the second miracle appeared.

A young cavalry sergeant was directing a small group of soldiers, forming a screening movement between the mass in front and the Khysids at their rear. As the pressure lessened, the sergeant rode to a nearby wagon and spoke to a young woman riding inside.

Wilcox urged his horse toward the wagon. The sergeant turned, saw Wilcox, and saluted him.

"Sir."

"You are?"

"Sergeant Justin Llewyllen, sir, of the Sixth Pennsylvania volunteers."

Wlicox again felt the rush of grief in his chest. This man's company, the entire regiment, had been the first attacked. "How did you get through the line?"

"We managed to fight house to house, sir, after General Wilcox's orders came down. He is a smart man, that general. Saved our," Llewyllen glanced at the woman. "I mean his orders saved us. We picked up Miss Sarah Clarke here, trying to help two wounded soldiers. Found the wagon and loaded the men we could into it."

Wilcox blew out his breath. "I'm General Wilcox, Sergeant." He thought the man looked about twenty. Wilcox peered into the wagon, then at the nurse. "Miss," he saluted her. "You have room for Tom Briggs?" He gestured to the young telegraph operator riding behind Embry.

Sarah smiled and nodded. "Yes, I could use the help."

Embry transferred Tom to Sarah's care. Wilcox took the canteen from his saddle and offered it to Sarah.

"We have water, General Wilcox. Please keep yours. We managed to raid some of the wagons for what we could use."

A thin smile crept across Wilcox's lips. "Good. Then this ambulance will be my headquarters for now. The fighting seems to have stopped behind us. Sergeant Llewyllen, get me whatever information you can."

"Yes sir." The man snapped a salute and beckoned for two other mounted enlisted men. "Come on," he ordered, and the trio rode toward Washington.

"And don't go much farther than the end of this mess!" Wilcox shouted at them. He turned to his staff. "Let's get moving."

~ * ~

"What the hell?" Gordo asked when his ears caught the stuttering of an airplane engine. "Give me that thing." He took the headset from the man trying to operate the radio and not having much luck with it. Gordo frowned. "This dial is for frequency," he explained with a sliver of impatience. "See."

"Warrenton base," Amber's voice sounded faint but recognizable.

"Gordo here, Amber, what happened?"

"Gordo, I've been hit. I'm almost out of fuel and there's smoke and oil in the cockpit."

"Dump the rest of your fuel and land the damn thing," Gordo ordered. "The field is cleared."

"I can't land in the field. If I crash, the others will have trouble landing and I can't make a second pass. I don't think I can stay conscious that long."

Gordo felt the hair on his neck stand up. His heart began to race. "Clear the field!" he shouted to the troops serving as the ground crew and waiting for the planes to return. "Get me the fire extinguishers Cc imported. You know where they are."

The men scattered as Crittenden, standing on the porch, watched the commotion. He began jogging toward Gordo but stopped as the P-40 came in for a landing.

"Get Dr. Reed," Gordo ordered the radio operator. "Then later I'll show you how to use this thing."

The sergeant saluted and raced from the field while Crittenden ran toward Gordo. The plane was coming in erratically and Gordo couldn't tell if the controls were damaged or if Amber was too injured to fly anymore. His ears caught the whistling sound of air being forced through the guns. She had fired them, he knew, for he had taped them as he had done to the P-40s in China. Tape prevented dust and water vapor from clogging the guns before they were fired.

She was landing on the road as she had promised, not in the field. Tears leaked from his eyes when the plane hobbled to a stop. It jerked to the right, before coming to rest against the side of the road, smoke pouring from the cockpit, ajar, but not opened. Gordo raced toward the plane, Crittenden on his heels.

But Gordo's ground crew had beaten him to the plane, the young engineers forcing open the cockpit as they had practiced with the spare P-40. He stopped, Crittenden at his side, as the men unbuckled Amber from the harness and lifted her body from the plane. Jessica Hoffman, a young woman working with Reed, followed him and two men carrying a stretcher.

Amber made a gesture with her hand as she was lowered gently onto the stretcher and Gordo could see the blood soaking her jacket and pants. The men carrying Amber moved her away from the plane, Reed walking beside them. He took a quick look at her wound before telling the two stretcher-bearers to take her to the hospital.

"Wound's not too bad, but she lost a lot of blood," he called to Gordo and Crittenden as he hurried after his patient.

Gordo switched his attention to the damaged P-40. The smoke was not as steady and the men were flooding the engine with foam. Gordo fought the urge to laugh. If it were not for the fact that the Confederate engineers were putting out the fire in the P-40, the scene could be China all over again.

~ * ~

It was almost as if the air battle ceased by mutual consent. The Khysid planes broke off and flew toward their home base. Marsden ordered that no one pursue. His squadron flew toward Warrenton Air Base.

Wilcox watched the planes disperse and shivered. He rubbed his hands together for warmth. Sarah offered him a cup of canned milk from the provisions Llewyllen's band had scavenged in the many abandoned wagons littering the retreat path.

"The wounded," he protested, even as his stomach growled.

"They have enough and you need your strength too."

He saw the others of his tiny command staff also drinking the milk and accepted the cup. The clouds in the western sky were over-spreading the area. He hoped it meant only an overcast night, not rain. Rain was the last thing they needed; his mind presented him with a road caked ankle deep in mud.

That meant no shelter, no rest, and no campfires. The army, slowly reforming around the nucleus of his tiny command, would have to keep herding the civilians before them.

Ahead were the reinforcements he had requested from Lee. He had feared seeing those men at Manassas and at Cheat Mountain. Now he prayed they were approaching from the west not as enemies but as welcome allies.

Twenty-one

Knowledge is the gift of the Realities.
Codex of Flowering Butterfly

November 1, 1961 (Universe 0)

Barstead prayed that the portal would hold until he got the remainder of the ISIR personnel across to the 1974 universe. He had sent Connie, Sam, and Alyssia to finish the task quickly. He explained the situation to Beaumont as he packed. Finally he gave the agent one of the immune-enhancing patches as Alyssia raced into his office to tell him Croll and his commandos were now in the parking lot. Barstead ordered everyone remaining into the wind tunnel, disconnecting the power source so it could no longer be activated. The tunnel had a massive steel door and two narrow, foot-thick windows to view experiments in progress.

Just as Barstead and the others entered and secured the tunnel, Croll and his men were outside its door. It was only a matter of time before they used explosives to open it. He, Beaumont, Alyssia, Connie, and Sam were trapped in the tunnel. Barstead checked the transfer device before trying to activate it, since the device had grown more erratic. The power source drained and did not fully recharge after each use. He knew he would be lucky to keep a portal open for the five of them to cross. He activated the device. The large hemispherical opening he was used to was reduced to a small hump.

"Take Arthur with you," he ordered the others. They dragged Beaumont through the rapidly shrinking opening.

"Come on, Julian," Sam shouted.

Barstead ducked low and squeezed through the opening as a massive explosion rocked the room. The steel door blew inward, coming to rest where the portal had stood as the power to the transfer device ceased.

Croll stormed into the room. He stared at the place where Barstead and the others had been, where the strange opening, like a door between worlds, had existed moments ago. The throbbing vein at his temple stood out prominently.

"Search the damned institute for whatever you can get. Bring it to me and when you finish, burn the place to the ground."

"Sir, the surrounding area is dry. The fire might spread."

"I don't care. Do it and let's get the hell out of here."

The officer left as Kraft entered the wind tunnel holding a thick report. "Looks like they made some notes on the process," he offered it to Croll.

Croll declined. "Later. Now I want word from Weber, beyond that communicator he managed to get to us."

"He's working on it."

"He better work faster."

Kraft shook his head. "He's in their camp. He has to be careful. I get the impression this General Crittenden is no pushover."

Croll grunted. "That's not what Weber says."

"Since when do you believe everything Weber says?"

Croll glared back at Kraft. "I don't. I just want him to think I do until I have one of those Jewels he's told us about. Once we know how these things called Source Gates operate, Weber is gone." Croll strode from the wind tunnel.

~ * ~

November 2, 1861(Universe 1)

A thin wedge of silver light hung beneath massive black clouds on the eastern horizon. To the west, the sky was obscured by mist. The clearing to the east renewed in Wilcox fear of more aerial bombing attacks. He and his new staff had spent a weary night along the thin ranks, separating the exhausted civilians from the enemy. Around three in the morning, Wilcox had called a halt to the retreat. Pickets were established and changed every two hours. Even Wilcox had managed some needed sleep.

He had little choice in calling for a rest period. Soldiers and civilians were falling in their tracks, sleeping on the ground as others stepped over them. But at least he detected no more Khysid troops behind him. The Khysid troops were securing the city, Wilcox suspected, but he refused to think about what that meant for anyone still alive within its confines.

He noticed that Llewyllen and his men were guarding the horses as the animals found forage in what remained of a wheat field. The farms and hamlets lining the escape route were empty of occupants. His soldiers checked a number of houses to find horses, wagons, carriages, and most goods missing, testifying to a hasty withdrawal by the owners.

"Word about the capital must have gotten to them," he muttered. The downed telegraph lines told him other damage was being done and he set his men on guard for any Khysid cavalry.

Gruber brought Wilcox a horse, saddled and ready to ride, but Wilcox insisted on walking. He would mount when it became necessary. The horse too could use the rest. He looked out over the wagons he had managed to collect as his men were rising and forming into straggling lines.

Fog hugged the ground, covering it in a white blanket, clothing his troops and the civilians in a dank mist. Wilcox shivered in the humid but chill air. Rain, he thought, might keep the flying machines on the ground, but it would be a disaster for his retreat.

"Let's move out," he shouted, and the troops began walking. Wilcox did not urge them to move faster. The men and the civilians still with the army needed to conserve whatever reserves they possessed. His troops and the civilians were spread across the area, even as he tried to keep them on the road to Monacacy. Wilcox, his staff, and the three ambulance wagons were in the lead.

Sarah Clarke had taken control of the care of the wounded and she seemed to be doing a good job. The small store of laudanum Gruber had found yesterday had helped men in the wagons. But two died last night and Wilcox had ordered the bodies hastily buried.

Ahead Wilcox could see nothing but mist and fog, rising from the ground in thin threads like wraiths leaving a grave. Suddenly, the wraiths took on a more solid appearance, and Wilcox ordered a halt. He raised his field glasses to his eyes and stared at the approaching column. His back muscles relaxed for the first time since fighting began.

A flag appeared from the mist carried by a bearer riding behind the officer at the head of the column. The gray uniforms of the soldiers blended with the fog and the approaching army seemed part of the dense atmosphere. Wilcox had seen a similar flag displayed at Manassas and at Cheat Mountain, where he had gone to confer with General Reynolds. He had never thought that he would be glad to see it coming toward him. Lee's reinforcements had arrived.

The infantry marching in the long column left the road at an order from the officer heading the march. The men began to filter though the ranks of the exhausted Union troops, filling in where there were gaps. Wilcox bit back tears, knowing some of these men had fought each other not that long ago. Whatever enmity they possessed seemed to be forgotten in the shadow of this new threat.

The officer at the head of the column and his escort halted. The man dismounted. He saluted Wilcox, who returned the courtesy. To Wilcox's eyes, the man in the ill-fitting gray uniform was the most unlikely general he had ever seen.

"General Wilcox, I am General Thomas Jackson," Jackson said in a soft voice, his hooded eyes taking in the condition of Wilcox's troops and the scattered bands of civilians dispersed among them.

Wilcox said. "So Lee sent you, General."

Blue eyes played across Wilcox as a minuscule smile turned up the corners of Jackson's mouth. "Yes, but I don't think a stand is what you have in mind."

"No, I need to get these people and troops as far away from the Khysid troops as I can. How did you get to us so fast?"

"By train," Jackson explained. "Tell me the situation and what happened in Washington," he requested as he fell in step with Wilcox.

The march resumed but was quickly interrupted by the hum of approaching planes. Union troops and civilians dropped to the ground in response. Jackson glanced around in surprise, for his men were still standing, bemused by the actions. Wilcox fell to the ground, pulling Jackson with him. Jackson's men did as their commander and hugged the earth.

"There's no cover from the aerial bombs," Wilcox explained. "We have played this charade before."

"Why waste ammunition on dead bodies, I see," Jackson intuited, his eyes darting toward the horizon to watch the flying machines. "But are we not lying in a too ordered fashion to seem dead?"

"Wish I knew," Wilcox answered. "I have no idea what we look like from up there. I've never even been in a balloon."

"The machines are moving into the clouds," Jackson announced as the planes gained altitude. "Why have they white stars on them?"

"They are ours, sir," Major Embry scooted toward the two generals. "They come from Warrenton. But others come from that field north of Washington." He pointed to the Khysids planes now on the horizon.

"Keep down and quiet," Wilcox ordered. He heard the whine as the Khysid planes lost altitude, approaching the massed pockets of soldiers and civilians in a strafing run. But the deadly maneuver was never completed for Marsden and his squadron came from the clouds with the mist-obscured sun at their back.

Jackson was on his knees gazing at the battle between the planes. “Look, an aerial ambush.”

Wilcox rose to his feet. “Move out now,” he ordered and waited for Jackson to stand. “Best we put distance between us and them.” He gestured to the sky with his thumb. “They are buying us time.”

“Like falcons,” Jackson said with a note of admiration.

The officers marched with their men. Wilcox was suddenly aware that at his command troops in both blue and gray started forward. He and Jackson marched in silence.

~ * ~

“Where are they getting those damned Messerschmitts?” Marsden grumbled into his headset.

“Cc hasn’t had time to find out,” Gray Eagle reminded Marsden. He felt cold each time he saw the German fighters. It was a coldness that had little to do with his ability to fly against them. Instead the fighters represented the echo of some horror he had yet to learn.

Gray Eagle tested the skill of a Messerschmitt pilot, knowing within the first ten seconds the man or woman was no match for him. Any well-trained combat pilot could tell within seconds of an engagement whether or not they could defeat the foe. Gray Eagle fired his cannon and the plane dropped from the sky.

But his P-51 shuddered and the controls grew unresponsive. Smoke leaked into the cockpit as

Gray Eagle realized he had been hit. “Rich, I have to ditch. I’ve been hit.”

“Are you hurt?” Marsden shouted into his headset.

“Shit no, just embarrassed. I lose a plane and will have to walk home.”

“Land safely, find a train,” Marsden replied. “I’ve got business on this end, copy?”

“Copy, Colonel.” Gray Eagle tore open his canopy and dropped from the plane as his P-51 began its death slide toward the ground. It accelerated beneath him, exploding before it struck the surface. Just as Gray Eagle’s parachute opened, a fragment from the explosion flew toward him, but he could not move away. The hot metal sliced through his chute and left a section of it flapping, speeding his descent.

Gray Eagle counted off the seconds and pulled the cord on his auxiliary parachute as his first one collapsed. The second chute opened, but he was covered in silk from the first one and unable to see where he was landing.

~ * ~

Look!” Jackson took Wilcox by the arm. “One of our flying machines has been hit!”

Wilcox felt his stomach clench, fearing for the man or woman in the airplane. He saw the body fall from it and the white parachute open.

“They have a means of escape,” he breathed relief.

Wilcox heard the collective gasp from those around him as Gray Eagle's parachute collapsed and the auxiliary chute opened. The troops and civilians were again running away from the plane as it fell from the sky.

"Embry, bring the man in that white canopy to us," Wilcox ordered. "He may be hurt."

Embry rode toward Gray Eagle.

~ * ~

Gray Eagle landed with the jarring technique he had been taught, grateful there was no wind. He tore at the fabric that engulfed him as both chutes covered his body, dragging him to the ground, and vowing to get the newer parachutes he had seen in other universes

He felt someone pulling the silk from him and rose to his knees when daylight appeared. He looked at a union major deftly rolling the parachute into a bundle. Gray Eagle stood.

"Thank you."

"I am Major Josiah Embry," the officer introduced himself. "General Wilcox sent me to aid you. Are you hurt?"

"No, but I need to get back to Warrenton. I'm Major Gray Eagle of the First Air Cavalry."

"It is indeed an honor to meet you, but haste seems in order. My horse," Embry pointed to his horse. He mounted and Gray Eagle swung up behind him, holding the rolled silk of the parachute between them.

"What is your status?" Gray Eagle asked as they rode at a canter toward the front of massed civilians and soldiers.

"We are holding our own, Major. Can that device that saved your life be repaired?"

"No, but we have others, better ones," Gray Eagle explained.

"May I ask that we retain the device you used for escape?"

"My parachute?"

"Is that what it is called?"

Gray Eagle nodded.

Embry directed his horse toward two men standing to the side of the road. "We can make use of the silk."

"It's yours, Major," Gray Eagle offered, suddenly aware that he ached. He had not escaped as lightly as he had first imagined. *Adrenaline is a wonderful thing until it wears off.*

Embry offered a salute to both generals and a hand to Gray Eagle. Gray Eagle dismounted. Embry followed, taking the parachute.

"Sir, Major Gray Eagle tells me his parachute cannot be repaired and he will require another. I thought we might make use of the silk."

"So, that device is called a parachute." The officer in blue studied Gray Eagle.

Gray Eagle saw the three stars on the shoulders of the man in the blue uniform and reasoned he was Wilcox. He saluted Wilcox and the officer in gray beside him. Wilcox was a tall bear of a man, with cinnamon hair and beard. His hazel eyes were alert despite the dark smudges beneath them.

Next to Wilcox the office in gray seemed to have slept in his uniform. His hooded blue eyes reminded Gray Eagle of something he had seen in a book years ago, but he could not place it.

"You are Major Gray Eagle?" the officer asked.

"Yes, sir."

"I am General Thomas Jackson."

Gray Eagle remembered what Gordo had told him about his meeting with Lee. Gray Eagle also remembered where he had seen the man standing before him. In a history book a universe away.

"It is an honor to meet both of you." Gray Eagle resolutely stamped down any feelings at crossing paths with Stonewall Jackson.

"Let's move," Wilcox ordered and Gray Eagle fell in step with the two officers. He was amazed that Wilcox and his troops were keeping up a rapid pace. "We have to move quickly, Major," Wilcox explained. "Between the enemy flying machines bombing us and you shooting them from the sky, we are in danger."

It had not occurred to Gray Eagle that the people on the ground might be hit by debris from the crashing planes. It should have, he realized, but the war he had fought was two decades away.

"We are usually not fighting directly over our forces," Gray Eagle explained. "Aircraft are used to sweep the skies clean for the bombers and to destroy enemy installations. And of course for strafing runs against enemy troops."

"Unfortunately, we are in the way," Wilcox sighed. "But with any luck, not for long."

"I have sent a rider to get word to General Crittenden that you are safe," Jackson told Gray Eagle. "In Frederick, you will be able to get a train to take you back to your base."

"Thank you, sir." Gray Eagle felt a flood of relief. The others would not worry about him when they returned to base.

"You are unafraid to fly again?" Jackson asked.

Gray Eagle, buoyed by his relief, answered. "Yes sir. Why, it's like falling off a horse."

Jackson cast Gray Eagle a dubious stare. "I doubt that, Major. I know of no one who fell a few thousand feet from his horse."

Wilcox snorted, while a few of the officers surrounding them laughed.

"It was the best analogy I could think of, sir." Gray Eagle took a step into something very soft and smelly. "Oh shit." He clapped his hand over his mouth, remembering that the Jackson of his universe was a dour man not given to cursing.

Jackson stopped and glanced at Gray Eagle's boot. "I suppose that isn't a usual problem for the Air Cavalry, is it, Major?"

"Thank God cows and horses don't fly," Embry chuckled.

"Embry," Wilcox growled.

Embry colored, but laughed despite the reprimand, as did Jackson. Gray Eagle shook the offending mess from his boot and continued walking. He decided he would have to re-evaluate the Jackson of this universe.

~ * ~

November 2, 1974 (Universe 10)

The plane trip to Chicago was uneventful and the charted bus was waiting for Barstead and the others at O'Hare Airport. Everyone settled in for the drive to Winchester, while Barstead read several magazines he had purchased at the airport before he boarded the bus. He was intrigued by the fact that personal computers were not yet available in this universe.

"Julian." Beaumont slid into the aisle seat beside Barstead. There were only twenty-two people, including Beaumont, on the bus.

"Yes?"

Beaumont sighed, held out his hands, and said. "Oh, I believe you now. No way I couldn't, but what I don't understand is how you learned about these alternate universes. Why did you even consider their existence as the solution to the ghost problem?"

Barstead shrugged. "It was the manuscript Hans Bechter gave to Amber."

"Why did he give it to her?"

"I've no idea." Barstead closed the magazine, placing it on his lap. "A better question is where he got it. It dates from before the Second World War."

Beaumont shrugged. “Bechter had some connection to the Nazi government, but it was never proven that he aided them. Still, he was permitted to immigrate to the United States.”

Barstead shot the agent a sharp stare. “Working for the Nazis didn’t stop scientists from being admitted to the U.S.”

“Weapons research.” Beaumont glanced away.

“Was that an answer or a reason?”

“Both.” Beaumont stared at the scientist. “If Bechter had some idea what was in that manuscript, and if he had it during the war, why didn’t he give it to the Nazis?”

“Even if he had, they couldn’t have built the device to open a portal. We couldn’t build it even with the manuscript and an actual transfer device. We had to find a Source Gate with the accompanying technical data to accomplish what we did.”

“It was a lucky break, wasn’t it?” Beaumont leaned his head against the plush seat.

“Very.” Barstead glanced out the window at the rush of concrete as the bus sped toward Virginia. “Almost as if it had been left for us. As if someone planned on us finding it.” He suddenly recalled Amber’s comments in Desiree’s house.

“Did Bechter plant the stuff?”

Barstead shook his head. “No, but there are a lot of unanswered questions. And you know what?”

“What?”

"I think General Crittenden may have some of the answers." Which was the main reason why Barstead planned to travel to Warrenton as soon as he crossed into that 1861 universe.

~ * ~

November 2, 1861(Universe 1)

Amber was restless. She didn't want to take the pain medication Reed had prescribed since it made her sleepy. Her wound was held together by staples and healing rapidly. If she didn't bend her leg, the pain was tolerable.

Reed had allowed her to return to the room she shared with the others, saying she would be fit to fly in about a week. From the tiny attic window, she could see the airfield and the new P-51s Rierdon had managed to locate. She was looking forward to flying those new planes, maybe even the lone Messerschmitt sitting to the right of the newly constructed east-west runway.

Harriette had just left after delivering lunch, saying that she wanted to see the planes returning. Amber knew the young woman wanted to fly them but had said nothing to Marsden. Reed seemed to think Harriette should work for him after her help with Joshua. Amber knew differently. Harriette belonged with the pilots, not with the hospital staff.

She pulled herself out of the padded chair and hobbled back to bed. It felt better to rest her leg on a pillow. She sat back against a second pillow and reached for her Palm-Com.

"Damn," she swore. She had forgotten that Weber had taken it the night she spent in the hospital. He had yet to return it and no one seemed concerned. But she was worried about the computer. She had stored a wealth of data in it though not any data dealing with what the Jewel told her in Bennett. That she kept in her head and a memory module hidden in her room.

The Luis, with Gray Eagle's help, had managed to grow a single Jewel-like crystal using the instructions she and Roger had supplied Gray Eagle. They stored it with the others in the security area of the Distillery Barn. Chen Lui had tested it yesterday. The crystal was functional. But this morning, as the planes left, she had limped to the storage area and replaced it with a glass ball Mary Frances had purchased in Warrenton a few days ago. Mary Frances was too busy convincing Crittenden to let her join the army to miss the bauble she had found so attractive.

Amber sighed and rubbed her leg. The effort to appear as if she were merely exercising and not attempting to hide something had drained her of some reserves. Crittenden had seen her, but she managed to convince him she was fine, despite the discomfort of her healing wound.

The overpowering urge to protect the crystal was the goad for Amber to steal and hide it in her room. She should have spoken to Crittenden, but she feared no one would believe her. Besides,

Crittenden knew nothing about what had happened to her and Roger in Bennett.

This crystal had to be protected and soon it had to replace the Jewel in residence in the Source Gate. Something was happening to that Jewel, she could feel it. It was as if a part of her felt a building of forces within the Jewel, establishing a deadly link, but to what?

If only she could speak with Gray Eagle, but he was on his way from Frederick. She would be grateful for his return. At least the Khysids had not destroyed the rails. In fact she wondered exactly what the Khysids were doing. Since they had taken over Washington and routed the Union army, there was little activity except pursuing Wilcox. She wondered when Crittenden would schedule another reconnaissance and who would fly it.

~ * ~

November 6, 1861 (Universe 1)

Gray Eagle returned brimming with news from his train ride and time with Wilcox. The Khysids had withdrawn into Washington and seemed to be securing the city. Wilcox, his troops and the civilians with them, were safe. He had joined Lee at Winchester before leaving for Philadelphia, the new Union capital.

Gordo, with Mary Frances' help, had managed to locate the dual-control Merlin and bring it to Warrenton. Rierdon, now a major in the Joint Army Air Cavalry, was busy expanding a group of men and women to help him locate and acquire goods, equipment, arms, and whatever was needed to prosecute the war. He called them the Pack Rats.

Reed was in the forefront of requesting medical equipment, ranting against the primitive state of medicine in the 1861 universe. He had demanded and gotten physicians to come and train at Warrenton. It had not been easy to convince the physicians of the need for special training, but with each success against disease, and the introduction of antibiotics, many were agreeing to the trip.

The tiny encampment was quickly turning into a major base. New, poured-foam housing was being erected, along with added sanitary facilities and water towers. Through all this, Weber worked alongside the others, seeming to have adapted to his present status. But Amber doubted the man had any intention of helping. He was enacting a charade. He may have fooled the others, but he didn't fool her.

~ * ~

"Are you certain of this?" Kester asked the man standing against the stairs of the abandoned tavern. The house had belonged to the Suratts, a fact Kester found amusing. The owners were now in Khysid hands. They had been recruited for his work, but Kester knew they were expendable.

"Yep." The man spat tobacco onto the ground. "Hear word about it all through Warrenton. Out there at the base for the flying machines, they got them something people are calling a Jewel, but in whispers. Don't make no sense to me, but you said you wanted anything I could find."

"Indeed I did." Kester reached his gloved hand into his pocket, removed a gold piece, and flipped it to the man. "Thanks, Colonel." The informant tucked the reward into his vest pocket. "I'll bring you more news when I hear it."

Kester nodded as the man mounted and cantered away. Kester untied his horse, swung into the saddle, and rode toward the remains of Washington.

~ * ~

It took Kester most of the day to reach Khysid Headquarters at the Embassy Club. Large earth-moving equipment scoured the streets of the empty city, scooping up debris and bodies and piling everything into massive trucks. Combat Engineers were tackling the job of constructing a defensive base big enough to support the influx of Khysid troops into the secured city.

Kester made his way through the mud and offal not yet removed. When he reached the Embassy Club, he was hot, tired, and dirty. He climbed the stairs into the soot-covered building, returning the salutes of the guards stationed around the building's perimeter.

"You look a sight," Colonel Hatar said, glancing at Kester in his civilian garb.

"Is General Sig in the secure room?"

Hatar nodded and gestured with her head. Kester strode along the clean floors, tracking the mud he had been unable to remove from his boots with him. He opened the door to the basement and raced toward the secure room, his heart pounding as he thought about what his informant had told him.

Kester entered the bustling nerve center of the invasion operation, standing at the entrance for a moment in order to locate Sig amid the welter of black uniforms. He found the general leaning over a computer while San sat before it, studying the updated readouts on the hanging screen.

"General San, General Sig," he saluted the officers.

Sig did not return the courtesy. "What is it now, Kester?"

"I have something for your ears only."

"Tell us quickly," San snapped. "We've got an invasion on our hands. Look, Sig, that area by the Naval Yards is a good place for establishing our naval section of the base."

Kester clenched his fists. He was carrying a potential bomb and the two of them were treating him as if he were the very dirt on his boots. He should've known not to trust San, even if she had named him as her second for the Challenge. Kester still wore no general's disk and most likely wouldn't unless he earned it through his own work.

"Very well then."

"General San, the resonance signal has begun again. This time it's stronger." A technician sitting opposite San and viewing the other side of the wafer-thin screen interrupted Kester.

San held up her hand for Kester to be silent. "Code alpha one, dash three, four, five, nine."

The screen she was viewing cleared at her verbal command and the complex graphics of the topology of the alternate universe mathematics appeared. Kester saw the winking red dot, reaching from one point to another. A second red dot was forming some distance away from the first, and the line from it snaked toward the first like a rat threading a maze.

"This makes no sense. Only another Jewel would set up this sort of resonance."

"The enemy has a Jewel at Warrenton." Kester dropped his bomb.

Sig jerked erect. "What?"

"One of my informants told me." He explained what the informant had learned from his trip to the base at Warrenton.

His superiors smiled, and Kester wondered how they could be elated at the news. "I don't understand. They have a Jewel, probably a Source Gate."

San nodded. "Oh, yes, they have a Source Gate, these lines and dots indicate it. The Jewel in Warrenton is reaching out to establish a link to ours."

"Why?"

"Occasionally a pair of Jewels will set up a resonance between them, just like temporal resonance can occur between universes. It's happening here. The Jewel in our Source Gate is recruiting the one in Warrenton to its use."

"But what does that mean?" Kester squinted at the two lines.

"In a few days, the two lines will meet and establish a link. How soon can you get shock troops ready, Sig?"

"Two hours."

"Get them ready on standby. As soon as this link is established, I want them to take the Warrenton base."

Kester glanced at the two generals. "It's heavily guarded."

"From without, Kester." San smoothed her lower lip with the tip of her finger. "But the link, once it stabilizes, will let us cross from here to Warrenton and come through their portal. Like the old back orifices of the primitive silicon technologies. They won't be able to close it and we'll take the base before they realize what's happened."

Sig eyes narrowed as he stared at the screen. "This explains why we couldn't locate the scientists. Somewhere they found a working Jewel."

"And we will use it against them." San relaxed in her chair.

Sig laughed. "And be rid of all opposition. How sweet to use what they think is their salvation to destroy them."

Twenty-two

Every spirit comes back every time.
Codex of Flowering Butterfly

November 10, 1961 (Universe 0)

Four cars rumbled onto the driveway of an old farmhouse outside of Warrenton. The owners of the house, an elderly couple, were vacationing in Florida. The drivers pulled the cars behind the house in order to screen their activity from the highway. They would spend the time until evening rehearsing their planned actions.

Croll and Kraft had arrived about three hours later. Croll called his special unit of commandos together and explained it was important to take some of the scientists as hostages, but Weber was to be killed. Every man in the squad had memorized Weber's photograph. Croll estimated it would take them about a half hour to secure the Warrenton base using automatic weapons. Weber's last communication suggested that the base was sparsely occupied.

The team made its way to an old barn, still in good repair, to wait for the agreed upon signal. As he waited, Croll fingered the tiny communicator Weber had slipped through to him several days earlier. Soon, he vowed, the technology the scientists had would be his, and no one would ever stand against him. He would use it as he saw fit. His mind spun a deadly fantasy while he waited.

~ * ~

November 11, 1861(universe 1)

The digital readout of Amber's watch said 1:15 a.m. She had gone to bed fully clothed so there was no need to dress before she sneaked from the house. Hugging the shadows around the porch, she wished Rierdon had not been so quick to supply lighting to the base and the fuel cells to run it. The sentries were visible, but so was she. Crittenden had instituted a policy requiring written permission to access the rooms housing the Source Gate. She had none and, in any case, the sentries would wonder why she was out this time of night.

With infinite care, she counted off their rounds before ducking to every shred of cover as she made her way to the distillery barn. Two more sentries guarded the entrance. There were also two inside guarding the door to the room housing the Source Gate, another recent precaution of Crittenden's. He had grown concerned once rumors had begun to circulate in Warrenton concerning the Jewel and the technology at the base.

She knew it was destined to get out about the activities at the base. “Try explaining airplanes and technology that appears out of nowhere and see what happens,” she muttered. “Now, to get rid of the sentries.”

She placed the EM Stinger on light stun. The men would be unconscious for only a minute or two, but that would allow her to get into the building. She recalled that, at dinner, Weber had been elated, babbling that he had some new ideas for upgrading the Source Gate. Amber had corralled Gray Eagle after dinner and confided her growing fears. He had promised to keep an eye on Weber, but Marsden and Crittenden had kept him busy with details of the setup of the Air Cavalry. She could wait no longer. She had to see what Weber was doing.

As she watched the sentries before the distillery-barn, she felt urgency growing with each minute she waited. The feeling of danger had crept over her slowly until she could no longer shove it aside. Whatever Weber was doing, he was endangering everyone. But she was being shunted aside, no one listening to her as she tried to explain her growing concern.

Amber counted the last round of the sentries and fired. The two guards dropped to the ground. She darted to the door, slipping inside before either regained consciousness. The building was warm and dry, kept so by an elaborate HVAC system. No one was around, since the Source Gate was rarely used between the hours of midnight and 6 a.m.

It seemed to her that her boots made noise no matter how hard she tried to be quiet as she entered the room housing the Source Gate. But if the noise was audible, it did not attract attention. Lights in the building were kept on around the clock, easing her path to the room she was seeking. As she approached, she realized the door was ajar. The humming sound of an activated Source Gate leaked into the hallway.

The guards lay dead beside the doorway. Her stomach muscles tightened as she continued inching her way to the door. She glanced inside. Weber stood before the Source Gate, operating the newly installed controls he had bragged about this evening. The Source Gate was fully activated. The softly glowing Jewel, suspended by five, thick fiber optic ropes, was cradled as gently as a newborn.

To Weber's left, the familiar beginnings of the hemispherical portal covered the space before the wall. Amber's breath caught as the portal cleared and she saw into a barn set in another universe. In that barn stood a squad of men dressed in camouflage with blackened faces holding automatic weapons and waiting before the opening.

The officer in charge of the soldiers hesitated, apparently not as confident on seeing the actuality of a portal as he had been with the theory. Behind him, Amber saw another officer in the uniform of an Army general and beside him Mark Kraft.

Next to Weber, on the wall, was a switch rigged to send a signal to activate the newly installed base alarms, but she would have to reach it. There was no switch outside the room. To reach the switch, she had to stop the commandos before they stepped into the room. Her EM Stinger was ineffective at this distance, so she ducked into the hallway and lifted a musket from one of the dead soldiers. Amber checked to see that he had loaded it, and stepped inside the room. She aimed the gun at the portal.

"Stay where you are!" she shouted.

Weber turned, swore, and started toward her as the lead commando overcame his reluctance and stepped across the threshold of the portal. Amber fired. The kick of the musket drove her backward several paces. The commando dropped to the floor of the room housing the Source Gate while those behind him scattered. His gun flew toward the console, coming to rest near it.

"She's got no other weapon!" Weber called as Amber reached for the second musket.

Ignoring the commando's gun, Weber pulled his EM Stinger and raced toward her. When Weber reached her, Amber swung the musket, knocking the Stinger from Weber's hand. He cursed and threw himself at her, while behind him the commandos poured through the stabilized opening. They collided with the pair, knocking them to the ground, and jumped over them. One of the commandos recognized Weber and fired a burst from his assault rifle at him. Weber took the brunt of the gunfire, but a bullet pierced Amber's shoulder. Her left arm went numb and she lay quiet, feigning death, while the men raced past her. The commandos continued along the corridor.

They seemed to know where they were going, suggesting that Weber had supplied Croll with a plan of the base. Amber bit her lips and crawled from beneath Weber when the last man exited the corridor. She used the door to pull herself erect, staggering into the room housing the Source Gate as she struggled against the pain of her wound. Her left arm hung limp and useless and pain burned in her shoulder. Against this new pain, the pain from her leg wound was not even a distraction.

“Stay away,” Croll ordered as he stepped into the room and fired a shot from his pistol.

She ducked aside, reached up, and pulled the switch to the alarm. Nothing happened.

“He disconnected it.” Kraft said as Croll stepped gingerly back into his own universe.

Neither man moved nearer the portal. She sensed that, despite Croll’s brief venture into the 1861 universe, he was afraid of the portal. She darted across the room to the controls.

“Shoot me and the portal goes.” She hoped she sounded convincing. She bit her lips against the sudden return of feeling and movement to her left arm. A throbbing pain coursed from her shoulder to the tips of her fingers.

“Damn you,” he cursed.

Her words bought her the time she needed. She activated the secondary alarm. The wailing klaxon rang across the base. Out of the corner of her eye, she saw Croll and Kraft scurry away from the opened portal.

Amber began the deactivating sequence, but the controls were unresponsive, even though Weber had not locked them. She glanced to her left and saw the portal taking on a strange appearance. She realized that Croll and Kraft were trying to escape what was happening to the portal. But just what was happening?

It was as if someone had put waves in a mirror. The images of Croll and Kraft disappeared, and the portal began to regenerate as if it had been cleared and restarted. She shook her head, wondering if her injury was affecting her mind.

"Who's there?" she called, hearing scraping sounds by the door.

"Stop!" Sergeant Gage ordered as he entered the room.

"It's me, Gage. I'm trying to close the portal. Weber let Croll's men through."

"Get away from it!" Gage ordered her.

Amber looked up from her actions to Gage. His face was drained of color, his eyes fixed on the portal. She turned to her left and saw the cause of his terror. Facing them was no longer a barn contiguous with the one in which they stood. It was a room filled with Khysid troops and housing another Jewel.

Amber felt the Jewel brush her mind. But unlike Bennett, there was no color or sound, just raw emotion and something like memory. “What is it?” she demanded.

“Destroy me.” The Jewel sang the words into her mind. “Destroy me, or all that you love, all that you care for will die.”

Amber turned to the Jewel. “How?”

“The gun from the dead man, use it. The Jewels have linked. Do it now!”

Amber did not question the command. Ignoring her pain, she reached for the gun the commando had dropped. It was lying a few feet from her. One of the Khysid soldiers stepped through the portal and into the room. He aimed his gun at her. Gage shot him and he dropped back through the portal. But not before he returned fire, a bullet striking Gage in the shoulder. Gage fell by the open door.

“Kill her!” A shouted order by a Khysid officer.

Ignoring a death sentence, Amber turned her back to the portal and lifted the gun above her head. She heard the Khysid soldier enter the room through the portal and fire his gun. As a bullet struck her in the back, exiting through her chest she staggered against the console but continued the downward motion with the rifle as she fell forward. The butt of the heavy automatic rifle struck the Jewel. The Jewel shattered in an eruption of blue-white fury, the ropes holding it separating and thrashing like electrified serpents.

Time slowed as light engulfed her and she could not breathe. For what seemed like minutes but were only seconds, a piercing brightness coursed through her injured body, filling her mind with a deluge of images and knowledge. It was as if the Jewel were draining itself through her. And she knew in that instant that it could not do this unless it was in some way part of her, had always been part of her.

"How can this be?" she whispered as she slipped to the floor.

The electricity in the room housing the Source Gate failed.

Barely conscious, Amber felt her chest. There was no pain, but her uniform was soaked with blood. She shoved her hand beneath her jacket and found smooth skin. There was no exit wound. At that moment she realized that her left arm no longer ached, nor did her shoulder or her leg. Her vision cleared, though she felt disoriented as she tried to rationalize what had happened to the injuries she had sustained only moments ago.

It occurred to her that the open portal was the only light source in the room. She rolled to her right side and looked at it. The Khysid officer who had shot her had retreated to his side of the portal and panic had set in at their end of the link.

"The link, that's what happened," she whispered as she realized what the Jewel had meant.

The Jewel beneath Washington had established a link with the Jewel in the Warrenton Source Gate. Amber understood some of the knowledge the Jewel had imparted to her. Not just understood, but remembered as if this had happened before. But there was no time for her to understand. The Jewel had done more, she knew. Somehow it had healed her wounds.

Before she could rise, the portal imploded, turning into foaming darkness with only a tiny silver-white vortex at the center. But the nightmare was not over. The vortex seemed to become a giant magnet and everything in the room acted as if it were made of steel. Whatever was not secured flew toward the portal, some of the items striking Amber on their way to the ravenous silver throat. She hunkered down, covering her head, but she too felt the pull. She reached to the side of the console for support.

It was like being downwind in a hurricane trying to fight your way up wind. She saw the door tear from its hinges and reach the vortex as she inched behind the console. She put the massive bulk of the machine between herself and the sucking maw of the vortex. The door crumpled as it was drawn into the tiny throat, while the machine before her strained against the screws anchoring it to the floor.

Gage slid toward the vortex. Amber reached out, grabbing him by his uninjured arm. She clung to him. As he began slipping from her hold, she tightened her grip and he drew her with him.

She screamed. "No!"

She and Gage were pulled toward the vortex, their speed increasing as they neared it. They spun to the base of the portal before the inward rush stopped as suddenly as it had started. The portal collapsed, leaving the two on the floor, before the stone wall.

Amber took a shaky breath, opened her eyes, and looked at darkness. All the lights in the building were out. For a moment, she lay next to Gage listening to his breathing. Then she managed to sit, reaching out to him and shaking his body.

"Sergeant?"

She still heard his breath, but he was unresponsive. The faint sounds of gunfire were audible now that the maelstrom in the room had dissipated. Light appeared in the corridor and Amber heard footsteps.

"Over there. The two guards are dead."

She recognized Reed's voice. "In here. Sergeant Gage is wounded."

Reed stood by the entrance to the room, holding aloft his electric lantern. He stepped inside calling. "Get in here now. We have an injured man."

"The commandos, where are they?" she asked. Reed's face took on a mask-like appearance in the wan light. The shadows from the lantern exaggerated the planes of his forehead and cheeks.

"They're being rounded up now," he rumbled while examining Gage. "What the hell are you doing here?"

"I knew Weber was up to something."

"Why didn't you tell Alex?" Reed looked up as two men entered. "Get this man to the hospital. He's been shot."

The soldiers loaded Gage onto a litter and left the room. Reed stood, reached down and grabbed Amber by the arm. He lifted her to her feet.

"I'm fine." But she realized her face and jaw ached.

"Come with me to the hospital now," Reed ordered. "I want to check you out. Give you a chance to meet Dr. Blackwell."

"Who's he?" Amber was forced to accompany Reed. He had not released her arm.

"She," Reed corrected. "Major Elizabeth Blackwell, a physician, sent by Lincoln."

"The name seems familiar," she said, wanting to tell Reed what had happened but suddenly afraid he would not believe her.

"It should. She existed in our universe as well and was a physician of some note or notoriety."

The pair left the room and hurried from the building. Additional light flooded the camp while soldiers assembled in one of the flat areas near the distillery barn. Amber watched the activity, feeling detached from everything surrounding her. Once at the hospital, she was left in the care of a petite Dr. Blackwell.

After a quick introduction, Blackwell stared at her blood-soaked uniform and asked. "What sort of a fight have you been in?"

"I was shot three times,"

Blackwell's eyes scanned Amber before she used the magnetic imager to trace a similar path. "I see no such injuries. Where did the blood come from? The imager indicates it's your blood."

"I know." Amber rubbed her temples, her head feeling stuffed with the recent events. "The Jewel healed the injuries somehow."

Blackwell shrugged. "Well, it didn't do a good job on your face."

"Oh, that happened later, when the vortex opened and stuff started flying around."

"I'll treat what I can, but from what I read on this device, nothing is broken, just what Walt calls soft-tissue damage." She placed the imager on the table. "I have no idea how you came to have your blood on your uniform, but you have no wounds."

"How long have you been here?" Amber changed the subject.

"Not long enough," Blackwell responded, lifting a paper packet and adding a handful of pills from a labeled jar sitting on a shelf. "These are for pain."

"I still have some pain pills to use for the shrapnel wound on my leg."

Blackwell swung on Amber. "You have no wound on either leg, according to the imager."

"It's gone now, doctor." Amber was confused and tired. "Everything is gone. We'll have to start over."

Blackwell came to Amber, cupped Amber's chin in her hand and stared at the young woman's eyes. "You haven't any brain injury, according to the imager, and your eyes are clear and reactive." She removed her hand. "Still, I want you to stay in bed for a day, just to make sure. These newfangled machines may not be as smart as Walt makes them out to be."

Amber realized the woman didn't believe her. "Dr. Reed said President Lincoln sent you. Women doctors are rare in this universe."

"Not as scarce as hen's teeth, as some would have you think. We are around, just not permitted to practice as do men." She tucked the packet of pills into Amber's hand.

"Why did Lincoln send you?"

"Because I told him to." She placed a TD patch on Amber's neck, discarding the container afterwards. "That will stop any infection. Now go to bed and stay there. I'll soon get my taste of the form of surgery Walt says we must use. I've had little training in the new methods." She strode from the room as Amber saluted her.

Alone for the moment, Amber allowed her mind to replay the events that had just occurred. She needed to see Gray Eagle and wondered where he was. She wondered what had happened to the men who had invaded the camp. Unable to find any answers standing in the hospital, she left to find Crittenden. But he found her first, in the person of Hargrove.

"General Crittenden wants to see you now!" Captain Hargrove shouted at her, beckoning her toward him. He was standing beneath one of the new lights. When she reached him, he stared at her and at her uniform.

She saluted him. "I'm not hurt," she said. "But I need to talk to General Crittenden." She turned toward the farmhouse. But Hargrove stopped her.

"Amber, you have a bullet hole in the back of your uniform."

"I have an exit one in the front as well," she retorted and continued her determined march toward the farmhouse.

~ * ~

"How many dead?" Sig stared at the shambles that a few moments ago had been the hub of the invasion.

"Twenty-three," one of the officers replied.

"How badly damaged is the Jewel?"

"It will take a day or so to assess, General Sig," a technician offered, standing just out of Sig's reach.

"Give me an idea," Sig demanded as he continued to watch the cleanup.

"I'd say power will be reduced to forty percent, if we're lucky."

"We better be lucky," Sig growled and stormed from the room. He climbed the stairs to the main floor. The large parlor was empty when he entered it. Brandy sat in a crystal decanter on a cherry sideboard opposite a mahogany loveseat. Two overstuffed sofas faced each other, a large cherry table between them.

Sig marched to the sideboard, poured a drink and plopped onto the loveseat as San entered the room. He stood, but she motioned for him to sit.

"I just heard." She sat opposite him.

"Shall I get you a brandy?" Sig asked.

She shook her head. "No. I want a complete assessment of the damage. How soon can we reactivate?"

"Probably not for a few days." Sig gulped his brandy. "You know we're trapped here until the Source Gate is on line. We've pulled the one from the 1961 universe. It was due here today."

"I've gotten word to the operatives in the buffer universe. They'll hole up until we can get them across." San rested her head on the back of the sofa. "How was the link broken?"

"One of the soldiers from the Warrenton base shattered their Jewel." Sig finished his brandy, rose, and poured another. "But Brul managed to put a bullet through her."

"Her?" San sat erect. "Interesting, she must have been one of the pilots."

Sig took another swig of brandy. "That's one less to trouble us."

"This puts us behind schedule." San managed to impart irritation into the sentence.

"And we've degraded another Jewel," Sig reminded her. "But we have others."

"Not as good as the one we almost lost."

Sig lifted his glass and smiled at San over the rim. "True, but I suspect the Jewel at Warrenton was the only one they had. Now they have none. They too are trapped and it's only a matter of time before we finish them off." He sipped his brandy, contented for the first time that morning.

~ * ~

November 11, 1961(Universe 0)

Croll pounded on the wall of the barn in

frustration. His men were gone and the opening sealed. That little bitch had alerted the camp, but she had done something else to the device Weber called a Source Gate.

“We still have one of the Jewels,” Kraft said into the quiet of the empty barn.

Croll turned to face him. “True, but we don’t have the instructions on how to use it.”

“We can reverse engineer it,” Kraft insisted. “If the ISIR people did it, so can we.”

“What about my men?” Croll demanded.

Kraft stared at the wall where the opening had been. “Let’s wait and see. They may succeed.”

“You don’t believe that for a moment,” Croll snorted.

“No, I don’t. But I don’t believe they will be allowed to stay in that universe either. That means someone will have to come and negotiate with us for their return.”

“Are you thinking what I’m thinking?”

Kraft nodded. “He went with them. He’ll be back, I can taste it.”

“I’ll not give up that device Weber sent.” Croll folded his arms across his chest.

“Call the lab in New Mexico and have them create a false report. The thing looks fragile. It could, say, be destroyed during testing,” Kraft suggested.

Croll unfolded his arms. “Indeed it could.” He glanced again at the wall. “I hope one of my men got Weber.”

"What if they didn't?"

A soft, silky smile lit Croll's features. "It would be better for him. They still hang you for treason in that world. Remember, there it's1861."

~ * ~

November 11, 1861 Universe 1)

Crittenden stormed into his office to find Amber standing beside his desk. "I've got a camp filled with fifteen soldiers from your universe, armed with automatic weapons. Never mind the damage they caused. What have you to say about this?"

Amber stood erect. "I knew Weber was up to something and I sneaked out to see what it was."

"Your uniform is covered in blood." Crittenden's mouth opened. He took two steps toward her. "Your face, what happened?"

"I think you better get Gray Eagle and Roger to hear this as well," she sighed, fatigue creeping into her words. She shivered despite the warmth of the office.

"Why?"

"Because you need to hear this and they already know what the Jewel did in Bennett."

Crittenden wiped his face with his hands. "What do you mean?"

"Please, it's important. We didn't even tell the others what happened in Bennett." She had to convince him to send for them.

He walked to the door and summoned Hargrove. "Send for Major Gray Eagle and Lieutenant Merit."

He shut the door and turned to Amber. “Sit down, Amber. You look as if you are about to faint.”

Amber slumped onto a sofa while Crittenden continued to pace behind her. His office was filled with twenty-first century technology but held nineteenth century furnishings. She thought absently that it looked elegant, not like the sterile offices she had seen in other universes.

The office, originally a parlor, had a small conservatory adjacent to it. Bea had had the doors removed and the original furniture clustered in the conservatory providing Crittenden with a less official area to entertain guests. It was growing light and the warmth of the room was a soporific. Amber’s head drooped. The sharp rap at the door stopped sleep from claiming her.

“Come in,” Crittenden barked. Gray Eagle and Roger entered. “Go, join Amber,” Crittenden ordered. “It seems we have a lot to discuss.”

Bea Crittenden entered the room after the two men, shutting the door behind her. She was dressed and Amber suspected the noise and gunfire had awakened her.

“Alex, what happened?”

Crittenden swung to face his wife. “I have something to deal with,” he said, but Bea scooted past him and hurried to Amber.

“My God, what happened?” she demanded.

From the look on Gray Eagle’s face, Amber suspected he was about to ask the same question. “Weber tried to aid General Croll to invade the base. I had to destroy the Jewel in the Source Gate to stop a link from forming and I got shot in the process."

Bea sat next to her, tracing the damage to Amber's uniform with her hand. "This is an exit hole, Alex." She pulled Amber forward. "There is a bullet hole in the back of your uniform."

"Hargrove noticed that too," Amber whispered.

Gray Eagle sat next to her and demanded. "What happened?"

She told him.

~ * ~

Barstead insisted on accompanying Wilcox and Lee on the train to the Warrenton Air Base, and Connie and Sam insisted on going with him. Beaumont, learning that his sister was at the base, demanded that he be allowed to accompany Barstead and the others. At any other time, the thought of speaking with people who seemed to have stepped from the pages of a history book would have excited Beaumont. Now all he could think about was Mary Frances and getting her away from this universe.

While the others chatted with the two generals, Beaumont sat alone, sipping coffee served by a porter. He did not expect the 1861 trains to have dining cars, but this train had several special cars designed for some rich financier and given to the Union government for Lincoln's use.

"You seem worried, Mr. Beaumont."

Beaumont glanced up to see Lee standing beside his seat. He rose. "I'm concerned for my sister's safety," he answered, feeling awkward in the man's presence. The Lee facing him was not the careworn image filling the pages of the history texts he had read. This man was vital, very much alive, and his eyes held genuine concern.

"I'm certain she is safe," Lee offered. "We will arrive in Warrenton within the hour. General Crittenden should have already received our message."

Beaumont sighed. "What will happen here, in this universe?"

Lee studied Beaumont for a second before replying. "General Wilcox and I mean to win this war, Mr. Beaumont. To that end, we can use all the help we can get. Any offer of aid will be accepted."

Twenty-three

To end one phase is to begin another.
Codex of Flowering Butterfly

November 11, 1861 (Universe 1)

Crittenden sat opposite Amber, his eyes closed in thought, his hands gripping the arms of his chair. Gray Eagle lingered on the edge of the sofa holding Amber's hand as she finished her tale.

"Where is this crystal, this synthesized version of the Jewel?" Crittenden asked when she stopped speaking.

"In the attic room I'm sharing with Kit and Harriette."

Gray Eagle released her hand. Her instincts had been accurate. They always were. He should have listened to her. "You feared Weber would destroy the crystal, so you hid it?"

"It was a fortunate choice," Crittenden observed. "When the storage area was searched after the raid, the container holding the Jewels was filled with debris. It appeared the other Jewels had been broken."

“We have to be sure, sir, that Weber didn’t send at least one of them to Croll,” Amber said. “The Source Gate has a built-in log program that records every transfer that drew on its energy. It also records an image of what was brought here or sent from here. We should be able to recover the data, even with the loss of the Jewel.”

Crittenden’s eyes widened. “When was that installed?”

“When Cc began to bring stuff across. He insisted we have such a log, so I put one in for him.”

Crittenden rubbed his forehead. “Why didn’t you tell me this before?”

She blinked. “I thought Cc did.”

Gray Eagle merely shook his head. He understood the sharpness of the question. Crittenden commanded the base and any action taken on it should have been cleared with him. But the ISIR people were behaving as if they were still at the institute. They were working for the same goal, but at cross-purposes. He suspected Crittenden was exasperated with them and he had a right to be so.

“General, it’s our fault. We’re not used to…”

“To what, Major? Being in the army? ” Crittenden stood. “But this is a military base under my command.” He glared at Amber. “Though one would be hard-pressed to think so. Amber, you do not act independently of your commanding officer."

Bea interrupted. “Alex, the child is exhausted.”

"Bea, she is not a child. She is one of my officers."

"I didn't realize what I did was wrong," Amber protested.

"Not wrong, perhaps, but it is what you call…" Crittenden searched for a word. "That late twentieth-century term Major Rierdon is always using… inappropriate."

Gray Eagle smiled at the idea of Crittenden picking up twentieth-century jargon, though he knew the man was being generous in his description. He should have used the word insubordinate.

Bea patted Amber's hand. "You take that medication Dr. Blackwell gave you."

"I need to take it with food," Amber explained.

"There is a large pot of pea soup in the main refrigerator. I'll fill a cup and heat it in the microwave for you."

Gray Eagle fought down the urge to chuckle. Crittenden must have read his mind. He shot Gray Eagle an annoyed stare. But Gray Eagle could not stop the smile spreading across his face.

"This is going to be a very strange and interesting war," he whispered.

"Major?" Crittenden continued to stare at him

"General, since Amber hid the version of the Jewel we made, we can rebuild the Source Gate. How this new one will behave is another matter."

"It will be safer," Amber insisted. "I think it won't be as powerful, but it also won't link with the Jewels the Khysids are using."

"Did you learn this from the Jewel before you destroyed it?" Crittenden demanded.

"Probably, but I can't sort out everything in my head." She rubbed her temples as if her head ached. Gray Eagle saw Crittenden's face soften as he watched her. Amber was a sight, with her blood-stiffened uniform and bruised face. Bea had prepared an ice pack while Amber had told her tale. The melted remains of the ice pack were residing in a large majolica platter.

Gray Eagle knew that he and the ISIR people had a lot to teach Crittenden and his people, but they had a lot to learn as well.

He stood. "Sir, may I make a suggestion?"

Crittenden nodded.

"Perhaps you might call a meeting of the ISIR people and we can discuss staying out of each other's way."

Crittenden stared at Gray Eagle. "Except for Margaret Aksawan and Chen and Marie Lui, I intend to get you all in uniform. Then you will stay out of each other's way or else. But those three absolutely refuse to join the army."

Gray Eagle shook his head at the man's determination, though the threat was somewhat hollow. Crittenden was firm, but fair, and Gray Eagle had seen no evidence of harsh treatment of anyone at the camp. Crittenden's idea of discipline was to keep everyone too busy to get into trouble. Problem was he had to regain control of the ISIR people, who were busy but running in all directions.

"This is a new form of warfare," Gray Eagle reiterated.

"Too new," Crittenden allowed, staring at the sun-filled windows of the room. "My God, what time is it?" Crittenden removed his watch, glancing at the face. "They're due here this morning."

"Who?" Gray Eagle asked.

Crittenden tossed the watch he held to Gray Eagle. "Wilcox and Lee, along with some of your ISIR people. The last group arrived. I received the telegram yesterday."

Gray Eagle caught the watch. He looked quizzically at Crittenden.

"Look at the watch, Major. It has shadows for hands."

Gray Eagle examined the watch. Both Amber and Roger stood and squinted at the holographic face.

"Where did you get it?" Gray Eagle asked.

"It was left for a friend by one of the members of the Triangle Club. The club member said it was to be used to kill him. My friend's name is Trevor Towsen and he was to be killed in a steamboat explosion. He took the watch when he escaped the steamboat, but the boat still exploded."

"I bet it's an RF device," Roger suggested.

"It's probably a signaling device for a fuse," Gray Eagle explained. "When did this explosion happen?"

"Before the war began," Crittenden told them. "If you open the back of the watch, you will find inside those little things you call microprocessors. One says laser optics, made in New Jersey."

Gray Eagle handed Crittenden his watch. "How long before Manassas do you suppose the Khysids were here?" Crittenden tucked the watch into his uniform. "As early as 1859, if my sources are accurate. And I must return this watch to Trevor some day."

Gray Eagle suspected his sources were accurate. "I don't understand."

Crittenden explained. "It seems the Khysids established an organization called the Triangle Club. I mentioned those clubs before, but not the details. The price of membership in the club was a human life. Three independent clubs existed as bases: one each in Richmond, in Washington and Baltimore. Trevor was instrumental in destroying the one in Richmond."

"But not Washington or Baltimore." Gray Eagle was beginning to see why those cities had fallen. "Richmond would have fallen too, but for this friend of yours?"

Crittenden nodded. "There is no club in Philadelphia. Mr. McBride had the city searched. It was one of the first things he did after the meeting at Manassas."

Gray Eagle understood. "The Khysids wouldn't be interested in Philly anyway," he said. "They had planned to take Richmond and Washington. Those were the capitals of the two countries in our war as well."

"Take the capitals, take the governments, and the whole of the country would have fallen quickly," Crittenden sighed.

"But our arrival threw a monkey wrench into their plans," Amber offered. "So did your friend when he destroyed the Khysid base in Richmond. I wonder how they originally intended to take this universe?"

"You, Lieutenant, can worry about that later," Crittenden told her. "Bea is right. You take that medication and get some rest. We will talk after supper."

"Are you angry with me?"

"Furious, but that will pass," he said. "Now what I just told you to do is called a direct order," he explained with the patience of a teacher trying to convince an obstinate child. "You are supposed to obey it without question."

"I think I can do that this time," she said.

Gray Eagle snorted, but Crittenden shot him a "be quiet" stare.

"Then do it, Lieutenant. You and Lieutenant Merit are dismissed."

The pair offered Crittenden a passable salute and left the room, ushered out by an anxious Bea. Gray Eagle shook his head in amusement.

"Both Rich and I will talk to them, sir. We'll talk to all the ISIR people. In our world, they would have had officer's training before being commissioned. At least some sort of basic training."

"Their training so far has consisted of aerial combat, more important to us than military protocol. But they will be interacting with others."

Gray Eagle glanced at Crittenden. "Like Generals Lee and Wilcox?"

Crittenden nodded. "Yes, them as well."

Gray Eagle said. "I see what you mean."

"I have no doubt about any of you or your loyalty, Gray Eagle. Amber risked her life to save this base. I want you to personally examine the damage in the room housing the Source Gate and report to me as soon as you finish. Only you will be allowed into that room."

"But if you trust us, sir?"

"I trust you, but no one must know about these incidents with the Jewel. A device that transmits information into a person's mind must be kept secret for now. All that we have learned so far must be kept within the confines of this room. Have you ever wondered if the Jewels used by the Khysids give them information as well?"

Gray Eagle shook his head. "Amber said the Jewel told her no Jewel would give the Khysids information on how to build a device to create portals."

"Interesting," Crittenden mused. "But does it tell them other things?"

Gray Eagle shrugged, aware of the cleverness behind the question. He knew Crittenden was head of Army Intelligence as well as the Air Cavalry. What was happening was indeed a new form of warfare, and Gray Eagle could think of no one better qualified to deal with it than the man standing before him.

"Gray Eagle, when you have time, I want you to teach me to fly."

"Sir?"

"I should have some idea what it is like to operate the flying machines. Colonel Reed says I'm fit."

Gray Eagle wondered when Reed had accepted a commission. Crittenden was wasting no time in getting those he needed into uniform. The color of the uniform depended on what was available. At this point, the color no longer mattered.

"And you will have a new pupil," Crittenden added. "Harriette Bouchard. I have just signed her commission."

Apparently the color of one's skin no longer mattered. Gray Eagle knew he had been accepted, but then his skills were needed. So were Mark's. With Harriette, Crittenden had broken a real barrier. Gray Eagle wondered if the man knew what he was doing. He knew, Gray Eagle's mind whispered.

"At your convenience, General, I will teach you to fly."

"Without interrupting the training of the others," Crittenden said.

"Yes, Cc just got us our first combat trainer, a dual control P-51. Now, I believe you also gave me an order about the Source Gate."

Crittenden returned Gray Eagle's salute. Gray Eagle left the office and stood on the porch. The day was bright and warm and the clear blue skies were empty of clouds. It was a great day for flying, he thought, once he finished his assessment of the Source Gate. He left the porch and stopped to look at the burgeoning airfield to the west. Yes, he thought, a great day to teach a Confederate general in the Joint Army how to fly.

~ * ~

November 12, 1861 (Universe 1)

Crittenden sat opposite Beaumont, listening to the man describe Croll. Finally he interrupted. "Mr. Beaumont, we know that Weber sent Croll one of the devices known as a Jewel. Also a device manufactured here to be used as a communicator."

Beaumont snapped forward in his chair. "If Croll builds a Source Gate…"

Crittenden shook his head. "He cannot."

"Why?" Beaumont let his gaze travel to the windows of the conservatory. It was mid-afternoon and the room was warm. His head ached with what he had just learned from Crittenden, and he was having trouble assimilating it.

"Mr. Beaumont," Crittenden gently summoned Beaumont's wandering attention. "General Croll lacks the technical expertise to engineer the device you mentioned. This we know."

Beaumont wondered how Crittenden knew that fact. But he had no doubt the man was speaking the truth. The sheer audacity of his grasp of advanced technology disoriented Beaumont.

"My sister wants to stay, sir. I can't refuse her wish and she wouldn't listen to me in any case."

"It is her choice."

"Yes." Beaumont rubbed the brocade on the arm of his chair. "But I can't stay. I feel I must return."

"In a few days, we will see to it that you are sent home. But I want you to speak with Croll about his men. Three are dead, two seriously wounded, and four more have minor wounds."

"You plan to send them back?"

Crittenden nodded. "I find their behavior and ideas rather repulsive. It's one thing to do your duty, but these men do not belong with us."

"What am I going to tell Croll?"

"If you would accept a little advice?"

A smile lit Beaumont's face. "From you, sir, always."

~ * ~

November 16, 1961(Universe 0)

"You can't go in there," the secretary commanded. Beaumont shoved past the woman, slamming the door in her face as he stormed into Croll's office.

Croll was on his feet dialing for security. "I'll have you shot."

"You do and Vance will kill you."

Croll held the phone, his hand still on the dial. "What?"

"You remember Carl Vance, everyone's favorite hit man?" Beaumont pulled a chair before Croll's desk and sat. "He owes me big time for a little matter two years ago. Anything happens to me, I even get a cold, and he nails you."

Croll returned the phone to the receiver. "What do you want?"

"To see you get your men back, the ones still alive. And I want the devices Weber sent to you, all of them."

Croll returned to his swivel chair and toyed with a pen. "I don't know what you mean."

"No fencing, Croll. They kept a log. One Weber was unaware of. He sent you a Jewel, a Palm-Com, and a communication device. I want all three of them, now."

"Pity I can only supply you with two," Croll's lips flattened against his teeth in a mummified smile. "I can give you the report on the thing you called a Jewel. Fragile item, seems my technicians destroyed it while trying to understand it."

Beaumont was uncertain if Croll was telling the truth, though he knew Weber had destroyed the others kept in storage. "I'll take the report and the other two items, Croll. You will inform my superiors I was on a special mission for you dealing with this liaison group."

"And if I don't there is always Vance? Tell me, Arthur, when did you become so smart and manipulative?"

"I was always smart, but working with you has made me manipulative. Now the items, if you please."

"I'll get them for you." Croll stood and went to the wall safe in his office. As he worked to open it, he spoke. "You must realize what knowledge those scientists have. The people in that universe, we can always make a deal. They need soldiers. We have plenty."

"They need to be left alone." Beaumont offered no further information.

"What about you?" Croll removed the communicator, the Palm-Com, and an inch-thick report. He walked to Beaumont and handed them to him.

"I have my duty to the president." Beaumont took the items and locked them in his briefcase.

"Which president is that, Kennedy or Lincoln?"

Beaumont stood. "Both," he said and left the office.

~ * ~

Beaumont waited near the visitor's center of Antietam Battlefield Park, stamping his feet to keep them warm. A spattering of wet snowflakes had made the day cold and miserable and the evening ugly. He hugged himself for warmth. Lights surrounding the center and the parking area offered the illusion of security. Beaumont had wondered why the meeting was here but learned it was for his convenience.

"Gentlemen to the end," he muttered

"You are Mr. Arthur Beaumont?"

Beaumont nearly left his shoes at the mention of his name. “Yes.” He chattered in the cold. “You are?”

“I am Major John Mosby.” The man, dressed in an officer’s woolen coat, offered Beaumont a salute.

Beaumont choked back a laugh. “I have the items, but the device called a Jewel was destroyed. There’s a report in the briefcase to that effect.” He handed the case to Mosby.

In turn, Mosby handed an object to him. “What is this?” Beaumont fumbled with the cover to the unfamiliar device.

“Something called a communicator. I believe there are written instructions with it. You are to summon us if you need aid.”

“Or if you need me,” Beaumont retorted.

Mosby shrugged. “You were not followed. We saw to that. Now I must leave, Mr. Beaumont.”

“It’s funny, you know,” Beaumont said in an off-handed way.

“What is funny, sir?”

“This whole thing began with a ghost. Now it ends with one.” Beaumont saw Mosby give a confused shrug. “Your counterpart in this universe was known as the Gray Ghost.”

“Indeed, sir, what a curious title. I rather like it.” Mosby saluted Beaumont and walked away.

Beaumont stood for a minute in the empty parking area as the snow turned to sleet. “It began with a ghost and ends with one,” he repeated. “No,” he amended. “It hasn’t ended. It’s just begun.”

~ * ~

November 17 1861(Universe 1)

Crittenden stood on the porch of the farmhouse watching Gray Eagle jog from the airfield. When he arrived at the porch, Crittenden said, “I have word from Mr. Beaumont. The Jewel Weber sent to Croll was destroyed.”

“Good. Did he get the other things back?”

Crittenden nodded. “Amber will be happy to have her computer returned, though I gather it too has been damaged.”

“Bulls in a china shop,” Gray Eagle grumbled. “The Palm-Com technology is almost seventy-five years ahead of them.”

“I issued her another computer yesterday. I also have these for you.” Crittenden handed Gray Eagle a box.

“What are they?”

“I have more than one set of insignia. I thought you might like those, Lieutenant Colonel Gray Eagle.”

Gray Eagle felt his eyes tear. “You giving away your old insignia?” he blinked rapidly.

“I want to start a tradition. Recycling, I believe it’s called.”

Gray Eagle took a deep breath. “I’ll be happy to wear these.”

“I have captain’s bars for Amber,” Crittenden added.

“You think that’s wise?”

“No, but it’s necessary,” Crittenden said. “We

are expanding and I can't put officers in charge whose only experience with flight is a balloon."

"Speaking of experience, sir, I have the dual control Merlin ready for another lesson. Come to the field."

"In a bit, Gray Eagle, I have some tasks to attend to."

Gray Eagle closed the box and shoved it into the pocket of his trousers. "I think you're going to want to see this, sir."

"See what?"

"Your first new pilot. He solos today."

"Who?"

"Elliott. Hard to believe, since he slept through his science courses at VMI, but he seems to have the knack for flying."

"Yes, I want to see this." Crittenden walked down the porch steps and followed Gray Eagle to the edge of the field.

The Merlin was taxiing along the runway. Gray Eagle watched the takeoff as Elliott left the ground and gained altitude. It was not perfect, but it was good, especially for a Confederate cavalry officer who had been riding horses a few months earlier. Gray Eagle remembered that a number of early combat pilots had been in the cavalry. Their success had been mixed. But he could tell by Elliott's flying that the young man was a natural.

"He'll fly a standard pattern and then land the plane."

Crittenden said. "In one piece, I hope."

"So do I," Gray Eagle replied.

Again the vision possessed Gray Eagle, like a giant hand crushing his stomach, but there was no change in the way his surroundings looked. The little Merlin was coming in for a perfect landing. But it was not alone. Behind it followed wave after wave of brightly colored P-51s. He could hear the throbbing of their engines as they raced overhead. His eyes caught the modifications, the startling changes that made them different from the machines he had once pointed skyward in another universe. And massed around them, like clouds of flying fish, were hundreds of unmanned craft of shapes he had never imagined. But stealthy, boxy or sleek, they flew as companions to their larger counterparts. He knew then they would fight the war imagined by military minds in more technologically advanced universes.

The tiny Jewel he carried grew warm in the medicine pouch lying against his chest. It would not be easy, he realized. But in time they would control the skies, the war, and in the end the linked fate of all the alternate universes.

Meet

Mary Ann Mogus

My formal education is in physics and biophysics subjects I taught at a university until retiring. But I've always been interested in archaeology, history, and forensics. I did work in archaeology and also served as a museum director for a short time. History and physics appear in my writings and include 'what if' ideas. My interactive murder mystery plays have been performed by nonprofit organizations as fund raisers. I write both fiction and nonfiction and also design and create jewelry and fiber arts and love plants.